Courting Trouble

Books by Deeanne Gist

A Bride Most Begrudging

The Measure of a Lady

Courting Trouble

Courting Trouble

A Novel

DEEANNE GIST

BETHANY HOUSE PUBLISHERS
Minneapolis, Minnesota

Courting Trouble
Copyright © 2007
Deeanne Gist

Cover illustration by Bill Graf
Cover design by Jennifer Parker

Published by Bethany House Publishers
11400 Hampshire Avenue South
Bloomington, Minnesota 55438

Bethany House Publishers is a division of
Baker Publishing Group, Grand Rapids, Michigan.

Printed in the United States of America

Paperback: ISBN-13: 978-0-7642-0225-4   ISBN-10: 0-7642-0225-1
Hardcover: ISBN-13: 978-0-7642-0394-7   ISBN-10: 0-7642-0394-0

Library of Congress Cataloging-in-Publication Data

Gist, Deeanne.
    Courting trouble / Deeanne Gist.
        p.   cm.
    ISBN-13: 978-0-7642-0394-7 (hardcover : alk. paper)
    ISBN-10: 0-7642-0394-0 (hardcover : alk. paper)
    ISBN-13: 978-0-7642-0225-4 (pbk.)
    ISBN-10: 0-7642-0225-1 (pbk.)
        1. Single women—Fiction.   2. Corsicana (Tex.)—History—19th century—Fiction.
I. Title.

    PS3607.I55C68   2007
    813'.6—dc22   2007007115

To my Groom,
whom I love with all my heart,
all my soul, all my mind,
and all my strength.

DEEANNE GIST has a background in education and journalism. Her credits include *People, Parents, Parenting, Family Fun,* and the *Houston Chronicle.* She has a line of parenting products called I Did It!® Productions and a degree from Texas A&M. She and her husband have four children—two in college, two in high school. They live in Houston, Texas, and Deeanne loves to hear from her readers at her website, *www.deeannegist.com.*

ACKNOWLEDGMENTS

The citizens of Corsicana, Texas, opened their arms to me and did all they could to assist me with my research. Many thanks to Bobbie Young, the precious gal who runs the Corsicana Historical Society. She gave up much of her time to me, answered my many, many questions and hooked me up with folks in the know—including Mayor Buster Brown. The Haynie brothers walked me up to Hickey Hill so I could see the oldest operating rig in the world—and one that was in use during the first oil boom in Texas.

Carmack Watkins was a particularly delightful old-timer who regaled me with stories and drove me out to the old brick yard where he had stored some "gumbo busters"—oil rigs from the early 1900s that could bust through Corsicana's black clay. He also had one of the original bois d'arc blocks that had once paved Corsicana's streets. He told me that when it rained, the blocks would stain your heels yellow, so Corsicanans became known as "yellow heels."

And a very special thanks to Clay Jackson, who dropped everything to meet me after hours and patiently answered so many of my questions about the early oil industry in Corsicana and Navarro County. When I asked him what oil smelled like, he looked kind of surprised, then shrugged. "I don't know that I could describe it, but once you smell it, you never forget it."

The next morning, he swung by my hotel with a jelly jar full of oil that he had tapped from one of his rigs—so I could smell it for myself. Can you imagine? Just walked out back and drew me up a sample. What a sweetheart!

Back in Houston, my dear sisters in Christ, Beth and Sabrina, hooked me up with three precious, godly women. Amy, Lisa and Angel: Thank you so very, very much. It is my fervent prayer that the Lord bless you abundantly.

My critique group for this book included two new members. A talented and insightful poet, Allison Smythe, and a highbrow intellectual with a fabulous sense of humor, J. Mark Bertrand. I have grown incredibly fond of both of them along with my returning critique partner, Meg Moseley. Y'all's fingerprints are all over this work. Thank you so much for sharing your expertise and time and talents with me.

Last, but certainly not least, I would like to thank Steve Oates and his sales and marketing team at Bethany House. They come out with both guns smoking and never look back. I am truly blessed to have such an awesome force behind me. I adore you all and so appreciate everything you do for me. Thank you, thank you, thank you!

PROLOGUE

CORSICANA, TEXAS
JULY 1874

THE COWBOY, GOLDEN-SKINNED, blond and blue-eyed, plunked down a wad of bills on the auctioneer's table. "I believe I'll take that lunch basket." He turned and picked Esther Spreckel-meyer out of the crowd with his intense gaze. "That is, if it's okay with Miss—"

"Es-sie!" her mother called.

The ten-year-old girl glanced at her bedroom door, then back at her "cowboy."

"I'd love to share my basket with you, sir," she whispered, "but if you would excuse me for just one minute? I'll be right back. Promise."

Flinging open the door, Essie left behind her make-believe Fourth of July celebration populated with figurines, baby dolls, and imaginary friends. "Coming, Mother!"

She vaulted onto the banister, slid all the way down, flew off the end and executed a perfect landing—feet together, back arched, hands in the air. Just the way those pretty ladies in the circus had landed when they jumped off the trapeze.

"*Essie.* How many times have I told you not to slide down the railing?"

She whirled around. "Papa! I didn't know you were home."

"Obviously." Her father shook his head. "When you are finished

9

with your mother, you are to write a one-hundred-word essay on the reasons females should not slide down banisters. It is to be on my desk before supper."

"Yes, Papa."

He tugged on her braid. "Go on now, squirt. I'll see you at dinner."

She flung herself into his arms. "I'll try to do better, I will. It's just so much fun. And I'm very good at it. I never fall off anymore. And if I'm going to be in the circus when I grow up, then I must practice."

He patted her on the back. "I thought you wanted to be a wife and mother when you grow up."

She offered her father a huge smile. "Oh, I do, Papa. I do. Didn't I tell you? I am going to marry either a cowboy or the ringmaster of a circus. But whoever he is, he's going to buy my box supper at the Fourth of July picnic."

Sullivan Spreckelmeyer blinked in confusion, but Essie had no time to explain. Mother didn't like it when she tarried.

chapter ONE

TWENTY YEARS LATER

ESTHER SPRECKELMEYER HATED the Fourth of July. This day above all others reminded her that everyone in the world went two by two. Everyone but her. She would have stayed home if she could have gotten away with it, but her father, the judge for the 35th Judicial District, expected his family to attend all social events.

Standing in the quiet of her family's kitchen, she determined that this year was going to be different. She had turned thirty last week and she needed a husband. Now.

She straightened the red-and-white gingham bow wrapped around her basket handle, then checked the contents one more time. Fried chicken, sweet potatoes, hominy, dill carrots, black-eyed pea wheels, deviled eggs, cow tongue, and blackberry tarts.

Cooking was of utmost importance to a man in search of a wife. Whoever bought her box supper today at the auction would need to know that with Essie, he'd be well taken care of.

Her father entered the kitchen, pulling on his light summer jacket. "What do you have in your basket this year, dear?"

She took a deep breath. "I don't want you bidding on it, Papa. Nor the sheriff, either."

Papa came up short. "Why not? What's wrong with your father or uncle winning it?"

"If the two of you bid, no one else will even try."

His gray eyebrows furrowed. "But no one has tried for years, other than that youngster, Ewing."

Essie cringed. Ewing Wortham was seven years her junior and used to dog her every step. At the ripe old age of ten, he offered two measly pennies for her basket. No one, evidently, had the heart to bid against him, and every year after he proudly bid his two cents. She could have cheerfully strangled him.

She'd received her height early and her curves late. Between that, her penchant for the outdoors, and her propensity for attracting the admiration of incorrigible little boys, her basket had been passed over more times than naught. Especially since Ewing had gone away to school.

Swallowing, she lifted her chin. "Nevertheless, Papa, I don't want either of you bidding on it."

"I don't understand."

"If neither of you bid, someone will step up to the task."

"Don't be ridiculous," her mother said, entering the kitchen and tucking a loose curl up under her hat. "No one's going to bid on your basket, Essie. Now let's go. We're going to be late."

Papa opened the door. Mama stepped through, the taffeta beneath her silk moiré skirt rustling. Essie gripped the edge of the table and stayed where she was.

"Are you coming?" Papa asked.

"Only if you promise not to bid."

He stood quiet for a long minute. It wasn't hard to understand why the people of Corsicana elected him term after term. Everything in his bearing exuded confidence and invited trust. His robust physique, his commanding stature, his sharp eyes, his ready smile.

"Come along, Sullivan," her mother called. "Whatever are you doing?"

He stayed where he was. "I'll have to leave during the auction, then, Essie. I would not be able to stand it if Ralph held up your supper and no one bid."

"That's not going to happen."

He tugged on his ear. "All right, then. Your uncle and I will slip away before your box comes up for auction—if you're sure."

"I'm sure."

But she wasn't. And between their arrival at the park and the start of the auction, Essie's self-assurance flagged. What if someone older than Papa bid? What if someone much younger than her bid? What if no one bid?

She glanced up at the blue heavens stretching across their small east Texas town and sent a quick prayer that direction. After all, she only wanted a husband, a house, and some offspring. Was that so much to ask? The Lord commanded His children to be fruitful, to multiply, and to populate the earth, and Essie intended to do her part.

Mr. Roland stepped onto the red-white-and-blue-festooned podium, stuck two fingers in his mouth and whistled. The piercing sound cut across the hum of the crowd, quieting the townsfolk as they gathered round. Essie placed a hand against her stomach to calm the turmoil within.

Boxes and baskets of every size, shape, and color covered the tables beside the podium. And though no supper had the owner's name tacked to it, everyone knew whose basket was whose, for the ribbons or doodads on a girl's box revealed her identity as surely as a stamped beehive identified Dunn Bennett china.

She adjusted her bon ton hat with its silk netting, handsome plume, and two bunches of roses all trimmed in red-and-white gingham. She had ordered it from the Montgomery Ward catalog specifically for this event, knowing it would set off her pale blond hair, which she had twisted tightly against her head.

Skimming the crowd, she swallowed. Papa and Uncle Melvin were nowhere in sight. Lillie Sue's box came up first and the bidding began in earnest, the young bucks all vying for the privilege of sharing a meal with the doctor's daughter.

Essie studied the unmarried men and widowers close to her age. There were not too many of them. Mr. Fouty, a cotton farmer from south of town. Mr. Wedick, a widower who'd outlived three wives so far. Mr. Crook, owner of the new mercantile. Mr. Klocker, Mr. Snider, and Mr. Peeples.

She cataloged every man in attendance, discounting the ones who were too old, too young, or too unsuitable in temperament or occupation. A silence descended and Essie turned to the podium.

Mr. Roland held her basket high. "Come on now, fellers, bid her up. If this basket belongs to who I think it does, you'll find something guaranteed to delight yer fancy."

No one offered a bid. Essie's stomach tightened. Her head became weightless. Blinking, she tried to see through the sunspots marring her vision.

"Now, boys. A basket like this is worth more than a pat straight flush. So, who'll start us off?"

Still no one bid.

Pretty little Shirley Bunting leaned over and whispered to her friend, "I cannot imagine why some old biddy would keep bringing her basket year after year when she knows nobody wants it. How embarrassing for her father."

Her friend nudged her and indicated Essie with her head.

Shirley turned, eyes wide. "Oh! Hello, Miss Spreckelmeyer. A lovely afternoon we're having, isn't it?"

Essie inclined her head. The girls hooked elbows and, giggling, disappeared farther into the crowd.

Someone yelled, "Where's Spreckelmeyer? Why ain't he speaking up? We're ready to bid on Betty Lou's."

Essie focused on the auctioneer, refusing to look anywhere else.

Mr. Roland scanned the crowd and stopped when he came to her. "Where's yer daddy, Miss Spreckelmeyer?"

She took a trembling breath. "He stepped away for a moment."

"Well, then, why didn't ya say so? I'll just put this here basket to the side, and when he gets back, you have him come on up and get it. I know he's good fer it."

She attempted a smile but wasn't sure it ever formed. The bidding on Betty Lou's basket commenced, followed by Beatrice's, Flossie's, Liza's, and the rest. By the time the auction finished and everyone dispersed, Essie's basket stood alone on the podium.

Slowly moving forward, she picked it up and walked home, never once looking back.

———————

Fredrick Fouty
Points of Merit:

- *Still has hair*
- *Has two young children, so our own offspring would not be too far apart in age*
- *Hardworking*
- *Loved his wife, God rest her soul*

Drawbacks:

- *Tight with his money*
- *Smokes*
- *Drinks spirits*
- *Only attends church on Sundays, but not Wednesdays*
- *Lets the children run wild*
- *Doesn't like pets*
- *Doesn't enjoy the outdoors*

Essie closed her eyes and tapped the top of her bronze Ladies' Falcon pen against her lips, trying to envision the men who had attended the picnic. Opening her eyes, she wrote Mr. Klocker's name down and proceeded to cover the ruled octavo notepaper with a list of his attributes and shortcomings.

Within the hour she had a comprehensive list of the eligible—and attainable—bachelors in Corsicana. She blew on the wet ink and stamped the pages with her blotter. There was something a little frightening about seeing the words in black and white.

Was this what men did when they considered whom they wanted to court? If so, what would a man list under the positive and negative columns concerning her? Whatever it was, she'd obviously come up short.

Placing her pen in its holder, she leaned back in her chair and studied the papers spread out on her desk. *Father, guide me,* she prayed. *Show me which one.*

But no answer was forthcoming.

Closing her eyes, she whirled her finger above the papers as if stirring some giant cauldron, then spontaneously landed her finger on the table. She opened her eyes.

Mr. Peeples. Leaving her finger in place, she leaned to the right so she could read what item she'd pointed to.

• *Bits of chest hair poke up out of his collar*

She snatched her hand away. Maybe she should sleep on it. Pray more about it. And in the morning, she would choose a man and launch her campaign.

———

Essie rapped on the back door of the Slap Out. It was a ridiculous name for a mercantile, but Hamilton Crook refused to call it Crook's Mercantile. Said it would be bad for business.

So everyone in town had offered their suggestions until some farmer came through exclaiming he was "slap out o' rum." Followed by another fellow who was "slap out o' salt pork and powder shot."

One of the regulars had chuckled and said, "You oughta call this place 'Slap Out'!"—never dreaming, she was sure, that the name would stick.

Essie pulled her shawl tight about her shoulders. The sun had risen, but it was too early for the store to be open. She had wanted to arrive in plenty of time to explain her idea without the risk of customers interrupting.

She knocked again and sighed. She had always hoped her married name would be something elegant, even regal. Anything was better than Spreckelmeyer, or so she'd thought.

Now she was beginning to wonder. Going from Essie Spreckelmeyer to Essie Crook had been the biggest drawback to choosing Mr. Crook as her future husband. Hard to say which name was worse.

The door swung open. Mr. Crook stood in his stocking feet, shirttail out, black hair completely mussed. "Miss Spreckelmeyer? What is it? What has happened?"

Goodness. He looked even younger than she had guessed he was. His youth was the other negative in his column, but she'd thought the gap between them was small. Now, inspecting him up close, she wasn't so sure.

A baby cried in a distant room. Mr. Crook stuck his head out the door, looking to see, no doubt, what disaster had brought the town's old maid to his back doorstep.

His gaze fixed on her bicycle propped against the building. "Has your riding machine blown a part?"

"No, no. I just need a short word with you, if you don't mind."

The baby's complaints turned from belligerent to downright frantic.

"Might I come in?" she asked.

He glanced toward the sound of the baby. "This is a rather awkward time for me. The store will be open in another hour. Perhaps you could stop by then?"

Her immediate instinct was to nod and scuttle away. But she needed a husband and she'd decided Mr. Crook would do quite nicely.

She pulled the screen door open and stepped inside, forcing him back. "No, I'm not sure that's a good idea. You go ahead and tend to yourself and the baby, though. I shall wait right here for you."

"Really, Miss Spreckelmeyer." He frowned, and already she found herself wanting to smooth down the patch of hair sticking straight out from his head. Perhaps it was a sign.

"I'm afraid I will be busy right up to store opening," he said.

"I understand. Run along now. I'll be here when you get back."

He hesitated.

She removed her shawl and hooked it on a hall tree. "Go on with you. I'll be fine."

She had to raise her voice to be heard over the baby's screeches.

After another second or two, he turned his back and disappeared up the stairs that led to his personal quarters.

The closing of a door abruptly cut off the baby's cries. A baby who desperately needed a mother. She squelched that thought for now. First things first.

She glanced around the narrow storage area. She'd never been in the back of the store before. It smelled of lumber, leather, soap, and grain. Empty gunnysacks lay piled in a corner. Shelves lined two walls and held a hodgepodge of tools and gadgets, dishes and jars, cloth and brooms. Harnesses, straps, and whips hung from ceiling hooks.

A couple of crates sat shoved against a wall with sacks of grain leaning against them. A wooden bar bolted the large barn-like door where barrels were delivered. The unvarnished plank floor beneath her feet had turned gray from exposure.

Mr. Crook's store was only two years old, the first competition the old Flour, Feed and Liquor Store had seen since opening in 1858. With the Texas Central Railroad now coming through town, businesses were popping up everywhere.

Essie moved through the curtained barrier between the storage room and the store, stepping onto the stained, varnished, and newly shined floor of the Slap Out. Sunshine seeped in around the edges of the drawn window coverings, filling the store with muted light.

She took a deep breath. This was her first taste of what her role as Mrs. Crook would be like. The large, still room invoked a sense of peace, tranquility, and rightness.

She belonged here. She just knew it. Mr. Crook might not have bid on her basket yesterday, but he needed a woman and helpmate. That baby needed a mother. And Essie was the perfect candidate for the job.

She just wished she could remember whose basket Mr. Crook *had* bought, but that entire auction was nothing but a muddle in her mind, as fragmented as an unfinished puzzle.

She strolled behind the counter, her bootheels clicking against the solid floor as she ran her fingers along bolts of wool, dimity, gingham, percale, linen, and lawn cloth. She skimmed her hand across balls of yarn in every color of the rainbow, then tapped one side of a scale, setting it to swinging and causing its brass pans to jangle.

She picked up a bottle of Warner's Safe Nervine—reading the label's claim of healing, curing, and relieving of pain—then set it back down and scanned the vast assortment of tonics, pills, and powders. She'd have her work cut out for her learning which medicine was best for what.

Beside these items, drawers and bins stretched from floor to ceiling across the middle section of the wall, each carefully labeled compartment filled with spices, coffee, tobacco, candy, buttons, peas, and most anything else imaginable.

And if she had her way, she would soon be proprietress over it all. But first, she must slip behind the lines, learn the lay of the land, and then take over to the point where Mr. Crook would become almost dependent upon her. Where he couldn't imagine life in the store without her. Once there, advancing from helper in the store to helper in the home was just a staircase away.

She smoothed her hand up the nape of her neck. She mustn't waver from her goal. She must stay strong in her purpose no matter how nervous she felt.

Still, subtlety would be the order of the day. She didn't want to scare him off by pushing too hard, too fast. Heading to the ready-made clothes section, she removed an apron from one of the shelves. Shaking it out, she tied it around her waist and mentally cataloged the boots, shoes, long johns, hats, bonnets, and handkerchiefs that lined the tables and shelves in this little nook.

She returned to the back room, picked up a broom and began to sweep the store, starting in the farthermost corner where the stove, chairs, and checkers had been set up. She was nearly finished with the entire floor when Mr. Crook came through the curtain.

His short black hair had been slicked down and parted in the middle, while square spectacles perched upon his nose. Rosy cheeks graced his oval face, making her wonder if she had been the one to put that color there.

He grasped the opening of his cassimere coat and tugged, drawing her eyes to the snappy plaid vest he wore along with a four-in-hand tie.

"Miss Spreckelmeyer? What are you doing?"

She looked down at the broom in her hand. "Oh. I just thought I'd make myself useful while I waited."

He strode forward and snatched the broom away. "That is quite unnecessary. Now, what emergency has brought you to the Slap Out at this early hour?"

She clasped her hands together. "No emergency, sir. I didn't mean to worry you."

"Then what is it?"

Stay strong. "I know things have been a bit difficult for you since Mrs. Crook's passing, and I thought I might ease your burden a bit."

He smiled warily. "Well, that is quite thoughtful of you, but Mrs. Peterson watches the baby and takes care of my meals."

"Oh no. I didn't mean that. I meant with the store. The other evening I saw you sitting at your desk burning the midnight oil, so to speak, and realized you must do nothing but work and sleep and work and sleep. I thought maybe if you had an extra hand, perhaps you could do some of that bookkeeping during the day."

He rocked back on his heels. "Are you, uh, asking for employment, Miss Spreckelmeyer?"

She gasped. "Good heavens, no. I had no intention of charging you for my assistance. I merely meant to give you a helping hand."

"I see. Well. I don't know what to say. That's very kind of you, but—"

"No need to say anything a'tall." Smiling, she patted his arm. "I'll just finish up with this sweeping here, then start dusting the shelves."

She took the broom back and put it to work on the last section of flooring, praying he'd be too polite to refuse her offer.

He removed a handkerchief from his pocket and dabbed his forehead. "Miss Spreckelmeyer, I really don't quite know how to say this, but—"

"Oh, now, Mr. Crook, no need to thank me. It's my pleasure."

"No, you misunderstand. What I was going to say was—"

Five succinct hammers sounded on the door. "Hamilton? You in there?"

Mr. Crook withdrew a pocket watch from his vest and popped it open. "Please, miss. I appreciate your concern and your very generous offer—"

She rushed to the door and gave the shade a good yank. It flew up, wrapping itself around a cylinder at the top, flapping as it rotated several more turns than was necessary.

"Oh, look," she said. "It's Mr. Vandervoort come for his coffee, and the beans are not even ground yet." She waved to the man outside, whose bushy gray brows rose in reply. "You go ahead and let him in," she said. "I'll do the coffee." She scurried to the bins, scooped out some beans and poured them into the mill.

Mr. Crook had not so much as budged.

She shooed him with her hand. "Go on."

Vandervoort jiggled the door. Mr. Crook glanced at him, then her, then moved to unbolt the latch.

"Wall, what's all the holdup about?" Vandervoort asked, pushing his way into the store. "Miss Spreckelmeyer," he said, touching his hat.

"Howdy, Mr. Vandervoort," she said. "We're off to a slow start this morning, but I'll have a fine pot brewing in no time."

"What're ya doin' here, woman?" he asked.

"I'm just temporarily helping out Mr. Crook. Seeing as he hardly has any time whatsoever to spend with his precious little baby girl and all."

Vandervoort harrumphed, then headed to his usual chair in the back.

Mr. Crook approached her. "Really, Miss Spreckelmeyer," he whispered. "I must ask you to stop this foolishness. I do not need any assistance."

Refusing to concede defeat, she girded herself with bravado, grabbed the grinder's handle and began to rotate the wheel. Little by little, coffee granules dropped into the hopper. "Well, it looks to me, sir, like you do need some help. Misters Richie, Jenkins, and Owen will be here any moment, and you haven't even started up the stove yet."

"That's because you threw off my entire morning."

"Pishposh. I did no such thing."

"Miss Spreckelmeyer, release that coffee mill at once."

She hesitantly let go and stepped back. "Well, all right, then."

"Thank you." He took a deep breath.

"You're welcome. I didn't know grinding up the beans was so important to you. But don't worry. I'm a quick study. I'll know your peculiarities in no time."

Without giving him a chance to respond, she bounced over to the stove and began to lay out the wood.

"Need any help with that, Miss Spreckelmeyer?"

"No, no, Mr. Vandervoort." She paused and looked up at him. "There is something you *can* do for me, though."

"Why, sure, ma'am. What is it?"

"You can do a better job of aiming your tobacco. That spittoon has a nice large mouth on it. Missing it smacks of sheer laziness, and I don't relish the thought of mopping up all that nastiness day in and day out."

He straightened. "Why, yes, ma'am. I'll do right better. Just see if I don't."

She reached over and gave his arm a squeeze. "You are such a dear. Thank you."

Hamilton Crook stared at the woman reprimanding his customer. She'd rolled up the sleeves of her olive-colored shirtwaist and wrapped a white apron around her grosgrain skirt. He knew his clothing, and hers were fine pieces. The shirtwaist sported the newest puff sleeves and choker collar while her skirt held tone-on-tone scrolling designs.

Her pinchback straw hat, however, was another matter entirely. With a wavy-edged top from which tulle poufs protruded, white flowers, fern and willow leaves surrounded vertically wired ribbon loops. Most impractical for store clerking.

He shook his head, peeking into the grinder to see how many

beans were left. Why in the blue blazes was the spinster daughter of the district judge doing charity work in his store? What was wrong with working in an orphanage? Or sharing a meal with old Mrs. Yarbrough? Or helping out with the church bazaar?

He looked around. To compensate for the name this town had *slapped* on his store, he made sure he not only kept it in tip-top shape with all the goods organized and grouped, but he also kept it clean and well stocked. Had there been complaints? Or was this do-gooder just a frustrated busybody who had singled him out as her next "project"?

Whatever the case, he needed to politely but firmly inform her that if he wanted help, he could well afford to hire someone. And that someone would not be an old maid who was notorious for wearing outrageous hats and who scandalized the town matrons by riding on a bicycle with her skirts hiked up to her knees.

chapter TWO

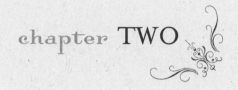

THE MORNING BROUGHT few customers, giving Essie plenty of time to dust the shelves, polish the scales, wash the windows, and grind the sugar. Mr. Crook sequestered himself in the back corner, nose buried in his papers. Essie hoped the smell of a clean store and a fresh pot of coffee brought a token of pleasure to his tedious task.

As she worked, Misters Vandervoort, Richie, Jenkins, and Owen took turns sliding checkers back and forth across a grimy board. Sometimes they pondered each move and sometimes they pushed the little discs without any apparent thought, but all the while they debated everything from the destiny of man to the finest bait for catching fish. No matter where the conversation strayed, though, it always came back to the topic on everyone's mind, the question of Corsicana's economic future.

"Wall, we gotta do somethin'," Jenkins was saying. "With cotton prices droppin' ever' day and Mr. Neblett's seed house shut down, this town's gonna shrivel up and die."

"What about putting up some brick buildings in the square?" Owen suggested. "That would attract businesses to town."

Vandervoort harrumphed. "Who's gonna want to build shops in a town with such a pathetic water supply?"

The bell on the door tinkled and the Gillespies' oldest boy ventured inside with a roll of hides under his arm. He wore a tattered corduroy coat with pockets vast enough to hold small game and oversized trousers folded up to reveal worn-out boots with so many holes it was a wonder they offered any protection at all.

"Good afternoon, Jeremy," Essie said, making her way to the counter. "What brings you into town today?"

The scrawny teener nodded slightly and doffed his old felt hat from his head. "Miss Spreckelmeyer. I come to ask Mr. Crook fer some oatmeal, rice, and cod liver oil, please, ma'am."

She smiled and patted the flat surface in front of her. "Well, Mr. Crook is working with his ledgers. Why don't you show me what you have."

Jeremy exchanged nods with the old-timers, then laid his hat on the counter. The checker game resumed and Essie caught a whiff of the young man, coughed a little, then tactfully breathed through her mouth.

One by one he unrolled his hides the way a fortune hunter might unfurl a treasure map. He smoothed out two raccoon skins, one rabbit, and one possum.

It was the possum that did it. Wrung out her chest like a tightly twisted mop. For she'd never known anyone to bother with skinning a possum. Most folks scalded them in boiling water, then scraped them hairless. And yet, the Gillespies had sent their eldest to town with an actual possum hide, of all things.

She fingered the raccoon, careful not to show signs of anything but admiration. She needn't look at the boy to recall how big his brown eyes looked within his hollowed-out face.

"Why, these are mighty nice, Jeremy," she said. "Did you do the skinning?"

"Yes, miss."

"Well, you're quite talented with a knife. I do believe these ear holes are some of the best I've ever seen. Should raise the value of these skins by a good twenty cents each." Her fingers moved to the animal's snout. "And would you look at that nose button? Still attached and everything."

He straightened slightly. "It all starts with how you insert the gamblin' sticks, miss. You gotta grip right firm-like and the tail will slide off the bone slicker 'n calf slobbers."

She stacked the hides carefully. "You don't fool me, Jeremy Gillespie. It takes more than tightly clamped sticks to skin an animal this cleanly. Now, how much oatmeal were you needing?"

She measured out the exact amount he asked for, not questioning for a moment whether or not Mr. Crook wanted the hides. When she started on the rice, Jeremy wandered over to the gun cabinet, keeping his hands clasped tightly behind his back.

Mr. Crook joined Essie. "What do you think you are doing, Miss Spreckelmeyer?"

"Lower your voice, Mr. Crook. I'm filling Jeremy's order. What does it look like I'm doing?"

"It looks like you are giving away the store."

"He brought in a trade."

Mr. Crook flipped through the hides. "These hides are worthless. I'll not trade good merchandise for—Great Scott!" He flung back the top three and stared aghast at the fourth. "What is that?"

"It's a possum."

"A *possum?*"

"Hush," she whispered, tying a knot around the top of a small burlap sack filled with rice. "Can't you see his family is starving? Just look at the boy."

Mr. Crook began to roll up the hides. "No. Absolutely not. I will not trade for these ridiculous skins. Go return those items to their appropriate bins. I will handle this."

She grabbed his arm. "Don't. Please, Hamilton."

His jaw slackened and it took her a moment to realize she'd used his given name. She'd been thinking of him in her imaginings as Hamilton, and it had accidentally slipped out.

Her face burned, but she remained firm. "Surely this one time will not hurt."

"The Gillespies have been charging all their purchases against this year's crop, and cotton is now at five cents on the Exchange and dropping. I cannot afford to extend any more credit to anyone. Especially not the Gillespies."

"How much for this rice and oatmeal, along with a vial of cod liver oil?" she asked.

"He wants liver oil, too? Ridiculous."

"How much?"

He picked up the two small sacks of oatmeal and rice, judging their weight in his hands. "Two seventy-five for these, plus twenty-five cents for the liver oil."

She quelled her reaction to the extravagant quote. Her family bought their grains by the barrel. She had no idea small portions cost so much.

"And the hides?" she asked. "How much credit for the hides?"

He held her gaze. "None."

He made to move past her, but she tightened her grip on his arm. "I'll replace your rice and oatmeal tomorrow from my own personal stock and pay for the liver oil with cash."

"Absolutely not."

"Why? What possible difference could it make?"

He leaned close. Whiffs of his shaving soap teased her nose. "I do not know what you think you are doing here, Miss Spreckelmeyer, but you are coming perilously close to overstaying your welcome."

She lessened the pressure on his arm, changing it to more of a caress, then softened her tone. "I'd like to purchase those hides you have for three dollars even, please, sir."

He studied her over the rim of his glasses. "You will have to buy them from Jeremy, then. I would not lower myself to carrying possum hides."

"It would wound his pride and embarrass me. Please. Just this once?"

He hesitated in indecision, then slowly straightened. "All right, Miss Spreckelmeyer. I will award the Gillespies three dollars credit for the hides . . . just this once."

"I'll pay you back."

"No. No you won't. But leave me out of the negotiations and make sure Jeremy understands not to set foot in here again with any more hides. Is that clear?"

For a moment she imagined what it would be like once they were a couple. She would fling her arms about him and thank him effusively for his consent. For now, she simply let the warm feelings flow freely through her eyes and smile.

She rubbed her thumb against his stiffly ironed sleeve. "Thank you. I'll always remember your kindness."

He jerked his arm away. She scooped up the sacks and called for Jeremy, asking him to bring her the liver oil. While she poured some into a small vial, she explained that he was fortunate to have brought those skins in when he did, for after today they wouldn't be taking any more hides for trade. Seemed Mr. Crook would no longer be stocking them.

———————

Essie ruined three hats that first week at the Slap Out. This morning a wall-mounted bracket lamp snagged the chiffon ribbon on her latest hat, bringing her up short like a dog on a leash.

"My stars and garters," she murmured, unhooking herself from the bronze sconce, then stuffing the trim back up into her Evangeline hat. "Here they are, Mrs. Quigley."

Essie laid ribbed hose, wool hose, leather stockings, and plain stockings on the counter. "This is our selection of boys' hosiery, the leather being the best, of course, giving fifty percent more wear than any of the others."

Mrs. Quigley picked up the plain cotton stockings.

"Those are some of the most satisfactory, ma'am. See the wide elastic hem at the top? That will help keep them from sliding down."

Mrs. Quigley squinted for a closer examination.

"They have double-spliced heels and toes, as well," Essie continued, "and are thirty-five cents each."

The Quigleys lived on the south side of town in a neatly kept house with a wide front porch. Mr. Quigley worked in the gristmill and had fathered a whole passel of youngsters. Three of them stood solemnly beside their mother, but Essie knew full well their behavior at school was less than pristine.

"And who is to be the recipient of these fine stockings?" Essie asked the boys.

"Grundy," the older one said. "He's always runnin' around without his boots on, tearing up his hose."

"Am not."

"Are too."

Mrs. Quigley silenced the boys with a look.

Essie smiled. "Well, I suppose we've all made a muck of our hosiery a time or two." She turned her attention to Mrs. Quigley. "Have you seen our new magic darner?"

She retrieved the little loom-like machine that would mend hosiery, silk, wool, or cotton. "It's small enough to fit inside your sewing basket and so easy to use, even the children could operate it."

By the time Essie was done, she had sold them three pairs of stockings, the magic darner, a pattern for a five-gored skirt, and several remnants of cloth.

After the Quigleys left, Hamilton joined her behind the counter and held up a satin rosette. "Did you lose this, by any chance?"

Her hand flew to the right side of her hat and discovered a gap. "Oh my. I seem to catch my trim on something every time I turn around." She took the rosette and tried to return it to its proper place but could not make it stay.

He chuckled. "Here. Let me."

She held herself perfectly still while he secured the flower back onto her hat. Her nose was mere inches from the buttons on his double-breasted fancy wash vest and the knot on his silk necktie. She breathed in the scent of his shaving soap, along with a hint of mustiness.

Her gaze veered to his raised arm and the damp stain on his shirt. The intimacy of seeing such a personal thing did queer things to her stomach. Blindly, she grabbed the counter to steady herself.

"There," he said. "That should hold, for a while, anyway."

She lifted her chin, the brim of her hat revealing his jaw, cheeks, and nose one linear inch at a time. She moistened her lips. The brown eyes behind his square spectacles were as warm as hot cocoa and at very close range.

"You have quite a knack for sales, Miss Spreckelmeyer."

"It's nothing, really," she whispered. "I just know everybody and what kinds of things they need, is all."

His mouth hinted at a smile. "That may be true, but there is a difference in knowing a thing and actually making the sale."

He stepped back and began to roll up the selection of hosiery Mrs. Quigley had decided against. "I have to admit," he said, "having you here this past week has been wonderful."

Her lips parted. "For me, too."

"Well, perhaps we should make the situation a bit more permanent?"

She sucked in her breath. "Yes. Oh yes."

He glanced at her and smiled. "Well, then. I shall pay you two dollars and fifty cents a week, starting now."

She blinked. "No. I mean, that's not necessary."

"Of course it is." He handed her the leather stockings and started on the wool. "You have a ribbon hanging down the left side of your hat."

She stuffed it back up. "Thank you."

"You're welcome." He handed her the rest of the hosiery and headed to his desk in the corner.

———

July gave way to August, and the hot summer sun broiled Collin Street. Hamilton forced himself to smile and nod from the Slap Out's front porch as horses, wagons, and townsfolk scurried to his competitor's establishment, causing dirt to surge upward in constant turmoil.

Word had spread early this morning that Charlie Gillespie and his boys had brought in a big black bear hide and traded it to the Flour, Feed and Liquor Store. Hamilton struggled to hide his chagrin.

The Slap Out faced east at the corner of Eleventh and Collin, offering him a clear view of the Pickens' place one hundred yards down on the opposite side of the road.

He squinted into the sunlight. Jeremy Gillespie bounded out of the Feed Store and headed down the street, straight toward him.

"Miss Spreckelmeyer!" the boy hollered, waving his hand high in the air. Essie had busied herself all morning dragging various goods outside in hopes of luring a few customers in, but even Vandervoort and his cronies had failed to make an appearance.

She turned at the sound of her name, then leaned far out over the railing, waving back. The unladylike position hoisted up her hems, exposing her petticoats and a pair of well-worn boots. Her backside poked out in an ill-mannered fashion.

"Hullo!" she yelled back.

The Widow Yarbrough, passing by, jerked her gaze toward the spectacle, then raised a disapproving eyebrow at Hamilton. He cringed with embarrassment.

Miss Spreckelmeyer's toes left the plank flooring, and for one horrid moment he thought she might tumble right over the side, but she managed to keep her balance and land safely on the porch, showing no distress over her near mishap.

"We caught us a bear," Jeremy exclaimed.

"I heard!" she answered. "You must tell me all about it."

"Oh, you gotta see her to believe her. I'd have brought her to the Slap Out first, but last month you done said Mr. Crook's got more hides than he needs."

"And so he does," she said.

"Not bear hides," Hamilton growled. "One can never have too many bear hides."

She glanced up at him, a confused expression crossing her face. "Well, we have no one but ourselves to blame, Mr. Crook. 'The miser is as much in want of what he has as of what he has not.'"

He stiffened. "There is no 'we,' Miss Spreckelmeyer. Furthermore, I am not a miser. And that black bear would have been mine if not for you."

Jeremy whipped off his hat. "Beggin' yer pardon, Mr. Crook. It weren't Miss Spreckelmeyer's fault Pa took the bear to old Mr. Pickens."

She smiled. "Oh, but I'm afraid it is, Jeremy. I didn't specify earlier that we are quite interested in large-game hides. It's only the small ones that we no longer stock."

Jeremy glanced between the two of them, then began to back up. "Wall, I'll be sure to tell Pa to bring the next one straight to you."

Like there will be a next one, Hamilton thought.

"Thank you," she said.

The Gillespie boy replaced his hat, then turned and hustled back to the Feed Store.

"I'm so happy for them," she said. "They'll have food a-plenty now."

Hamilton pushed his glasses up his nose. "Do you have any idea how much money you have cost me?"

She blinked. "Nonsense. No one is going to actually purchase that bearskin. Why, it would cost a fortune."

"That may be so, but folks far and wide will go to the Feed Store to have a look at it, now, won't they? And while they are there, they will make other purchases and then have no reason to come to the Slap Out."

"Hmmm. I see what you mean." She thrummed her fingers against her skirt. "Well, we will simply have to come up with something better."

"Better than a black bear hide?"

"Yes." She hooked her hands behind her, throwing her shoulders back and calling attention to the pale blue dimity shirtwaist she wore. It was a ready-made that he kept in stock and he'd easily sold three times the number he normally did. He felt certain it was because the style suited Miss Spreckelmeyer, and other women thought it might flatter them, as well.

She took a few lazy steps toward him, her head cocked to the side, a blond wisp escaping her coif. "Any ideas?" she asked.

He frowned. She stood close, so close that he could see each and every nuance of color in her blue eyes and smell the hint of clove she used for fragrance. He could even hear her breath coming and going in regular intervals.

"Perhaps we should have a contest," she murmured.

His frown deepened. "There is no 'we.'"

"Or a tournament."

Hamilton studied her. He knew full well she was after a husband and he had no interest whatsoever. He hadn't meant to encourage her. Had not, in fact, realized until it was too late that when he praised her for her performance, she took it in a much more personal manner.

But in the month since Essie had forced herself on him and the Slap Out, his sales had soared—at least until she'd sent his business across the street to gawk at a bearskin.

Never had he seen such a salesclerk, though. She sold leather pre-server to the carriage and harness dealer. Sold books on midwifery to the doctor. Sold fancy goods to the ladies.

And even though she freely squandered inventory on those in need, his profits had soared.

As a shopkeeper she would do, but as a wife? Never. Hamilton knew he could do much better than the town spinster. Still, he had to tread carefully.

He was an outsider to Corsicana, and though the townsfolk tutted behind their hands over Miss Spreckelmeyer's unorthodox tomboyish ways and her ridiculous hats, she was a local and they were quite fond of her. Treated her much like they did Cat, the town stray.

If the tabby showed up on their porch, they'd give her warm milk. If a storm was brewing, they'd give her shelter for the night. If mischievous boys were mistreating her, they'd interfere on her behalf. But their sympathies did not extend to the point of actually taking her home and calling her their own.

No. Miss Spreckelmeyer was the town spinster and he, for one, deserved better.

She noticed his scrutiny and her eyes brightened. "A checkers competition. What do you think about that?"

"I think, Miss Spreckelmeyer, that you and I need to have a talk."

Her face softened. She took another step forward. He took one back.

"All right, Hamilton. When would be a good time for our . . . talk?"

That was another thing. Calling him by his given name when he'd not given her leave to do so. No wonder the men of this town had shied away when she came calling. Never had he met a more forward, unpredictable and impulsive woman. And from such a good family, too. For their sake and for the sake of his good standing in the community, he would be sure to let her down gently.

"Tomorrow evening," he said. "After store closing. Would that suit?"

A soft sigh escaped her lips. "Yes. Yes, it most certainly would."

———————

Essie could not believe her good fortune. Had she known how easy it was to bring a man to heel, she'd have done so years ago. But then, perhaps it had nothing to do with "fortune" and everything to do with God's plan for her life. Finally—*finally*—His plan was bearing fruit.

She laid her new summer skirt and shirtwaist across the back of her bedroom window chair, careful not to crease or wrinkle the freshly ironed garments.

She knew how much Hamilton liked it when she wore ready-mades from their store, and she wanted to be sure to please him tomorrow. For tomorrow, after store closing, he was going to declare his intentions.

Oh, how she wished she could wear one of her lovely hats, but she'd given up on trying to wear them in the store. If she were to don one now, it might spook him.

She laid a white linen detachable collar and matching cuffs on her toilet table, the only concession to extravagance in the ensemble she was preparing. Glancing in the mirror, she caught her reflection. The reflection of the soon-to-be Mrs. Hamilton Crook.

chapter THREE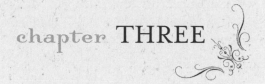

ESSIE GROANED, CLUTCHING her stomach and curling up tightly on the bed. Mother dipped a cloth in cool water, then wrung it out. Essie eyed the array of clothing hanging limp on the chair so far away.

Mother draped the cloth across Essie's forehead.

"I have to get up. Mr. Crook is expecting me."

"You cannot. You're too sick. Besides, you've no business forcing yourself on that poor man. I cannot imagine what you have been thinking to make such a spectacle of yourself. It's downright embarrassing."

"Please, Mother. You've made your opinion on this crystal clear, but I haven't changed my mind. I'm going to continue working at the Slap Out for as long as Mr. Crook will have me."

Her insides gurgled and she slapped a hand over her mouth. Mother pulled the chamber pot from under the bed, uncovered it and held it while Essie emptied her stomach again.

There was nothing for it. She'd have to send word to Hamilton that she would not be in to the store today. Nor to their little tête-à-tête afterward.

———

"I'm telling you it *is* here. Miss Spreckelmeyer said so. She knows how I have been waiting and waiting for that book. You must locate it straightaway, sir. I insist."

Mrs. Lockhart punctuated her demand with a thump of her cane, sending a ripple up her arm, across her shoulders, and through her sagging middle.

Hamilton forced a polite smile. "I will look yet again, ma'am. Do you happen to remember the title of the work?"

"Certainly. Don't you think I'd remember what volume I ordered?" The elderly woman pinched her lips together revealing a spider web of creases and folds around her mouth. "Honestly. I detest dealing with such simplemindedness. When is Miss Spreckelmeyer to return?"

"As I said earlier, she's taken ill today. I expect her to return as soon as she is able."

"Well, it can't be soon enough. Now hurry it up, young man. Miss Spreckelmeyer would have had the book all wrapped up and tied with string by now."

"The title, Mrs. Lockhart. It would be helpful to know the title."

"I told you that already. Will you *please* pay attention. It is a work by Mrs. Bertha Clay entitled *Clarabel's Love Story*."

"Yes, ma'am. If you will excuse me, I'll check once more in the back."

He allowed a scowl to cross his face the moment he stepped through the curtained partition. *Clarabel's Love Story*. What in heaven's name did that old boiler want with a love story and where in the blazes would Essie have put it?

He'd already checked all the lower shelves and he couldn't imagine it being on any of the high ones. Still, he upended an empty fruit crate and climbed on top to better see the upper shelves. He shoved aside lantern holders, trunk locks, and carving tools, awakening dust motes long in hibernation, then picked through sulphur candles, butter molds, and nursery-bottle fittings.

As he searched, his hand brushed against a familiar eight-inch rod attached to the bottom of a black suctioning device shaped like a bowl. Much to his surprise, it had arrived in the post mere days after his wife's passing. The order had been of such a delicate nature, his wife had not even told him of it.

When he'd first unpacked the contraption, he'd researched it in his catalog. The advertisement claimed that this "bust developer" would build up and fill out shrunken and undeveloped tissue and form a rounded, plump, and perfectly shaped bust. In the weeks following its arrival, he'd eyed most every woman in town, speculating about which mystery lady in Corsicana, Texas, had decided to compensate for her lack of that greatest charm, a bosom. But the owner of the enhancer had never come forward to claim her purchase, and it had been sitting on this shelf ever since. He smirked at the memory, then returned it to its place on the shelf and continued his search for Mrs. Lockhart's novel.

The bell on the door jingled and voices in the store increased in volume. Saturday was his busiest day of the week. He couldn't waste any more time on the book. He returned to the front and told Mrs. Lockhart she would have to come back Monday.

"Well," she said. "I had planned to fill an order today, but perhaps I should go to the Feed Store instead. Mr. Pickens always knows where *his* inventory is."

"My sincerest apologies. From now on I will be sure to coordinate the location of all my stock so that both Miss Spreckelmeyer and I can find it at a moment's notice."

Through round spectacles, she scrutinized him from the part in his hair to the tips of his boots. "See that you do. I shall be back first thing Monday morning."

The rest of the afternoon went much the same. Miss Lizzie wanted a woman's opinion on what color would suit her best. She went down the street for Mrs. Pickens' advice—and cloth.

At just past three, Preacher Bogart arrived wanting Miss Spreckelmeyer to describe to his wife the new baptismal pants Essie had mentioned. They evidently had boots sewn right onto them, like wading pants except nicer. Hamilton looked them up in the special-orders catalog but could find no such thing. The Bogarts went to the Feed

Store to see if Mrs. Pickens had ever heard of them.

An hour later, Mr. Bunting wanted Miss Spreckelmeyer's advice on whether to buy his wife a brooch pin or a hair charm for their twenty-fifth wedding anniversary. Hamilton gave his opinion, but Mr. Bunting decided to ask Mrs. Pickens.

Even Vandervoort and his cronies were out of sorts. Miss Spreckelmeyer had promised to play the winner of their checkers match, for none of them had yet beat her. They grumbled over their game until closing, then left without saying good-bye.

By the time Hamilton locked the door, he'd made fewer sales for the day than he had in months. Especially for a Saturday. He pulled down the shade on his front door. Perhaps he should consider what Miss Spreckelmeyer was offering him. She was a bit on the muscular side, a bit on the bossy side, and a bit on the eccentric side, but she certainly knew how to close a sale.

Essie arrived at the store Monday morning at her normal time. Her ailment had lasted only a day, leaving Sunday for her to regain her strength and her anticipation. She'd taken great care with her toilet this morning, donning the clothes, collar, and cuffs she'd planned to wear Saturday and taking extra care with her hair.

Hamilton opened the back door. "Essie," he said. "I'm so glad to see you."

She stood as still as a hunter who had his prize quarry in range. Hamilton had used her given name. And in the very next breath, all but said he'd missed her.

He stepped back, widening the door. "How are you feeling?"

"Much better. Thank you." She crossed the threshold and plucked her apron from the wall hook. "I'm so sorry about Saturday. How did it go?"

But he didn't answer and she looked up. Her hands hesitated. She had been blindly tying the bow of her apron behind her, causing her shirtwaist to temporarily tighten across her chest.

His gaze rested at the very place her buttons strained. She drew a breath, startled. Never before had he made his interest so clear.

She quickly finished her bow and fluffed her apron, reveling in the rapid tempo of her pulse.

"Everything was all wrong without you," he said, his voice sinking into an intimate register. "The customers were disconcerted. The coffee came out too strong. The fancy-goods department was in shambles before noon. And," he took a deep breath, "sales were down."

In the windowless storage room the shadows were deep and the corners dark. If she were imagining this moment, it would be the perfect time for him to take her into his arms. But she wasn't imagining it and she wasn't quite sure how to encourage him.

"It's all right," she said. "I hardly ever get sick and I'll have everything fixed up quicker than a hen on a hot griddle."

Yet she didn't move, knowing that the moment she did, the mood would be broken.

He took a thorough survey of her person. "You're a passable-looking woman, Miss Spreckelmeyer."

"Essie," she said, barely above a whisper. "Please, call me Essie."

————————

Essie's mother had always told her not to stare at a man. *"How can he get a good look at you if you're always staring at him?"* she would say. Remembering this advice, she was careful to keep her gaze on anything but Hamilton.

Yet she'd felt his regard all day, whether she was helping customers, weighing items, or wrapping purchases. When he asked her to clean out and organize the storage room, she put it off as long as possible, not wanting to be out of sight or out of mind.

Instead, she settled down for a match of checkers with Mr. Owen, while Misters Vandervoort, Jenkins, and Richie gathered round to offer advice to their friend. They were playing the best of five games. Owen was down by two.

"You be red this time," he said.

She began placing her pieces on the dark squares closest to her.

"What'd the judge think of last month's meeting, Miss Spreckelmeyer?" Mr. Richie asked.

"Of Corsicana Commercial Club?" she asked, putting the last checker in place. "He was pleased the members voted in favor of tapping some shallow artesian wells. Otherwise, we would continue to be a one-staple community with no hopes of bringing in new businesses."

"Anything happen so far?"

Essie moved between her own pieces, edging closer to Mr. Owen's with each turn. "They put together a water-development company and took bids from various contractors."

"What'd they say?"

"That three wells will give us a flow of 750 thousand gallons of water a day."

Mr. Jenkins whistled.

"Better not do that, Lafoon," Mr. Vandervoort warned.

Mr. Owen froze, his big, pudgy fingers resting on a black disk.

"She wants you to jump that, 'cause soon as you do you'll be in a worse spot than you are now."

"Well, if I don't, I'll lose three pieces."

Vandervoort shrugged. "Do what ya want, then."

Owen jumped Essie's piece, opening the lane to his king row. She moved that direction.

"How they gonna get that much water to flow up through them wells?" Mr. Richie asked.

"Papa said they wouldn't need any pumping installations at all. Said there is enough natural pressure to fill standpipes and storage tanks. Crown, please, Mr. Owen."

Scowling, he crowned her checker. "What about the seed house? Any word on what the town's supposed to do with that vacant monstrosity now that Mr. Neblett's gone belly up?"

"No," she sighed. "I'm afraid there was no news on that front."

A few minutes later, she won the match.

"That's it," Owen said. "I'm goin' out front to whittle awhile. Y'all comin'?"

The men shuffled outside. She put away the checkers, wiped off the board, then glanced up to find Hamilton staring at her from his desk chair.

"You ought to let them win once in a while," he said.

"I've tried, but then we get to talking and I forget to make bad moves."

He raised his hands above his head, arching his back.

"Tired?" she asked.

"A little."

"Can I get you some coffee?"

"That sounds good."

She chose a black enamel cup from those hanging beside the stove, knowing it was Hamilton's favorite. She handed it to him, basking in her intimate familiarity with his likes and dislikes.

"Thank you," he said, taking a sip.

"You're welcome."

The hum of conversation from the front porch filtered through the walls. His foot dislodged a burlap bag leaning against his desk, causing the beans inside to shift and resettle.

Rolling back his chair, he slowly pushed himself to his feet. "Why haven't you ever married, Essie?"

Blood rushed to her cheeks. *No one ever asked me.* But she couldn't say that. "The right fellow never did come along, I guess."

Every impulse she had urged her to close the gap between them. She stayed where she was.

"You look nice today," he said. "Tidy. Did you do something different?"

Yes. Yes, I did. "No. Just the same ol' me, I guess."

The town cat's meow made them both jump.

Hamilton frowned. Essie smiled.

"Cat!" she said. "What are you doing in here?"

She scooped up the short-haired, scrawny animal and rubbed her nose against its neck. "You looking for some attention?"

Hamilton stared at Cat, the color draining from his face.

"What is it?" she asked.

He took a hasty step back and plopped down in his chair.

"Nothing. Nothing at all. Did you finish up in the back room?"

"No. I haven't even started. I'll go do that now."

"Thank you. And take that . . . that stray with you."

―――――――

Essie started with the top shelves, dusting, organizing, wiping down and cataloging while humming "I Just Started Living." Hamilton had almost made a declaration. Right in the store in the middle of the day when anyone might have walked in.

He hadn't said anything about talking with her after closing, but she hoped he would. If he didn't lose his nerve. She smiled. He always seemed so appreciative when she accomplished some task around the store. So she was determined to get as much of the back room done as she possibly could.

Her fingers strayed to a black rubber bowl. Pulling it off the shelf, she discovered it had a long, straight rod attached to its bottom. *What in the world?*

Was it a stand of some sort? A rain catcher? A candy dish? Whatever the thing was, she wiped it clean, then made a note to herself to ask Hamilton. He'd certainly know.

―――――――

Hamilton locked the door, pulled down the shade and took a deep breath. He'd studied Essie all day long. She had a strong, symmetrical face, with high cheekbones and bold lines—nothing delicate about it. Her cheeks dimpled when she smiled, her lower lip was fuller than the upper, her blue eyes were a bit too large, and her nose was a bit too thin.

What he couldn't determine, however, was what kind of shape she had hiding under that skirt. He knew her legs would be long. He just didn't know how much meat they'd have on them.

He'd seen her calves when she rode her bicycle—shoot, the whole town had seen them and there wasn't an ounce of extra padding on them.

A woman ought to be soft. Voluptuous. Something a man could

cozy up to. Not wiry and hard and muscular.

Oh, she had curves up top. Nothing overflowing, but nothing that would require an enhancer, either. Her stomach, however, was as flat as an iron. Would it be as hard?

He'd almost reached out and touched her today. Just to see.

But the woman already had wedding bells clanging in her head. He'd best not make any advances at all until he was sure. Absolutely sure that he could live the rest of his life with a woman he truly just did not find attractive. He'd managed to tolerate her bossy nature during working hours, but could he do the same every day and every night for the rest of his livelong days?

The thought gave him pause. He knew all about bossy women. His mother had ruled the roost while he was growing up, henpecking her husband and sons until Hamilton could hardly stand it anymore. He'd promised himself he would never, ever marry a mouthy woman.

Essie wasn't mouthy, exactly, just stubborn. And old. And set in her ways. A man liked to have a young, fresh gal on his arm. One he could shape and mold. One who would make the days go by quick and the nights go by slow. Not a woman who'd be turning gray a few short years after the nuptials.

If his conscience would let him, he'd write a list of all she offered and all she didn't. But that would be too cold. Too mercenary. Too unforgiving, by half.

He could hear Essie in the back throwing out a bucket of cleaning water. Humming to herself off key. He had perfect pitch and tuned the church organ by ear every Sunday before services. He could not abide an instrument that was so much as an eighth of a step off. Essie was a full half step off.

Maybe he should make a trip up to the wholesalers in Dallas. Get away for a few days. Think through exactly what he wanted to do.

"Hamilton?"

He turned. She might have been tidy earlier, but she was a mess now. Her blond hair stuck out in tufts, her hands were red from scrubbing, her apron was filthy, her face was smudged.

"Guess it's time we call it a day," he said.

She clasped her hands in front of her. Waiting. For something. He racked his mind. It wasn't payday. Wasn't . . . anything.

"Did you want something?" he asked.

She licked her lips. "Did you?"

"No. Not that I can think of."

"Oh." She shifted her weight. "I cleaned up all the top shelves and half of the middle ones."

"Excellent."

"I guess I'll finish the rest of them tomorrow."

"That'll be fine."

Still she stood there.

He adjusted his glasses. "Well. Good night, then."

She sighed. "Good night, Hamilton. I'll see you in the morning."

———————

Back home in front of the mirror, she pulled the pins from her disheveled hair. The candle on her vanity guttered in the breeze from the open window.

She was losing him. She could feel his hesitation. His doubt. His second-guessing. She had to do something. Fast.

She said her prayers, then climbed into bed. Was it because she got sick? Because she beat Mr. Owen at checkers? Was Hamilton still sore about that bearskin?

Whatever it was, she knew the quickest way to his heart was through his store. She must do something drastic. Something that would bring the town to his store in droves.

chapter FOUR

MORNING DEW DECORATED the lawns of Essie's neighborhood. Dappled sunlight from the eastern sky splashed onto the shimmering blades butted together like an endless green carpet.

She kept to the road, her strides long and brisk as she headed to the Slap Out, beseeching the Lord to give her a revelation. Some idea, some inspiration that would cultivate customers as numerous as the grass in these yards.

The screams of a child jerked her out of her reverie. Scanning the area, she spotted a young boy and girl in the vacant lot toward the end of the street.

The boy, who couldn't be more than six or seven, had placed himself between the girl and whatever was frightening them. Arms spread in a protective gesture, he stumbled back. The girl continued to scream and peer around his shoulder.

Lifting her skirts, Essie sprinted to them. As she approached, she recognized Emily Wedick, one of the many Wedick girls, and Harley North, an orphan who lived in the state's facility just outside of town.

"What is it?" Essie gasped. "What has happened?"

Harley, brown eyes wide with terror, pointed to a large, flat rock surrounded by weeds. Napping on top of its smooth surface was one of the most gorgeous prairie king snakes she had ever seen.

"Hush!" she whispered, laying a hand on Emily's shoulder. "You must hush at once."

The screams subsided into whimpers.

"Quickly, run next door and ask Mrs. Pennington for a gunnysack. Hurry."

The freckled girl darted away to do Essie's bidding, her long red braids flapping behind her.

"Is it poisonous?" Harley asked, his bare feet sticking out of trousers a good three inches too short.

"No, no. On the contrary, it is one of the finest snakes you'll ever see."

During her snake-collecting days, she and Papa had invented a rating system. The yellow-bellied water snake ranked higher than the ribbon snake. The hognose above the water. The rat above the hognose. The speckled king above the rat. And the prairie king above them all.

This snake was an exceptional specimen, with the smooth, dry scales of a recently shed skin. As it glistened in the morning light, she noted spots of chocolate brown speckling its beautiful tan hide, and its small head wore brown lightning bolts.

The girl finally returned and handed an empty flour sack to Essie.

Holding a finger to her lips, she silenced the children. With slow, quiet steps, she advanced, loosening her hold on the flour sack until it gaped open, then, with her free hand, snatched the three-and-a-half-foot reptile from the rock.

Emily screamed. The snake writhed and twisted in Essie's hand, spraying her with musk, but never attempted to bite her.

She lowered the king into the flour sack, knotted the opening, then spoke to it in a soothing voice. "Hush, now. It's going to be all right."

"Golly, Miss Essie," Harley said, his eyes wide. "What are you gonna do with it now?"

The snake hissed and wove around.

"I'm not sure. Are y'all okay?"

"Yes, ma'am," he said, though the girl still hovered behind him.

"Why don't you walk Emily home, Harley? Think you could do that for me?"

"I reckon."

"Go on, then. I'll take care of the snake." She waved them off, then headed back home. She'd have to bathe after being sprayed, which would make her late for work. But she wasn't worried. It was no coincidence the Lord had dropped this piece of manna from heaven. She'd prayed for something better than a black bear hide, and she'd gotten reptile royalty.

Everything was going to be fine now. Just fine.

———

Essie set the flour sack, snake and all, just outside the back door of the Slap Out.

"Sorry I'm late," she said, entering the storage room.

Hamilton hoisted a bag of grain onto his shoulder, then turned. "Is everything all right? You're not sick again, are you?"

"Good heavens, no. I hardly ever get sick." She tied her apron on. "I figured I'd go ahead and start on the rest of these shelves. You think you could mind the store without me for a while?"

He nodded. "So long as Miss Lizzie doesn't want any more fabric, I can. But if it gets busy, then come on out front with me."

"Will do."

The entry door jingled and he strode through the partition. As soon as he cleared the curtain, she grabbed a peach crate, wiped it down and laid a bed of newspaper in the bottom. Rummaging through the shelves, she found a small bowl, an empty cracker box, and a piece of poultry netting.

Outside, she scoured around for a limb, cleaned it and returned to organize the king's crate. Once all was in readiness, she opened the bag and poured the lightly floured snake into the crate.

He coiled immediately, lifting his head high and furiously buzzing his tail.

Essie smiled. "You don't fool me. I've known the difference

between a rattler and a prairie king since I was knee-high to a grass-hopper."

The reptile whirred in reverse, darting inside the open-ended cracker box, buzzing away. The front door jingled again.

Essie placed the mesh screen across the opening, weighing it down with a couple of rocks.

"You hungry? Well, you better stop your fussing, then. I have no intention of feeding you anything until you settle down. You hear?"

The quivering tail rat-a-tat-tatted against the wall of the box.

———

Essie's stomach growled and she glanced at the clock behind the counter. Almost noon. They'd been unusually busy for a Tuesday. Neither she nor Hamilton had had time to do anything other than wait on customers and it still hadn't slowed. A couple of women were perusing Hamilton's selection of garden teas, and old Mr. Mapey was just walking in.

"Hmmm," Mrs. Lockhart said, spinning the catalog toward Essie. "What about this one?"

Essie looked at the title Mrs. Lockhart pointed to with her crooked, wrinkled finger. She'd finished reading *Clarabel's Love Story* in one day and wanted another of Mrs. Clay's novels.

"Beyond Pardon," Essie read. "I'm not so sure. Sounds a bit, um, questionable, don't you think?"

The woman's face wilted in disappointment.

Essie absorbed her surprise at Mrs. Lockhart's tendency toward such silly books. She should undertake a more improved course of reading. "What about *Ivanhoe* by Sir Walter Scott?"

Mrs. Lockhart crinkled her nose and squinted at the catalog through her spectacles. "What about *Only One Sin?*"

Good heavens. "Well. I suppose everyone's sinned at least once."

The elderly woman straightened, a triumphant look upon her face. "Perhaps even twice!"

Essie nodded. "Shall I order—"

A crash, a scream, and a shocking curse from the back room

brought everyone to a standstill. The curtained door swished open. Hamilton stood at its entrance, face flushed, eyes snapping with violent anger.

His gaze found Essie at once. "Get back here."

She stood frozen to the spot.

"Now!"

She jumped. "Would you excuse me for a moment, Mrs. Lockhart?"

The woman's regard bounced between Essie and Hamilton, her eyebrows going up. "Of course, dear. I'll just look over the book list a little while longer. You'd best go on, though."

Hamilton's shoulders rose and fell like a bellows breathing a flame to life. He clenched the curtain open with a balled fist, then released it as she slipped by him, cutting them off from curious stares.

Grabbing her arm none too gently, he propelled her around some fallen buckets and toward the peach crate. "Just what the blazes is that?" he hissed.

"A snake?"

He swore. "I know what it is, Essie. I meant what is it doing here?"

She touched her stomach. "Hamilton! You mustn't curse."

His eyes narrowed. "Essie Spreckelmeyer, I will commit a much more grievous sin than that if you do not explain yourself immediately."

She knelt beside the crate and lifted the top just a crack so he could glimpse the speckled treasure within. "That's our bearskin."

"What are you talking about?"

"When everyone hears what we have, they'll come from all over to see it."

"You expect me to put that thing out there where my customers are? Woman, are you demented or just plain stupid?"

She sucked in her breath. "There is no need to get testy, Hamilton. This is an excellent plan." She snapped the crate lid shut. "Why, it's even an answer to prayer."

"An answer to prayer? *Satan* uses snakes, Essie, not God."

She rose to her full height and brushed the dust from her skirts. "Don't be ridiculous. God made it and He gave it to me."

"Then you can jolly well take it back home with you. I'll not risk injuring one of my customers."

"No, no," she said, clasping her hands in an effort to remain patient. "It's not a rattlesnake. It's not poisonous at all. It's a prairie king snake. They're quite harmless and not nearly as irritable as other kinds of snakes."

They stood facing each other, the only sound that of the snake's tail buzzing inside the cracker box.

"Then why is it rattling?" he asked.

"It's only shaking its tail, trying to scare off its enemies. You would, too, if you'd been living in the wild all this time and suddenly found yourself confined to a cracker box. It will settle down."

"And what if it doesn't?" he said, his voice rising.

"Hush," she whispered. "Someone will hear you."

"I want that snake out of here."

She grabbed his shirt-sleeve. "Don't you see? It's perfect. Most snakes have scars from encounters with their enemies. But this one— this one has no bobbed tail, puckered wound, healed sore or anything. It's as if God had been protecting it all this time just for us. Why, never have I caught such an exquisite specimen."

"*You* caught that thing?"

She cocked her head. "Well, of course. Where do you think I got it? The Flour, Feed and Liquor Store?"

He yanked his arm free. "It will scare more customers away than it will bring in."

"I don't think so. Especially if we have a snake-naming contest."

He crossed his arms.

"Everyone can submit names for the snake," she explained, "and then we can put it to a vote and whoever wins can receive a prize from the store." She tapped her fingernail against her apron. "But it must be a big prize. Something that will generate excitement . . . and sales, of course."

"A prize? Like what?"

"Oh, I don't know. A pocket watch or a brooch or a . . . a camera!

That would be perfect. It would appeal to men, women, and children alike."

"A camera? That's way too much money. I'm not giving away a camera."

"I'm not talking about a new order. I'm talking about overstock. Why, you have a Hawkeye Junior up on the shelf right there. Never been opened. I found it when I cleaned up yesterday."

He scanned the shelves, then grabbed a large rectangular box. "This thing costs seven dollars and twenty cents."

"Well, yes, but to keep using it, the customer will have to buy glass plates, which cost ninety cents each, or a roll of film, which is fifty-five. Besides, you have two Hawkeyes out in the store going nowhere."

He glanced down at the peach crate and scratched the back of his head. "I don't know, Essie."

"I do. We'll get the whole community involved. We can take nominations for names this week, give everyone the following week to cast their vote, and announce the winner of the prize the Saturday after that. Townsfolk will talk about the contest in their parlors, at their dinner tables, and at their social club meetings. And if for no other reason than curiosity, they'll come in to see the snake."

She held her breath. She knew it would work. She'd make sure of it.

Handing her the camera, he sighed. "All right, but you're in charge of that serpent. I'm not cleaning its cage or feeding it or running this contest. You'll have to do it all. And if it upsets my customers, it goes. Is that understood?"

She grabbed his lapel, gave him a quick peck on the cheek and then released him before he could blink. "Oh, thank you, Hamilton. You'll not be sorry, I promise."

Scurrying out of the storage room, she returned to the counter and placed the camera underneath. "Now, Mrs. Lockhart, I believe you were wanting to order *Only One Sin* by Mrs. Bertha Clay, is that correct?"

But Mrs. Lockhart ignored the catalog. "Is everything, um, all right, dear?"

"Why, yes." Essie glanced at the other customers eyeing her curiously. "Oh, you mean *back there*?"

Mrs. Lockhart gave her a nod.

"Yes, ma'am. We have everything all settled now."

"Do you, indeed?"

"Yes, ma'am."

"Splendid, splendid!" She patted Essie's hand. "Now, I should like to order *Only One Sin*, *Beyond Pardon*, and *A Mad Love*, please."

The following morning, Essie arrived at the store before Hamilton came downstairs. She slipped in the back door, lit a candle and set it down beside the king's crate.

After the initial shock of his capture had worn off yesterday, the snake had settled down and not rattled his tail at all. He'd even begun to nose around his new home of wood, tree limb, and newsprint. The final test would be whether or not he would eat. She'd had snakes before that had been so shocked by captivity, they'd refused to feed.

Opening her drawstring coin pouch, she lifted out a live white mouse by its tail and placed it in the crate.

Soon as it hit the newspaper, the mouse scurried to the corner, quivering. The snake poked its head out of the cracker box, forked tongue searching the scented air. Essie nodded, willing him to strike. The king stiffened, then shot forward and grabbed its prey, swallowing it whole.

Praise the Lord, Essie thought. *All will be well.*

chapter FIVE

HAMILTON WRAPPED UP two dozen finishing nails. "That'll be ten cents, George."

The young carpenter reached into a deep pocket of his brown duck overalls and pulled out a handful of change, all the while keeping his gaze on Essie.

Boys of every size and shape stood shoulder to shoulder, surrounding her like staves in the side of a barrel. She held the snake in her hands, letting it coil around her wrist and slither up her arm and onto her shoulder.

The boys watched wide-eyed as she took the snake by the neck and held it out for them to touch. A couple of the braver ones ran their fingers along the smooth, dry scales.

"That's one strange woman," George said. "Ain't natural the way she's so brash."

Hamilton agreed but refrained from saying so. The snake had definitely created an uproar, which had been good for business, but not so good for Essie. He wondered how a girl with so much smarts could have no sense of propriety. Her mother was well-known for being socially correct in every way. The poor woman must succumb to vapors on a regular basis over the behavior of her daughter.

Still, the snake brought in crowds of children and with them came their mothers, milling around, gossiping and shopping. So as long as customers came to watch, he'd ignore the unseemly side of the spectacle.

He glanced back at George, surprised to see the man's face bright red.

"Meant no offense," George said.

"None taken."

The man quickly paid for his purchase and hurried out the door just as a stranger entered. A tall cowboy. He stood inside, taking a quick survey of the store. The snake caught his eye immediately, but he soon pulled his gaze to Mrs. Tyner and her maiden daughter, Miss Sadie. Approaching them, he doffed his hat, laying it across his chest, and bowed slightly.

Both women simpered. The cowboy winked at the older woman, then looked the younger up and down.

"How-deeeeee-do," he said, slow and lazy.

Miss Sadie's cheeks filled with color and Mrs. Tyner hustled her back to the dry goods section, where Mrs. Lockhart examined a bolt of cotton.

The man strolled through the store, bowing, smiling, and "howdy-do"ing every woman regardless of age, shape, or size. His spurs jangled with each step and scraped Hamilton's carefully polished floor.

The cowboy paused at the stove and introduced himself to Vandervoort and his cronies. The whole shop grew quiet, the patrons craning to overhear the conversation. The ladies pretended to fiddle with various sundries as they marked every move the cowboy made and whispered furiously to one another.

He set his hat down and unhooked a tin cup from the wall, then poured himself a cup of coffee. After taking a sip, he wandered over to where Essie was holding court. Hamilton drew satisfaction in advance for what he knew Essie's reaction would be to the philanderer. She was not one to have her head turned by a pretty face and charming manners. No, she'd set him in his place, all right.

The cowboy stood like a captain on the quarterdeck, his feet spread wide. He took another sip of coffee. Essie glanced up, her lips parting as she gaped at the wrangler.

The snake, forgotten in her hands, slithered up her arm, across her shoulder, behind her neck, and back around, draping itself across her like a winter scarf. It glided down her chest, calling attention to her womanly features as it lifted its head into the air.

The man tracked the reptile's progress, and the corners of his mouth crooked up. "My name's Adam. Adam Currington. And if your name's Eve, I do believe I'm in a whole passel of trouble."

"Her name ain't Eve, mister," young Harley North said. "It's Miss Essie."

His smile widened, forming large brackets on both sides of his face. "Eve. Essie. That's mighty close, if I do say so myself."

"You cain't call her that lessen she gives ya permission. 'Til then, you'd best be calling her Miss Spreckelmeyer."

His eyebrows lifted. "Spreckelmeyer? The judge's daughter?"

She nodded, still in a daze.

He set his coffee on a barrel and stepped through the circle of boys. Lifting his palm like a beggar, he let the snake pass from her chest to his hand, then up the length of his arm where it crinkled his blue shirt and coiled around muscles that were clearly accustomed to heavy work.

"I do believe this is the prettiest catch I've seen in a long, long while," he drawled.

Hamilton scowled. The cowboy wasn't looking at the snake. He was looking at Essie. What the blazes was wrong with her? Couldn't she see he was all talk? A man with looks like that could want only one thing from a spinster woman.

Hamilton came out from around the counter, but Mrs. Lockhart intercepted him.

"I've been suffering from a most troublesome headache, Mr. Crook. Might you have something for me?" she asked.

He hesitated, glanced at Essie in frustration, then changed directions and headed to the medicinals.

The cowboy from Essie's childhood dreams had materialized before her very eyes. And, oh my, but he was even more beautiful in the flesh.

The prairie king ventured from the man's arm on up to his neck. Its head disappeared momentarily while it circled around only to return again to the front.

The tail end of the three-and-a-half-foot snake still clung to her neck, effectively tying her to Mr. Adam Currington. The king lifted its head, testing the air with its forked tongue. She reached out and the pet glided across to her hand. Currington moved closer, letting the snake encircle them.

"What's its name?" he whispered.

"He doesn't have one yet. We're in the middle of a naming contest, actually. Would you like to enter?"

"You gonna be the judge?"

"One of them."

"Is there a prize, too?"

She nodded.

He stroked his finger along the snake's back where it crossed her shoulder. "Yes, ma'am. I surely would like to play, then."

His hat had left an indention in his blond hair, bringing out a few streaks of brown that matched the brows framing his blue-green eyes. When he smiled, the coppery skin crinkled around their corners.

"I'm afraid you'll be well on your way by the time the winner is announced," Hamilton said, startling Essie into taking a step back.

She gathered up the snake, which Mr. Currington released reluctantly, then squeezed through her audience of children to place it back in its crate.

The stranger stuck his hand out toward Hamilton. "I'm Adam Currington, one of the crew that's been hired by the Commercial Club to dig a few water wells for y'all."

Disappointment surged through Essie. "You're not a cowboy?" she asked, placing two rocks on top of the mesh lid.

He retrieved his coffee and rested his weight on one leg. "Well, I reckon I am, ma'am. But it gets mighty hot and lonely on the trail, so I decided a change might be nice."

"You're a drifter, then," Hamilton said.

Essie frowned. "Mr. Currington, this is Hamilton Crook, proprietor of the Slap Out."

"Howd—"

"Lookit here, Miss Spreckelmeyer," Jeremy Gillespie hollered, charging into the store with six of his twelve siblings behind him, chattering in excitement. Withdrawing his hands from the large pockets of his jacket, he held two live mice suspended by their tails in one hand, three in the other.

Sadie Tyner screamed, startling everyone including Jeremy, who loosened his hold on the mice. Three of the five fell with a thump to the floor and scattered in all directions.

One of the furry critters scampered between Adam's legs and he jumped back, sloshing coffee onto his sleeve. The judge's daughter dove for the mouse, stretching out full length on the floor and knocking Adam's feet right out from under him.

He pitched sideways to keep from landing on her, spraying coffee in the general direction of heaven. His shoulder clipped a barrel as he hit the floor, knocking over a box of ball bearings. The metal balls scattered onto the wooden floor, pinging with each bounce.

As he rolled out of their way, he found himself pressed cheek-by-jowl against Miss Essie. The gal had managed to trap one of the escapees in her outstretched hands, then, quicker than a flea, she hopped up and ran with it to the back, giving Adam no nevermind at all.

The youngsters had taken up the chase like hounds after a fox, barking and squealing and shouting. The scrawny little miss who'd started the ruckus with her scream hadn't let up. She'd vaulted onto a table of ready-mades, knocking shoes, hats, long johns, and bonnets onto the floor. One of the old beans pushed the girl's mother behind him, shielding her with his body—as if that was going to accomplish anything.

Adam sprang to his feet and raced through the store, grasping women by their waists and lifting them onto any available surface, whether it be table, counter, barrel, or chair. The one with a cane he was particularly gentle with, excusing himself even as he placed her on a countertop.

He heard her sigh like a schoolgirl just before he saw Essie storm out of the back room with a small cage and a black bowl that had a rod attached to it. She set the cage down in front of the teener who'd brought in the mice—and still had two dangling from his fingertips— then thrust the bowl contraption into the hands of a bowlegged old John standing wide-eyed by the checkerboard.

"Here," she shouted over the commotion. "Use this."

"I see one!" one of the youngsters hollered. Essie pushed the man in that direction, then scanned the floor looking for the third mouse. Her gaze halted abruptly and she flew across the room to a small gap between some shelves and a wall of bins.

The fancy-pants proprietor stood dazed, motionless, and as worthless as a milk bucket under a bull. Adam hurried over to catch the mouse Essie had spotted, but before he could reach her, she knelt down on all fours and squeezed her arm into the crack between the shelves.

The space was too dark and narrow to look into, so she pressed her ear against it and blindly felt inside.

"Need some help?" he asked, squatting down beside her.

"I have it, sort of."

"Sort of?"

"The very tip of its tail is underneath my finger. I'm just trying to . . ." She clamped her tongue between her teeth, then gasped. "Botheration!"

She leapt up, searching the floor around them. A lump beneath her skirt caught his attention. The pesky thing was climbing her petticoats like a ladder.

"Hold still!" he hissed. She froze and he flicked up her skirt, sliding his hand between the dark serge and white petticoat underneath before latching on to the varmint.

When it dawned on him where his hand lay, he glanced up at her face, trying to gauge her reaction. He might have long been floundering in the mire of sin, but she looked like somebody'd shown her a fifth ace in a poker deck.

A thunder of boots on the wooden floor at the other end of the store drew his attention. The old cuss with the newfangled mouse catcher spun around like a button on a privy door, trying to capture the wily rodent.

The children shouted. One of the women swooned. A quick survey of the room assured him no one was taking notice of him and Essie.

Keeping a tight hold on his own mouse, he rotated his hand so his knuckles rested against her leg, layers of soft, ruffled petticoats shielding her skin from his touch. He was in no hurry as he drug his hand down her long, long leg.

For a moment, her expression turned soft and dreamy. She was a ripe one, all right. But she was the judge's daughter and possibly Mr. Prissy Pants' betrothed. She must have remembered this herself, for she suddenly jerked away from his touch.

He pulled his hand out and dropped her hem, taking in the dips and swells of her landscape as he stood.

"Did you . . . did you get it?" she whispered.

"Right in the palm of my hand, sweetheart."

A cheer rose up from the other faction. "He caught it! He caught it! Mr. Vandervoort caught it!"

Adam gave her the mouse and gently squeezed her waist. "They're calling for you, Miss Essie. You'd best go see to them."

Essie helped Mr. Vandervoort put the last mouse into the cage while the children all spoke at once. The cowboy lifted the women by their waists and set them back on solid ground. The sound of his pandering voice, full of false solicitude, turned Hamilton's stomach.

The last time he'd experienced this kind of anger was when his older brothers had bent the tip of a willow tree to the ground and told him to grab on with both hands and feet. They let go and left him clinging upside down for what had seemed like hours.

He still remembered how helpless he'd been, stuck atop that tree with no way of getting down. If anything, this was worse.

The front door wrenched open and Sheriff Dunn stomped in. "What in tarnation is going on?" His hollering brought silence as quickly as a gavel in a noisy courtroom.

Dunn was a solid man. Not tall, not short. Not fat, not thin. Just solid. His gray, bushy moustache hid his mouth and made Hamilton want to sell him a moustache comb and scissors every time he saw him.

Gripping his rifle, Dunn scanned the room, taking in the Gillespie boy and then halting altogether on the cowboy.

"Uncle Melvin," Essie exclaimed, hurrying toward him. "There's no need for distress. Just a little game of cat-and-mouse."

Vandervoort let out an amused bark.

"Crook?" the sheriff asked, still keeping his attention on Currington.

"Everything's fine," Hamilton answered.

The tension in the room dissipated with his words, only to be replaced with a resurgence of excitement as Essie, Vandervoort, and the children all started explaining what had happened. The cowboy helped the last two women from their perches without a word, then picked up his hat and slipped out the door.

Hamilton noted the sheriff missed none of it, though he appeared to be listening to Essie's explanation.

"So you see, it was really my fault," she continued. "I had told the children that anyone who brought in a mouse for our snake would receive a chance to actually feed it."

With Currington gone, the sheriff relaxed and rubbed his neck. "Looks like a twister went through here. You catch 'em all?"

"Yes, we did. And I'll have this mess cleaned up in no time."

He smiled. "I know you will."

Sheriff Dunn was Mrs. Spreckelmeyer's brother and a lifelong friend to Mr. Spreckelmeyer. As Essie's uncle, he held particular affection for her. Hamilton suppressed the urge to roll his eyes, irritated over the sheriff's partiality to Essie almost as much as he had been over the cowboy's easy banter.

"Want to see the mice?" she asked.

"I'd rather see the king."

She grabbed his hand and pulled him toward the snake's crate.

After a long look, the sheriff whistled his appreciation. "That's a beauty, sugar. You catch that all by yourself?"

"She shore did," little Harley said. "This thing here had me and Emily Wedick scared something awful. But Miss Essie snatched it up with her bare hands and stuffed it in a gunnysack. She didn't scream or nothin'. And she caught two of them mouses, too."

Dunn chuckled. "Well, if she keeps this up, I just might have to deputize her."

Some of the women snickered and Mrs. Tyner, who a few moments earlier had been perched on the counter, put her hands on her hips and snorted.

"Of all the ridiculous things," she said. "A woman deputy, indeed."

Sheriff Dunn straightened his spine, having no tolerance for disparaging remarks concerning his niece.

Old Vandervoort jumped in, waving the bust enhancer in the air triumphantly. "Well, I'll tell you something. I ain't never seen a mouse catcher that works so good as this one. Where'd you get this, Miss Essie?"

Miss Sadie Tyner took one look at the thing and gasped, clapping a hand over her mouth. Hamilton appraised the girl, comprehension dawning, only to blush profusely when Miss Sadie caught his speculative perusal. Blood drained from her face.

"Why, I found it gathering dust in the back," Essie answered. "Would you like to purchase it?"

"I surely would," Vandervoort replied, tucking it under his arm like a fancy gentleman's riding crop.

"Me too," Mr. Owen said. Followed by seconds from Jenkins and Richie.

"Wonderful. Hamilton?" Essie turned to him, flushed with pleasure. "If you'll write their orders, I'll start cleaning up this mess."

He snatched the bust enhancer out of Vandervoort's grasp. "This isn't for sale."

"Oh," Essie replied. "Well, all right, then. We'll just order Mr. Vandervoort one, too."

"No," Hamilton said, beads of sweat forming on his brow. If these ladies figured out what this was he'd be ruined.

Essie frowned at him.

Shaking, he wanted nothing more than to toss her out on her backside. He cleared his throat. "I'm afraid . . . that is, I'm sorry, but the firm that made them has . . . has failed."

Miss Sadie pressed a handkerchief to her brow, looking faint, but apart from Hamilton, no one took notice.

"Oh no!" Essie said. "Are you sure?"

"Quite sure." Turning his back, he stomped to the storage room and shoved the enhancer back up on the top shelf.

———————

Settling herself onto the piano stool in the parlor, Essie allowed her fingers to move across the keys, playing Beethoven's "Für Elise" by heart. Since childhood, Essie had whiled away the hours sitting at the keyboard. And this was the piece she always played when she wanted to indulge a particular fantasy—an idyllic afternoon being romanced by her imaginary beau.

During the prelude, they picnicked beside Two Bit Creek and fed each other bites of egg salad sandwiches. His lips grazed her finger accidentally. She blushed and pulled her hand away.

As the interlude began, they swung up onto their horses and raced neck-and-neck around Waller's Bend, their mounts stretching and straining forward. At the last moment, she bent down, urging the horse forward, and pulled ahead of her cavalier. She hadn't realized, of course, that he had held his horse back, allowing hers to win.

The piece moved into a crescendo, and she pulled her mount to a stop. He drew his horse next to hers and brought her hand up to his lips for a kiss.

A knock at the front door interrupted her musings, but not her music. She softened the notes while her mother answered the door.

"Hello, Melvin. Sullivan's back in his office."

"Actually, Doreen," he said, "I was thinking to enjoy this mild weather we're havin'. Would you mind telling him I'm waiting for him on the porch?"

"Not at all."

Essie moved into the final lines. Her mother and Uncle Melvin had talked during the part of the music where she married the man of her dreams. Now she and her "husband" sat at a dinner table with a horde of their offspring gathered round. He said a prayer of thanksgiving. For their meal. For their children. And for their everlasting love.

She left her finger on the final key until all sound faded. This past month, Hamilton had played the part of the gallant in her dreams, but tonight he'd been replaced by Mr. Adam Currington.

The cowboy embodied the very thing dreams were made of. Exceptional looks. Exceptional charm. Exceptional . . . everything. A man like him would love the out-of-doors. Animals. Riding. Fishing. She closed her eyes, reliving their shared intimacy, feeling once more the tingles that had run down her leg this morning.

Dusk settled in, but she didn't light a lantern. Instead, she sat still on the piano stool, unmoving in the growing dark. A breeze fanned the curtains along the front wall, bringing with it Papa and Uncle Melvin's voices from the porch as they discussed the prophecies of Isaiah. The conversation eventually drifted from Scriptures to town happenings. When Adam's name was mentioned, though, Essie's senses came to attention.

"You know much about him?" the sheriff asked.

"He told the Club he'd lived in the desert so long he knew all the lizards by their front names and was ready for a change."

Essie smiled. Sounded like something Adam would say.

"Well, he sure had all the ladies at the Slap Out in a twitter."

"I can just imagine," Papa said with a laugh.

"Speaking of ladies in a twitter," the sheriff continued, "how's things between Crook and our girl?"

"Strangest thing," Papa said. "Doreen was so sure Essie was making a fool of herself chasing after him up at his store and all—"

"I wouldn't say she was chasing him, exactly."

"—but I'll have you know he approached me after church last Sunday and asked to come speak with me this week."

The creaking of Uncle Melvin's rocker came to a stop. "Is he going to make a declaration, do you think?"

"What else could it be?"

Essie's heart galloped.

"Think he's good enough for her?" Uncle Melvin asked.

"If Essie thinks so, then I don't see I'll have much choice."

The rocker started creaking again. "I reckon so. He was good to his first wife. Runs a clean place." He sighed. "I hope the young'uns take after Essie, though."

Papa chuckled. Essie slipped from the parlor and up to her room, savoring this momentous news. She pushed all thoughts of Adam Currington firmly from her mind.

Mrs. Hamilton Crook. Mrs. Esther Crook. Mrs. Crook.

O Lord. Thank you, thank you, thank you.

chapter SIX

HAMILTON LOCKED THE Slap Out's door and let out a sigh, savoring the stillness that came at the end of a busy day. After a pause, he turned to where Essie was tallying votes. The snake-naming contest had brought more trade than any tactic he'd ever tried in the past.

She sorted the final votes into neat stacks on the barrel that normally held a checkerboard. Banjo, Willie Waddle, Laddie, Colonel, and Butcher were the names still in contention.

"Doesn't look like the Willie Waddle stack is doing too well," she said.

"Thank goodness. I can't imagine how such an undignified name made it into the top five."

She smiled. "There's no accounting for taste."

He refrained from commenting.

She wore a navy-and-white shirtwaist with novelty buttons and puff sleeves. Her blond hair had begun to loosen from its pins, but ever since the catastrophe with the escaped mice, she'd curbed her behavior some and, for the most part, conducted herself with total propriety.

The woman might be unconventional. She might be too outdoorsy. She might be plain looking. But she sure could bring in the customers.

The stairs creaked and a moment later Mrs. Peterson peeked in. Alarm flashed through him. She'd been looking after baby Mae since his wife's death and never disturbed him unless it was urgent.

"Mrs. Peterson?" he said. "Is everything all right?"

The frumpy woman entered from the storage room, carrying Mae in her arms. "I'm sorry, sir, but I cannot stay late tonight. My grandson turns two today and my daughter's having me over for the celebration. Had you forgotten?"

Relief poured through him. "Well, yes, I'm afraid I did. But you go ahead, of course." He took Mae and saw Mrs. Peterson out the door.

The baby kicked her legs and waved her plump arms up and down. At some point in the last seven months, Hamilton had gone from being angry at the child for Eleanor's death to treasuring her for the link she provided to his late wife.

"Oh, Hamilton," Essie said, staring at the baby. "Look how big she's gotten."

"Has she? It's hard to tell when you see her every day."

Shifting in her chair, Essie opened her arms. "May I?"

"Certainly." He handed her the baby.

Essie smiled and stroked Mae's cheek. The baby turned her head and took Essie's little finger into her mouth. "Oh, my goodness. I can see you're a hearty eater."

Watching Essie coo and cuddle Mae brought an unexpected tightness to Hamilton's chest. Mrs. Peterson was an old woman. Fifty, at least, maybe older. She looked nothing like Essie when she held the baby.

Essie looked soft and womanly and, for the first time ever, downright attractive. The tightness in Hamilton shifted slightly into something he'd not felt in quite a while.

Mae grabbed a piece of Essie's hair and yanked, freeing it from the pins. Essie laughed and bent over, rubbing noses with his baby.

"Ummmmm," she said. "There's nothing quite so yummy as a baby's neck." She nibbled on Mae's neck, eliciting a squeal of delight from the baby.

Hamilton swallowed.

"She smells like oatmeal," Essie said, then looked up when he didn't respond.

Mae pounded and pushed against Essie's chest, molding the fabric of the shirtwaist to her curves. Tendrils of hair fell across her shoulder and down her back. Her blue eyes, framed with what he now realized were exceedingly long lashes, shone with joy. Dimples framed her mouth.

Bending down, he placed one hand on the back of her chair and the other on top of the barrel, and kissed her while she clutched his baby in her arms.

It was a fleeting kiss, the barest of touches, really. But when he pulled back, he pulled back only an inch. Just enough to see her lips, smell her scent, feel her breath.

He acknowledged his desire, then cupped Essie's chin and kissed her again. This time with the intention of finding out just exactly what the town spinster was made of.

Mae began to protest and Essie pulled back. "Hamilton," she whispered, "I'm not at all sure this is proper."

He felt a quick pang of guilt. Whether it was due to feeling desire for a woman he didn't love or for feeling desire at all, he didn't know.

"You're right," he said, straightening and pushing his glasses up his nose. "My apologies."

A look of confusion crossed her face. "Oh, please don't apologize. Never tell me you're sorry, Hamilton. Are you?"

He lifted Mae into his arms. "I'm afraid I won't be able to help you tally these votes tonight, Essie. Perhaps we could do it in the morning?"

She rose, concern etched onto her face. "Are you angry with me?"

"Not at all."

"You're acting angry."

"No, I'm not. You know what I'm like when I'm angry and this is not it."

She tucked her hair back up into her pins. "I see. Well, then, I'll just, um, let myself out. Good night, Hamilton. Good night, Mae."

———

Essie reread the paragraph for the umpteenth time, but still her thoughts wandered. She glanced at her mother, envying her ability to sit calmly in her parlor chair stitching an ornate *S* on the corner of her handkerchief, as if she hadn't a care in the world. As if it were only another ordinary Sunday afternoon.

"Is the book not to your liking, dear?" she asked.

"Where is he, Mother?" Essie asked.

"I have been thinking," she said. "I don't believe I shall plant morning glories along the front verandah next year. Have you noticed how many bees they attract?"

Essie looked out the parlor windows, accepting her mother's none-too-subtle change of topic. "I like the sound of their humming. It's soothing."

"It's distressing. And a constant reminder you could be stung at any moment. No, I shan't plant them so close to the house again. Have you any suggestions for their replacements?"

Essie sighed. "No, Mother. I haven't the slightest idea."

She and Hamilton had announced the snake's name and the winner of the camera yesterday amidst much fanfare and excitement. By day's closing they'd had record sales. But Hamilton had been distant and distracted.

Essie had been beside herself with excitement. He'd kissed her. All that was left was for him to make his declaration to Papa. He'd said nothing of their kiss all day yesterday, nor should he. But she'd relived it a thousand times in her mind.

This morning she'd taken great care in preparing for church. He'd treated her the same as he always did, greeting her and her family with the friendly politeness he greeted everyone else with. But the entire time, she knew he would be coming to the house today to make his declaration, for he'd told Papa he'd be by before the day was up.

Turning the page, she surreptitiously smoothed out the pieces of paper she'd inserted into the book. *Fredrick Fouty, Charlie Wedick, Winston Peeples, Hamilton Crook.*

She paused, reviewing the assets and drawbacks she'd assigned to Hamilton. If she redid the list today, she'd have so much more to put in his "asset" column.

"Did you hear the news at church?" Mother asked.

"I'm sorry?" Essie said, looking up from her musings. "Did you say news?"

"Yes. I heard that Ewing's coming home."

"Ewing? Ewing Wortham?"

"Mm-hmm. He's to graduate from that fancy Bible college in Nashville in another few months, and our church is considering him as a replacement for Preacher Bogart once he retires."

"That would be awfully strange, wouldn't it?" Essie shook her head. "Seems like yesterday he was running around in short pants and pulling the girls' pigtails. I can't quite picture him at the pulpit, can you?"

The knock was abrupt, causing Essie to jump. In a slow and unruffled manner, her mother set aside her stitching and answered the door.

"Good evening, Mr. Crook. Won't you please come in?"

"Thank you, Mrs. Spreckelmeyer. I was, uh, wondering if I could visit with the judge for a few moments?"

The sound of his voice filled Essie. She closed her eyes, wanting to commit to memory every detail of this life-changing occasion.

"Yes, he's been expecting you. If you would like, Essie is in the parlor and I'm sure she'd be glad to keep you company while I tell him you are here."

Essie stood as he entered.

He still wore his Sunday clothes, his hat grasped tightly in his hands. "Miss Spreckelmeyer."

"Mr. Crook," Essie said. "Please, sit down."

They both sat while her mother went to get Papa.

"Yesterday's winner was quite the topic at church this morning, I noticed," she said.

He nodded. "I'm so glad Willie Waddle was not the winning name. Having a pet snake is bad enough. But having one named

Willie Waddle would have been more than I could bear, I'm afraid."

"Well, Colonel is a grand name, I think."

"Yes. Yes, I agree." His gaze caught, then narrowed on her book. "Is that one of Mrs. Lockhart's novels?"

Essie sighed and placed the closed book on the table beside her. "I'm afraid it is. She's foisted it on me, insisting I read it. I have been trying for an hour to get past the first few pages but haven't had much luck."

"I should hope not."

Silence.

"How is Mae today?"

He smiled. "Fine. Just fine. She's such a good baby, you know."

Essie returned his smile. "She's lovely, Hamilton. Very much like you."

His eyes widened and Essie could have ripped her tongue out. Oh, where was Mother? "May I get you something to drink? Some lemonade, perhaps?"

"Yes, please. If it's no trouble."

She hurried from the room and with fumbling fingers poured the lemonade. Upon her return, she found Hamilton studying Mrs. Lockhart's novel. She froze, tray in hand.

Hamilton snapped the book shut, the edges of her personal papers peeking out. "I must admit, it has been very interesting reading after all."

"Hamilton," she said, placing the tray on a nearby cart. "Let me explain."

"Mr. Crook?"

They both started at Mother's beckoning.

"Judge Spreckelmeyer will see you now. Won't you come this way?"

Essie placed a hand on his arm. "Wait—"

He shook off her hand, his eyes frosty and distant. Mother glanced between the two of them before escorting him out, their footsteps echoing down the hall.

Moments later her mother returned to her chair and gave Essie a brief, questioning look before plying her needle.

Essie picked up the book. Her hands shook so badly, she immediately sat and rested the novel upon her lap. The clock chimed the quarter hour, then the half hour.

Her father's door opened.

"Thank you so much for seeing me, Judge."

"Anytime, Crook. Anytime. Good day, now."

"Good day to you, too, sir. And thank you."

The front door opened and closed. The sound of Hamilton bouncing down the porch steps reached the ears of those in the parlor. When all was silent, Papa stepped into the room.

Mother lowered her stitching. Essie clutched her book.

He looked first at Mother, then at her. "He asked if the Slap Out could be granted a license to act as a post office."

Essie waited, but he said nothing more. "Is that all he asked for, Papa?"

His entire face showed his distress. "I'm sorry."

"A post office," Essie repeated. "Well. Will you give it to him?"

"It's not my decision, ultimately, but I agreed to initiate the paper work and to give him a recommendation to the state."

She nodded. "Good. That's . . . why, it's wonderful news. I know he's thrilled. Thank you, Papa."

"Squirt," he whispered.

But she'd already left the room.

———

"I'm going up to market in Dallas for a few days," Hamilton said. "Do you think you can handle things while I'm gone?"

Essie paused before slipping a bolt of fabric onto the shelf. "Of course. When were you thinking of leaving?"

"Right now."

"Right now! But . . . but what about Mae?"

"Mrs. Peterson has agreed to stay with her while I'm gone. I've already sent my trunk to the station."

"Oh." Essie looked around the store, trying to get her bearings.

Since their incident in the parlor, she hadn't known quite what to do or say. He'd been completely unapproachable, either barking at her or ignoring her.

"Hamilton, about yesterday—"

"I won't be away for more than two or three days and will be back before Saturday, in any event."

"I see." She straightened a stack of handkerchiefs on the table.

"Well, good-bye, then." He pushed his glasses up.

"Good-bye, Hamilton. Godspeed."

ES: DELAYED STOP BE BACK MONDAY STOP HAVE BIG SURPRISE STOP HC

Essie pressed the telegram against her heart. Absence really did make the heart grow fonder. She slipped the telegram back into the envelope and placed it in her apron pocket.

She'd never been sent a telegram before. It was heady, receiving such a thing. And he wasn't mad anymore. Was even going to bring her a surprise to make up for their little misunderstanding.

She raised the shade and propped open the door to the Slap Out.

Essie held the mouse catcher high over her head, gently twirling it in a circular motion. Each boy crowding around her had placed his name in the black bowl at the end of the rod.

"Mr. Vandervoort?" Essie asked. "Would you like to do the honors?"

He looked up from the checkerboard. "Why, shore, Miss Essie." Standing, he hitched up his trousers and looked the group over. "All these fellas brought in a mouse?"

"That's right. You pick a name from the bowl, and that's who gets to feed Colonel."

Vandervoort raised his hand and fished inside the bowl.

"*Essie!* What in the blue blazes are you doing?"

Essie jumped. Vandervoort jumped. The children jumped.

"Hamilton! You're home!"

He strode to her, his hair mussed, his complexion windburned, his eyes furious. He snatched the mouse catcher out of her hand, spilling a couple of names from its bowl.

She had no idea what he was angry about and she didn't care. She was so very glad to see him. "Mr. Vandervoort?" she said, never taking her eyes off Hamilton. "Whose name did you draw?"

"Lawrence's."

She turned her attention to Lawrence. He was about six years of age and from one of the better families in town. "Congratulations, Lawrence. You won! Would you like me to show you how to feed Colonel?"

"He will have to wait," Hamilton said. "I must see you in the back."

She smiled. It was so good to have him home. "Of course." She glanced at Lawrence. "I'll return in just a moment."

Hamilton grasped her arm and propelled her to the storage room. As soon as they made it through the curtain, he spun her around.

"What's the matter?" she asked.

He shoved the mouse catcher toward her. "Hold this."

She took it.

"Don't move."

He disappeared into the store and then returned with the catalog in hand. He slammed it onto a barrel. "Page two hundred thirty-one," he said, then swept back into the store.

Frowning, she put down the mouse catcher and turned to page 231 in the catalog. Strewn across the top of the page in large, bold letters were the words: **THE PRINCESS BUST DEVELOPER AND BUST CREAM.**

She touched her hand to her lips, quickly skimming the advertisement. A drawing of the mouse catcher accompanied a lengthy explanation of the product. *A new scientific help to nature . . . will produce desired result . . . comes in two sizes . . .*

She moved her attention to the second half of the page. *BUST CREAM . . . delightful cream preparation . . . forms just the right formula for wasted tissues . . . greatest toilet requisite ever offered . . .*

She closed her eyes. Mortified. It could not be. Oh, how would she ever face him again? Any of them. But, no, the others didn't know what it was, either. Why, they had even wanted to order some.

What a scandal that would have been if those old-timers had bought bust developers and started chasing mice all over town with them. Choking, she opened her eyes and picked up the developer, examining it. She placed it over herself, then jerked it away, embarrassed. Horrified. Fascinated.

Did it actually work? Who had ordered it? And why had the customer never picked it up? She quickly did a mental count of the women in town, but she couldn't imagine anyone ordering such a ridiculous thing. She slipped it back up on the top shelf.

Nothing in all her born days had prepared her for how to handle a situation such as this. But Hamilton was home, and he had a surprise for her. And nothing was going to keep her from that surprise—not even his understandable anger about her innocent mistake.

She stepped out from behind the curtain. Hamilton was waiting on a petite woman Essie had never seen before. He glanced up and turned a startling shade of red. She felt her own skin flush.

He excused himself and headed toward her. A surge of excitement shot through her. She'd seen married couples share moments such as this. Communicating with each other across a room and at a level that no one else could match.

As embarrassed as she was, she could not help but enjoy the thrill of sharing this intimate moment with him. He stopped in front of her, shielding her from the view of others.

"I don't know what to say, Hamilton. I'm horrified."

"You didn't know."

"I certainly did not. But whose is it?"

Red stained his cheeks again. "The order was placed without my knowledge. It arrived after Eleanor passed, and I had no way of discovering whose it was."

"Did you see how much it cost?"

"I know. I can't throw it out because someone in this town has paid for it. So I'll just have to keep it up on that shelf until it is claimed. But in the meanwhile, I don't think we should be using it to trap mice and have drawings."

Essie could not stop a tiny chuckle from escaping. "Of course not."

He frowned. "This is not the least bit amusing, Essie."

"Miss Spreckelmeyer?"

Essie peeked around Hamilton to see Lawrence, mouse already in hand. She crooked a finger at him and took his free hand. "Would you excuse us a moment, please, Hamilton?"

"Yes, yes. Hurry it up before he drops it."

She smiled and led Lawrence to Colonel's cage.

"First," she said, "you must remove the mesh top from the crate."

The other boys gathered around. Lawrence handed her the mouse, then placed the two rocks on the floor and lifted off the mesh top. Colonel tested the air with his forked tongue, but otherwise didn't stir himself.

Lawrence retrieved the mouse, holding it by its tail.

"Drop it in," she said.

"Will it hurt the mouse?" he asked.

"How animals obtain their food is designed by God," she said. "He made the mouse and He made the snake. We must trust that He knew what He was doing."

"Will the mouse go to heaven?"

She hesitated only a moment. "I pray it is so."

He dropped the mouse into the crate. Colonel clamped his mouth around it, then proceeded to swallow it whole. The boys made noises of approval.

A sound behind them caused Essie to turn. The new customer Hamilton had been helping swooned. Jeremy Gillespie caught the woman. Her alabaster skin was as smooth and white as a china doll's, her rich black hair startling in its contrast.

Hamilton rushed to her side. "Darling? Darling? Are you all

right?" He took her from Jeremy and patted her cheeks. "Katherine? Can you hear me?"

Cold swept through Essie's innards, spreading to her limbs. She stood.

Hamilton found Essie with his gaze. "Can you do something? She's fainted."

Essie moved by rote to the medicinal section and took some smelling salts from the middle shelf, then poured cold water into a tin cup. A cousin. An in-law. A sister. *Please, Lord. Let it be a sister.*

A crowd of people had gathered. She excused herself and they made a path for her. Hamilton took the salts and waved them under Katherine's nose.

She was a shapely woman. Soft and lush, where Essie was hard and firm. Small and petite, where Essie was tall and long. Pale and fragile, where Essie was sunburned and tough.

Her eyes fluttered open. "Hamilton?"

"I'm here, my dear. I'm here."

She smiled at him. This was no cousin or in-law or sister.

Trembling, Essie knelt opposite Hamilton. She dipped her apron into the cup of water and swabbed the woman's face.

A tiny bit of color returned to her cheeks. "Thank you."

"Of course," Essie said. "Are you better, ma'am?"

"Yes. But I think I'll just rest a moment. Such a shock, you know. That poor little mouse."

Essie lifted her gaze to Hamilton.

He swallowed and looked down at the woman. "Katherine? I'd like you to meet my store clerk, Essie Spreckelmeyer. Essie? This is my new wife, Katherine Crook."

chapter SEVEN

ESSIE'S HEARTBEAT ROSE. Her breathing grew labored. The blood drained from her head down to her stomach, leaving her dizzy and slightly ill.

But she would not faint. She refused to succumb. Her mind gave her body strict orders to settle down, but it would not listen. She wiped her face with the corner of the apron she'd just used to wipe Katherine Crook's. *Mrs.* Katherine Crook.

How could he? she thought. He'd kissed her only last week. Surely he'd not been engaged this entire time?

"My goodness," she managed, hoping her voice did not betray the upheaval within her. "This is a surprise."

Mrs. Crook had closed her eyes again, oblivious to the introduction and the undercurrents it provoked.

Hamilton's glasses had slid to the end of his nose, giving Essie an unobstructed view of his eyes. He looked so different without his glasses. So young.

His hands were full, so Essie reached over and pushed his glasses up where they belonged. "Congratulations," she whispered.

"Essie," he said, but she lightly touched her finger to his mouth, shushing him.

"I believe your wife has fainted again. Perhaps you should take her upstairs and when she awakens introduce her to your . . . your baby."

To her horror, a sheen of tears glazed her eyes. She dare not blink or they'd fall and her humiliation would be complete.

"Katherine and I have known each other since childhood," Hamilton said. "We ran into each other in Dallas. It was as if we hadn't been apart for more than a day or two, so quickly did our rapport return. I had no idea she'd been married, much less widowed. And, well, one thing led to another and—"

"Hamilton," Essie said, nodding toward the crowd gathered around them.

He glanced up and scowled, then slid his hands beneath his wife, lifting her as he rose to his feet. "Essie, will you follow me, please?"

No, Hamilton, no. You cannot ask me to follow you while you carry your bride up those stairs and across the threshold.

But she rose and went with him through the curtain, as far as the stairs.

"Hamilton," she said.

He paused, his wife limp in his arms. The gold band encircling his fourth finger jumped out at Essie. She looked at Katherine's hands, but they were still hidden inside her gloves.

"I think it best if I stay with the store," Essie said. "Mrs. Peterson will know what to do. If you need a doctor, have Mrs. Peterson come and tell me. I will see to it."

His Adam's apple bobbed. "Essie, I don't know what to say."

"Go on. We'll be fine down here."

"Are you sure?"

"Absolutely."

"You're a marvelous woman. Any man would be lucky to have you." He hesitated, as if weighing his words. "I also know you to be rather competitive and if you'd allow me, from one friend to the other, I think you should know: The man likes to do the chasing, Essie."

He turned his back, walked up the stairs and disappeared across their threshold.

Essie sat in her window seat, a place of succor since childhood. A tiny alcove carved out of her bedroom wall with a soft cushion to sit on and fluffy pillows to lean against. It was her cleft in the rock, a place where she could hide within the shelter of His wings.

Moving aside some papers, she tucked a crocheted blanket about her feet and looked out the window on the flower gardens below. Gardens she and her mother had planted, with buds arranged by color so they would make a pretty picture when they bloomed. But summer and the hot Texas sun had overbaked the blossoms, leaving brown, shriveled patches in place of once-vibrant colors.

She touched the glass that separated her from the out-of-doors, and nature's display blurred as she refocused on her hand. Her ringless hand.

He had married a childhood friend. A widow.

Why, Lord? Why does she get two husbands when all I want is one?

It didn't make sense. She'd be such a good wife and mother. Why was God keeping her from doing the very thing He made her for? Surely it couldn't be because she'd made some silly little list.

She laid her forehead on her upraised knees. What was she going to do now? She couldn't just up and quit working in the store. That would be too obvious. Too humiliating.

But Essie had thought of it as her store for so long that she wouldn't take kindly to changing things around simply to suit the new mistress.

Yet Hamilton's wife would want to do things her way. And like it or not, Essie would have to oblige her. Perhaps she could get herself fired. But, no, she didn't want to sabotage the store or Hamilton.

So she'd stay. And she'd work. And she'd quit, just as soon as she gracefully could.

Cranking open the window, she took a deep breath. The breeze lifted the papers littered at her feet. She slapped them down with her hands before they flew away, then gathered them up.

81

Hamilton Crook
Points of Merit:

- *Has an infant who needs a mother*
- *Has a new store and needs a helpmate*
- *Cared for his wife, God rest her soul*
- *Attends church*
- *Would profit from having a hometown girl in his store*

Drawbacks:

- *Horrid last name*
- *Younger than me*
- *Never see him outdoors*
- *Works past the supper hour (but that would change once he married me and had some help)*
- *Doesn't have any pets*

She folded the pages in half, then ripped them down the middle without even looking at the other men on her list.

———

It would have been so much easier if Essie could have hated the new Mrs. Crook. But no one in their right mind could hate Katherine Crook. The petite woman epitomized kindness and sincerity. She spoke softly. Listened intently. Laughed easily.

Essie was completely intimidated. Hamilton was completely captivated.

Only a week had passed, but Katherine had easily won over the old cronies. Her only fault was her opinion of Colonel.

In Katherine's mind snakes were synonymous with Satan. She could not distinguish one from the other. And Colonel must have sensed it somehow, for he'd quit eating.

The snake had grown an inch, he'd remained calm and tolerant—never striking in anger—then for no apparent reason he'd stopped feeding. Essie had tempted him with several different mice at several different times of day. No luck.

Perhaps the crate had become too confining. She didn't know, but she had to free him. And she'd need to do it now while the fall weather was still mild.

The boys in town were crushed. They'd grown very attached to Colonel. Particularly the little orphan, Harley North. He'd come so far since she'd seen him screaming in fear that long-ago morning. Now he couldn't get enough of the prairie king.

He, Lawrence, and Jeremy entered the Slap Out as solemn as if someone had died.

"Hello, boys," Essie said.

They congregated around Colonel's crate.

"Can we hold him one last time?" Harley asked.

"Of course," Essie said, removing the mesh top. While the boys took turns holding and petting the snake, she moved his crate to the back and cleaned it.

"Are you all right?" Hamilton asked, closing the large barn-like door that had been flung wide during a delivery of pork barrels.

Essie picked up an empty gunnysack. "A little sad, I suppose. He's a wonderful snake."

"I'm sorry."

Sorry for what? she thought. *For having me underfoot all the time? For the awkwardness between us? For ever hiring me in the first place?*

"I've been thinking, Hamilton," she said, playing with the string at the top of the burlap bag. "Since Colonel's leaving and all, I thought maybe it would be a good time for me to move on, as well."

"What do you mean, 'move on'?"

"Quit," she whispered.

He said nothing. She looked up and felt a pang of guilt. He looked so torn. He had to know she couldn't stay, no matter how successful she was at selling his goods.

"You don't have to go," he said.

"You know I do. But I thank you. I haven't had such a grand time in forever and a day."

"When do you have to . . . leave?"

"I'll stay through Saturday."

"So soon?"

"I think it best. But if you ever need anything, if Katherine gets sick or something, just send word."

He surveyed the storage room as if its shelves would offer him a compromise of some sort.

"Well," she said, lifting up the gunnysack, "I'd best get this over with."

The boys placed Colonel in the sack, and Essie knotted the top.

"Maybe we ought to bring the mice, too," Jeremy said. "We could let 'em out close to where we free Colonel. Then he won't have to go so far to find some dinner."

They walked through town with Jeremy carrying the snake and Lawrence carrying a sack of mice. They passed the men drilling the community's new water wells. Adam Currington took off his hat, swiped his brow with the back of his hand and waved.

He stood tall and lean, silhouetted against the blue sky. His shirtsleeves were rolled up, his hip cocked. He placed his hat back on his head, adjusting it until he had its brim at just the right angle.

The boys waved back, hollering out a greeting. Essie tucked her chin. They continued walking for a good half mile until they reached the banks of Two Bit Creek.

The sounds of town had faded, replaced by the gurgling of the creek, a woodpecker searching for bugs, two squirrels playing chase. Birds of vivid blues, yellows, and reds flitted from tree branch to tree branch, each chirping over the other.

"What do you think about this spot?" she asked.

The boys looked around. "It's a right nice place, Miss Essie," Jeremy said.

Lawrence poured the mice on the ground like a schoolboy releasing his marbles from a pouch. They scurried in all directions. Jeremy untied his gunnysack, lifted Colonel out and placed him on the ground. The snake froze, tongue darting, then slithered through the weeds toward the stream and disappeared beneath some brush.

Essie envied Colonel's freedom to go where he wanted. To do whatever he fancied. Accountable to no one.

Harley buried his face in her skirt.

She stroked his hair. "Maybe I'll take you boys snake hunting one day soon. Would you like that?"

Lawrence sighed. "My ma probably won't let me. She makes me do girly things, like play the piano."

Jeremy nudged his shoulder.

His eyes widened. "Oh. I didn't mean nothing by that, Miss Essie. You aren't like other girls."

I know, Lawrence. I know. "Come along, we'd best be heading back."

They had just made it to the dirt road outside of town when the sound of a wagon made Essie shade her eyes.

"Lookit, Miss Essie!" Harley yelled. "It's the peddler man!"

The boys took off running, Essie right behind them. Levi Baumgartner pulled his horse to a stop, causing the pots and pans in his wagon to clang. "Whoa, Clara. Whoa."

A black-and-white dog put two paws up on the wagon's sideboard, barking and wagging his tail.

"Howdy, Mr. Bum!"

"Well, it is Lawrence, a clever *shaygets*, to be sure. What are you and your friends doing way out here?"

"We were lettin' our snake go on account of he quit eatin'," Harley said, trying to catch his breath.

Mr. Baumgartner chuckled, then tipped his hat. "Miss Spreckelmeyer. A delightful surprise." He was not an old man, but he looked like one and spoke like one. He had lines on his brown face and a thick black beard covering his chin.

"Hello, Mr. Baumgartner," she said. "Welcome to town."

"Thank you. How is Pegasus?" he asked, eyes twinkling.

"Wonderful. She's in excellent health."

Jeremy looked up from petting the horse's nose. "Who's Pega Siss?"

"That, my boy," the peddler replied, "is the name of Miss Spreckelmeyer's bicycle."

"Your ridin' machine has a name?" Harley asked.

"Of course," she said. "My horse has one. Why shouldn't my bike?"

The dog barked, distracting the children.

"Can we play with Shadrach?" Lawrence asked.

Mr. Baumgartner set the brake lever and gave a command in Yiddish. The border collie sailed off the wagon and into the circle of boys. They chased the dog, then laughed as the dog chased them. After a while, Shadrach collapsed at his master's feet, panting, back legs extended, tongue hanging out like a bell pull.

"Whatcha got in yer wagon this time?" Jeremy asked.

Mr. Baumgartner opened up the back of his wagon, pushing aside brooms and tinware and a whole tub of shoes. "I have a hunting knife with a seven-inch clip blade," he said, handing the knife to Jeremy.

The teener held it reverently, touching his thumb to its tip, and a drop of blood instantly appeared. "She's a beauty."

He gave it back to the peddler without even asking the price, for whatever it was would be too much.

"What about me?" Harley asked.

Mr. Baumgartner handed him a china dog no bigger than his little finger.

"It's Shadrach!" Harley exclaimed, showing the treasure to the rest of them. "You ought to get your pa to buy this, Lawrence. He could buy you whatever you want."

Lawrence frowned. "He don't like buying from the peddler man."

Jeremy nudged him.

"What?" Lawrence asked. "What'd I do?"

"Nothing, boy," Mr. Baumgartner said, ruffling his hair. "You've not done a thing. But you've also not asked about Miss Spreckelmeyer. Don't you think she might like to see what I have in this wagon?"

Harley wrinkled his nose. "Oh, don't start showing your ribbons and stuff or we'll be here all day."

"Ah, but Miss Spreckelmeyer is special. It's not the ribbons that catch her eye. Only the goods that promise excitement or adventure will intrigue our fine German *shiksa*."

The boys peered into the covered wagon, and Essie felt herself respond to his teasing. "Did you bring me some excitement and adventure, Mr. Baumgartner?"

He bowed. "For you, I bring the world."

Harley snorted. "That won't fit in yer wagon!"

Mr. Baumgartner's black eyes lit with mischief before he disappeared inside the canvas bonnet. They heard him shifting trunks and goods, murmuring to himself in a language they didn't understand but loved to hear.

Finally he jumped down from the bed. "I have something especial for you."

Essie took the bulky offering and examined it. The block of wood looked to be eight inches in length and five inches wide. It had leather straps with buckles across the top and a long rope on each side. Also attached to the sides were four wheels made of boxwood—two on each side.

"What is it?" she asked.

"Wheeled feet," he answered.

"What?"

He drew out another block of wood exactly like the one she held. "You strap them onto your shoes. Like a bicycle, except for the feet."

Essie stifled a giggle. "Truly? That's truly what they are for?"

"Try them."

"But how do you pedal?"

"You don't. You just . . . go."

She looked between him and the wheeled contraption, tempted beyond belief. They were still outside of town and no one but these boys would see her.

"You must all swear to secrecy," she said.

Jeremy grinned. Lawrence made an *X* over his lips. Harley saluted.

She looked at Mr. Baumgartner. "I'm going to break my neck."

"That's what you said about the bicycle." He patted the wagon bed. "Here. I'll help you put them on."

Jeremy made a stirrup with his hands and boosted her up onto the wagon. Mr. Baumgartner placed one of the blocks of wood against his thigh, guided her booted foot on the block, then strapped her in.

When all was ready, Mr. Baumgartner handed her the ropes that were attached to each block. "Hold on to these."

He and Jeremy set her on the ground and held on to her elbows.

She lifted up the ropes of one block like a marionette. "That can't be right," she said.

Mr. Baumgartner scratched his beard. "Perhaps we use the ropes to pull you."

"You've never seen them used?" she squealed.

"Who needs to see them used? They have wheels. You strap them on and go."

She arched a brow. "How?"

"Give me the ropes. I'll be the horse. You be the cart."

"Absolutely not. You'll pull my feet right out from under me."

"Then bend your knees and lean forward. Jeremy? You get behind her and push. Give me the ropes, shiksa."

She handed him the ropes. Jeremy grabbed her waist.

"You ready?" Baumgartner asked.

Essie bit her lower lip. "Giddy-up!"

Jeremy pushed, the peddler man pulled and Essie screamed, landing with a *thunk* on her backside, skirts tangled.

Baumgartner let out a string of Yiddish, clearly chastising Jeremy for dropping her.

She raised her hands in the air. "I'm fine, I'm fine. Help me up."

They helped her up.

"You pull, Jeremy," Baumgartner said, grabbing her waist tightly. "Hold on to me, Miss Spreckelmeyer."

Essie locked on to his wrists. "Go!"

Jeremy pulled, Mr. Baumgartner steadied, and they rolled about a foot before her skirts became tangled in the wheels and both she and the peddler ended up in the dirt.

"Botheration!" Essie said. "I need my bicycle skirt. Here, help me up."

They did. She wadded up one side of her skirts and handed them to Harley. The other side she handed to Lawrence, instructing the boys to keep her hem away from the wheels.

They tried again but as soon as Jeremy increased his speed, he jerked her feet forward and they all went tumbling.

Mr. Baumgartner whistled for his dog and positioned him in front of Essie. "Here, Jeremy. Give Miss Spreckelmeyer the ropes and take my place behind her. Shiksa, hold on to Shadrach's tail. He will pull you more smoothly, I think."

"Won't that hurt him?"

"No, no. Won't hurt him at all. Boys, grab on to her skirts."

When all was in readiness, Mr. Baumgartner gave Shadrach the command to go and off they went. This time they made it almost six yards before falling.

"Yes! Yes!" Mr. Baumgartner said. "You have it. Now, again without me. I am going after my wagon."

By the time they reached the edge of town, Essie could travel almost twenty yards without falling.

"We're going to have to stop now, boys, or our secret will be out," she said, breathing heavily.

"Oh, one more time, Miss Essie!" Jeremy said. "Nobody can see us from here. Please?"

"All right. But after this, we really must stop."

It was their best run yet. Shadrach got to going so fast, Essie let go of his tail, Jeremy let go of her waist, and the boys let go of her skirt. Freedom. Blessed freedom. Just before reality struck.

"I don't know how to stop!" she said, rounding a bend in the road. "Look out!" she screamed.

But it was too late. She'd barreled right into Adam Currington, knocking him clear to kingdom come.

chapter EIGHT

ESSIE LAY FACEDOWN in the dirt—her scraped chin throbbing, her palms embedded with gravel, a tear in the elbow of her shirtwaist. But her pride suffered a worse blow than all those put together.

Shadrach reached her first, sniffing and whining. Jeremy, Lawrence, and Harley arrived fast on the dog's heels.

"Are you all right, Miss Essie?"

"Bee's knees, you were goin' fast!"

"Do you think Mr. Bum will let me give 'em a try?"

Essie planted her hands beside her shoulders and pushed up. She hadn't risen very far when strong hands clasped her waist and lifted her to her feet.

Her legs wobbled and Adam drew her up against his side. "Woman, what the fiery furnace are you doin'?"

She pushed a hunk of hair out of her eyes. "I'm so terribly sorry, Mr. Currington. Are you all right?"

Chuckling, he smoothed the rest of the hair away from her face. "Well, Miss Essie, I must admit, you shore know how to sweep a man clean off his feet."

The sparkle in his blue-green eyes conveyed genuine teasing rather than the patronizing tolerance townsfolk usually showed her.

She felt herself smiling in response. "I assure you, that was not my intention."

He touched a finger to her chin. "You look like you been fightin' a bobcat in a briar patch."

"I'm fine, thank you. You can let go now."

He continued to hold her. "What are those things you're wearin'?"

"Wheeled feet, I'm afraid."

"You shoulda seen her, mister," Harley said. "Shadrach was pullin' her and—"

Jeremy shoved him. "Hush up. Yer sworn to secrecy."

Harley slapped a hand over his mouth and gave Essie an apologetic glance.

Adam quirked an eyebrow, a slow smile creating deep grooves on either side of his mouth. "Well, now, I like a woman with a few secrets." Leaning over to better see her shoes, he grabbed a handful of skirts and started to lift.

She swatted him.

"Now, Miss Essie," he said, snatching his hand back. "You threw me so high I could've said my prayers before I hit. Surely yer not gonna keep me from seeing these wheeled feet, are ya?"

"I'm not entirely sure it would be proper, Mr. Currington."

He pulled her more tightly against him. "Call me Adam," he whispered in her ear, then placed his arm beneath her knees, scooped her up and sat her on the ground. "Now, show me."

But there was no need to, for the large blocks of wood protruded from beneath her skirts.

Adam pushed aside her hems and turned her foot this way and that. "Woman, has the heat addled your think box? It'd be safer to walk in quicksand than to wear these things."

He began to unbuckle them.

Mr. Baumgartner came around the bend, pulling his wagon to a stop. "Take your hands off her," he said, jumping to the ground.

Adam stilled and rose slowly to his feet. Shadrach growled.

"It's all right, Mr. Baumgartner," Essie said. "Mr. Currington was simply helping me with the buckles."

"Jeremy will help you," the peddler said.

Jeremy immediately loosened the straps and handed the wheeled feet to Essie.

She scrambled up, ignoring the soreness in her muscles. "I plowed over Mr. Currington by accident."

"What are you doing way out here?" Mr. Baumgartner asked him.

"I was lookin' for the judge, actually." Adam turned his attention to her. "I saw you pass by earlier and thought you might know where he is."

"He's not in his office?"

"No, ma'am."

"What's the matter?"

"We were drilling and when we got about a thousand feet down, oil started fillin' the water hole. We tried to seal it off, but it's runnin' uphill, and it'll be deep enough to wash a horse's withers if we don't do somethin' quick."

"Good heavens." She handed the wheeled feet to the peddler. "Can you give us a ride to town?"

"*Ye.*"

"Come on, Mr. Currington." She headed to the back of the wagon, Adam right behind her. "Jeremy, go tell my mother that Mr. Baumgartner is in town and to set an extra plate for supper," she shouted over her shoulder.

Adam tossed her in the wagon, closed the hatch, then leaped over it, knees and feet together. Never had Essie seen such a graceful vault. It took her a moment before she registered his boots were covered in oil.

She quickly grabbed a dripping pan hanging nearby and set it under his feet to keep him from ruining the wagon. The merchandise stacked around them formed a turreted and private alcove. The wheels of the wagon groaned in protest to the pace the peddler set, dirt forming a cloud in their wake.

Adam braced his hand on the floorboards behind her, his shoulder bumping hers with each sway of the cart. He stared at her, but she looked at her lap, out the back of the wagon, and at the various trunks beside her before finally turning to him.

"I must look a fright," she said.

"I do believe you have the longest eyelashes I've ever seen in my whole entire life."

"I do?"

"Yes, ma'am. You surely do."

The wagon continued to rock, her skirts inching toward him with each bump of their bodies. There was no room to scoot away, so she corralled her encroaching hem and tucked it tightly beneath her legs to keep it from touching his trousers.

"Who's the peddler man to you?" he asked.

"Excuse me?"

"Why does he get to sit at your supper table tonight?"

"Oh, I don't know," she said. "Papa has a great deal of respect for God's chosen people. Mr. Baumgartner always stays with us when he comes through town."

"Stays with you? He gets to stay with you, too?"

"Why, yes."

Adam surveyed the interior of the wagon. "Well, I think I might seriously consider becomin' a peddlin' man if it means I would get to sit by you at supper and sleep near you at night."

Essie straightened. "Mr. Currington. You mustn't say such things."

"Now, don't go gettin' all stiff with me, Essie. I'm just a mite jealous, is all."

Jealous? Of what? But the wagon pulled to a stop before she could voice the question.

Adam stuck his head out the back. "I gotta go, sugar."

They'd stopped at the field bordering Twelfth Street where the water well was being drilled. Her father, along with several other town leaders, had crowded around it.

Adam started jogging toward them. "Much obliged for the ride, mister," he said over his shoulder.

Essie began to climb out of the wagon, but Mr. Baumgartner came around back, stopping her. "You'd best stay put, shiksa. Out there is no place for a woman."

"Papa won't mind."

"No, but some of those other *goyim* might."

She hesitated, wanting to see for herself what was happening. But perhaps the peddler was right. She'd been the focus of much speculation after Hamilton had come home with his new bride. And her current disheveled state would definitely raise eyebrows. She didn't savor bringing down any more unfavorable talk.

She'd just have to wait until Papa came home to find out what exactly was going on.

Mother took great pains to look after Mr. Baumgartner's dietary restrictions. She prepared the biscuits without lard and kept the milk well away from the meat.

Essie swallowed her bite, then dabbed each corner of her mouth with a cloth. "How much oil is coming out of the well?"

"It's all over the place," Papa answered. "The ground is so saturated it caught fire twice already."

"How?" she asked.

"Umphrey dropped his match on the ground after lighting his cheroot. We'd barely extinguished that blaze when a spark from the forge started up another one."

"Mercy me," Mother said.

"The boys are digging a massive sump a few yards away from the well so they'll have someplace to drain the oil. Hopefully that will help."

Mother began to collect platters from the table. Essie stood to help.

"Is the water well ruined?" the peddler asked.

"No, we just need to keep drilling. Once we get past this oil-bearing stratum, we should find water. It'll slow things down, though."

"Are you finished, Mr. Baumgartner?" Essie asked.

He leaned back and patted his stomach. "Yes, shiksa. It was excellent, as always. *Dank*."

She removed his plate while Mother stepped to the sideboard and spooned peach cobbler into some bowls.

"Everyone's up in arms over the delay," Papa continued, "but I'm going to send a sample of our crude to Pennsylvania for evaluation."

Mr. Baumgartner twirled his finger in his beard. "Are you thinking to drill for oil instead of water?"

"I think it's worth investigating."

"And if the oil is good, what will you do?"

Papa shared a smile with the peddler.

"Isn't it election year?" Mr. Baumgartner asked.

"It is."

"Are you thinking to hang up your robe and become an oil tycoon?"

Mother paused in serving dessert.

"Oh, that might be a bit premature at this point," Papa answered.

But Essie wasn't fooled. The men dipped their spoons into the warm peach cobbler, its sweet fragrance filling the dining room.

"You're going to drill for oil, aren't you, Papa?"

He didn't answer and she wasn't sure if it was because his mouth was full or because Mother was in the room. But his eyes shone when he looked up at Essie.

She served herself a bowl and sat down.

"What happened to your chin?" Papa asked.

"I took a bit of a tumble this afternoon."

"In the store?"

"No."

"Off your bicycle?"

"No."

"Then where?"

She glanced at Mr. Baumgartner. He paid particular attention to his dessert.

"Out by the creek," she said. "We were freeing Colonel and I, um, stumbled."

Mother tsked. "For heaven's sake, Essie."

"You never could get the snake to eat?" Papa asked.

"I'm afraid not."

"A shame. He was a beauty."

———————

Essie hunched over the massive mahogany desk, adding the column of figures one more time. Papa was knee deep in campaigning for another term, which left her with the task of gathering information on oil production.

The "water" well was producing 150 gallons of oil a day, and the analysis from Pennsylvania came back pronouncing the crude as having "definite commercial value." So Papa had organized the Sullivan Oil Company and made extensive leases for mineral rights near the water well. Essie had tried to persuade him to call the company Spreckelmeyer Oil, but he thought his first name sounded better.

He entered the office, loosened his four-in-hand tie and collapsed into a chair opposite Essie. His jovial face showed signs of fatigue and his blue eyes had lost a bit of their sparkle.

"Long day?" she asked.

"My mouth hurts from smiling so much," he answered. "What about you?"

"I finally got those estimates you were waiting for." She slid the papers she was working on toward him. "Excavating the oil would be fairly simple. You could drill a well with two men. It's what to do with the crude afterward that's the problem."

He studied her figures. "This says we could complete a well for about five hundred dollars."

"That's my best guess, anyway, but that doesn't include storage tanks, pipelines, a refinery, and the manpower that goes along with it."

He handed the papers back to her. "All we need to do is hit a gusher or two. Once that happens, word will get out and the oilmen will come running."

"And what will you do with the oil in the meantime?"

"Put it in whatever we can find or dig some more sumps. Too bad we can't find some way to store it in Neblett's old seed house."

"Papa, there's no guarantee you'll find more oil."

"True. But let's assume we do. Think of what it would mean for our town—our entire state."

Essie leaned back in the huge leather chair. "Oil is useless unless it can be turned into kerosene. All the refineries are up north."

"I know." He wound the tie around his hand. "The whole thing appeals to me, is all. Working outside. Getting my hands dirty. Striking that big one."

She propped her arms on the desk. "But you're going to be sixty soon. You can't be taking on something like this at your age."

"Says who? Noah was five hundred before he went into shipbuilding." He shrugged. "Besides, I think the discovery on Twelfth Street bears looking into."

They were kindred spirits, the two of them. She understood his desire to take a risk, to challenge the odds, to try something new.

"This is a bit more serious than betting a little pocket money on Mr. Mitton's horses," she said.

"A bit."

"How are you going to do all this and still fulfill your civic duties?"

"Maybe God has something else in mind for us both."

He said nothing further, just held her stare.

She began to shake her head. "Oh no. I'm a woman. Working in a mercantile is one thing. Running an oil company is something else altogether. Mother would have a fit."

"You're the best man for the job. I'll handle Mother."

"And the men in town?"

"I'll handle them, too." He nodded toward her chin. "You want to tell me what really happened while you were releasing Colonel?"

She touched the scab that had started to form. "I tried out some wheeled feet that Mr. Baumgartner had in his wagon."

He absorbed that bit of information, and the twinkle that had been absent when he'd entered the office was back in full force. "You trading in your bicycle?"

"No. Just supplementing."

He chuckled. "You better not let your mother catch you."

She raised a brow. "I thought you could handle Mother?"

"I can . . . up to a point." He stood and walked to the door. "I've arranged for a man by the name of Davidson to come down and look the oil field over."

"Where's he from?"

"Pennsylvania. He'll be here within the week."

If Mr. John Davidson was surprised to see Essie accompanying him and Papa to the fields, he didn't say so. Nor did he include her in any of the conversation.

But Essie preferred it that way. Being invisible had its uses. It allowed her to size him up as they walked the one block from the railway station to Twelfth Street, and Papa always appreciated the unguarded impressions she collected due to being ignored.

The oil scout wore no suit, coat or tie, but simply a cotton shirt and belted trousers. Mud frosted his boots and hat, while a neatly trimmed moustache made him look older than she suspected he truly was.

"Will you be doing sample digs or running tests in the ground?" Papa asked.

"Neither. I'll just be looking."

"For what?"

"Well, there's no real science to it. I personally use a little geology, a little doodlebugology, and a little common sense."

"Doodlebugology?"

"That's a method oil scouts employ by using wiggle sticks, forked limbs, doodlebugs, that sort of thing." He smiled. "There's one man by the name of Griffith who puts this platelike thing in his mouth that has coiled springs protruding from it. I can't tell you much about its workings, but when he stands over oil, there's a little lever that turns around. And that's where he recommends his customers drill."

Essie and Papa exchanged a glance.

"I mostly look at the surface of the field and the vegetation in the area. You go to any oil field and you'll see it differs a little bit from the surrounding territory."

A strong, unpleasant odor coming from the oil began to pervade the air about the time they reached the intersection of Dallas and Twelfth. Turning south on Twelfth, they continued down the plank sidewalk, past the Poker Palace and Rosenburg's Saloon.

Men wove around them, horses waited patiently at hitching rails, and someone on a piano played "Do, Do, My Huckleberry, Do." Mr. Riddles came out of a domino parlor, gave her a sidelong glance and tipped his hat. Most decent women wouldn't be seen east of Beaton Street, but she was with Papa, and folks were used to her coming and going as she pleased.

The sidewalk ended, and several yards later the field began. Mr. Davidson tramped right across the oil-covered ground. A giant earthen pit on the east side of the field held thousands of gallons of oil, with more trickling in.

Mr. Davidson walked the perimeter of the field, then picked up a piece of wood the size of a broom handle. He peeled off the bark and started jabbing it into the ground, working it down as far as he could before moving to the next spot.

The water well at this location had been finished, finally breaking through the oil-bearing strata and into water at around 2,500 feet. Adam and the rest of the crew had moved on to drill the second and third wells on the other side of town.

Mr. Davidson tossed down his stick and headed toward Essie and Papa.

"What do you think?" Papa asked.

The oilman looked out on the field like a mother hen preening over her chicks. "Well, Judge, if it were mine, I'd be drilling on it before the week was out."

chapter NINE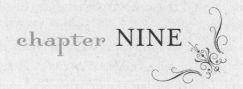

ESSIE BUMPED DOWN Beaton Street, pedaling Pegasus—Peg, for short—over the old bois d'arc blocks paving the street. The wooden surface alleviated one problem—dust—and created another—discomfort for every vehicle traveling down the jarring road.

Turning east onto Jefferson Avenue, she waved at Mr. Mitton as she passed his wagon yard. She longed to pull over and admire the thoroughbreds he boarded in stables so fine the locals referred to them as "Mitton's Hotel," but she needed to speak with the artesian well drillers. She continued on past the icehouse, the county jail, and the Anheuser-Busch Beer Depot, the smell of horses from the wagon yard still lingering in the air.

At the edge of town she spotted two men kicking down a well while Adam watched, wiping the back of his neck with a bandanna. Sweat rolled off the cable-tool boys as they each placed a foot in the stirrups hanging from a fifteen-foot log.

The rig sat underneath a high tripod of poles and looked like a child's seesaw made with a tree trunk instead of a flat piece of wood. She noted the fulcrum was way off-center, and one end of the log was fastened to the ground.

The other end of the log—where the men in the stirrups were—projected up into the air at about a thirty-degree angle and was so far away from the fulcrum that it held a surprising amount of spring. The men grabbed on to the tree and threw their weight into the stirrups, forcing a heavy iron bit, which dangled from a cable between them, into the ground to break up a little of the earth.

They quickly repeated this motion over and over until one man took a break and Adam replaced him. Moisture stained Adam's blue shirt beneath his arms and between his shoulder blades. Essie stopped Peg and laid her on the ground. Brushing dust from her calf-length split skirt, she advanced on the men. "Good afternoon," she called.

The drilling stopped, and Adam jumped from the stirrup to approach her. "Miss Essie. Aren't you as purty as a little red wagon?"

She smiled. "I don't believe I've ever been compared to a wagon before, Mr. Currington."

He made no effort to hide his perusal of her, from her red-trimmed Benwood hat all the way down to her bicycle boots. "You ever seen a little red wagon?" he asked.

"Of course."

"Then you know there ain't nothin' purtier."

"I know no such thing," she said, shaking her head and passing him by without pause.

He hastened his stride to keep up with her. "You ride that thing all the way from your house?" he asked, glancing over his shoulder at her riding machine.

"I most certainly did." She stopped a few feet away from the rig. "How do you do?"

The other two men doffed their hats.

"Miss Essie, this is Mr. Pugh and Mr. Upchurch. Fellas, this is Miss Spreckelmeyer, the judge's daughter."

Mr. Upchurch's whip-thin body surprised Essie. She would have thought drilling required more muscle. Perhaps his legs, hidden in the folds of his waist-overalls, were thicker than the rest of him. The removal of his hat revealed a head shaped like an egg and just as smooth. What hair he lacked on top he made up for with his moustache.

Mr. Pugh, a stocky and solid man, scowled, bringing his black eyebrows together in such a way that she couldn't tell where one brow ended and the other began.

"Gentlemen," she said, "I'm sorry to interrupt, but I wanted to contract you for another job when you are finished with this one."

They glanced at one another.

"I would like you to drill a well about two hundred yards south of the one on Twelfth Street. This one would not be for water, however, but for oil."

A beat of silence. Mr. Pugh recovered first. "We have us another job already scheduled. Over in Waco. Besides, we drill water wells, not oil wells." He crammed his hat back on and began bailing loose rock and dirt out of the boring hole.

"How long will you be in Waco?" she asked.

"Longer than you wanna wait," Pugh answered.

Mr. Upchurch remained motionless, hat in hand.

Essie turned to Adam. "I need two drillers. Do you know where I might find some?"

"Who's providing the grubstake?"

She hesitated. "The payroll, you mean? My father, but I'll be running the project."

He rubbed his jaw. "Don't you think your pa's saddle is slippin' a bit? This is cotton and cattle country. The judge has as much chance of a future in crude as a one-legged man in a kickin' contest. If it's oil he's interested in, he'd be better off in cottonseed oil."

"We're not looking for a business partner, Mr. Currington. We're looking for drillers."

The men exchanged glances.

"Never mind," she sighed. "I'm sorry to have disturbed you."

Adam grabbed her wrist. "Whoa there, filly. Not so fast. Rufus?" he asked, still holding on to her. "What if you and Arnold went to Waco without me? Then I could see about rustling up somebody else to help me with Miss Spreckelmeyer's well. What do you think?"

Upchurch rubbed his egg-shaped head with a handkerchief and looked at Pugh.

"You saying you'll work for a *woman*?" Pugh asked.

Adam scrutinized her again. She tugged her hand free.

"Now, Rufus. I wouldn't be workin' for just any woman. I'd be workin' for this here woman. And I have to tell ya, the thought don't bother me none a'tall."

Mr. Pugh gave a sound of disgust. "Just what are me and Arnold supposed to do, then?"

"You'll find somebody. Same as me."

"What are you gonna drill with?"

Adam thought a minute. "He's got a point there, Miss Essie. They'll be taking this rig with 'em. I'd have to build you one of your own."

"That would be fine, Mr. Currington. Can you come by the house tomorrow to settle on the details?"

"It'd be my pleasure."

————

Adam arrived late in the day, standing on Essie's porch, spit and polished in a crisp white shirt, red neckerchief, and blue denim trousers with brass rivets at the pocket corners.

He removed his cowboy hat. "Afternoon, Miss Essie."

"Mr. Currington. Please, won't you come in?"

She led him to Papa's office and poured them each a glass of lemonade. "Thank you for coming."

He guzzled the beverage in one prolonged swig. Head back, eyes closed, Adam's apple bobbing. Swiping his mouth with his sleeve, he sighed. "Ah, darlin', my throat was drier than a tobacco box. Thank ya."

She accepted his glass. "Would you like some more?"

"Not right now."

"Well." She took a sip of hers, then set it on the tray. "I've put together a list of materials I'm assuming we'll need to construct a rig, but I thought you should take a look at it and see if I left anything off."

He set his hat in a chair and perused the list she gave him.

"The lumber I'll purchase from Mr. Whiteselle," she said. "The cable and drill bit can be made down at Central Blacksmith Shop."

"And the stirrups?"

"The carriage and harness shop."

He handed the paper back to her. "You're gonna need the smithy to make a few more down-hole tools," he said.

"Like what?" She picked up Papa's pen and dipped it in an inkwell.

"Metal connectors, rope sockets, a sinker bar, jars, and an auger stem."

Still standing, Essie leaned over the massive desk, scribbling furiously on the parchment, forgoing the precise lettering she'd learned at the Corsicana Female College.

Adam hovered over her shoulder, watching. "Make sure the lumberyard gives you hemlock, ash, or hickory for the spring pole and something sturdy, like oak, for the fulcrum."

After several moments, she replaced Papa's pen and blew on the paper. When she straightened, Adam stayed put, his eyes a translucent mosaic of blue and green.

"Why do you do that?" she asked, baffled.

"What?"

"Crowd me."

"Am I crowdin' you?"

"You know you are."

"I don't mean to. It's just that when I stand right close I can smell them cloves you use in your toilet."

She caught her breath and glanced at the door, open only a crack. "You're not supposed to notice that kind of thing," she whispered.

A smile lifted one side of his mouth. "I notice everything about you, Miss Essie."

"Why?"

Shaking his head, he took a step back, putting a proper distance between them. "The fellas in this town are either blind or fools. Maybe both."

She frowned, searching his expression. "Your pardon?"

He pointed to the list on the desk. "We're gonna need a weight to anchor the butt end of the spring pole. If you don't want to pay the smithy to make you one, I can see about finding a heavy boulder or somethin'."

"Do you think you could come with me when I place these orders?" she asked, glancing at the parchment. "That way we'll be sure to get exactly what we need."

"You tell me when and I'll be there."

———

The clink of iron reached Essie and Adam well before they arrived at Mr. Fowler's Central Blacksmith Shop. They paused just inside the dark, cavernous building, allowing their eyes to adjust. A blanket of heat and hazy smoke swaddled them, along with the smell of burning coals.

With his back to them, Mr. Fowler worked the bellows while the tip of his poker turned from red to white and flames danced. A dirty, once-white apron string wrapped Fowler's waist like Cleopatra's asp, dividing his blue shirt from his waist-overalls. Releasing the bellows, he removed the iron from the flame and hammered on the hot metal, sending sparks in all directions. He'd barely managed half a dozen strikes before having to return the poker to the fire.

"Howdy, Miss Spreckelmeyer," he said, looking up and moving toward them. He gave Adam the once-over. "And you're one of them water-well drillers, ain't ya?"

"Good morning, Mr. Fowler," Essie said. "And yes, this is Mr. Currington. He's going to stay on and build another rig, but this one will be for Papa."

When the men leaned in to shake hands, Essie was surprised at how much taller Adam was. She'd always thought of Mr. Fowler as a huge man. But she realized now the bulk on him was more from tickling the anvil than from height.

"Your pa has a hankerin' for a water well out in his own backyard, then?"

"Not exactly," she said, glancing at Adam. "He's going to drill for oil."

Mr. Fowler stared at her a second, then doubled over with laughter. She schooled her face, knowing full well his reaction would have been vastly different had Papa been the one stating their purpose.

"Now, Mr. Fowler," she began.

He silenced her with a raised hand, sobering, his mirth replaced by a mask of professional gravity. She motioned to Adam, who held their lists and diagrams, when out of the corner of her eye she caught Mr. Fowler cracking another smile.

She arched an eyebrow.

"Sorry," he said.

There were other smithies in town, but J. T. Fowler was among the most capable and enterprising. And once he realized she was serious, he would not only fill her order but he'd do it quickly, expertly, and with respect.

"Here's what we're gonna need," Adam said. He spread the piece of parchment on a rough wooden counter and began to explain everything. Mr. Fowler nodded and asked a few questions, his amusement vanishing as he became absorbed in the details. When they had finished, he gave Essie a conciliatory smile.

"I'll get started on this right away," he said.

Outside, the sun was so bright Essie shaded her eyes. Adam glanced back over his shoulder at the blacksmith's shop, shaking his head.

"Thank you, Mr. Currington."

"Call me Adam. And it was my pleasure," he said, winking as they headed down Eleventh Street.

"Shall we go see about the stirrups?" she asked.

"We can do that, but Mr. Weidmann's kitchen is one block over on Collin Street. How 'bout we take a detour and have us some o' that fruitcake he makes? I can smell it clear from here."

As he said the words, her nose registered the delectable aroma of fresh bread and something indefinably sweet.

"It's still morning. Won't you spoil your dinner?"

"No, ma'am. I've found there's never a bad time for a visit to Mr. Weidmann's bakery."

Town activity had picked up with the advancing morning. Wagons trundled up and down the street, stirring up dust, horses cutting between them. The stray tabby, Cat, darted past Essie and Adam. Men conversed about everything from the price of cotton to the November election to the abandoned seed house.

Being the judge's daughter, Essie knew most everyone, so they were forced to stop and chat a few times along the way. She introduced Adam as one of the artesian well drillers, explaining he'd decided to stay in town awhile longer.

The townspeople looked at him askance, displaying forced politeness.

"I don't believe the folks of your town like me very much," he whispered after they broke away from a conversation with the school superintendent and the wainwright.

"It's not that. They would simply prefer it if you had been born here."

"How long you reckon it'll take before they forgive me for that slight?"

"Oh, I would think twenty years should do the trick."

He shook his head. "More like forty, you mean."

They shared a smile, and he opened the bakery door.

"Ach, look at this fine German *mädchen* who comes to see me." Mr. Weidmann circled around his table to take hold of Essie's shoulders and kiss both her cheeks. "*Wie geht es Ihnen*, Fräulein Spreckelmeyer?"

"I'm fine, Mr. Weidmann. And you?"

"I am good. Very, very good." He turned, grabbing Adam, and gave him the same greeting he'd given Essie, bringing a shade of red to the cowboy's cheeks. "You watch out for this one, Fräulein. Eternally hungry for my fruitcake, he is. Pesters me night and day."

"Is that so, Mr. Currington?"

"I'm afraid it is, ma'am," Adam said, patting his stomach.

"*Ja,*" said Mr. Weidmann. "I will get you some."

The bakery was more of a kitchen than anything else, but it had a small table pushed into one corner. Adam pulled out her chair and she sat, relishing the smells of vanilla, apricots, dates and pineapple.

Mr. Weidmann brought them each a large slice of cake resting on brown paper. "I am sorry, but I have no plates or forks."

"It's all right. This will be fine." Essie broke off a portion with her fingers, while Adam lifted his entire piece and took a large bite.

"So tell me, Mr. Currington, how does a cowboy end up drilling water wells?"

"Just decided to do somethin' different, I guess."

"But why?"

He took another big bite, slowly chewing the confection, his carefree manner diminishing. "It happened a while back."

Mr. Weidmann washed and chopped cherries on the other side of the room, paying them no mind. So for now, the two of them had the place to themselves.

"What happened?" she asked.

"I grew up on a ranch. My pa was a cowboy and my grandpa before him. So I been steer ropin' since I was ankle-high to a June bug."

She took another nibble, waiting.

"A couple of years ago, a big ranchman in Gonzales County asked me to be the trail boss for his yearly drive from San Antonio to Abilene, Kansas. It was my job to plan the route, to decide when to stop, where to bed down, where to cross creeks, that kinda thing."

"I've heard that only the top cowhands make those kinds of trips."

"I reckon that's so." He picked at a splintered piece of wood on the rough table. "We had two point men ridin' up front directing the lead steer, then the swing and flank boys along the sides, with the tail riders bringin' up the drag."

"How many were in the herd?"

"Eighteen hundred. Everythin' went fine 'til we reached Waco. Then a gully washer came. It rained 'nough to have everybody wishin' they'd grown fins instead of feet."

"What did you do?"

"All that rain made it too dangerous to cross the Brazos. We had no choice but to wait 'til the river went down. We lost so much time,

I decided we'd go east to Shreveport instead o' Kansas. Last thing I wanted was to get stuck in the middle o' winter. Some o' the other fellas disagreed, so I told 'em I'd get the herd there in good shape or I'd take off my spurs and never make another roundup."

She rested her hands in her lap, no longer interested in the fruit-cake before her.

He scratched the top of his head, causing his blond hair to stand up a little on the right. "We got across the Brazos okay, but then Spanish Tick Fever took hold of the herd and the farther we went, the more we left behind. Dead."

"Oh no."

"By the time we hit the Trinity River, we only had five hundred left." He swallowed. "And when we reached Shreveport, we had fewer than a hundred."

"But that wasn't your fault."

"I was the trail boss, and I'd given my word. So I sold my horse and saddle."

She gripped her hands, hiding them in the folds of her skirt. A cowboy's horse was more than a source of transportation. It was his constant companion. A friend he could talk to and confide in.

More than his mount, though, the cowboy prized his saddle—and quite often it cost more than the horse itself. It was undeniably the very last thing he parted with.

"I'm so sorry, Adam."

He pushed the crumbs of his fruitcake around with his fingers. "You gonna eat that?" he asked, indicating her abandoned piece.

She slid it toward him. "Is that when you started drilling?"

"No. I got a job on a wagon train carryin' goods to Memphis, Tennessee. Then I started loadin' and unloadin' merchandise for the riverboats. Did that 'til about six months ago."

"What happened then?"

"A showboat pulled in and I met up with Pugh and Upchurch."

The last of the cake was gone. She folded her paper in half, then in half again, trapping the crumbs inside. She did the same for his, wondering what his father's and grandfather's reactions had been.

If they had taught him everything they knew, how could they have let him give up something he so clearly loved? But to ask would be intrusive.

A woman came in to place an order with Mr. Weidmann. Adam dropped a coin on the table, then he and Essie slipped out. This time Essie didn't reprimand him when he took her elbow and stayed close enough to smell the cloves she used in her bath and for her to smell the Yankee shaving soap they sold at the Slap Out.

chapter TEN

WATCHING ADAM CONSTRUCT the rig these last few weeks reminded Essie of her embroidering. Just as every stitch she took revealed more of the final picture, each piece of lumber Adam added gave more definition to the rig.

She suggested they hire Jeremy as helper. If scrawny Mr. Upchurch could manage it, then Jeremy certainly could. Adam protested, though, saying the teener was nothing but a farm boy.

Her crossed arms betrayed her determination. "You'll have to train him, then."

Jeremy was eager and hardworking, as she knew he would be, and so proud of earning ten whole cents a day. For all his previous bluster, Adam set about training the boy as if he hoped to make a top hand out of him, never hazing or harassing, always answering his questions patiently and offering plenty of encouragement.

Adam tightened the second stirrup they'd hung on the spring pole. "You ready to give it a whirl, Boll Weevil?"

Jeremy grabbed on to the pole. "You say when."

"Go!"

They jumped into the stirrups, and the pole bowed down and up, responding to their lead. The shade of a bois d'arc tree in the corner of the field didn't quite reach the workers. Some of its bright yellow leaves fell to the ground—many blowing into a freshly dug oil sump next to their new rig.

Essie watched the man and boy bounce a few more times, then clapped. "It's working! All we need now are the cable tools."

They stepped out of the stirrups.

"How long before Mr. Fowler's got 'em ready?" Jeremy asked. He looked as if he'd grown four inches over the summer, but only in a vertical direction. He'd not added any meat or muscle to his spindly frame, and his loose clothing made him look even thinner.

"He said he'd have the tools by first o' next week," Adam answered.

The three of them admired their handiwork before Essie finally stirred herself. "Well, Jeremy, I guess you'll have yourself a few days off before the real work begins." She handed him his first wages.

"That's right," Adam said. "And come Monday, you be ready to sweat like a hog butcher in frost time."

"I'll be here and ya won't hear me complainin' none." Jeremy palmed the bag of coins, testing its weight. "Fer now, though, I'm gonna go over to the Slap Out and get the young'uns a sassperilly candy. Boy, won't they be surprised!"

He took off running, shirttail flapping, skinny legs pumping. They watched him disappear across the open field, down the dirt road and on into town.

"You sure were right about him, Essie. He works hard as any I seen and was all swoll up like a carbuncle just now, wasn't he?"

"He did seem pleased. I wish I could see the expression on those children's faces when he comes home with candy. I imagine it'll be their first."

"First? They ain't never had candy?"

"I wouldn't think so."

Adam loosened the bandanna from around his neck, wiped his face, then looked at the now-empty road. "Yes, sir, that boll weevil 'uld do to ride the river with."

She smiled. "Well, would you like to follow me to the house and I'll give you your wages, as well?"

Mischief transformed his face. "Actually, ya know what I really wanna do?"

She found herself shaking her head.

"I wanna ride your wheeler. Would ya mind?"

Glancing at Peg, she worried her lip. "It's not as easy as it looks. You can't just swing into the saddle and say 'giddy-up.'"

"So teach me."

"What?"

"Teach me."

"Here?" she squeaked.

He scanned the area. "No, we probably ought to go out there where you practice on your wheeled feet when you think nobody's lookin'."

She took a short breath. "How do you know about that?"

With a shrewd smile, he took her elbow and steered her toward her bike. "I already done told you, I notice everything about you."

———

"The knack of balancing is really all that needs to be *learned*," Essie said, holding Peg by her handlebars. "The rest comes with patience, perseverance, and practice."

Adam stood with one hip cocked, his arms crossed in front of his chest and an indulgent smirk on his face. The breeze stirred up a few fallen leaves and shook more from the branches above them.

"You're not taking this with the proper amount of seriousness," she said. "I don't want you to fall and hurt yourself."

"Just show me how it works, Essie."

He rolled up the sleeves of his blue cotton shirt, then made sure it was securely tucked in to the denim trousers hugging his hips. Dust dulled the shine of his big silver belt buckle, but it still managed to capture a glint from the setting sun. She could tell how proud he was of it by the way he hooked his thumb behind the belt.

She wondered if he ever wore suspenders like the other men. If he had, she'd never seen him.

"Well, first," she said, "I'm going to have you coast down this gentle slope. When you take your seat and proceed, don't grasp the handles too tightly, and *never* lean on them."

The sun blazed onto the grass-covered incline, but the ground was still a bit moist from recent rains.

Adam straddled the vehicle, grabbing the handles as if they were horns he had to wrestle with.

"It's not a bull, Adam. Relax your grip."

He complied.

"Now, if you lose your balance and start to fall, touch the ground with your toe on whichever side the machine is falling to right yourself again."

He nodded.

"Remember, don't use the pedals. The incline will give you plenty of speed for balancing and steering."

"Relax my hands and no usin' the stirrups."

"Exactly. Are you ready?"

An excited smile spread across his face. "My heart's beatin' faster 'n a grasshopper in a chicken yard."

"You don't have to try it, Adam."

"Step aside, ma'am. I got some dust to churn up."

Releasing the handlebars, she backed away. In one fluid motion, he spread his legs wide and rolled down the hill in perfect balance, as if he'd been riding for months.

It had never occurred to her that he would manage to stay balanced so long. But he had, and in another couple of yards the slope would turn into a full-fledged hill.

"Whoooo-wee!" he hollered, his momentum picking up. He stayed aright even as he accelerated before finally hitting a rut and flying through the air, bicycle and all.

He tightened his grip and tried to hug the machine with his body the way a person would when jumping a horse.

"Don't lean!" Essie cried. "Angle your legs out! Keep the wheels straight!"

But he curled into the bicycle as if man and machine were one, then crashed to the ground. The crunch of metal blended with his gasp as the jarring contact of wheels and ground knocked the wind out of him.

He swerved out of control, fell in a tangled mess and slid down the hill before slowing to a stop just feet before he'd have collided into a tree stump.

Essie hiked up her skirts and raced to him, slipping on the grass. "Oh my goodness!"

He lay motionless on his back, his silver buckle winking in the sun.

"Adam, Adam!" She skidded to a stop and fell to her knees. Moisture seeped from the damp ground through the fabric of her brown skirt and petticoats where she knelt. "Can you hear me? Are you all right?" She touched his forehead, brushing hair out of his eyes.

Groaning, he tried to spit a leaf out of his mouth. She snatched it away.

"That saddle o' yours hit me in the caboose and sent me fer a flight to Mars."

"Don't move," she sighed in relief. "Just tell me what hurts."

He opened one eye. "I'm achin' in a lot o' new places."

She swept a quick glance down the length of him but saw no obvious injuries. "Anyplace in particular?"

Both eyes opened. The sun reduced his pupils to mere pinpoints. The rays of his blue-green irises were like the spreading of peacock feathers.

"You gonna kiss it and make it better?" he asked.

Her hand stilled, but her heart thar-rumped. "I'm serious, Adam."

"You think I'm not?" He turned his head and gently nipped the inside of her wrist, prompting a reaction in places far removed from her hand.

She snatched it away. "You mustn't say—or do—things like that."

"Why? Because I'm the hired hand and you're the boss's daughter?"

"Because I'm a woman, you're a man, and only engaged couples do such things."

"That ain't so, Essie. Lots o' couples do it, and not 'cause they're

117

engaged, but because they like each other. And it feels real nice. And it chases away the loneliness. You ever get lonely, Essie?"

Yes.

He recaptured her hand, nuzzling it like a horse searching for a sweet, the stubble on his cheek abrading her palm.

"Them married folks," he said, "they never think about us. What it's like to go without bein' touched. Without bein' loved." He raised himself up into a sitting position. "You ever been kissed?"

Once.

"I'd shore like to kiss you, girl."

And try as she might, she could not deny her interest in kissing him, too. How could she not? She'd never seen a more beautiful man. And never had one made her insides jump the way he did. Certainly Hamilton hadn't. Not even once.

And Adam was right. She did grow tired of relying on stray animals and the occasional child for a scrap of affection. She longed for more. Much more. But no matter what he said, contact of a personal nature was not done unless the man had spoken to the woman's father first.

But she'd let Hamilton kiss her and he'd not spoken to Papa . . . or to her. So perhaps couples did share such intimacies without parental permission.

She reviewed in her mind some of the young courting couples in town. Shirley Bunting and Charlie Ballew. Flossie Shaw and Dewey Taylor. Lillie Sue Gulick and Hugh Grimmet. Every single one of those girls had been looked at the way Adam now looked at her.

He placed a hand at the base of her head, tunneled his fingers into her hair twist, and pulled her toward him. She did not resist.

"Close your eyes," he whispered before covering her lips with his.

This was *nothing* like the kiss Hamilton had given her. It was all movement and coaxing and lushness. She rested her hands against his shoulders to keep from falling.

He grasped her waist and slid her close. It happened so quickly, she had no time to protest.

Wrapping his arms fully around her, he released her lips only as long as it took for him to angle his head in the opposite direction and swoop in to kiss her again.

She completely gave herself over to the experience, relishing the warmth and pleasure it induced.

"Open your mouth," he murmured.

"Wha—?" She never finished the question, shocked into stillness. He gave her no quarter, no time to assimilate, no time to react. Only took and gave. Gave and took. And, oh my, but it was heady.

Breaking the bond between their lips, he buried his face in her neck. He smelled of salt and sweat and man. She hugged his head against her, registering the texture of his thick, beautiful hair, the feel of his day-old beard scratching her skin.

"I'll be hanged, but you're sweet," he said, finally releasing her.

And when he did, her sanity returned. She scurried back like a crab, plopped down, then touched her hair, appalled to find it tumbling about her shoulders.

"It's all right, darlin'," he said, scooting himself next to her again. "Easy, easy. I'm not going to hurt you."

He reached for her.

She grabbed his wrist. "No," she breathed. "We must stop."

He froze, his arm caught between the two of them by her hand. "Nothin' will happen, Essie. I just wanna kiss you a little longer."

"Nothing will happen?" She released him and pressed a hand to her chest. "Something is already happening."

Groaning, he pulled her back within his embrace. "Don't say no, girl, please." He showered quick kisses along her hairline and tugged on her ear with his lips.

She slid her eyes closed, longing to give in. He latched on to her neck with his mouth. The delicious reaction that provoked was frightening and unexpected.

She shoved him away and jumped to her feet, stumbling backwards.

He stayed on the ground watching her, propping himself up with one hand, his eyes simmering with sensual promises. She turned and raced up the hill, leaving him, the bicycle, and a temptation so strong that surely she'd burn in hell for even contemplating surrender.

———

Essie had to force herself not to run down the deserted dirt road on the outskirts of town. She slipped behind a tree to straighten her loose hair—but it was her loose behavior that made her hands shake.

Her mother would expire on the spot if she were to ever find out. Essie could not even imagine what kind of retribution such a tawdry deed would provoke.

Once, when she was a girl, she had overheard one of the men in town say Widow Edmundson had an itch, and all his friends had laughed in response.

Later that week, she'd seen their parrot, Joe, scratching himself with his beak. So she'd taught it to say, "Joe has an itch."

Joe started saying it all the time. And when he did, Mother would turn redder than blazes and Papa would muffle his amusement. Essie had to break a switch off a tree, then bring it to her mother for a whipping.

Essie never understood what she'd done wrong. She'd taught Joe to say lots of things and had never gotten in trouble. But now, with the aftereffects of that kiss still humming through her body, she had a very good idea what exactly an itch was.

Mortification seeped into her being. What if Adam told the men in town that *she*, the town's old maid, had an itch? Tears sprang to her eyes. Surely he wouldn't.

Dear Lord, please, please, don't let him tell anyone. I promise not to ever, ever do that again. Just don't let anyone find out. Especially not Mother.

She'd almost reached the bend in the road that would take her into Corsicana. She slowed her step, knowing she couldn't just brazenly walk through town. Someone would see her and they'd know. Know what she'd been doing.

She brushed the dirt from her skirt but could do nothing about the two spots of moisture covering her knees. Nor could she wipe away the shame of her wanton response to Adam's kisses.

Stopping, she looked back over her shoulder, but Adam was nowhere to be seen. She'd half expected him to ride up on her bicycle and poke fun at her.

Because clearly he'd kissed before. Probably more than once or twice. And clearly, she had not. So why did that make her feel embarrassed when she'd been taught such virtue was a badge of honor?

But she knew why. By her very nature she wanted to be the best. At everything. Including kissing. And she would never know how she measured up, because she would never ask. And she would never do it again.

chapter ELEVEN

CUTTING BACK AND FORTH through the woods around town had made Essie's route home three times as long, but she didn't begrudge one single step, thankful for the protection the trees and brush had offered. She stood within their shelter, gauging the final leg of her journey. It was a good hundred yards to her house, and wide open.

She removed what few pins she had left in her hair, stuck them in her mouth, then finger-combed her hair once again, pulling it together at the back.

When she had all within her grasp, she twisted until it coiled up like a snake against her head and then transferred the pins into strategic spots. The style was severe and sloppily done. Anyone who knew her well would know she never wore it this way, but it would have to do.

She stepped into the open just as Mrs. Lockhart rounded the bend. Would the woman see something different? Something she oughtn't? Essie forced herself to walk in a sedate manner.

"My dear, dear girl," Mrs. Lockhart said, "how have you been?"

"Very well, thank you. And you?"

The elderly woman touched Essie's arm. "Such a surprise how Mr. Crook married up so fast to that woman from Dallas. I haven't had a moment alone with you since. How are you managing without him?"

"My work in the Slap Out was temporary from the start. I was just helping out until he could find someone permanent."

Mrs. Lockhart tsked. "You needn't feed me that twiddle-twaddle. I know a budding romance when I see one." She shook her head. "Why, look at you, so stiff and stern." She patted Essie's hand. "I always have preferred the stories where the woman wounds the man, not the other way around."

Essie glanced at her home. So close, yet so far. "Yes, well, perhaps the new Mrs. Crook will be able to recommend one from the catalog for you."

"Very commendable of you to say so. Commendable, indeed." She tilted her head. "Have you read the book I loaned you?"

"No, ma'am. Not yet."

The woman brightened. "Well, you must do so right away. Might teach you a thing or two about how to hold on to a man once you have him."

A spurt of defensiveness surfaced, giving Essie an overwhelming urge to explain exactly who had left whom this very afternoon, but she didn't dare.

"Don't give up, dear. However, you must desist from that ridiculous hairstyle. Much too off-putting for attracting a man." She glanced up and down Essie's frame. "And these tomboyish ways of yours have gone on long enough. Why, just look at your skirt. A mess, to be sure. I insist you read Mrs. Clay's novel. She's all-knowing about these things." Mrs. Lockhart punctuated her pronouncement with a tap of her cane, then continued on her way.

Essie made no pretense about moving sedately any longer. She all but ran the rest of the way home, flew through the front door and right into her mother.

"What on earth?"

"Oh, I'm sorry, Mother. I wasn't watching where I was going."

Her mother took Essie in with a glance, and her eyes filled with misgiving. "What has happened?"

"Nothing. Nothing at all."

"What happened to your hair?"

Essie touched the back of her bun. Still intact. "It came loose when I was out riding and I lost some of my pins. This was the best I could do under the circumstances."

Her mouth tightened. "You fell off your machine, didn't you?"

Essie said nothing.

"Where? In town?"

"No."

"Well, thank heaven for that, anyway." She continued to examine Essie, disappointment evident in her expression. "I have prayed and prayed about the way you cavort about town on that thing. Have you no shame whatsoever? Do you ever wonder why you are an old maid?"

Essie sucked in her breath.

"I'm sorry to be so blunt, but it is time to face the facts. Look at you. Thirty years old and not a prospect in sight. A confirmed spinster. And it's no wonder when you drag in with mud on your skirt and your hair in shambles."

Essie swallowed back the hurt. "My hair is not in shambles."

"It is! And do you even care? Is that bicycle so important you'd rather have it than a man? Than babies of your own?"

Essie flinched. She would, of course, rather have a man and a family, but must she really choose between that and her love of the outdoors? Surely it wasn't an either/or decision.

"Is it something I've done to make you act this way?" Mother asked.

"Of course not. It's nothing to do with you."

"It's everything to do with me. You're my daughter. A reflection of me and all I stand for. And what about your father? If you haven't a care for what people think of you or me, what about him? He holds a very important position in this town. Have you no appreciation for how hard he works? For the constant insinuations he puts up with on your behalf?"

Try as she might, Essie could not ignore the sting her mother's words inflicted. She knew from long experience that keeping silent was the quickest way to end these "discussions." But they never ceased to hurt. Deeply.

Mother sighed. "Your father wants to see you right away in his office, but do not even think about going in there until you have at the very least put your hair to rights."

"Yes, Mother." She hurried up the stairs.

———

Essie sat in one of the upholstered armchairs opposite Papa's desk, catching him up on their progress.

Mother stuck her head in the office. "Mr. Currington's here." She stepped back and allowed him entrance before Essie had a chance to compose herself.

He'd cleaned up, shaved, and combed back his hair, though it was still wet. How many pairs of those riveted, double-seamed denim trousers did he own?

She brushed a dried piece of dirt from her sleeve, wishing she'd had time to do more than re-pin her hair and change her skirt. But Papa had called for her before she'd had a chance to wash. As a result, she felt like a goose to Adam's swan.

His cowboy boots thumped against the hardwood floors as he crossed the room to shake Papa's hand. "Sir."

"Essie tells me you've made quite the progress."

"Yes, sir." He pinned her with his gaze. "I'm glad she's pleased with me."

Feeling a slow blush move up her neck, she glanced at Papa. He, fortunately, did not notice the double entendre, nor even look her way.

"She's been singing your praises all afternoon," he said.

"Has she now? Well, I'm mighty glad to hear that."

She scrutinized the papers she was holding, praying that she could make it through this meeting without exposing her feelings.

"Have a seat, son."

"Thank ya, sir." He sat in the chair beside her, boots together, knees wide apart. "I stopped by the smithy's on my way over."

Adam went on to explain to Papa how the down-hole tools

worked, when Mr. Fowler would have them ready, and when they should break ground.

"Will Jeremy slow you down, do you think?" Papa asked.

"Oh, he may be slim as a bed slat, but he's a hard worker. And I'd rather have that than somebody that's always sittin' on his endgate. We'll get along fine, I reckon."

"Excellent. Essie? Do you have anything else?"

"I think that about covers it." She stood and circled around the desk, withdrawing Adam's wages from one of the drawers.

Both men stood.

"Here you are, Mr. Currington," she said. "Thank you for all your hard work."

He took the pouch. "It's been my pleasure, Miss Spreckelmeyer."

"Yes. Well. I'll walk you to the door."

"No need, ma'am."

"I insist." She led him down the hall and stepped out onto the front porch with him, closing the door behind them. She touched a finger to her mouth, indicating the open windows.

They walked to the white picket fence outlining the yard. Only when they reached the gate did she dare to speak, and even then in a whisper. "Where's my bicycle?"

"It was purty bent up, girl. I toted it down to Fowler's."

"Why? What was wrong with it?"

"The frame was kinked some. He'll have it fixed in no time."

Touching her waist, she looked in the general direction of the blacksmith's shop. "What did you tell him?"

"The truth."

She snapped to attention. "You *what?*"

"I told him the truth, Essie. I've learned it's best not to make my stories wider than they are tall."

"But . . . but—oh dear. We'd better go back inside and talk to Papa. He'll know what to do."

She turned around, but he grabbed her wrist. "Hold on, there, girl. I told him I tried your machine out and that it threw me forked-end up."

"Oh. That's all?"

"That's all."

"Nothing else?"

"Nothin' else."

It was a moment before she realized he still held her wrist. She pulled loose and examined her fingernails.

"I can't court ya proper-like, not with you being the judge's daughter and all."

She looked up. "What has that to do with anything?"

"I'm a drifter, Essie. Nobody wants a drifter comin' to call."

She hesitated only a moment. "I do."

His expression softened. "Yer pa would squirt enough lead in me to make it a payin' job to melt me down."

"You don't even know him."

"I know he's up for reelection. I know he's mighty powerful in these parts. I know him and the sheriff use the same toothpick. I know it'd only take a nod from either o' them and I'd be doing a midair ballet from a cottonwood."

Disappointment wilted her shoulders. She didn't think it would be as bad as all that. Truly, Mother would be more of a problem than Papa. Even though she acted it, she wasn't so desperate to see her daughter married off that she'd settle for just anybody. And a drifter would definitely fall into the "just anybody" category.

Essie also knew Papa's tolerance level dipped awfully low before an election. If Adam were to ask permission now and Mother put up a fuss, Papa would capitulate simply because it was easier.

"It don't mean we can't see each other," Adam said.

"I thought you said—"

"I said we can't court. I never said nothin' about spoonin'."

"You mean, secreting away behind my parents' backs? So that no one knows?"

"Now, I don't know as I'd say that, exactly. Let's just say we'd be keepin' things private fer a while."

"You mean until after the election?"

"That'd be better, I think."

"I don't know, Adam. Perhaps if I spoke with Papa first."

"No! No, don't do that. It ain't right. The man's supposed to do the talkin'. When it comes time, I'll go to him. Promise you won't say nothin'."

The front door opened and Papa came down the steps, settling his hat on his head. "You still here, Currington?"

"Just finishin' up a few particulars with Miss Spreckelmeyer, sir."

They stepped apart and Papa passed between them. "Good day, then."

"Same to you, sir."

"Bye, Papa."

They waited until he'd walked several houses down, then Adam turned back to her. "Promise me, Essie. I mean it."

"No, Adam. I'm sorry. Either you speak to my father and court me properly or we don't court at all."

He stepped through the gate. "Suit yourself, then."

He started down the sidewalk, his lazy gait capturing her attention and her imagination. Panic took hold. She knew without a doubt he wasn't just walking out of her yard, he was walking out of her life.

He was handsome. He was charming. He was an outdoorsman. And if she didn't take him up on his offer, there might never be another one—from anyone.

"Adam?" she called.

He hesitated, then waited while she hurried to him.

"Perhaps I was a bit hasty," she said.

Tipping the brim of his hat back, he shifted his weight onto one foot but offered her no encouragement.

"If I agree to this, um, private courtship, you'll speak to my father after the election?"

He gave a slow nod. "Yes, ma'am. I surely will."

She glanced up and down the street. Papa had long since turned the corner. There were no carriages, no horses, no people to witness her surrender.

Election Day was almost seven weeks away. What possible harm could come from keeping their courtship a secret for those few weeks?

"Very well, then. But I want to be the one to pick up my bicycle when it's ready."

"If that's what you want. Maybe when we pick everything else up Monday morning, Fowler will have that for us, too."

She nodded.

He rubbed his neck. "I'm sorry I messed it up."

The tension that had gripped her only moments before eased. "It wasn't your fault. I didn't expect you to go so far down the hill."

"I did purty good, then?"

"You did outstanding."

"Why, thank you, ma'am." Winking, he pinched her chin, then continued down the sidewalk. "I'll swing by here first thing on Monday, then," he called over his shoulder.

An unexpected lethargy fell over Essie. She thought about her mother's diatribe. It had a sharper edge to it than usual. She had actually verbalized what had heretofore been unspoken in their house: the word *spinster. Old maid. No prospects in sight.*

But she did have a prospect. And she thought of him constantly, reliving their first meeting at the Slap Out. His unexpected interest. His disillusionment over that cattle drive. His devotion to building her a rig. His bicycle ride down the hill. His kisses afterward.

Essie straightened her cuffs. Mother had certainly been wrong about the bicycle in this instance, for it was that very vehicle that had brought her and Adam together.

She wondered where he was. What he was doing. What he'd spent his wages on. Was he thinking of her as much as she was thinking of him?

The weekend dragged as she waited for Monday to arrive. On Saturday, she finished all her washing and ironing, helped Mother put up some pumpkins, and baked some bread.

She wondered what denomination Adam was, for she'd never seen him at church, and this morning was no exception. Something else for Mother to complain about once he expressed his intentions.

Without her bicycle, Essie grew listless. She could practice her wheeled feet, but she wasn't in the mood. She could take little Harley snake hunting, but she didn't much feel like that, either. She'd invited Papa to go fishing, but he and Mother were going to the Dunns' for their weekly Bible study.

The house was quiet with them gone. No breeze stirred the curtains. She sat on the front porch for a while, waving to her neighbors as two by two they went here and there.

She went inside and played the piano, but even that didn't hold her interest for long. Spying Mrs. Lockhart's novel on the table, she thumbed through it, wondering what secrets it held—if any.

Taking it upstairs to her bedroom, she fluffed her pillow, curled up in bed and began to read *Clarabel's Love Story*.

Clarabel was a tough, passionate woman jilted by a lover who was too poor to marry her. Distraught, she married the first "acceptable" man to ask her—a stodgy Oxford graduate. The match was so distasteful, the couple moved to separate homes only three days into the marriage.

Clarabel exhibited strength in supporting herself but never forgot her original suitor. Later, he returned a wealthy man and they engaged in an illicit affair. Love triumphed when the Oxford man died.

Essie closed the book, her mind in a whirl. The sentiments expressed in the novel were completely unacceptable in life as she knew it. But Mrs. Lockhart was a respectable, churchgoing matron. And she had knowingly given the book to Essie, suggesting, even, that Essie emulate Clarabel.

But didn't Mrs. Lockhart find it shocking? The point of the entire novel was to raise her romantic standards by lowering her moral ones.

Perhaps Adam was right. Perhaps there really were couples who did such things. Even right here in Corsicana.

Was that why she had never married? Had her decency scared men away? She thought of the numerous weddings that had been performed this summer. Had those brides given themselves to their men before the vows were spoken?

She placed the book on the bedside table and lay back on her bed, watching the light and shadows of twilight fight for dominance on her ceiling.

The darkness eventually won.

chapter TWELVE

ONCE ADAM AND JEREMY started drilling, Essie's presence at the field was superfluous. She could take lunch out to them each day, but she didn't want Adam to think she was "chasing" him. So she only took lunches out on Fridays.

This Friday was no exception. She dressed casually, but carefully, in a new bicycle dress she'd made. The dark Turkish trousers fell below her knees and were so full that when standing they appeared to be a skirt.

She buttoned a matching double-breasted jacket over her vest, collar, and tie to accommodate the cooler weather that had begun to settle in. Holding her tongue between her teeth, she pinned on a modest, fur-trimmed hat with two shortened peacock feathers the color of Adam's eyes, then checked herself in the mirror.

Fashionable but not overly done. The quintessential modern woman.

She skipped down the stairs, running her finger along the banister and bumping it against a series of old nails sticking out every few inches. As a youth she'd slid down the banister more times than she could count. One time she fell off halfway down and sliced open her chin.

Mother made Papa drive nails into the railing, leaving about an inch of each nail sticking up. The family had become so accustomed to them, they didn't even notice them anymore. She really ought to have Papa remove them.

In the kitchen, Essie took some boiled eggs from the icebox, along with three jars of tea, and nestled them in a basket with frog legs, cheese, potato croquettes, pickled okra, and fig tarts—all made by her own hand.

After securing the basket to her bicycle, she headed to Twelfth Street. It had been two weeks since Peg's repair. Plenty of time for Essie to get used to the new clicking noise Peg made with each rotation of the wheels.

But she simply couldn't keep the sound from registering. Instead of causing concern, however, the noise reminded her of Adam and the passionate kisses they'd shared. Neither she nor Peg would ever be the same again.

She glanced up at the sky. Clouds bunched together like suds in a washtub, obliterating the sun's rays and graying the town. On main thoroughfares, she had some protection from the wind. But once she left the shelter of the buildings, the blustery weather threatened to tip her and Peg over.

She tucked her chin and squeezed the handlebars, fighting the wind at every turn. It battered her hat, whipping against the brim and straining her hair where it was pinned, but she didn't dare let loose of the bike. Fat raindrops began to plop from the sky as she reached the field.

Adam saw her coming, left the rig and jogged to her. "Better slide off yer saddle, girl, before them clouds open up."

She relinquished the bicycle to him and they ran for cover, slipping beneath the thickly clustered, arching branches of an old magnolia that formed a leafy cupola clear to the ground.

He hastily propped Peg against the tree's trunk, grabbed Essie around the waist and pulled her flush against him. "Quick, before the boy comes."

He captured her lips with his and gave her a hurried but thorough kiss. "By gum, I've missed you," he said, then released her as Jeremy approached.

"Hey, there, Miss Essie," Jeremy said, bending down into their shadowed haven. Earthy smells rose from the dormant soil they'd disrupted with their presence. A gentle tapping of rain began to sprinkle the leaves sheltering them.

Still trying to recover her composure, the best she could do was nod a greeting.

Jeremy zeroed in on the basket secured to her bike. "You bring us some lunch?"

She stared back at him, totally devoid of words.

A slow, delicious smile crept over Adam's face. "Don't be teasin' us, now, Miss Essie. That boy there's a mite narrow around the equator and I'm so hungry I could eat a sow and nine pigs."

She blinked. "What? Oh. Of course. Help yourself."

Jeremy began to loosen the rope binding the basket to her bike, his back to them. Adam took a leisurely surveillance of her, from her skewed hat to her bicycle boots and back up again, not bothering to disguise his interest.

She flushed hot, then cold, trying to think what Clarabel would do. And in the next moment found herself examining him with the same boldness he'd used with her.

He'd been still before, but she detected a subtle tensing of his muscles as she pored over him. Cowboy hat. Lifted brows. Wide lips. Shadowed jaw. Extensive shoulders. Molded chest. Silver buckle. Cocked hip. Massive thighs. Cowboy boots.

From the corner of her eye, she saw Jeremy releasing the final knot on the basket, so she swept her gaze up to Adam's and forgot to breathe. She'd never seen such heat, such desire, such impatience in a man's eyes.

It filled her with a surge of power. And the upper hand shifted from him to her. She knew it. He knew it. And it released in her something she hadn't known she possessed.

Wickedness? she thought. Perhaps.

"I have something sweet for you today," she said.

135

Adam's lips parted.

Jeremy turned around. "You always bring somethin' sweet, Miss Essie."

She held Adam's gaze. "So I do. So I do."

Adam swallowed.

Essie took the basket from Jeremy. "Shall we sit?"

Jeremy plopped down.

Adam jumped forward and grabbed her elbow. "You'll get your skirt dirty."

"It's all right," she said.

"If I had a jacket, I'd lay it out for ya."

She breathed in the smell of him, part sweat, part salt, part shaving tonic. "I know."

He increased the pressure on her elbow for a mere second before helping her settle on the ground. Gone was the teasing banter that came so easily to him, replaced with an intensity that she knew she'd caused.

Her mother was wrong. She wasn't undesirable. She may be thirty and she may ride a bike, but she'd caught the attention of not just a man, but a gorgeous man. A man who could have his pick of any woman he wanted.

"Oh, lookit this," Jeremy said. "Frog legs. My favorite."

Essie spread a small, square cloth over her skirt. "I didn't realize you favored them. You should have told me sooner."

Jeremy took a big bite. "Hmmmm. Where'd you catch 'em?"

"Not far from where we let Colonel loose."

Adam paused. "*You* caught the frogs?"

"Of course," she said, unscrewing the jar of pickled okra and popping a piece into her mouth. "I'm not as good at catching them as Jeremy is, though."

"You do all right, Miss Essie," Jeremy responded.

A gust of wind broke through their barrier, lifting the cloth on Essie's lap. Adam clapped a hand on her leg to keep the napkin from blowing away.

He surreptitiously caressed her through her skirts. "Careful, girl. You're fixin' to lose somethin'."

She glanced at Jeremy, then lifted her cloth, dabbing the corners of her mouth. "I'll be careful."

Adam smiled. "Where'd you learn to catch frogs?"

"At my grandpa's farm. He has a place out near Quitman. I used to go there every summer."

"By yourself?"

"Well, Mother would take me, but she never stayed the way I did. First day of summer, she'd wake me up early in the morning and we'd take the train. Then Grandpa would pick us up in a carriage pulled by two palomino horses."

"I never rode in a train," Jeremy said.

"Where would you go if you could?" Essie asked.

He put a chunk of cheese in his mouth. "Don't really know," he said around his mouthful.

"What did you do up there all summer?" Adam asked her.

"Lots of things. Grandpa's syrup mill was my favorite, though. The horse would walk in circles all day turning the mill, pressing sweet juice out of the sugarcane. Sometimes I'd help pour the juice into big vats where they slowly cooked it, and this wonderful aroma bubbled up from it."

"You ever get to have any o' that syrup?" Jeremy asked.

"Yes. They'd pour it into jugs or tin buckets, and at the house I'd get to eat ribbon cane syrup on Grandma's hot, buttered biscuits."

Rain started to leak into their haven, causing the three of them to scoot closer to the trunk of the tree.

"My grandpa ain't nothin' like that. He don't do nothin' but drink the day away."

Essie had known Jeremy since he was a tiny baby, and this was the first time she'd ever heard him so much as mention his grandfather—Corsicana's town drunk.

"You have a grandpa, Adam?" he asked.

"Shore do."

"He drink?"

"Shore does."

Jeremy took a gulp of tea from his glass jar. "Is he a drunk?"

Adam dug around in the basket for a boiled egg as if Jeremy had asked him nothing more than if the sky was blue. "Nope. He likes to look at the moon through the neck of a bottle, but he knows his limits. Best cowboy that's ever lived."

"He the one what taught you ropin'?"

"Him and my pa."

"You ever seen Adam rope?" Jeremy asked Essie.

"No, I haven't."

"You gotta show her, Adam. Miss Essie'd be impressed. 'Course, she'd want you to teach her how, though."

Adam glanced over at her. "I'll teach her. I got a whole passel o' tricks I could show her."

He took a bite out of his egg, and Essie looked down. The advantage had somehow shifted back to him.

The rain stopped, but a few gusts of wind rustled the big, glossy leaves around them, loosing random droplets of water. They finished their meal, leaving not so much as a crumb behind.

"That sure was good, Miss Essie," Jeremy said.

"Thank you."

She took a sip of tea, then reached for the lid, but Adam snagged the jar from her, turned it to the exact spot she'd touched with her lips and drank deeply, finishing all that was left.

"That was mighty sweet," he said, handing the jar back to her and scraping his mouth with his sleeve.

A crack of thunder reverberated above them.

"You may as well head on out, Jeremy," Adam said. "As long as the Old Man up there is stompin' on his campfire and sending sparks a-flyin', we ain't got no business under that tripod o' poles."

Jeremy's eyes lit up. "You sure?"

"I'm shore, but when the lightning stops, you come on back."

"I will." He hesitated. "What about Miss Essie?"

"I'll stay here with her until everything settles down."

"That okay with you, Miss Essie?"

She schooled her expression to show none of the commotion going on inside her. "Of course. I'll be fine."

Jeremy stood and brushed the backside of his waist-overalls. "Well, thanks again, Miss Essie, and I'll see ya later today, Adam."

He ducked out into the field, and she listened to his rapid footfalls splashing through the puddles until they were no more.

Adam said nothing, just looked at her. The tension inside her built. She thought of how bold she'd been earlier and felt herself blush. What in the world had she been thinking?

He picked up a corner of her skirt and gave it a gentle tug. "Come here."

And so she had her choice. She could take her bicycle and leave or she could scoot over next to Adam and learn some new and unsearchable things. Things she might never have another chance to experience if she didn't seize this opportunity.

Stiff. Stern. Old maid. Spinster.

That's what she was and what she would continue to be unless she secured this man's interest. And if that meant allowing him to steal a kiss or two, so be it. In fact, she found the idea more than a little thrilling.

She shuffled over on her knees. As soon as she was within reach, he caught her to him and brought them both to the ground.

"I was so afraid you were gonna say no," he said, then covered her lips with his.

Her hat forced her head into an uncomfortable angle. His belt buckle dug into her. Her shoulder landed in a small puddle. None of it mattered.

She wrapped her arms around his neck and kissed him back with everything she had. He held her tight, one hand between her shoulder blades, the other at the small of her back.

An explosion of thunder from far away slowly faded like a music box that winds down. A moment of silence as the earth stilled in anticipation of once again being quenched of its thirst. A gradual tapping of water on the leaves above and the ground outside increased in sound and speed, culminating in a waterfall from heaven. So much.

So fast. The soil could not absorb it all at once.

"Your hair," he said. "Can I see your hair?"

Wrenching the pin from her hat, she flung them both to the side and sat up. She tugged at her pins until her hair fell down her back, then ran her fingers through it, savoring the freedom of having it loose.

He sat up and cradled her face with his hands, his eyes smoldering. "You are beautiful."

He kissed her again with an exquisite gentleness that undid her more than the earlier impatience. He tasted every inch of bare skin he could. And when he'd finished with her face and neck and hands and fingers, when he'd finished smelling and stroking and worshiping her hair, he placed her hand over the buttons of her double-breasted jacket and left it there.

If she removed it, her modesty would still be intact, with her vest and shirtwaist remaining. She slowly undid the buttons. He pushed the jacket off her shoulders and down her arms. Then waited.

She unhooked her vest.

He freed her of it, then unfurled her tie and slipped it from her collar. Nothing they'd removed allowed him access to more than he'd had before. But the act of disrobing made her feel vulnerable. Wanton.

He kissed her again. His hands took liberties and she allowed it. Relished it. Wanted more of it. And that's when she heard Papa's voice.

"He and Jeremy must have run for shelter," Papa said, "but if I know Adam, they'll be back. He doesn't waste a moment of daylight."

Essie gasped. Adam touched a finger to her lips, then held her still against him. When had it quit raining?

"Well, I have to confess, you were right and I was wrong. Currington looks to be on the up-and-up."

It was Uncle Melvin. She felt Adam tense. Panic filled her. If they were caught, Papa could be reasoned with. But Uncle Melvin always swung first and asked questions later.

The two men discussed the progress of the well and what they'd do if they hit a gusher. What they'd do if they didn't. How far they were in the drilling. How much farther they had to go still.

Adam's thumb made a circular motion on her waist. His breath tickled her hair. After what seemed a lifetime, Papa and Uncle Melvin left the field, passing right by the tree.

She and Adam stayed still and huddled together for several minutes. When they were sure all was safe, Adam pulled back but did not release her.

"You all right?" he asked.

"I think I'm going to cast up my accounts."

He smiled. "Me too." He pecked her lips. "Come on, I'll help you with your things."

He did not allow her to do anything for herself. He hooked all the hooks, buttoned all the buttons, and tied all the ties. By the time he had finished, they were both as worked up as they'd been before.

He threaded his hands through her hair, cupped her head and kissed her. Thoroughly.

"By jingo, but you are sweeter than a honeybee tree." He kissed the end of her nose. "I'm afraid you're gonna have to put your hair back up. That's one thing I can't do for ya."

"My mother is going to know."

He searched for her scattered hairpins and plucked them from the ground. "No, she won't. I'll make sure ya look as prim as a preacher's wife before ya leave."

She took more care with her hair this time, tucking it into a French twist. Adam watched unabashedly, handing her pins as she needed them. She picked up her hat.

"Wait," he said, pulling her to her feet. He drew her against him and kissed her again. "Come to the show with me."

"What?"

"There's a ten-cent show at the Opera House tonight."

She sucked in her breath. "A ten-cent show? But those are the low-comedy shows. I've never been to one in all my life. Besides, I thought you said we couldn't openly court."

"We can't, but we could meet there. Like it was an accident or somethin'.." He rubbed his thumb along her jaw. "Please?"

She vacillated, afraid of what would happen if she went. Afraid of what would happen if she didn't. She might very well lose him if she refused. And to lose him now would be unbearable.

Her mother's words once again droned through her mind. *"No one's going to bid on your basket . . . not a prospect in sight . . . spinster . . . old maid."*

"I'll be there," she whispered.

He kissed her again, helped her get her hat on straight and sent her on her way.

chapter THIRTEEN

ESSIE HAD NO IDEA what to wear to a ten-cent show. When Papa took them to the Opera House to hear a concert or soloist, she and Mother always dressed in their finest. Surely that would not be the case for the low-comedy shows.

By the same token, she wanted to look nice for Adam. It was their first official outing, clandestine though it was. She threw yet another dress on her bed and reached for a pale blue crepe de Chine. It was made in princess effect and covered with black chenille polka dots. The waist was tight-fitting and the vest would show white lace at the neck, which would be duplicated at the edge of the sleeves and in a flounce at the bottom of her skirt.

She put it on, turning around and looking over her shoulder into the mirror. She could wear her hat of blue tulle with black chenille dots and a black bird-of-paradise. She'd had it specially made to match the gown.

"Essie?" Her mother tapped on the door.

"Come in."

Mother opened the door, glancing at the clothing heaped on the bed, draped over the chair, and slung over the footboard. "What are you doing?"

"I'm going to play piano with the orchestra at the Opera House before tonight's performance and then again between acts."

"Play at the Opera House? But why? What happened to Mr. Graham?"

"He's playing the cornet between acts, and reverting to piano during the actual program."

"I don't understand. You've not played for them in years."

"No, but you know how Mr. Creiz has been trying to persuade me to become a permanent member of the staff orchestra ever since Mrs. Graham has taken ill and Mr. Graham has been hinting at retiring."

"Well, yes, but you're not actually considering it, are you?"

"No, no. I'm just helping him out tonight." Essie picked up a brown velveteen and slipped it on a hanger.

"I thought you were going to the card party in Pinkston with us tonight."

"I'm afraid that will no longer be practical," Essie said. "I'd have to go on horse now since you'll have the carriage and by the time I arrived, there would only be an hour or so before it was time to turn around and head home."

"Well, for heaven's sake. I wish you'd checked with me first. Your father is campaigning. It's important the entire family attend these socials."

Essie placed a ribbon collarette in her drawer and slid it closed. "I'm thirty years old. An old maid. Remember? Perhaps I should start acting like one."

Mother stiffened. "Just what is that supposed to mean?"

A breeze from the window sent a starched linen cuff flitting to the floor. "Old maids don't check in with their mothers. They make their own plans. Live their own lives. You know. Like Aunt Zelda."

"Don't be ridiculous." Mother picked up the cuff and slapped it back onto the toilet table. "Zelda's eccentricities shamed the entire family. She was a constant source of embarrassment."

"Was she? I always remember her as being a great deal of fun."

"You are still living in my home, young lady," Mother said, stepping to the window and yanking the gossamer curtains together.

"I'm not a *young* lady anymore."

Mother frowned. "Nevertheless, you will do me the courtesy of checking with me before you make any plans."

Essie folded a corset cover. "I will do you the courtesy of *telling* you my plans when I've decided what they are."

"I don't like your tone, Esther."

Essie straightened. "Don't you? Well, please forgive me."

Mother narrowed her eyes. "What is the matter with you?"

"Nothing. I guess your little lecture a couple of weeks ago has me considering exactly what my role is now. And my responsibilities."

"Nothing has changed, dear."

Essie smoothed a piece of fur trimming one of her cloaks. "You're mistaken, Mother. Everything has changed."

Essie guided Cocoa to the left when she reached Tenth Street and headed to Molloy's Livery. Remembering what Adam had said about not making his stories wider than they were tall, she had gone straight to the Opera House after leaving the oil field that afternoon. She'd asked Mr. Creiz, the leader of the orchestra, if she could play with them this evening.

He'd immediately agreed. She'd explained she didn't want to play during the actual performance, since she'd not rehearsed with them, but instead just at the beginning and during the interludes. He had been delighted.

She pulled Cocoa to a stop just inside the livery's gate. A lad of twelve or thirteen rushed out to help her dismount.

"I'm not sure how late I'll be," Essie said.

"Don't matter none, miss," he said. "She'll be here when you get back, no matter what time it is. What's her name?"

"Cocoa."

"I'll take good care o' her."

Essie slipped him a coin, then went around to Hunt Avenue and approached the front entrance of the Opera House just as the orchestra, in full regalia, came out, all talking at once. The swarm of men wore deep blue suits and hats with light blue braid and a red sash tied about their waists.

She stopped the trombone player, a large man always ready with a smile. "Mr. Collier?"

"Oh, howdy, Miss Spreckelmeyer. Tony says you're gonna play with us tonight."

"Just during the in-betweens. What are you doing out here?"

"We're fixin' to parade up and down Beaton Street."

"You are? Why, I didn't know you did that."

He leaned in and whispered, "We always do that before the girlie or minstrel shows. Helps get the attention o' folks on the street and brings in a bigger crowd."

Essie flushed. "I had no idea. I . . . I'm afraid I was unprepared for that."

He laughed. "Oh, we don't expect our guest players to do that. Just us regulars."

When they reached Beaton Street, Mr. Creiz signaled for attention, raised his baton and gave a count. They started in on "Sweet Rosie O'Grady" and set off down the street. Essie stood back, unsure of what to do.

Mr. Crocket's drum kept the rhythm, while the piercing notes of the brass carried above all the other instruments. They passed the barbershop, the jewelers, and the hardware store. Men poured out of the Bismarck Saloon, yelling encouragement to the orchestra and hooking up behind them.

Her social circle was so small, she often forgot about this side of town. The side where churchgoing women rarely went. And never without escort. She didn't recognize one single person, other than the orchestra members. And they had always been just this side of respectable.

She began to question the wisdom of her plans. Perhaps she needed to go back to the livery and ride Cocoa out to Pinkston after all. Instead of meeting Adam tonight, she could play cards with men and women her parents' age. A few were her age, too—but they all had spouses and children and homes of their own.

"A penny for your thoughts."

She turned. Adam stood close behind her, freshly pressed and smelling of Yankee soap. His crisp white shirt contrasted sharply with the deep golden hue of his skin. His cowboy hat could not shade the brightness of his clear blue-green eyes.

She still couldn't quite believe that just hours ago she'd been wrapped in his arms and he in hers. How she looked forward to the time when they could openly court. When she could walk into church on the arm of the handsomest man in town. Her. Essie Old-Maid Spreckelmeyer.

"Hello," she said, a bit of shyness creeping over her.

He removed his hat. "You look mighty nice."

"Thank you." *So do you.*

He stood silent. Serious. "I've been thinkin' about ya all day."

She warmed at his words.

"Wonderin' if you were gonna come. Wonderin' if you didn't, how I'd not even wanna stay for the show. Wonderin' if you did, how I'd keep my hands to myself."

Her pulse picked up.

"I didn't expect you to get here before me. Have ya been waitin' long?"

She shook her head. "I arranged to play piano for the orchestra tonight, so I had to come early."

His face fell. "The whole time?"

"No, no. Just between acts."

They stood on the steps, adjusting to the newness of what was happening between them.

"Did ya tell your folks where you were goin'?"

"I did. They're playing cards with some friends out in Pinkston tonight. They don't suspect a thing."

"When will they be back?"

"Late."

The words settled around them like the last brush of sunset before night falls.

"I wanna kiss ya right here. Right now."

She surprised herself by answering, "Me too."

He slipped his hand into hers. "Come on, Miss Spreckelmeyer. We'd best be joinin' the fun, else we might miss the show altogether."

"What if someone sees us?"

He cocked his head. "Would you join the fun if you were with Jeremy?"

"Yes, I'm sure I would."

"Then we've nothin' to worry about."

He pulled her by the hand, down the steps and into the street. She savored the intimacy of it. Never, ever, had a man led her around in such a way. Always, they took her elbow. Occasionally touched her waist. But this—this was so much more personal.

She lifted her skirt to keep up with his long strides. The orchestra now played "Daddy Wouldn't Buy Me a Bow Wow," and the crowd of revelers had grown larger and noisier. Adam took the two of them into the thick of it. Folks bumped and jostled her from all directions.

Adam kept his hand in hers, hiding them within the folds of her jacket. She checked the men and women crowded around them and caught the attention of George Bunert, the harness maker, staring at her from a few feet away.

She shook her hand free. "Hello! How are you?" she shouted above the noise, waving.

He wove around a few people to reach her, then removed his hat. "I didn't expect ta see ya, Miss Spreckelmeyer."

They had to shout to be heard. "My father had to be in Pinkston this evening, so I am here on his behalf to visit and greet his in-town constituents."

"By yerself?"

"No, no. Mr. Currington, my father's driller, is here with me."

She tried to introduce the two men, but the noise level made it nearly impossible, and the crowd ended up separating Mr. Bunert from them. She lost sight of him as Adam tugged at her jacket and bent his head to her ear.

"You wearing all this stuff to protect you from me or the weather?"

She smiled. She'd chosen to wear her three-quarter-length coat, knowing it would be dark when the show was over and the ride home on Cocoa would be cold.

Instead of answering, she indicated his shirt-sleeves. "Aren't you cold?"

He reclaimed her hand. "No, ma'am. Not when I'm with you, sugar. Not when I'm with you."

His thumb drew a circle on her palm. She darted a quick look around, but no one gave them any notice. And they wouldn't see anything untoward if they did. His hidden caress continued and though it was no more than a simple gesture, its very secretiveness in such a public place was in many ways more potent than what they'd shared underneath the tree.

He winked and began to sing with the crowd.

"I'll be so glad when I get old,
To do just as I likes,
I'll keep a parrot and at least,
A half a dozen tykes;
And when I've got a tiny pet,
I'll kiss the little thing;
Then put it in its little cot, ,
And on to it I'll sing:
Daddy wouldn't buy me a bow wow! bow wow!"

He raised her hand above her head and simultaneously spun her at the waist. When she completed her turn, he positioned her directly in front of him, face forward. The crowd had grown and become more packed together. Adam placed his hands at her waist, his thighs bumping against the back of her legs as they walked in unison to the music.

The orchestra began to make a horseshoe turn and head back to the Opera House. She reveled in the festiveness of the men. The excitement of having this cowboy with her. The anticipation of what the evening would bring.

When they reached the steps, the orchestra stayed out front, continuing to draw more folks in. She turned her face toward Adam. "I have to go. Where will I meet you?"

"*What?*" he said.

She saw his mouth form the word but could not hear him over the noise.

He leaned down and put his ear next to her lips, his cowboy hat concealing her from view. Instead of repeating her words, she took his earlobe in her mouth and tugged. His hold on her loosened and she slipped from his grip, running up the stairs and glancing back just before entering the Opera House.

She smiled to herself. Judging from his expression, no meeting place would be necessary. He'd find her.

chapter FOURTEEN

MR. MIRUS TOOK Essie's coat and waved her up the steps of the wide stairway that led from the street level to the mezzanine. Several offices and club rooms opened off this second floor and were divided by portable walls that could be taken down to form a large dancing area for the annual Fireman's Ball. She expected she'd be attending the next one with Adam.

She continued on up the steps to the third level and entered the theater. All light and gold leaf, it rivaled anything in Dallas or Houston. A carpet covered the entire main floor, giving it an air of splendor. Recessed in the center of the ceiling was what everyone referred to as "the sun"—a large cluster of mirrored electric and gas lights.

Essie made her way down the east aisle, enjoying the stillness of the auditorium. There were no benches, only wicker seats with backs. She glanced up at the box her father owned. This would be the first time she'd view a show with someone other than him and from some other vantage point.

Just as she reached the bald-headed rows and descended into the orchestra pit, the crowd began to enter. The men were noisy, rowdy, and not at all like the patrons she was accustomed to. She didn't see one single woman.

Feeling awkward and a bit conspicuous, she picked up the sheet music on the upright piano and focused on the pieces she'd be sight-reading. A few minutes later the rest of the orchestra joined her but did not take the time to tune up. Instead, the lights dimmed and Mr. Creiz conducted them in the prelude.

The music moved quickly and robustly. Essie's fingers flew across the keys, and by the time they hit the crescendo she was out of breath. The men whistled and stomped. The lights went out. The curtain rose.

Essie slipped through a side door in the pit, skirting the auditorium and entering the deserted lobby, where statues and friezes of nymphs, cherubs, and winged figures decorated the hall. The gold carpet cushioned the sound of her heels.

She found Adam by the balcony steps. He beckoned her over and she hurried to his side.

"Come on," he said, ducking under the rope that cut off the balcony entrance.

"It's closed," she said. "No one else is up there, are they?"

"No, ma'am." He lifted the rope. "It's reserved. For the two of us. Now, hurry before someone sees us."

She dipped under the rope and followed him up the steps. At the top, the sudden darkness disoriented her. He grasped her hand and tugged. Instead of leading her to the first, or even second, row of seats, he settled them into the buzzard roost at the very back of the deserted balcony.

The stage had been transformed into a fancy ballroom, complete with flamboyant wall sconces, chandeliers, grand paintings, and gigantic windows. A lovely woman in a lavish gown sat center stage, earnestly visiting with an imaginary gentleman.

Her voice was high, affected, and gushingly southern. "Ah, so kind of you to find me this charming nook, Mistah Rushah. I feel *some* bettah now, thank you. And I believe I *would* like a cup of chocolate." She waved her handkerchief and called after the imaginary man, "Vewah *light* refreshments, Mr. Rushah, *vewah* light!"

Adam rested his arm on the back of Essie's chair, running a finger along her shoulder. She pretended not to notice. But behind her schooled features, she was paying very strict attention.

When the imaginary gentleman left the stage, the southern belle's manner changed entirely. She leaned back on the settee, sighed, and spoke to the audience in a natural voice. "Thank goodness that insipid specimen is gone. That ponderous old Smith came down full weight on my foot!"

She thrust her foot before her. "These slippers are several sizes too small but so Parisian, you know." Sitting up, she took a furtive look around. "I don't believe anyone is looking. I'm going to slip this one off—just *got* to stretch my poor toes a little!"

The woman crossed her legs and began to slowly lift the hem of her skirt. The men in the audience shouted and whistled. When she'd exposed one stocking-clad leg up to her knee, she bent forward.

The neck of her bodice gaped, causing another roar of approval from the men. She ran her hands down her calf and made quite a show of removing her shoe.

Essie watched with horror and fascination, her heart hammering in her chest. Adam's hand made its way to the back of her neck. He slipped a finger inside the top edge of her collar and moved it back and forth like a pendulum.

"Gracious!" the belle exclaimed. "I've danced a hole as big as a dollar in my stocking." She leaned back and lifted her foot in the air, exposing her toes and rotating her ankle round and round. A profusion of petticoats teased the men, offering them brief glimpses of her legs.

"My, what a relief to have that shoe off," she sighed.

Adam leaned closer, placing a kiss on Essie's neck. She caught her breath, then closed her eyes as he continued his foray, only to reopen one eye when the actress continued with her monologue.

"Here comes an English lord," the actress said, "strutting with importance, like the peacock he is."

Adam touched her chin, turning it toward him and gaining her full attention. He lowered his lips to hers.

"I'm going to shock him," the actress said. "Shatter his delicate English nerves. I'll play the wild, woolly Western girl."

Their kiss deepened and he slipped his arms about her. She touched his face, exploring it as if she were blind. Learning the texture of his skin, the angle of his jaw, the softness of his eyebrows.

"We believe in women's rights out West, Lord Catchum." The actress's voice had turned loud and nasal. "Disgusting? Not a bit. Did you ever see any Western women? Didn't? Missed the experience of a lifetime. They're awful smart. I'm a specimen."

The armrest bit into Essie's side. Adam took her hands and placed them behind his neck, then he began to explore *her* face, but with his lips.

"Why, they know as much about business as the men do. Yes, sir, they doctor, practice law, and extract teeth without pain. Then they make things red-hot for the saloon people—especially in Texas."

The men in the main gallery below them hooted and bellowed.

Adam's hands roamed, igniting an intense, deep desire. She didn't scold him for his boldness but instead wondered what he'd do if she were just as bold with him.

"How do they look? Purty well, as a whole. Most of them got rather big waists, but then, there's lots o' air out there in Texas that's got to be breathed, and they couldn't do it harnessed in an eighteen-inch belt."

Adam groaned and rested his forehead against hers. "I don't know how much more o' this I can take, sugar," he whispered.

"You want to stop?" she asked. "Why?"

He grasped her head between his hands and kissed her hard on the lips. "Let's get outta here."

"The orchestra."

"Leave it. You shouldn't be playin' for this kinda show anyway."

He picked his hat up off the seat next to him, put it on, and ushered her to the exit. Pausing, he pulled her against him and kissed her soundly one last time while cloaked within the theater's darkness.

"I'll overlook your breach of propriety in not proposing to me," the actress scolded. "You look startled, Mr. Catchum."

Adam released her. "Come on," he whispered.

They'd almost made it down the stairs when Adam stopped short.

Uncle Melvin stood in the lobby, his widened gaze tracking their descent, his sheriff's badge twinkling in the gaslight. For a moment he was frozen like one of the statues, but he quickly came to life.

"Just what do you two think you're doing?" he hissed, striding toward them, displeasure evident in his expression.

Essie caught her breath, her pulse shooting up to an alarming level, and she quickly touched the back of her hair to make sure all was in place.

Adam held up the rope.

Forcing down her panic, she slipped under it. "Good evening, Uncle."

"Don't 'good evening' me. What's going on?"

"Why, nothing. I'm playing incidental music with the orchestra, but Adam came to tell me he didn't think it a good idea for me to stay."

"What were you doing in the balcony?"

"I couldn't very well sit in the auditorium with the men."

Uncle Melvin glanced between the two of them. "Why didn't you stay in the pit?"

"I tried, but when the woman on stage began to remove her slippers, I became uncomfortable and retreated to the balcony."

He absorbed this bit of information and she hoped the barrage of questions was over and that he wouldn't catch her in her lies. She wasn't sure how much longer she could create answers without tripping herself up.

"What about you?" he asked Adam.

"I saw her outside during the before-show parade. When she left the pit, I followed to make sure she was all right."

Mr. Garitty, president of the Opera House, joined them. White hair encircled the sides of his head, leaving the top shiny. "Is there a problem, Sheriff?"

Uncle Melvin turned. "Did you know Essie was playing in the pit tonight?"

He shook his head. "Not until I saw her during the overture and asked Mirus about it."

"She has no business being here."

"I agree. If I'd known earlier, I would have warned her."

Essie touched Uncle Melvin's sleeve. "I'm sorry. I'll be sure to ascertain what show is playing next time. But no harm done. Adam has said he wouldn't mind seeing me home."

The sheriff scrutinized her. After a moment, he moved his attention to Adam. "I'll take her home, Currington. You can return to the show."

"It's no trouble for me, sir," Adam said.

"Nor me."

Adam looked at her. "Well, then. Good evening to you, Miss Spreckelmeyer." He touched the rim of his hat and pushed through the main entrance of the theater, the door clicking shut behind him.

———

Essie guided Cocoa out of the livery to where Uncle Melvin waited. So far, she'd managed to keep her irritation in check. But she was not at all pleased at having her evening cut short.

They rode together in silence. When they turned onto her street, the anticipated lecture began.

"That was a fool thing you were doing back there, girl."

She said nothing.

"What possessed you?"

"I've never been to a ten-cent show. How was I to know what it was like?"

He tipped his hat back and scanned the sky. "You're not talking to your pa. You're talking to me. So quit stretching the blanket. You know good and well there's a reason you ain't never been to a ten-cent show. Now, what were you doing there?"

"I went there for a clandestine meeting with an unsavory man," she snapped. "What do you think I went there for?"

He yanked his horse to a stop. She kept going.

"You better stop that thing right this minute or I'll hobble your ears."

She stopped.

He pulled up next to her. "Your mother's been tellin' my Verdie that you've been acting something awful lately. I'd never have believed it if I hadn't seen it with my own eyes. What's gotten into you?"

"Oh, I'm sorry," she sighed. "I didn't mean to bite your head off."

He touched his ankles to his horse's side. She did the same.

"Wanna talk about it?" he asked.

"Not particularly."

"Well, I don't know if I'm gonna give you a choice this time."

She looked down at the reins in her hands. "I'm just tired, is all."

"Tired? Of what?"

"Of being pestered for riding a bike. Of being scolded for acting like a man when I'm helping Papa with the business. Of having my every move criticized. Mother called me an old maid, you know."

He sucked in his breath. "That ain't true."

"Oh, but it is." A rush of renewed anger swept through her. "And that's when I decided that if I was going to live the rest of my life in that house, then I was going to make a few changes. And it was going to start with Mother."

They rode into her yard and he watched her dismount. "Just what is it you plan on doin'?"

"I'm not a child, Melvin. I'm thirty years old. It's time to cut the apron strings. Live my own life. And if that means playing the piano at the ten-cent show, then I will do so. And I don't care what Mother or anybody else says."

She walked Cocoa to the barn, suppressing the urge to say even more. Melvin dismounted and followed, holding Cocoa while Essie shoved the bar up and pulled the massive barn door open.

"Thank you," she said, reaching for Cocoa's reins.

He didn't release them. "Go on inside, girl. I'll put her up for you."

"No. I know you have things to do. I can do it."

He touched her elbow. "You'll ruin your gown. Now, go on."

She hesitated. "You sure?"

He nodded. When she reached the back door, she looked at her uncle. He stood by the barn, watching her.

"Are you gonna tell Mother where I was?"

"I thought you didn't care about her opinion anymore."

She fingered the buttons on her coat. "I don't. But that's no reason to borrow trouble."

He took his time answering. "Those ten-cent shows can get purty rough, Essie. Tonight's was not so bad. But most of the gals up on that stage—or worse, the ones in the audience—aren't even fit for a drinkin' man to hole up with. If you start playin' piano for them, the fellas are gonna think you're something that you're not."

She dropped her gaze.

"Is that what you want? You want your name to come up right alongside the names of those saloon gals who bare more hide than an Indian?"

"Of course not," she whispered.

"Then you better tell Creiz you ain't playing for any more of them ten-cent shows."

"Yes, sir," she replied, then slipped inside and gently closed the door behind her.

———

Melvin put Cocoa to bed, then returned to the Opera House. As town sheriff, he tried not to stray too far from the ten-cent show, in case of trouble. But he'd never expected to find his niece in attendance.

Moving into the lobby, he headed to the west wall, trying to reconcile in his mind what all she'd said to him, none of which bode well.

He wished he'd not revealed his presence to her. That way, he could have followed and seen for himself what was going on, if anything. With Currington involved, though, their actions were immediately suspect.

Essie might be thirty years old. She might think she was all grown up. But she always saw the good in people. Never the bad. And if Currington had designs on her, she'd be a sitting duck.

Melvin positioned himself against a column in the theater's lobby and waited. When the show ended, the men poured out. Adam was easy to find, being taller than most.

Melvin pushed his way through the crush and grabbed Adam's arm. "You got a minute?"

They stepped to the side, letting the others swarm past.

"Sheriff," Adam said.

According to the judge, this boy was hardworking, responsible, and good with Jeremy. So what was it that just didn't sit right?

"I wasn't happy to see my girl here tonight," Melvin said.

"No, sir. I felt the same way when I saw her." Adam shook his head. "She's awful smart about some things, but I'm thinkin' she wouldn't be able to tell the skunks from the house cats."

Melvin pulled a toothpick out of his inside pocket and worked it in between his teeth. "And which are you, Currington? A skunk or a house cat?"

Adam took a hard look at the sheriff. "I'm not gonna take offense at that 'cause I know yer just concerned about Miss Spreckelmeyer. But if anybody else had asked, I'd o' kicked 'im so far it would take a bloodhound six weeks just to find his smell."

"You threatenin' me, son?"

"Just statin' a fact, sir."

"Well, then, let me state a fact for you," he said, pointing the toothpick at Adam. "I put a lot of stock in my girl. I find out somebody's been playin' her, and he'll end up shaking hands with St. Peter. I can promise you that."

"I'll be sure to pass that along, sir." Adam touched his hat and headed down the stairs to the street.

chapter FIFTEEN

ESSIE THOUGHT OF ADAM constantly, yet she still forced herself to stay away from the fields until Friday. She knew Jeremy wouldn't have given her presence a second's notice, but she didn't want to risk being discovered, nor risk losing Adam by being too forward.

Hamilton had said men liked to do the chasing. So she'd decided if Adam wanted to see her, he'd figure out a way. Only, he hadn't.

Maybe he had decided to lay low for a while after their close call at the Opera House. Whatever the reason, she'd not seen hide nor hair of him.

But no matter, for today was Friday and today she'd take the boys some lunch. She wanted to wear a skirt instead of her bicycle costume, so she left in plenty of time to walk out to the Twelfth Street fields.

The sun warmed her skin, counteracting the briskness of October's air. The few trees sprinkling town offered bouquets of red, yellow, and orange foliage.

She hoped she hadn't overdone it with her toilet. The grayish green gown she wore had a short Louis Seize coat with a cutaway that opened widely onto a double-breasted white vest with two rows of buttons. A large cravat of white chiffon draped her bust, and a green straw hat trimmed with ribbon and black plumes perched smartly atop her head.

Adam didn't even try to conceal his pleasure at seeing her. He stepped back from the rig, wiped his neck and forehead with his large red handkerchief and tracked her progress as she approached.

He took in her attire and her hat. She felt a spurt of pride. Hats were her one weakness. The wider, the taller, the more ornate, the more she liked them.

And wearing a fabulous hat would be rather pointless if the rest of her ensemble was lacking. So, she found herself indulging in the very latest of fashions.

"Miss Essie," he said, "you are the purtiest thing I ever did see."

"Hello, Adam. And thank you."

"What'd ya bring us?" Jeremy asked.

She handed him the basket. "Why don't you go pick us out a spot of shade. We'll be right there."

Jeremy grabbed the basket and hustled toward the big bois d'arc tree.

"Where ya been?" Adam asked. "How come you haven't been out here all week?"

"I didn't want to be in the way."

He flicked a quick glance at Jeremy. "I'm thinkin' it's the boy that's in the way right now."

Me too, she thought.

He looked her over again. "You have any idea how bad I wanna kiss you?"

Yes.

"We're gonna have to do somethin' about that. I can't keep going days and days without seein' ya, and then havin' to mind my manners when I do."

"Hey!" Jeremy yelled. "Y'all comin'?"

Adam removed his hat and made a low, courtly bow. "Miss Spreckelmeyer? Will ya do me the honors?"

He held out his arm, and she hooked her hand inside his elbow. Tucking his arm in, he covered her hand with his and walked her toward the tree. Instead of keeping the requisite distance between them, she leaned into him. With each step her body brushed his upper arm. He ran his thumb over her knuckles.

Jeremy had found the cloth she'd brought and had spread it out for them to sit on. "She brought us some sandwiches."

"What kind?" Adam asked, helping her settle.

"Fish, looks like."

She smoothed her skirts. "One moment, Jeremy. I'm sure Adam will want to say grace first."

Jeremy retracted his hand.

Adam looked a bit startled, then bowed his head. "God bless the grub. Amen."

"Amen."

Essie frowned at his abbreviated, awkward prayer. Even hungry, he should have taken time to properly thank the Lord.

The boys didn't seem concerned, though, and dove into the food, drinking deeply of the tea and wasting no time in finishing off all that she had brought. For the most part, they restricted their conversation to expressions of appreciation. But that was just fine with her.

A married woman might receive such compliments often enough to take them for granted, but for Essie it was a rare occasion. Even when she did receive a kind word on her cooking, she usually had to share the credit with her mother. But these Friday lunches were all her own making, and watching Adam devour them was a special pleasure.

"You goin' to the Harvest Festival, Miss Essie?" Jeremy asked, slowing down. Once dessert was the only thing left, he usually tried to delay the return to work as long as he could.

"Of course. I wouldn't miss it."

"I heard they're gonna have a tightrope walker this year. Is that what you heard?"

"Papa told me he was a peg-legged man and that he's going to walk the rope with a cookstove strapped to his back."

"No foolin'? Did ya hear that, Adam?"

"Shore did." He had finished and lay on his side, propped up on his elbow. He made no secret of studying her.

"The Commercial Club's done asked Adam if he'll do some

ropin'. He's gonna be part o' the show, too."

"Is that so?" She shot Adam a questioning look. "Well, I hadn't heard that."

"Yep. He's been practicin' ever' day now." Jeremy sank his teeth into a molasses cookie. "Why don't ya show Miss Essie some o' yer tricks?"

A slow smile crept onto Adam's face. "Would you like that, Essie? Would you like to see some o' my tricks?"

"Say yes, Miss Essie," Jeremy said. "You'll take a shine to it. I know ya will."

A warmth spread inside her. "I believe you're right, Jeremy. I believe I'd like it very, very much. Please, Adam. Will you show me?"

"It'd be my pleasure, ma'am." But he didn't move. "Why don't ya go get my rope, Jeremy."

The boy jumped up and headed over to the rig.

"How much longer 'til Election Day?" Adam asked her, lowering his voice.

"Not until after the festival."

"I can't keep this up for another month. I wanna see ya tonight. And tomorrow night. And the night after that."

Her pulse began to race. What was he saying? That he wanted to speak to Papa before the election or that he wanted to meet secretly with her on a more frequent basis?

Jeremy returned with what looked to be a twenty-foot rope. Adam coiled it loosely and stepped out from beneath the tree. The moment he cast the rope, it began to whirl, never once touching the ground.

He didn't look at what he was doing but kept his attention on her. The rope responded to the merest flick of his wrist. He kept his loop low and parallel to the ground, spinning it around the outer perimeter of his body—round the front, the side, the back. Then he switched hands and spun the rope to the other side and back to the front, where his right hand once again took over.

Keeping the spinning loop low and in front of him, he jumped in and out with both feet. At one point he stayed inside the loop and brought it up over his body until he had it twirling high above him.

He did figure eights to the side. He made the loop larger and larger and even larger before bringing it back to a more normal circumference. He rolled it over his left leg just above the knee and then under.

He spun it high above his head and held it there for so long that she lowered her gaze from the rope to him. With a start, she realized he was still looking at her.

"Come here," he said.

She could no more resist than if he were the Pied Piper himself. She rose and stood before him.

"Closer," he said.

She took a step forward.

"Closer," he whispered.

She moved into his space.

The rope came down, encircling the two of them and trapping them inside its magic.

"I want to see you," he whispered.

"When?"

"Tonight."

"How?"

"The Opery House?"

She gave a slight shake of her head. "Too risky."

"The creek?" he said, keeping his voice low.

"Jeremy and some of the other boys fish out there at night."

He paused. "The magnolia tree?"

Her heart began to hammer. "What time?"

"Eight o'clock." He whipped the rope back up above them, and she returned to the blanket.

————————

She sat in corset and drawers, staring at herself in the toilet table's mirror. This was not like going to the show. At the Opera House, she could pretend they'd gone with the intention of watching the performance.

But there was only one thing to do beneath the shelter of that magnolia tree. And heaven help her, she wanted to . . . and she didn't.

Perhaps it was more a question of *how much* she wanted to do. She loved the kissing. The feel of his arms wrapped tightly around her. The smell of his soap. The texture of his hair. The exclamations of marvel he made when they were sharing intimacies.

Yet each time, his hands had become more bold. And instinctively she knew that this time, if she went, he might not be satisfied with touching her through her gown.

She smoothed her hands down her figure. Clarabel may have allowed it. Other girls in Corsicana may have allowed it. But could she allow it? And if she didn't, would she lose him, along with her chances for marriage?

But he'd not spoken of marriage. Nor of what he would do to support them. Nor had he spoken of love.

Perhaps they should discuss those things tonight. First. And then what? What if he spoke of marriage and commitment and love? What then?

She ran a brush through her hair. Then he should be willing to wait.

So why was she trying to decide whether or not to wear the corset cover in her hope chest? The one she'd made herself all those years ago and put away for her wedding night?

Setting the brush down, she removed her everyday corset cover from a drawer in her wardrobe and determinedly buttoned it on.

Slipping away from the house had been no trouble. Mother and Papa had invited the mayor and his wife over for a game of dominoes.

She'd told Papa she was going to do some night fishing at the creek, and she fully intended to do so. After she met with Adam.

Wearing an old, worn skirt and shirtwaist, appropriate for fishing, soothed her conscience. She'd not taken any pains with her hair or her toilet. She wore no hat.

And she wore her ugliest and most threadbare underclothes. She'd die before she let anyone see them. That ought to keep her honest.

The oil field was abandoned and dark. The crickets clattered so loud they almost drowned out the other trilling insects. But the frogs gave them some serious competition, and a thrush that had yet to go to bed played its flutelike song.

Essie's boots crunched across the brown grass, her fishing rod and tackle box gripped firmly in her hand. Taking a deep breath, she bent beneath the magnolia's branches and pulled up short.

Adam stood leaning against the trunk of the tree, but it was the blanket and pillows he'd spread out on the ground that drew her attention.

"How did you get those here without someone seeing?" she whispered.

He stepped forward and took her rod and box. "Are we going fishing?"

"I am. A little later, that is."

He set the items on the ground and led her to the blanket. "I didn't want ya to have to make explanations if your gown got dirty, so I brought us a blanket."

"And the pillows?"

He gave a rakish smile and shrugged.

She swallowed. "Adam, I—"

"Shhhh. Sit down and tell me about yer week. I want to know what ya did ever' minute you were away from me."

They sat on the middle of the blanket, facing each other, Indian style.

"But our voices will travel," she whispered. "Someone might hear and come investigate."

"We'd hear them long before they'd hear us. But we can whisper if it'd make you feel better," he said, taking both her hands in his.

"Yes, please."

"So, what'd ya do last week?" he whispered. "Start with what happened when the sheriff hauled you home."

She lowered her chin. "He was very concerned."

"'Bout what?"

"About me attending the ten-cent show."

"He's only tryin' to protect ya."

"I know. I just wish they'd all leave me alone."

"Did he say anythin' about me?"

"No. I'm sure it never crossed his mind that we had gone to the balcony to, um, be alone together."

He smoothed a tendril of hair from her face. "I've relived our time in the Opery House a hundred times in my mind."

"You have?"

"Well, shore. Haven't you?"

She slowly nodded her head.

He raised their clasped hands to his lips, kissing her knuckles. "I remember the honeyed taste of yer lips." He bit the tip of her finger. "The smell o' cloves in yer hair." Next finger. "The feel of yer hands on my shoulders." Third finger. "The feel of my hands on yer—"

She flung herself free, grabbed his cheeks and pulled his lips to hers.

He moved her to his lap. "Ah, just as sweet as I remembered," he mumbled.

There was no him. No her. Only them. It lasted forever. It didn't last long enough.

"Oh, Essie. You're killing me, darlin'," he breathed.

She tried to see his eyes in the dark, but couldn't. "What?"

"I'm wantin' you something fierce, girl." He cupped her chin. "Do ya know what that means?"

"I think so."

"Lemme show you."

She said nothing.

"Please."

"We're not married."

They were still whispering. The sounds of the night creatures paled in comparison to the roaring inside her as right and wrong waged war.

"But we will be," he said.

"We will?"

He grasped her shoulders and leaned back where he could see her. "Well, o' course. What'd you think?"

Euphoria bubbled over inside her. "You never said anything."

"Maybe not with words, but I've sure as shootin' shown ya."

She wrapped her arms around his neck. "Oh, Adam. I love you."

He clamped his mouth to hers and they tumbled to the ground, stretching out on the blanket. It was much, much later before she realized he'd never said he loved her, too.

chapter SIXTEEN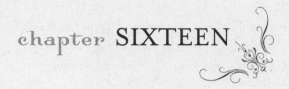

MELVIN HEADED TO Twelfth Street, an unlit lantern in one hand, a rifle in the other. He'd meant to get out there much sooner, but he'd been held up by two bar fights and a runaway horse.

He pulled his hat low. He was gettin' too old for this.

The night was unseasonably warm for October but still cool enough to be comfortable. He'd seen Currington earlier this evening with a pouch slung over his shoulder and thought the drifter had decided to move on without tellin' the judge. So Melvin followed him.

And what he'd discovered was much worse than if the cowboy had skipped town. What he'd discovered was that no-account preparing himself a little love nest.

Melvin wondered who the poor, gullible thing was this time. He'd seen girls fall a hundred times before and would probably see a hundred more before he was through. But it never ceased to rile him.

He pictured the young gals in town who had been flirting with disaster lately—Ruth Smothers, Carrie Quigley, Lorna Wedick. There were plenty right now for Currington to choose from. Girls whose parents were blind to what their "little angels" were up to.

And it always fell to him to be the bearer of bad news. Blast Currington for putting him in this position. He'd planned on being inside their hidey-hole before the couple had shown up.

That way, he'd avert the disaster; he'd make sure the gal knew she'd be better off standing in a nest of rattlers than giving herself to a no-good drifter; and he'd run Currington right outta this town.

It'd be too late for that now. Instead, he'd be taking Currington and his girly home to her mama and papa. He hoped it wasn't the Smothers girl. Her mama had enough vipers in her brood already with those boys of hers without having to deal with one of the girls.

He slowed his pace and approached quietly, but he needn't have bothered. The two of them were making enough noise to wake the dead. He paused right outside the tree, disgusted at the sounds coming from inside.

"Currington?" he barked, readying his rifle.

A gasp and a scramble.

"Get out here."

No response.

Melvin set the lantern on the ground, struck a match and lit the wick.

"I'm comin'," Currington answered.

He stepped out from beneath the tree, shirttail hanging and an unfastened silver belt buckle peeking from between the shirt's opening.

Melvin's insides started to churn. "Who you got in there?"

"How'd ya know we were here?" the boy snarled. He was blazing mad.

Well, good. That made two of them.

"Who you got in there?" Melvin repeated.

Currington eyed the rifle and clamped his mouth shut. Melvin could hear frantic movements coming from inside the shelter. Whoever it was evidently had some repairing to do.

"Come on outta there," Melvin said, none too gently.

More scrambling.

"Who is it, Currington?"

The boy refused to speak.

"Either you come out here on your own, girl, or I'll come in there and drag you out."

She whimpered.

"Give her a minute, Sheriff," Adam said, his tone more threatening than respectful.

Melvin checked his impatience, then after another moment decided he'd waited as long as he was gonna. "That's it." He pulled back the branches.

Squealing, the girl curled her knees up under her skirts, wrapped her arms around them, and bent her head. Long blond hair flowed loose down the back of her worn shirtwaist. She rocked herself.

Squinting his eyes, he studied her. The girl was familiar, but with her face hidden, he couldn't quite place who it was. Grabbing the lantern, he held it high. Evidence of lost innocence spotted the blanket.

Blast.

"Come on," Melvin said, more gently this time. "Come on out."

She raised her head. Air rushed out of his lungs. No. No! Not *Essie.*

Distress, humiliation, and stark terror played in rapid succession across her face.

He plunked down the lantern, then dropped the branches and rifle. "You son of a—"

Currington took a step back, bringing his fists up, but not fast enough. Melvin threw a punch, sinking it hard into the boy's jaw.

"No!" Essie screamed.

Adam started to fall back, but Melvin grabbed his shirt, hauled him upright and hammered him another one. This one had a satisfying crack accompanying the blow and sent the cowboy flying.

"Stop it! Stop it right now!" Essie screeched. "I mean it!"

She threw herself at Melvin and tried to hold him back.

He grabbed her shoulders. "Did he force you?"

Her eyes widened. "No, no. Of course not."

"You can't mean that, Essie."

"It's true." She hung her head, avoiding his eyes.

He glanced behind her. Adam knelt on the ground, holding his face, blood leaking from his nose.

Melvin hauled her against him, hugging her tight. "What the blazes were you thinkin'? Sneaking off to meet some good-for-nothin' drifter? He's not worth two hairs on your head. What possessed you to do such a thing?"

She was crying. Hard. He was nearly crying himself.

"I love him," she said. "We're going to be married."

"You better believe you're gonna be married! If I don't kill the snake first."

Melvin slammed his eyes shut. In his mind's eye he saw Essie's dishevelment. Unbound hair. Wrinkled skirt. Shirtwaist buttoned unevenly. How in all that was holy did this happen? How was he gonna tell his sister? Or his best friend?

Anger roiled inside him. He glared at Currington, but the cowpoke must have known better than to make eye contact. Essie sniffled and took choppy breaths.

Melvin petted her head. "Go on back under the tree and make yourself presentable. You look a mess."

She pulled away from him, keeping her chin tucked.

"Take the lantern," he said.

She turned, saw Currington's blood, and rushed to his side. "Are you all right?"

He didn't answer her.

"Let me see." She pulled his hand away from his nose and sucked in her breath. "Oh, Adam. Oh, darling. Is it broken?"

He shrugged, then grimaced.

She lifted her skirt and ripped off a portion of petticoat. "Here. Try to apply some pressure."

Taking the fabric, he tenderly pressed it to his nose.

She whirled on Melvin, fury coming off her in waves. "How could you? How *could* you?"

"You're lucky he's still breathin'."

She narrowed her eyes. "*You're* lucky he's still breathing." Whipping up the lantern, she disappeared beneath the tree.

Her betrayal hit him square between the eyes. He'd known her, loved her, protected her for thirty years. And in the blink of an eye she switched her loyalties. To this slag. And now, they'd be married. He'd have to put up with this fly-by-night for the rest of his days. At church. At parties. At dinner tables. He snarled.

Currington lifted his pain-coated gaze, then rose to his feet. He buttoned his shirt, tucked it in, and fastened his belt.

Melvin should have killed him. Hung him. Beat him to death. Something more than a couple of well-placed punches.

Essie stepped out from the tree. Her hair was all pinned up, her shirtwaist back in order, her fishing pole and tackle box in her hand.

A defiant light came from her eyes. Not a tear to be seen.

"Let's go," Melvin barked.

Adam's bleeding had, for the most part, stopped. She tore off a fresh piece of petticoat. He accepted it and touched it to his nose, then took the fishing pole and tackle box for her.

The walk home had never seemed so long. She vacillated from being shamed to furious to scared out of her wits. Surprisingly, it wasn't facing her mother that scared her the most. It was facing Papa. Because she knew he'd be crushed. Disappointed with the daughter that had never—in his eyes—done any wrong.

The things that Mother always nagged her about were often the very things Papa was most proud of. But not this time. This time they'd both be shocked. Horrified. Enraged.

She didn't want to face them. How could she, knowing they'd find out what she had been doing?

She was so worried about the confrontation, she hadn't even had time to assimilate everything that had happened between her and Adam. The mysteries that had been revealed. The mysteries that had not.

Would they be married tonight? By her father? Would Adam be joining her in her very own bedroom? And have breakfast with the family in the morning? How awkward.

She glanced up at him. He looked neither left nor right but

straight ahead, his expression hard, his nose swollen. She slipped her hand into his.

He looked down. A slight softening touched his eyes and he squeezed her hand.

She loved him. He loved her. Whatever happened, they'd face it together.

When they approached the house, Uncle Melvin cursed.

"The mayor's still here," he said, then scowled at their clasped hands. "Let go of her and let me do the talking."

Adam released her hand and put some distance between them. They entered the house and the two couples in the parlor looked up from their game of dominoes.

Mayor Whiteselle owned the brick and lumberyard south of town. He was one of those rare persons who liked everybody while still being genuine. Of medium build, he had ears that stuck out from the side of his head, a rapidly receding hairline and a thick brown moustache. He and Papa stood.

"Well," Mother said, "hello. Come on—" She looked at Adam's nose and the blood splattered on his shirt front. She jumped to her feet. "What happened?"

"He ran into somebody's fist," the sheriff said.

"Oh dear."

"Essie said she'd get him fixed up," Uncle Melvin continued.

All offered words of concern, except Papa. He knew Uncle Melvin too well to be fooled.

"Essie, why don't you take Adam to the kitchen," Papa said. "Maybe the rest of us ought to call it a night."

They began to put their game away, and Adam followed Essie from the room.

As soon as they were in the kitchen and out of earshot, he grabbed her hand. "I'm sorry about this, girl. I have no idea how the sheriff found out."

She suppressed the panic she felt and put on a brave face. "Well, no sense in worrying about it now. Things will be bad at first, I'm sure, but my parents love me. They'll settle down once the shock has passed. We'll just have to weather the storm together."

She realized with a start that his nose was crooked. It hadn't been crooked before.

"You all right?" he asked. "I mean, did I hurt you . . . very much?"

She looked down, embarrassed. "I'll be fine," she whispered.

He squeezed her hand. "I'm sorry."

She bit her lower lip. "How's your nose?"

"That sheriff may be a man-eater, but he'll find me a tough piece o' gristle to chew."

"You sit on down, then," she said, dropping his hand. "I'll break up some ice."

She'd just finished wrapping ice chips in a cloth when she heard the mayor and his wife leave. Her parents and the sheriff immediately joined them.

"Is it broken?" Mother asked.

"I haven't examined it yet," Essie answered, not wanting to alarm Adam.

"Sit down, Doreen."

Mother hesitated at Uncle Melvin's command. She looked between the four of them. "What? What is it?"

Papa pulled out the chair across from Adam, keeping his hands on its back even after Mother sat in it. Essie handed the compress to Adam and stood behind him as he placed it on his nose.

"I'm sorry to have to bring you this news, Doreen, but I found Currington and Essie in a compromising position this evening."

Mother frowned. "Essie is constantly compromising herself with the townspeople."

"Yes, well." Uncle Melvin cleared his throat. "Fortunately, no one from town saw this one. Only me."

"Then what's wrong?"

Papa slowly straightened, his eyes widening.

Uncle Melvin nodded his head. "She's been ruined, Sullivan. I'm sorry."

The knuckles on Papa's hands turned white from clenching the chair. His face tightened and he skewered Adam with his gaze before returning it to Uncle Melvin. "By force?"

Melvin shook his head in the negative. Papa's lips parted in shock.

Twisting around in her chair, Mother looked up at Papa. "What is happening, Sullivan? I don't understand."

"Is this true, Essie?" Papa asked.

She swallowed as her father stared at her in disbelief. "Yes," she whispered, unable to deny the truth.

His expression transformed into something fierce and frightening. He moved his steely gaze to Adam. "I trusted you. Stood up for you when others were quick to judge. And you repay me by taking advantage of my most treasured possession?"

His tone rose higher and higher with each accusation. Adam met Papa's gaze without flinching but offered no rebuttal.

Realization dawned on Mother. "No. No. You can't mean . . ." She gaped at Essie. "You haven't . . . you didn't let him . . . oh, Essie. No. Surely even you wouldn't be so foolish?"

Straightening her backbone, Essie took a deep breath. "I love him and he loves me."

"Mercy me. What are we going to do, Sullivan?"

"Yours was the fist he ran into?" Papa asked Melvin.

"It was."

"I wish it had been mine."

Essie pressed her fingers to her mouth. *Oh, Papa.*

Mother stood. "They must get married. At once."

But Papa was shaking his head. "No. She'd be bound to him for the rest of her life."

"She's already bound to him! In God's eyes they are one."

Warmth flooded Essie's face. She glanced at Adam. He'd not moved nor said a word. Just held the ice compress to his nose and watched.

Papa slammed his fist on the table. "No, Doreen. Marrying him because they had relations is a senseless reason to wed. We would be shackling her to a philanderer. I won't do it. We will run him out of town."

"No!" Essie said.

"And what if she is with child?" Mother cried at the same time.

A swell of silence followed her question, its implications echoing in all their minds. Mother turned solid red, as did Papa and Melvin. Essie parted her lips, stunned. So much had happened so fast, she'd not seriously considered the possibility.

She glanced at Adam. He was watching her, gauging her reaction. She touched her stomach and smiled tremulously.

"Tell him, Melvin," Mother said. "Tell Sullivan they must wed."

But Uncle Melvin said not a word.

Papa stormed out of the room and slammed into his study. Mother quickly followed. Essie stood frozen, listening to their shouts, though she could not tell what they were saying. Never in her entire life had she heard her parents yell at each other.

Adam reached for the chair beside him and pulled it out for her. She plopped down.

Uncle Melvin strode to the window above the washbasin and looked out. The glass reflected back his hard expression.

In a few moments, Mother and Papa returned.

Papa's face was flushed, his eyes murderous. He slapped the Bible in his hand onto the table. "Stand up, you two, and prepare yourselves to speak your vows."

chapter SEVENTEEN

ADAM LOWERED THE compress from his nose and rose to his feet. "May I say somethin'?"

Papa did not respond. He didn't need to. If he'd been a dragon, he'd have been breathing fire.

"With all due respect, sir," Adam continued, "I think it's a mistake to be sayin' the vows tonight."

Roaring, Papa lunged at him, but the table stood between them. Uncle Melvin grabbed Papa.

Essie jumped to her feet.

"Don't get me wrong, sir," Adam said, taking a step back. "I wanna marry her. But I don't wanna shame her."

"Well, it's a little late for that, isn't it?" Papa shouted.

"Papa, please," Essie said.

"Shut your mouth!" Papa yelled, jerking free from Melvin's hold.

She sucked in her breath, unable to control the moisture springing to her eyes. Never had Papa said such a thing to her or raised his voice, for that matter.

"What I'm tryin' to say, sir, is that if we marry hurry-up like, it'll create talk. And there's no reason to. The only people that know about me and Essie having our weddin' night two jumps ahead o' the ceremony are here in this room."

Papa ground his teeth.

"If we marry tonight, like this, the whole town'll know. And I just don't see why we should put Essie through that."

Mother touched Papa's arm. "He has a point, Sullivan."

"What are you suggesting?" Uncle Melvin asked Adam.

"That we announce our intentions. That I court Essie all proper-like. And that we marry at the end o' the month or somethin'."

Essie's heart swelled. He was willing to wait for her to be his bride in order to protect her from any vile gossip.

"Perhaps that would be best," Mother said.

Papa looked ready to explode. He glared at Adam. "You will conduct yourself with complete propriety. You will not so much as kiss her until the vows have been spoken."

"Papa," Essie exclaimed.

"I told you to *be quiet!*" he bellowed.

Adam stiffened. Essie stumbled back.

"Sullivan," Mother hissed under her breath. "Be reasonable."

"Be reasonable? Be reasonable!" He jabbed a finger in Adam's direction. "He has tumbled our daughter and you want me to be *reasonable?*"

Mother gasped. "That is quite enough!"

"It doesn't even come close to being enough. Enough would be stringing him up by his personals on the nearest cottonwood tree!"

Mother pressed a hand to her throat.

"Sullivan," Uncle Melvin said, his voice low.

The two friends exchanged looks. Essie dashed away a tear, only to have another fall.

"I mean it, Melvin." Papa took a deep breath. "If they have to marry, I *will not* have him touching her until after the vows have been spoken."

"I'll honor yer wishes, sir," Adam said. "All courtin' will be done in full view of chaperones."

Papa stood breathing like a horse who'd run a lengthy race.

"There," Mother said, tugging her cuffs. "That's settled. Now let's pick a date. I think it needs to be sooner than later in case Essie is in a family way."

Everything was happening so fast. No one was asking her what she wanted. It was to be her wedding, after all.

"How 'bout during the Harvest Festival?" Uncle Melvin suggested. "Everybody will be there and it wouldn't be the only attraction, so to speak, which will give folks things to talk about other than the wedding."

Essie frowned. She *wanted* her wedding to be talked about. She wanted it to be a grand affair, not some peripheral event that would take second fiddle to the fair.

"The Harvest Festival," Papa agreed. "Now get out of my house."

"Papa!"

Adam gave her arm a quick squeeze. "Yes, sir." He turned toward her.

She forced herself to relax. The details of the wedding could be worked out later. For now, she wanted to set Adam's mind at rest.

She'd always heard that eyes were the windows to the soul, so she let down her guard, exposing her heart, and allowed him to see into the very core of her being. *I love you.*

His expression softened. "I'll see you tomorrow, girl," he whispered and winked.

Uncle Melvin followed Adam down the hall, their footsteps ringing on the wooden floor. When both men had left, Papa turned to her.

"Get to your room," he ground out. "This minute. Before I say something I regret."

Grabbing her skirts, she ran up the stairs, then slammed her bedroom door shut.

———

Essie crawled beneath her covers, pulling them clear to her neck and drawing comfort from their shelter. Neither Mother nor Papa had come upstairs yet. She wondered what they were saying to each other. About Adam. About her. About what had happened.

She thought back to all the times her father had been in volatile situations. As a judge, there had been plenty of them. And never, ever, had she seen him lose control—though in several instances it would have been warranted.

So to witness it now, and know she had been the cause, filled her with remorse. She'd not really thought about how her decision to give herself to Adam would affect others. She had naïvely assumed it would only affect her and Adam.

And now it was too late. For the rest of their lives, Adam and Papa would remember this night. And so would she.

Now that she was alone, she allowed the tears that had been pressing against her all night to flood her eyes. She wanted Adam and Papa to get along. To like each other. Respect each other. Befriend each other.

How long would the rift between them last? A lifetime? Surely not. But Papa was a judge by occupation. It's what he did. And when he made his decisions, he did so with firmness and finality.

Would this bitterness extend to his grandchildren? She couldn't imagine that it would. But then, she couldn't have imagined Papa's actions tonight, either.

She thought of the reassuring smile and wink Adam had given her before he left. Would the very things that she found charming be things Papa would resent most? Oh, she hoped not. Because if Adam tried to suppress those things, he'd be suppressing his very self.

The stairs creaked and she tensed.

"Oh, Sullivan," came Mother's muffled sob as she and Papa reached the top of the stairs and walked past Essie's door. "What will we do if—?"

"Shh," he soothed, though his voice cracked as he whispered, "We'll trust God, that's what we'll do. And we'll pray. . . ." Their door clicked quietly closed and she heard no more.

Rolling to her side, Essie bunched her pillow beneath her head and closed her eyes against a new wave of tears. A cricket outside her window called loud and longingly for its mate.

For the first time in her life, she heard its distress. Its edge of desperation. And she, too, realized that after tonight no one could comfort her the way Adam could. No one. She'd so much like to be held in his arms right now.

She allowed herself to review in her mind the consummation of their relationship. Because of the darkness beneath the magnolia, she had no images to recall, only sounds. Touches. Feelings.

At first it had been marvelous. Yet as things had progressed, she'd found some of the intimacies not to her liking. And some downright painful. But she'd not wanted to disappoint Adam. So she'd allowed him free rein. But in truth, she'd felt more like a martyr than a partner.

Perhaps that's why the marriage act was referred to as a duty. She sighed. What a shame, for it had started out so wonderfully.

She touched her flat stomach through her nightdress. Could it be . . . might she really be with child? Would the intimacy they'd shared result in the miracle of a baby? Part her? Part him?

She wondered what their child would look like. She pictured the three of them going to church together.

Drifting off to sleep, she realized she'd never asked Adam what denomination he was. She'd need to do that first thing.

———

Essie could not believe she'd slept so late. Trying to decide what to wear the day the town would find out about her betrothal—while simultaneously knowing it was also the day after her parents had caught her with her lover—was extremely difficult.

She wanted to choose something light and carefree and flattering. But she didn't dare. So she chose a taupe cashmere house gown perfectly suitable for home wear, yet also very becoming. It had a small, snug-fitting yoke of black velvet at the waist and a modest high collar of the same velvet. The sleeves were tight-fitting with pointed cuffs at the wrist.

All was quiet except for subdued voices coming from the partially open door of Papa's study. Taking a deep breath, she walked past it without looking in, making a beeline for the kitchen.

"Essie?" Papa called.

She stopped, turned around, and pushed open his door. Mother and the sheriff sat opposite Papa's large desk. Mother's eyes were red and when she looked at Essie, a fountain of tears tumbled from her eyes. Pressing a hanky to them, she jumped up and hurried from the room.

Uncle Melvin slowly stood. "Mornin'."

A spurt of anger she didn't even realize she'd been harboring for him jumped to the surface. She did not answer his greeting.

He glanced at Papa. "I'll see you later," he said, then hesitated in front of her. "Essie, I . . ."

She lifted her chin but focused her eyes on some distant spot over his shoulder.

"I had to do what I did," he said. "Surely you see that."

What she saw, though, was the image of her beloved uncle breaking Adam's nose. "Shall I walk you to the door?" she asked, her tone perfectly modulated.

Sighing, he placed his hat on his head. "No, thank you. I'll see myself out."

She stepped out of his way, then met her father's gaze.

He looked as if he'd aged ten years in one night. She noted for the first time that he had almost as many white hairs as gray. His jowls were loose. His eyes dull.

"Come in, please," he said. "And shut the door behind you."

Her stomach did a somersault. She closed the door.

"Have a seat."

So formal. She smoothed her skirt beneath her and sat in the upholstered chair across from him.

"I'll cut right to the chase." He took a deep breath. "Currington has skipped town."

She frowned. "What?"

"He's gone, Essie. Pulled up his stakes. Flew the coop. Squirreled off."

She shook her head. "You're mistaken."

"I'm afraid not."

She thought of the smile and wink Adam had bestowed upon her last night. "I don't believe you."

"Jeremy came by this morning when he didn't show up for work. So I had Melvin go to the boardinghouse. Mrs. Williams said Currington packed up late last night, paid up the rest of the month's board, and left. We've scoured the town for him. He's gone."

"There's some other explanation. I'm sure of it." But all of a sudden, she wasn't sure of anything.

Papa leaned back in his chair, steepling his fingers, and waited. Waited for her to accept the truth.

But she couldn't. Adam loved her. She knew he did. She raced through her memory, trying to recall when he'd told her that very thing. And her stomach began to feel queasy. For though she had expressed her love for him, he had never actually said those words to her. Had only implied it. By his actions.

She took a fortifying breath. "He said he'd come see me today and he meant it. I've no doubt he'll be here any moment."

"The word of a man who takes advantage of women is worthless."

She shot to her feet. "You've done something," she cried. "After I went to bed last night. You threatened him, didn't you? Or offered him a bribe. Tell me."

Papa's face cleared of all expression. "Upon my honor, I did nothing of the kind. Nor did your mother. Nor did your uncle. That scallywag tucked his tail and ran. Leaving you at the altar without caring for one moment whether or not you are carrying his child."

She wrapped her arms about her stomach, wondering who had moaned. Then she realized it had been her.

Papa remained seated, not a shred of sympathy or compassion on his face. "You are relieved of your duties with Sullivan Oil."

Falling back into the chair, she shook her head. "What?"

"Your mother was right. It's my fault all this has happened. I've given you entirely too much freedom and have encouraged you to disregard the dictates of society. That stops now."

"No, Papa."

He leaned forward, resting his arms on the desk. "I am handing you over to your mother. Your actions will be dictated by her. And I will endorse and support every decision she makes."

Essie grabbed the arms of the chair. "Please, Papa, please. Don't do this. I . . . I know I've hurt you. I know I've shamed you. But please. Mother will squash me. She'll stomp out every bit of pleasure I have in life."

His mouth tightened. "I'd say you've had more than enough *pleasure* lately to last you a lifetime."

She sucked in her breath. Had he slapped her across the face, she couldn't have been more hurt. But instead of the tears that she expected, an all-encompassing anger swept through her.

"How dare you," she said.

He slowly rose, squaring his shoulders and letting her see the formidability that she'd always known was there. Never before, though, had it been directed toward her.

"No," he said. "How dare *you*."

———————

She waited all day, but Adam never came.

Skipping breakfast the following morning, she rummaged through her father's box of tools, little caring for the recklessness with which she handled his things. Finding a hammer, she grasped it, retrieved a tiny block of wood from the woodpile, and stormed into the house.

She slammed the door. Kicked over a chair in her path. Stomped up to the top stair and began to remove the nails in the banister.

She could hardly see what she was doing, so blurred were her eyes by desperate, angry tears. But no matter what, those nails were coming out. Today. Now. This very minute.

One by one she jerked them free, sending them flying. Disappointed at the puny tinkle they made when landing.

Mother came rushing from the back of the house and stopped short.

Essie paused and seared her mother with a look that caused the matronly woman to take a step back.

"Let me make myself perfectly clear, Mother," Essie said, not even trying to staunch the flow of her tears. "If I want to slide down the banister, then I will slide down the banister. If I want to teach a parrot to curse, then I will teach a parrot to curse. If I want to give myself to every man in the county, then I will give myself to every man in the county. And I dare you—no, I *beg* you to come up here and try to stop me."

Sorrow and tenderness consumed Mother's features. Papa jerked open his study door, his face livid.

"No," Mother said to him.

He stopped short, his chest pumping like the cable tool on Adam's rig. "I will not—"

Mother narrowed her eyes, bringing Papa's words to a sudden stop. He whirled around and slammed his door shut behind him. Mother left the way she had come. Essie returned to her task, albeit with a little less oomph.

Moments later Mother came back and strode directly to the bottom stair. With a hammer and wedge of wood, she began to remove the nails on the lower part of the banister.

Essie swallowed, then proceeded with her task. Each nail brought them closer and closer to completion and closer to each other. It was Mother who removed the last one.

They stood face-to-face on the middle steps. The white, smooth skin that her mother took such pride in was splotchy and swollen.

She offered the nail in her hand, palm up. Essie took it and defiantly flung it across the entry hall. It ricocheted from wall to wall to floor, finally rolling to a stop.

"Oh, Essie," Mother said. "I'm so, so sorry, baby."

For what? Essie wondered. For the nails? The restrictions? The critical things she'd said to Essie over the years? Or was she sorry that her daughter's dreams and future hopes had been shattered by a man who had used her and left her for greener and younger pastures?

"For what?" Essie choked.

"For everything," Mother said. And then she opened her arms.

Essie hesitated only a moment before falling into them, sobbing, wailing, expending the anguish that consumed her.

Mother held her. Rocked her. Patted her head.

She heard Papa's door open. And she knew that the two of them were staring at each other over her shoulder, grieving simply because their daughter was.

chapter EIGHTEEN

ESSIE'S LEGS BEGAN TO fall asleep. Still, she stayed on her knees. Bargaining, for the most part.

If you bring Adam back, I promise to spend more time in your Word. I'll read it more, memorize it more, dwell on it more.

She racked her brain for the sorts of things that would please God.

I'll do more service for the church. I'll clean the sanctuary, bring plants for its beautification, teach Sunday school. If only you'll bring Adam back.

She rested her forehead on the edge of the bed.

I'll spend several days a week at the State Orphan's Home. I'll care for the children, teach them some skills, shower them with affection. Please, Lord. Bring Adam back.

She wondered if she was carrying his babe. On the one hand, she wanted a baby so badly she could hardly credit it. And at the moment, she couldn't care less what the townsfolk thought of her bearing one out of wedlock. But she knew she would care one day.

She didn't want the child to grow up with the stigma of being a bastard. She'd never known one personally, but she'd heard they were treated like outcasts. She couldn't imagine her friends and neighbors doing so. Or maybe she could.

Yet she could not bring herself to pray that there was no babe.

Instead, she continued to implore God to bring Adam back.

She considered confessing her sin of fornication, but she wasn't sure she was truly sorry for it. She knew she should be. But she wasn't, entirely.

Oh, she was sorry for the pain it caused her parents. She'd be sorry for the pain it might cause her unborn child—if there was one—and the shame it would bring to her parents. But she couldn't be completely sorry she'd learned what happened between a man and a woman.

She'd always wondered and now she knew.

"I'm sorry that I'm not sorry," she whispered. "But please, please, won't you still bring Adam back to me?"

Her bargaining turned into begging.

A knock sounded on her bedroom door. "Essie?"

Essie stayed where she was. The door squeaked open.

Her mother entered and sat on the edge of her mattress. "Come sit by me for a moment."

Icy prickles of pain bombarded her legs and feet when she joined her mother on the bed. A penance, perhaps.

"You need to come downstairs and eat."

"I'm not hungry."

"Just the same, you've not eaten all day."

Essie wondered if she'd be bound to her mother's schedule for the rest of her life. If she would be living in this house, this room, until her parents' deaths and then her own.

It wasn't a bad place, but she didn't want to live in her father's house. She wanted to be like other women. She wanted to "leave and cleave." But there was only one way to achieve that. And her ticket to freedom had abandoned her.

Please, God. Please.

"The ladies at church are going to sell some baked goods at the Harvest Festival," Mother said. "They need someone to work the table for them. I told them you would help."

Yesterday Essie would have agreed without a moment's hesitation. Today she resented her mother making arrangements on her behalf.

"I'm not sure I'm attending the Harvest Festival."

"Of course you are."

"In the future, I do not want you offering my services to anyone without my permission."

Mother sighed. "If you mope about on the heels of Mr. Currington's sudden departure, people will put two and two together. You must pretend nothing has happened."

"I cannot."

"You must."

"I will not."

Mother rose. "Yes, you will, Esther. Yes, you will."

Essie refused to eat.

"I'm fasting," she told her mother, then she wedged a chair underneath her doorknob and read her Bible.

She read Ecclesiastes.

"'Vanity of vanities, all is vanity.' . . . Whatever my eyes desired I did not keep from them. I did not withhold my heart from any pleasure. . . . I said of laughter—'Madness!'; and of mirth, 'What does it accomplish?'"

She memorized verses, then chapters. She ignored her mother's pleas to come out. Her father's commands to unbar the door.

Hours turned into a day, then into two days. Still she read. Memorized. Fasted. Christ had gone without food for forty days. Surely she could share in His sacrifice.

She wasn't worried about her baby—if there even was one. She had complete faith that God would take care of it. She was, after all, fasting. An endeavor that God would honor by protecting any babe He'd created.

Papa kicked the door open, his face red. Whether from anger or exertion, she wasn't sure. She stared at him, unmoved and unrepentant. Mother led her to the kitchen and fed her.

The food did not settle well and left her stomach shortly after reaching it. She had no energy. No interest in bicycling. No will to do anything other than sleep and read her Bible.

For the first time, she realized what a burden she must be to her parents. All she'd ever done was make mistakes, and that was probably all she'd ever do. She should have long ago left the nest. Yet here she was, still in their home. Eating their food. Encroaching on their privacy. Spending their money on fine clothes.

In the weeks that followed, she restricted herself to the simplest of attire. Dark skirts, white shirtwaists, no hats. She tried not to eat too much, so as not to be a burden. She worked harder than ever before around the house and garden.

She gathered all her hats and put them in burlap bags.

"What are you doing?" her mother asked.

"I'm going to give my hats to the poor," she said, descending the stairs with three bulky sacks.

Mother pointed to a corner of the hall. "Set them there. I have some things to give away, as well. I'll put yours with mine."

The next day the bags were gone. Essie wondered what it would be like to see someone else in town wearing one of her hats. She wondered if she'd care.

She took a basket of bedding out to the clothesline. Her mother joined her.

"There is no babe," Essie said, pinning one corner of a sheet onto the taut wire before securing its other corner.

Mother paused, a pillow slip in her hand. She offered no response, good or otherwise.

———

Essie chose another pecan from the bucket, cracked it open, then began to pick out its fruit. The sun had risen more than an hour ago, and she had been on the porch shelling pecans long before the first glimmer of light had touched the sky.

In an effort to ward off the cool breeze, she adjusted a blanket thrown about her shoulders.

Her mother pushed open the screen door and stepped out onto the back porch. "The Harvest Festival is today."

The day Essie was supposed to have married Adam. She placed a shelled nut into a bowl at her side.

"Have you decided what you are going to wear?" Mother asked.

"I'm not going." She cracked another nut.

"You'll miss the tightrope walker."

"I'm no longer interested in such frivolities."

Mother eased into a rocking chair. "Essie, dear. I think it is time we had a talk."

Essie raised a brow. "I believe it's a little late to be discussing the birds and the bees, don't you?"

Mother blushed but remained steady. "Actually, I would venture to guess there is quite a bit you don't yet know, but that is not what I wanted to talk about."

The sun touched a corner of the porch but offered no relief from the chill in the air. Essie's fingers ached from the cold. She ignored it and harvested another pecan.

Mother moistened her lips. "Young women are taught that losing their virtue is synonymous with losing their right to marry." She paused. "I want you to know, your father and I do not agree with that line of thinking."

The pecan Essie was picking splintered. She popped the ruined fruit into her mouth, its dry texture rough and hard to swallow.

"What I'm trying to say is, if you think you can no longer marry because of what happened between you and that young man, then I think you will find that is not the case."

"Oh, Mother," Essie said. "What you and Papa believe about such things means nothing. It is what the man in question believes that is at issue. And I would venture to guess, no man wants used goods. Besides, I cannot credit any man wanting me, chaste or no."

"I have complete faith that God has someone for you."

Essie rolled her eyes. "Are you quite through?"

"You do not have to give up your zest for life," Mother said, leaning forward. "You needn't give up your hats, either, simply because you made a mistake."

"Perhaps I want to give those things up. Perhaps I am tired of adventure and extravagant hats and wild living. It has brought me nothing but ridicule and scorn. I cannot believe that you, of all people, are trying to discourage me from living decorously."

"Oh, Essie. I am merely pointing out that to try and mold yourself into some image the town has of a 'proper woman' is no way to experience God's grace. You have made a mistake. Well, it wasn't the first and it certainly won't be the last."

"That's not the way you raised me. Why the sudden change of heart?"

"Maybe I've come to realize that, under the circumstances, riding bicycles and sliding down banisters are not really worth worrying over."

"Well, it doesn't matter anyway," Essie said. "My new life of works and quiet living will please God. No more mistakes for me."

The sun edged closer, teasing the hem of Essie's gown.

"You cannot make yourself righteous by simply changing your behavior," Mother replied.

Essie stiffened. "I'm sure I don't know what you mean."

"What I mean is that when Christ died on that cross, He took your sin upon himself. The very one you committed with Mr. Currington. As well as all the ones you have committed in the past and will commit in the future."

Cracking another pecan, Essie stuffed down the lump rising in her throat.

"Have you so little appreciation for His sacrifice that you would fling it back in His face by trying to earn your way to heaven?" Mother rose.

Essie's fingers stilled.

"Tell me this, dear. What good is God's mercy if we never have need of it?"

She reentered the house, leaving Essie alone. Her hands lay still. A half-shelled pecan rolled from her fingertips and clattered onto the porch. The sun slowly climbed up her skirt and onto her lap, blessing her with warmth for the first time in a long, long while.

Buggies filled the roads. Single buggies, double rigs, and even some "Hug-Me-Tight" carriages with barely enough room for two. Horses of all kinds pranced through the streets, kicking up dust as they clip-clopped amongst the throng.

A giant tent had been staked out on Ninth Street. Beneath its shelter were rows of tables and booths selling every kind of goods imaginable. Children pulled taffy. Women circled around quilts. Men bet on the horse race that was to be run later in the day.

Mr. Lyman had parked his old wagon next to the tent, the perfume from his spicy chili pervading the air. He stirred his concoction in a large iron cauldron over charcoal coals. Bowls of chili were five cents each with an added bonus of all the crackers you could eat for free. His dog, Wolf, lay at his master's feet, never leaving his side.

A rope high up in the air stretched taut, spanning the street between the balconies of Keber & Cobb's Confectionery and Castle's Drug Store. A mule-drawn street car gave its "last call" warning for potential riders.

The excitement of the atmosphere began to draw Essie in. She wore a dark wool skirt and white shirtwaist beneath her simple cloth cape and velvet collar. Her hat was dark and modest.

When she'd returned to her room this morning, two of the sacks she'd discarded earlier leaned against her bed. Inside were the hats she'd told Mother to give away. She assumed Mother had given the missing third sack to charity.

Essie wove through the aisles underneath the tent, looking for the table where she was to work. The ladies from her church had set up a baked-goods booth, and Essie was to help man it for a few hours. Just like she'd told God she would. Only, He hadn't delivered His end of the bargain.

She passed Mr. Weidmann's booth where people lined up to buy fruitcake. She waved to him, but he was so mobbed with customers, he didn't see her.

At long last, she found her table. Sitting behind it was Katherine

Crook. Hamilton's beloved wife. She wore an exquisite gown of broadtail fur and moiré combined in an intricate design. A high collar of chinchilla was surrounded by a lower collar of Russian sable, both framing her delicate face.

Her hat, however, did not live up to the gown's requirements. Instead, the flat design with very little ornamentation appeared incongruous with the rest of her costume. Still, Essie's ready-mades were pauper's fare next to hers.

"Well, hello," Essie said.

"Miss Spreckelmeyer." Her tone was polite but cool.

"I'm supposed to help sell at this booth. Are you coming or going?" Essie asked, circling behind the table.

"I just arrived. I didn't know you were to be working with me. I'd heard you were, um, indisposed."

"Had you? How very strange." Essie looked over the goods on the table and began to rearrange them.

"What are you doing?"

"I'm grouping the goods so that they will be more pleasing to the eye and so they will make more sense to the customer." She put the meringue pies on one end and the frosted cakes on the other.

"You'd best take note, my dear," Hamilton said, stepping up to the table. "Essie has quite a knack for sales. I've no doubt the hours she works will be the most profitable for the booth."

Katherine clicked her tongue. "Honestly. You say the most ridiculous things sometimes."

Essie looked up in surprise. "Hamilton. My goodness. How are you?"

A healthy color tinged his round cheeks, no doubt from the brisk weather. There was nothing cool about his gaze, though. It conveyed warmth and kindness. She smiled in response.

His square spectacles had slid down his nose so that their upper rims divided his irises in half. She longed to push them back up so she could see his brown eyes without interference.

He tipped the brim of his derby. "You haven't stopped by the Slap

Out in ages. Haven't you missed me, Essie? I've certainly missed you."

Out of the corner of her eye she saw Katherine stiffen. Flustered, Essie didn't know how to respond. For the truth was, she hadn't missed him at all.

chapter NINETEEN

HAMILTON DRANK IN the sight of Essie. There was something different about her. She was more reserved. More circumspect. More . . . refined.

He'd have expected her to wear her most outrageous hat to a festival such as this. Yet she wore a very understated hat and a somber costume.

She had greeted him with eloquence instead of exuberance. She rearranged the items on the table in a slow, deliberate manner. He liked this new Essie. He liked her very much.

"What has kept you away?" he asked.

"I've been . . . busy."

"Drilling oil wells?"

"Not anymore. Papa decided it wasn't proper and has banned me from them."

"Really?" Katherine said. "That's not quite how I heard it."

Essie glanced at her, but Katherine busied herself placing oatmeal cookies in a tin container.

She'd been a model wife, his Katherine, and he loved her to distraction. But he discovered she'd developed a penchant for gossiping. She had an uncanny ability to pluck out two completely unrelated events and connect them together in the most absurd fashion.

Take Essie, for example. Her father's endorsement of her role in his new oil venture had Katherine's tongue twanging. Then Jeremy would come to the store and inadvertently mention something that intimated a relationship brewed between Essie and the cowboy who worked for Sullivan Oil—which was ridiculous, of course. Hamilton had seen for himself the type of women Currington had favored, though he couldn't very well tell Katherine that.

When the drifter left town unexpectedly and the judge reversed his decision to let Essie work in the oil field, Katherine decided it was because Essie and Currington had been involved in a licentious relationship.

Hamilton had never heard of anything so preposterous. And the more he tried to defend Essie's honor, the more adamantly his wife justified her theory. It had progressed to the point where he wasn't sure if Katherine was able to separate the truth from whatever fantasy she had concocted within her mind.

"Mrs. Lockhart misses you," he said.

"I miss her, too."

"Well," Katherine said, "I can't imagine what you were thinking, Miss Spreckelmeyer, to perpetuate the decline of a churchgoing woman. Were it up to me, I'd refuse to order those scandalous books she's so attached to."

Hamilton frowned. "But it isn't up to you, is it, my dear? It's up to me."

Essie looked between the two of them. "You must admit, Hamilton, they are shameful. Mrs. Crook is right about that."

Katherine pulled back, causing her chin to collapse into folds against her collar. "And just how would you know that?"

A hint of a smile touched Essie's lips. "She insisted I read one. *Clarabel's Love Story,* I believe it was. Quite shocking."

Gasping, Katherine sent him an *I-told-you-so* look.

He suppressed a groan and did what he could to repair the damage. "That was very businesslike of you, Essie. I can't seem to impress upon Katherine the value of familiarizing herself with the items we carry. Yet you were always so good at that."

"Oh, nonsense," Essie said. "I read that book long after I quit working at the Slap Out. And I'm sure the customers just love Mrs. Crook." She stayed Katherine's hand. "You might want to put those pralines next to the divinities. Don't you think it would be more attractive that way?"

Katherine slammed the pralines back down where she'd had them, breaking one in half. Essie gave her a confused look.

"Well," Hamilton said, "it was good to see you again." He turned to Katherine. "I'll come back for you after a while." He held her gaze for a moment, telegraphing his thoughts: *And be nice.*

She huffed and turned her back.

———

Essie had forgotten how much she enjoyed selling things. Didn't matter if it was a bag of nails or a piece of cake. She loved the challenge. And the people. And the competition.

"Mr. Vandervoort!" she exclaimed. "How in the world are you?"

The old nester sauntered up to the table, then coughed up and swallowed an accumulation of phlegm. "Well, Miss Essie, things are pretty dull in the Slap Out without ya. No snakes, no mice—" he leaned forward with a teasing light in his eyes and whispered, "—and no 'mouse catchers.'"

Essie caught her breath.

He winked, then said more loudly, "Yep. I surely did want me one o' them mouse catchers. But Hamilton wouldn't sell me one to save his life."

She bit her lip, but not before a giggle escaped.

"What?" Mrs. Crook said. "You're in need of a mouse catcher, Mr. Vandervoort?"

Patting his chest, he chuckled. "Oh, I don't know that I'm in need o' one, exactly. But I shore would like another gander at it. That Hamilton won't let me have so much as a peek."

"You mean, we have what you want and he won't sell it to you?"

"He has his reasons," Mr. Vandervoort said, rocking back and forth on his feet.

"Well, perhaps I could help you the next—"

"Can I interest you in some tutti-frutti?" Essie interrupted, picking up a square and offering it to him. "Or perhaps some penuche? Mrs. Whiteselle made it, you know."

"Excuse me, Miss Spreckelmeyer," Katherine said. "I believe Mr. Vandervoort and I were in the middle of a transaction." She smiled at him.

"It don't matter none," he said. "I think it already sold, actually."

"No," Essie said under her breath.

He nodded. "You didn't know? Well, shoot. I was hopin' you could tell me who the lucky owner was. I'd surely like to know."

Covering her mouth with her hand, she couldn't suppress her amusement. "That is too bad of you, Mr. Vandervoort. For shame."

He guffawed. "Ah, Miss Essie. You gotta come have a cup o' coffee with me and the boys. We still talk about the day that cowboy came into town and wound you up so tight with the snake that you ended up dropping all those mice."

Mirth fell from her as quickly as if she'd been doused with a bucket of cold water. "I didn't drop the mice."

"Well, maybe you didn't. But that feller shore did tangle you up." He picked up a square of tutti-frutti and handed her two pennies. "We'll see ya later."

She watched him walk away, images of that day flashing through her mind.

"They do talk about it quite often," Mrs. Crook said. "Seems it was the first time they ever saw the cat capture your tongue."

Essie dropped the pennies into a cigar box. She had no idea anyone else had been watching the two of them. But of course it made sense that they would have been the center of attention. Adam had not only been a stranger, but he'd been a gorgeous stranger. Every man and woman in the place would have tracked his every move.

He wasn't so perfect now, though. He had a crooked nose. She wished they all could have seen that.

"It was the same man who worked on your father's oil rig. A Mr. Currington, I believe?"

Nodding politely, Essie scanned the crowd for a potential customer.

"I do declare, he turned every girl's head in town. But it was evidently young Shirley Bunting who claimed to have captured his heart."

Essie whipped her head around. "What makes you think that?"

A knowing smile touched Katherine's face. "Hadn't you heard? He was to escort her to this festival. She purchased fabric to make an autumn jacket in honor of the occasion. That's how I know."

Essie didn't believe it. She would have heard something. But she'd been so absorbed in her own little dreamworld that she hadn't noticed much of anything since Adam began his seduction of her.

"You're a bit pale, dear. Are you all right?" A look of realization came over Katherine. "Oh no. You didn't have . . . *feelings* for him, did you?"

Essie forced herself to take slow, deep breaths. "No, no. Of course not. Whatever gave you such an impression?"

Katherine cocked her head. "Well, it only makes sense, him being so handsome and all. And the two of you working so close together right after Hamilton jilted you."

Essie stiffened. "I don't know what you're talking about."

"No need to get defensive, dear. Hamilton told me all about how you chased after him, no matter how many times he tried to discourage you."

Mortified, she couldn't believe he had shared such a thing with Katherine. A spurt of anger shot through her.

She imagined them sharing other intimacies, then talking about her, laughing as they discussed what a pathetic old maid she was. The fragile palisade she'd erected around her heart began to crumble.

"Mr. Currington left town rather quickly, as you well know." Katherine looked left and right, then leaned close. "The night he left, he came knocking on our back door to settle up his accounts. There had been some trouble. Woman trouble. And the sheriff was running him out of town."

Essie felt like an exposed possum caught in the open while a hunter took aim with his shotgun. Too bad she couldn't "play dead."

"Unbeknownst to Hamilton, I had come down the stairs in my stocking feet to make sure all was well. I stopped when I heard the men's voices." She licked her lips, warming up to her story. "I could tell Hamilton was angry. He'd never much liked Mr. Currington, you know."

"No," Essie said. "I hadn't realized that."

"Yes, well. He asked who the woman was, but all Mr. Currington said was that she wasn't the kind you pay for. Nor was she the kind you'd want to marry. Too old, he said."

Breathing grew difficult. The tent, the crowd, the tables began to close in on her. She needed to get out. She needed air.

"At first I thought it was Shirley, but she's just a young little thing. I wonder who it could be?" Katherine gave Essie a penetrating stare. "Whoever it was, he was clearly using her to slake his thirst for pleasure. Why else would a man like that toy with an older woman?"

She knew. This woman knew Essie's secret. Or at the very least, she strongly suspected. If Essie were to run, all would be confirmed.

"Poor Shirley," Essie managed. "She must be devastated."

Katherine chuckled. "Hardly." She indicated someone with a nod of her head.

Essie turned. Shirley Bunting, in a form-fitting jacket of satin merveilleux shot in copper shades, walked by with an entourage of men trying to gain her favor. The young woman laughed and teased and flirted.

"Well," Essie said, hearing her voice tremble and hoping Katherine didn't notice. "I'm so relieved. It would have been tragic for her to have found out Mr. Currington was stringing her along while pursuing interests elsewhere."

Katherine raised a brow. "I do believe, Miss Spreckelmeyer, it wasn't Shirley he was stringing along. But someone else. Someone older." She smirked. "But clearly, not wiser."

———

Essie strode from beneath the tent and headed to Mr. Lyman's wagon for some chili. Anything to occupy her hands and her mind. Had Katherine Crook known Essie well, the game would have been up. But she didn't. And hopefully, Essie had bluffed her way through these last three hours without giving herself away.

The animosity Katherine held toward Essie was as clear as the sky above. What she couldn't fathom was the reason for it. Why would Katherine dislike her so completely?

It was Katherine, after all, who got the man. Not Essie. It was Katherine who'd had two husbands, while Essie hadn't had so much as one. It was Katherine who ran the store with Hamilton, while Essie had no purpose in life whatsoever.

It didn't make any sense. Nevertheless, she'd have to be very, very careful. One little slip and all would discover her shameful secret. She'd told herself it didn't matter what the townspeople thought, but it did.

It mattered a lot. And not just for her sake, but for her parents' sakes. It would ruin Papa's chances for reelection, just a few days away. And it would reflect badly on Mother. The women of her circle would somehow think it was Mother's fault.

"One bowl, please," she said, handing Mr. Lyman a nickel and patting Wolf on the head. The dog lifted his nose and slapped his tail against the ground in appreciation.

"Here ya are, Miss Spreckelmeyer," he said. "You better go on now. The peg-legged man's fixin' to walk that rope."

She glanced over at the crowd that had begun to form and headed toward them. The thick, hearty fare tasted like no other chili she'd ever had before. She welcomed the warmth it provided as the sun began its descent.

Up on the balcony, she could see several men strapping a cumbersome cookstove to a man's back. The crowd around her chattered with excitement.

"Miss Essie," someone called.

She turned. "Jeremy!"

He wove his way through the crowd until he reached her side. "It's mighty good to see ya," he said. "I shore do miss those lunches you used to bring us."

"I miss them, too," she answered, smiling sadly as she thought of the picnics she'd shared with Adam and how much she'd enjoyed them.

She looked Jeremy over. All that cable drilling had added breadth and form to his once-skinny body.

"What happened with you and Adam?" he asked.

She stiffened. "What do you mean?"

"Well, golly, Miss Essie. Anybody could see y'all were sweet on each other."

She forced a laugh. "Oh, don't be silly. We were just friends."

"I don't know," Jeremy said, looking at her askance. "I seen the way you two would get yer heads together and whisper-like. And his eyes would light up like firecrackers when he'd see ya comin'."

Did they? she wondered. It made her feel a little better that Jeremy had seen something, too. At least she hadn't been the only one to imagine an interest that clearly wasn't there.

"I'm afraid you're mistaken, Jeremy. We were just friends."

"Well, if ya say so, but you shore never looked at me the way ya looked at him. And you and me is friends."

She cleared her throat. "Yes, well."

"He was gonna rope fer everybody today. Remember?"

Yes. He was also going to marry me today. She tried to put the thought from her mind.

"I could o' watched him do them ropin' tricks all the day long. That new feller that works with me now? He ain't near so easy to get along with."

"Oh? I'm sorry to hear that."

"Maybe if ya bring him some lunches, too, it'll improve his disposition some."

She smiled, then froze as she caught sight of Katherine and Hamilton standing a few feet away. Hamilton's attention was focused on the tightrope walker. Katherine's was focused on Essie.

Her heart started to pound, wondering how much the woman had heard, if anything.

"Lookit!" Jeremy said, pointing. "He's fixin' to go."

Essie turned and shaded her eyes. The man began to slide across the rope one foot at a time, his wooden leg stiff, his other leg bending for balance.

The crowd hushed, not daring to breathe as he inched his way across the rope. The stove was obviously heavy and awkward. It looked to Essie as if it was not evenly distributed across his back, but a bit heavier on the left.

He teetered. The audience gasped, then held their breath until he regained his balance. His clothes were as black as the stove, making the rope slashed across his body more pronounced.

The farther he came to the halfway mark, the more the rope sagged, giving in to the tremendous weight. The man wavered again, far to the left.

Essie sucked in her breath. He windmilled his arms, but the stove interfered with his motions. He leaned to the right but overcompensated, and the stove shifted.

Before anyone could so much as react, the man fell with a crash to the ground.

chapter TWENTY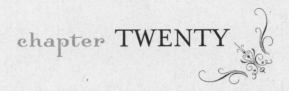

WOMEN SCREAMED. Children buried their eyes in their mothers' skirts. Men rushed forward.

"Let me by," Essie said, shoving aside those in her way.

When she finally broke through, she saw that the stove had landed on top of the man, trapping him beneath. He was still alive, but just barely. Blood pooled beneath his mop of dark hair, accentuating the clammy whiteness of his face.

Her father and Dr. Gulick bent over him. Uncle Melvin shooed the crowd back.

"Do you want a preacher?" the doctor asked.

No answer.

"Can you tell me where you're from?" Papa said.

Still no answer.

The crowd parted, making way for Preacher Bogart. He knelt beside the dying man. "Do you know Jesus Christ, son?"

The man's eyes fluttered open. "Please," he gasped. "A rabbi. I am a Jew."

A fleeting look passed between the men.

Papa caught sight of Essie. "Get me a rabbi."

They exchanged the briefest of glances, knowing full well there was no rabbi in Corsicana, Texas. But there was a Jew.

She whirled around and fought her way through the press, heading to the north side of the tent where she'd seen the peddler's wagon.

"Mr. Baumgartner! Mr. Baumgartner! Come quick," she screamed.

He jumped from his wagon seat where he'd been trying to see over the crowd and raced toward her. Grabbing his hand, she pulled him behind her.

"The rope walker," she said over her shoulder. "He's asking for a rabbi."

Mr. Baumgartner increased his speed so that by the time they arrived he was pulling Essie behind him.

Papa and the preacher stepped back. Mr. Baumgartner touched the man's forehead and spoke over him in Yiddish.

The man visibly relaxed, said a prayer in Hebrew, and died.

Mr. Baumgartner closed the man's eyes and then looked at Papa. "His Hebrew. It was perfect."

Papa placed a consoling hand on Mr. Baumgartner's shoulder.

"I wonder if he had any kids," little Harley North said, startling Essie. She'd not even noticed him standing next to her. He looked up. "If he did and there's no mama, then they'll be orphans. Like me."

She lifted him into her arms and hugged him close. He encircled her with his arms and legs, pressing his face into her neck. The boy was too young to have witnessed something so horrible. Still holding him, she walked away so the men could do what needed to be done.

———

For the first time in its history, the festival closed down early and the horse races were postponed. Essie set Harley in a chair at her mother's kitchen table, placing a plate of cookies and a glass of milk before him.

"Is this where you eat with yer ma and pa ever' meal?" he asked, his gaze touching the gingham curtains framing a window, the indoor water pump Papa had installed for Mother, and the fancy Sunshine cooking range in the corner.

"Yes, it is."

"Golly. I wish I had somethin' like this. We all eat in that big ol' ugly room with nothin' but tables and chairs."

She smoothed back the black hair covering his eyes. He needed a haircut. "You snack on these cookies while I go put on my bicycle costume," she said. "Then I'll give you a ride home on my handlebars. How does that sound?"

"You're leavin'?" His eyes widened and he grabbed her skirt. "What if the judge comes home? Or yer ma? And they see me eatin' their food?"

"It'll be all right, Harley. You just tell them Miss Essie gave them to you. They won't mind."

"Ever'body minds. Nobody wants a orphan in their kitchen. Nobody."

She frowned. "That's ridiculous and not the least bit true. Why, I want you in our kitchen and I'm somebody."

His eyes darted to the back door.

"Hush now, and eat up. I'll hurry. I promise." She pried his hand from her garment and quickly made her way upstairs.

Removing her skirt and petticoats, she began pulling on a short skirt, bloomers, and leggings. The wonder in Harley's voice as he'd examined their kitchen provoked feelings of compassion and not a little guilt. She'd just this morning resented their home, thinking of it more as a prison than anything else. Yet little Harley would give his eyeteeth to live here.

She fastened the final button of her boot. She had already taken so much time, she didn't want to delay any longer. Not bothering to change her shirtwaist or hat, she came out of her room, heard voices, and quickened her pace.

Harley stood on a chair before a table with an apron wrapped twice around his little body. He pounded a lump of dough with one fist and then the other as if he were trying to annihilate it.

"I'm makin' some biscuits, Miss Essie," he exclaimed, his eyes bright.

Smiling, Mother cracked an egg into a bowl. "Watch what you're doing, Harley, or else you might miss the dough and deliver a fatal blow to the table."

Realizing the trip to the orphanage would wait, Essie removed her hat, picked up the empty plate and glass Harley had snacked from earlier and carried them to the washbasin. Then the three of them continued with dinner preparations, Mother and Essie doing most of the work and Harley doing most of the talking.

"What do ya think they'll put on the peg-legged man's grave? 'Here lies a man with one leg. If ya knows where he's from, please make his mark here.'"

Essie and Mother exchanged glances.

"You think he has family?" Harley continued. "Do Jews have families, Miss Essie?"

"Yes, of course they do," Essie answered.

"How do ya know? He only had one leg. Ladies are awful picky. I'd bet they'd want their fella to have both his legs."

"You can't judge a man by the way he looks," Essie said. "A good man without legs would be a far better friend than a bad man with both his legs intact. It's not what's on the outside that counts, but what's on the inside."

"Unless you're a orphan. Nobody wants a orphan no matter what he looks like on the inside."

She started to contradict him, then held her tongue. What he said had some truth to it. Folks put a lot of stock in family backgrounds. If someone from a good family were to marry an orphan, there would be a scandal of huge proportions.

Still, she had come from a good family, and nobody'd wanted her. They'd especially not want her now. Now that she was a full-fledged spinster. And a ruined woman.

But Harley was different, she told herself. He had his whole life ahead of him. And who could resist him, orphan or not?

"That's not true," she said.

"Is too."

"Is not."

Harley studied her for a moment, then opened his mouth as wide as he could, showing her every single tooth and his tonsils to boot.

She blinked.

"Well?" he asked. "What do you think? Am I purty on the inside?"

She smiled. "The best I've ever seen. And that's the truth."

"Really?"

"Really. Now, use this pin and roll out that dough." She positioned the roller in his hands. "Start in the middle and work your way to the edges."

He couldn't manage it, so Essie placed her hands over his and guided him. With Mother puttering around behind them, Essie could almost pretend Harley was her son. Almost.

She thought of Adam and once again tried to imagine what their child would have looked like. Or what a child of hers with Hamilton would have looked like. What would it be like to have her stomach swell as it held a life that God had knitted together with His own hands?

She inhaled, then stopped herself midstream. Harley needed a bath.

"Maybe the peg-legged man was a orphan," the boy said, "and that's why he was by hisself."

"Possibly." She moved the roller to a thick section of dough. "Here, try to spread it out evenly. Like this."

The dough started sticking to the pin. Essie sprinkled it with flour.

"You sure are good at this, Miss Essie. How come you ain't married?"

She heard Mother pause in the middle of chopping some carrots.

"I don't know," Essie answered softly.

"Ain't ya purty on the inside?"

Mother resumed her task with sudden vigor.

No, Essie thought. *I'm not.*

He twisted around when she didn't answer. "Lemme see."

She shook her head.

"Come on. Open up. I'll tell ya the truth."

She glanced at Mother, but the woman acted as if chopping vegetables required every bit of her attention.

Essie slowly opened her mouth.

Harley studied her for so long that she became embarrassed and closed her mouth. *See, I told you so.*

"Well," Harley said, "I ain't never peered inside o' anybody before. Only horses. And I can tell ya this, yer insides is a whole lot purtier than Mr. Mitton's horses. And he boasts somethin' awful about them beasties."

"Thank you," she whispered.

"Miss Essie, do ya think ya might could wait 'til I get a little taller? Then you and me could marry up, seein' as how we both think the other 'un is purty on the inside."

A rush of affection for the boy filled her. "Well, Harley. Those are some mighty strong words to say to a lady. So, I'll tell you what. When you get a little, um, taller, if you find that you are still interested, why don't you ask me again?"

"You're just sayin' that 'cause you don't wanna marry no orphan." His shoulders drooped.

"No, no, that's not true. It's just that you are supposed to speak with my father first. But I think you probably ought to wait a few years before you do that. All right?"

"All right. And as soon as they let me, I'll start votin' fer him, too."

She smiled. "He'd like that very much. Now, put the rolling pin aside. It's time for the biscuit cutter."

———

They ended up riding Cocoa to the State Orphan's Home. After the excitement of the festival and the big dinner they'd fed Harley, the boy could barely keep his eyes open. He'd have fallen asleep and tumbled off the bicycle's handlebars, so they'd taken the horse instead.

"Listen, Harley," she whispered. "Do you hear that cricket with evenly spaced chirrups?"

"Uh-huh."

"That's a temperature cricket. If you count the number of chirps within a fifteen-second span, then add forty, you can calculate the temperature outside. Let's try it. Ready? Go."

She silently counted. "I counted sixteen. That would mean it's fifty-six degrees outside. How many did you count?"

A soft snore escaped Harley as he relaxed against her. She wrapped her cloak more tightly around them, trapping their warmth inside. The stench of his dried sweat breached the covering. The boy reeked, but she'd not had time to give him the promised bath. She planned to return to the orphanage tomorrow to see he received both that and a haircut.

A nighthawk darted by, startling Essie with its sudden, erratic advance. Its nasal *peent* cut through the drone of insects. Essie couldn't see it anymore or the female it was trying to impress, but she could hear the explosive ruffle of its wings as it dove toward the ground, swooping upward at the last possible moment.

She suppressed her irritation. Wasn't there anywhere she could go without being constantly reminded of males and females and their courtship rituals?

The entire world goes two by two, Lord. All except for me. Why? Why did you cut me out of my inheritance?

And now it was too late. She was ruined. Even if the Lord sent a man her way, she'd not be able to marry him without confessing she'd given herself to another.

And that would be the end of that. So why even bother? She would have to resign herself to life as a spinster.

But she didn't want to. She couldn't quite let loose of that elusive dream. She wanted it so badly. Was Mother right? Would a man be willing to accept a woman who'd been used by another? She didn't think so.

What if she didn't tell him? What if she pretended he was the first?

She discarded the thought immediately. Even if he never found out, she would know. And God would know. Deceit simply wasn't an option.

She sighed. It was a waste of time to contemplate such things anyway. Her chances for catching a man were over. Over. The sooner she accepted it and moved on, the better.

They crested a hill, and Cocoa blew a gust of air from her lungs, shaking her mane. Essie steadied her.

The full moon backlit a conglomeration of buildings nestled at the bottom of the hill. She could just make out the superintendent's residence and the children's dwellings behind it. Barns and sheds sat tucked toward the back edge of the property, a picket fence encompassing all.

Cocoa's hooves crunched the gravel path. A clapper rail called out in evenly spaced clicks. As Essie neared the gate, she realized it wasn't a bird she heard, but the rhythmic creak of a rocking chair on the superintendent's front porch.

And whoever was rocking had stopped and headed toward the fence. "Who goes there?"

She pulled her mount up. "Essie Spreckelmeyer. I have Harley North with me."

"Miss Essie?" he asked.

She squinted, trying to see who it was. "Yes. Who's asking?"

"Ewing Wortham."

"Good heavens. You're back from Bible school in Tennessee?"

"That's right." He moved next to her, then lifted his arms.

She relinquished Harley to him. The boy stirred, then settled against Ewing's shoulder.

"Are you a preacher, then?" she asked.

"Only if someone hires me as one."

Slipping off Cocoa, she tied the horse to a fence post. "How long have you been home?"

"Only a few hours."

They stepped through the gate and headed to the boys' dormitory.

"Oh my. Were your parents even here? Most folks were still at the festival."

"It was pretty quiet," he said, boosting Harley up.

"Is he heavy?"

"No, he's fine. Ma said there were a few stragglers that hadn't made it back. Which one is this?"

"Harley North. We don't know much about him. A farmer from Blooming Grove brought him into town a couple of years ago saying his parents had died of smallpox."

They reached the cabin where the boys slept.

"I'll get him settled, Miss Essie."

She stroked Harley's head. "Thank you. I'll be back tomorrow to check on him. The accident today upset him."

"I heard it was pretty bad."

"It was awful. It happened so fast, Ewing. And right in front of all those youngsters. Once the shock of it wore off, the menfolk formed a tight ring around the man, shielding him from view, but by that time the image of that poor soul resting in a pool of blood, all crushed and broken, was indelibly stamped in my mind." She shook her head. "I'm sure it will be a long time before any of us sleep soundly through the night."

"Did he have anyone with him?"

"Unfortunately, no. Ends up the name he went by was one he'd adopted as a performer. They're still trying to find out who he was and where he was from. But no matter what, this town will see to it that he has a proper mourning and burial. Mr. Baumgartner is instructing us in the Jewish traditions for such things."

A pig frog grunted several times in rapid succession. A gnat buzzed in her ear.

"Well, I suppose I ought to head on home," she said. "Good night and thank you for helping me with Harley."

"If you'll wait a minute, I'll walk you back to the gate."

"That's all right."

"I insist." Before she could respond, Ewing hurried into the dormitory.

It was so dark, she hadn't been able to have a good look at him, but she remembered him well. He was six or seven years younger than she was, and they'd both attended the one-room schoolhouse together as children.

He'd been a pest, always wanting to come with her when she went fishing or hunting. It used to drive her to distraction. He'd been noisy and easily sidetracked, while she'd been very serious about her pursuits. And she still hadn't quite forgiven him for bidding his measly two cents on her box suppers all those times.

The door creaked open and he crept out. "Sorry it took so long. I didn't know which bed was his."

"Did he wake up?"

"Only for a moment. He's fallen back asleep now, though."

She turned toward the front gate, but he stopped her. "No, Miss Essie, come this way."

"Why?"

"I'm going to saddle Rosebud and escort you home."

"Oh no, Ewing. That's not at all necessary. I wander these hills alone all the time."

"Not when I'm around, you don't."

She smiled. "Really. I'll be fine."

"Miss Essie, I don't mean any disrespect, but I'm saddling up Rosebud. If you leave ahead of me, I'll have to push that ol' girl in order to catch up. You wouldn't want to distress her like that, now, would you?"

She placed her hands on her hips. "You haven't changed one single bit, Ewing Wortham. Still blackmailing me into letting you tag along. Didn't that Nashville Bible school teach you anything?"

"Yes, ma'am. Taught me to take care of our women. Now, come on and help me with Rosebud. She always liked you better anyway."

All Essie wanted was to go home and crawl into bed. Instead, she resigned herself to doing the polite thing and followed the "preacher."

chapter TWENTY-ONE

MOISTURE COLLECTED AGAINST the walls of the barn. Essie tugged her cloak together to ward off the chill, yet it did no good. The smell of leather, hay, and muck filled her senses. Ewing lit a lantern.

Oh my, but he's grown up, she thought. Gone was the chubby, freckled kid who'd dogged her every move, and in his place was a young man. Still light-haired, still quick to smile, still on the short side, but there wasn't anything boyish about him, nor was there an extra ounce of flesh to be seen.

"You must be a cyclist," he said, eyeing her short skirt.

"Yes."

"It's quite popular in Nashville."

"You ride?" she asked.

"It was forbidden."

He pulled a saddle off a rack, threw it over the mare's back and began to cinch it up. The horse swiveled her head around and bit him.

"Rosebud, no!" Jumping back, he rubbed his arm and shot Essie a glance. "I told you she didn't like me."

Suppressing a smile, Essie hugged herself to keep warm.

"Push the barn door open for me, would you?" he asked, slipping a bridle over the horse's head.

They walked the horse to the front gate, where she retrieved Cocoa and mounted up.

"It sure is good to be home," he said, inhaling deeply.

"You didn't like Nashville?"

"I loved it. Never seen a prettier place. But it gets mighty cold in the winter. Mighty cold." He pulled up short. "Shhhh. Listen."

She stopped.

"You hear that? You hear that beetle?" he asked.

A noise much like a squeaky hinge sounded over and over again.

"That's a pine sawyer," he said. "You know how I know that?"

She shook her head.

"You taught me."

"I did?"

"Yes, ma'am. You taught me to listen to all the night creatures."

"I was probably just trying to get you to hush up."

He chuckled. "You cut me to the quick, Miss Essie."

They rode in silence, she with a new ear to the nocturnal. The animals and insects of the night were as familiar to her as breathing. She had no recollection of teaching their identities to Ewing.

"So what have you been doing with yourself since I've been gone—besides bicycling, that is?" he asked.

"Nothing much, I suppose."

"Now, why is it I don't believe that?"

She didn't respond and he allowed the conversation to lag. Something she'd never known him to do before. Maybe that school had taught him a thing or two, after all.

They arrived at her house and he would have gone all the way to the stables with her, but she stopped him.

"Let me put her away for you," he said.

"No. Don't you remember? Cocoa doesn't like you, either."

He huffed. "I'd forgotten."

"Good night, Ewing. And thank you for seeing me home."

He tipped his hat. "My pleasure, ma'am. I'll see you tomorrow."

"What?"

"You said you were going to check on Harley. I'll be there, too."

"Oh. Of course. Well, tomorrow, then. Good night."

He made no move to leave, so she left him staring after her as she guided Cocoa round back.

———

"I wanna take some flowers to the rope-walker's grave," Harley said, pulling a gooey handful of pulp and seeds from inside a pumpkin.

He and Essie were cleaning them out for Lester, the orphanage's cook. He'd set them up in the dining hall, now empty apart from the two of them and their pumpkins. She scraped the sides of hers with a spoon.

"I'll take you," she said, "but you'll need a bath and a haircut first."

Scrunching up his nose, he paused. "The feller's dead. Why should he care what I look like?"

The screen door at the front of the dining hall squeaked open, then slapped shut. "If Miss Essie says it's time for a bath and haircut," Ewing said, entering, "then you don't argue. You simply do it."

"Howdy, Ewing," Essie said, then turned back to her task. "Harley, have you met Mr., um, Preacher Wortham?"

Harley shook his hand, trying to dislodge a pumpkin seed. "I met him," he said, accidentally slinging the seed off of his hand and onto her cheek. "I didn't know he was a preacher, though."

Ewing spun a chair backwards and straddled it. "Ewing is fine."

Her hands were a mess, so she brushed the seed with her shoulder but could not get it off. Ewing leaned his chair forward on two legs and plucked the seed from her cheek.

"Thank you."

He smiled.

"Cook's gonna make some pumpkin soup," Harley said.

"Y'all need any help?" Ewing asked.

"Not with the pumpkins, but Harley might need some assistance with his bath."

"I don't need no help. I can do it."

"Just the same, will you help him, Preacher?"

"Be glad to. And don't call me Preacher. Doesn't sound right coming from you."

"But neither Ewing nor Mr. Wortham is the correct form of address."

"Ewing will be fine."

She wasn't so sure about that, but calling him by anything other than his given name did seem a bit bizarre.

She shot a surreptitious glance in his direction. Wouldn't the girls in town be agog when they saw how he'd changed? It wouldn't be long before he'd marry one of them. She wondered which one it would be.

"I'm all done with mine," Harley said. "What about you, Miss Essie?"

"I've still got a little ways to go. Why don't you and Ewing go on to the creek and wash up. When you return, I'll be finished here and ready to cut your hair."

Ewing stood.

"You gonna wash, too?" Harley asked him.

"Might as well." He picked up a rag and wiped the boy's hands off. "We'll be back shortly."

"Take your time."

———

The water was cold as a Tennessee winter. Ewing dove under, then shot back up with a roar. Harley stood naked and shivering at the edge of the creek.

"Come on in. Feels great."

"Preachers ain't supposed to lie."

"I'm not lying. It does feel great. It feels great to be clean and to smell nice. Now, come on."

"How 'bout we just say I did. Nobody'll know."

"Miss Essie will know. And then we'll both be in trouble." He could see the boy wasn't going to make it in past his ankles. Striding out of the water, he swooped Harley up.

"No, no! I'm gonna freeze." The boy kicked and screamed.

Ewing kept right on walking. Harley put up such a fight that by the time Ewing managed to dunk him, they were both warm from the effort.

But it didn't last long. He had to soap the boy's hair and body two or three times to remove all the dirt. His lips turned blue before they were finished.

He toweled them off with worn fabric that was too old for someone's rag basket and had therefore been donated to the orphanage.

"Here's some clean clothes. They might not fit just right, but they'll keep you warm for now."

He'd never heard someone's teeth actually chatter, but Harley's were clacking up a storm. He'd known all along that they'd need a fire after their swim, so he'd laid some kindling in advance. Now he bent to light it, then pulled on his trousers, shirt, and jacket.

Harley huddled in his oversized clothing and fed the flames with dead leaves and pine needles.

"You must be something special to have Miss Essie looking after you this way," Ewing said.

He shrugged. "Me and Miss Essie is friends, is all. We go fishin' together. She ain't never made me take a bath before, though."

"Well, she's taken a shine to you. Anybody can see that."

"I akst her to marry me."

Ewing lifted his brows. "Did you? What'd she say?"

"She said I had to wait 'til I was taller. Then I could ask her again."

The smell of freshly burned pine spread throughout the clearing. Ewing blew on the flames and they surged upward. "Has she had many beaus?"

"Lots o' fellers like her."

"Who?"

"The sheriff. The peddler. The shopkeeper."

"What shopkeeper?"

"Mr. Crook."

"Never heard of him."

"He runs the Slap Out. So did Miss Essie for a while. That's where she took the king snake we caught. You shoulda seen it. His name was Colonel."

"What happened to it?"

"Me and Miss Essie and Jeremy let it go free."

"Jeremy? Jeremy who?"

"You know. His granddaddy's the drunk?"

Ewing nodded. "Gillespie. You're talking about Jeremy Gillespie?"

"I don't know. He works on Miss Essie's oil well. Him and that cowboy fella by the name o' Adam. The one what likes Miss Essie. 'Cept he cut outta town real quick-like."

"Who did? Jeremy or Adam?"

"Adam. Ain't you payin' attention?"

"I'm trying." Ewing scratched his jaw. "So this Adam fellow. He was sweet on Miss Essie?"

"She liked him, too. She never came to see me once when he was in town. I saw her plenty o' times, but she was always with him and didn't even know I was there. She even let him ride her bike. He crashed it and ever'thing and she still let him kiss her. I saw."

Kiss her? And he'd left town in a hurry? But Ewing let those questions go unspoken and instead asked another, more important one. "Does Miss Essie know you saw her kissing this man?"

"Nope."

"Have you told anyone else what you saw?"

"I tol' Jeremy."

"Anybody else?"

"Well, I tol' you just now."

Ewing rested his elbows on his knees. "Harley, there are some things a man does, and some things he doesn't. He does protect the womenfolk. So if you were spying on Miss Essie—"

"I wasn't spyin'!"

"Excuse me. If you accidentally saw Miss Essie with a man and feared for her safety, then it would've been okay to have kept your eye on her. But once you realized she wasn't in any danger, keeping an eye out for her changed into spying. And that's something a man doesn't do."

"How can ya tell she ain't in danger?"

"When she kisses him back."

"Now, how am I supposed to tell who's kissin' who?" Harley said, clearly exasperated.

"Was she struggling, Harley?"

The boy looked off into the distance as if recalling what he'd seen. "No. Can't say that she was."

"Then she was kissing him back and it was time for you to leave. All right?"

"All right."

"And one more thing."

Harley looked at him.

"A man never, ever, kisses and tells. And not just when he's doing the kissing, but when he sees someone else doing the kissing. I don't want you to ever, and I mean *ever*, breathe a word about Miss Essie and this cowboy to anyone else. You understand?"

"Yes, Preacher."

Ewing ruffled the boy's head. "All right, then. Let's put this fire out and go get you a haircut."

————————

Something had happened at the creek. Essie could sense the change in Harley and Ewing immediately. A camaraderie. An easiness.

She tied a sheet around Harley's neck, glad to know he had a new friend, especially one who would be so close by.

They were once more in the dining room, but this time it held a handful of children doing chores. A girl about ten years old in a tattered brown sack dress wiped grime from the windows. A boy a little older than Harley placed chairs on top of the tables while another followed behind with a mop.

Ewing had just finished stacking the chairs closest to him, when he twirled one around and straddled it.

"That crick was cold, Miss Essie," Harley said. "I don't ever wanna do that again."

Thank you, she mouthed to Ewing.

He winked.

The gesture so startled her, she dropped her scissors. He grinned and did it again.

"You ever cut a fella's hair before?" Harley asked.

"What? Oh. Yes. Of course. I've cut my father's many a time. Now, sit still."

She picked up the scissors and concentrated on her task. She couldn't fathom why in the world Ewing would wink at her. That would be like, like *Jeremy* winking at her. She shook her head. Ewing might have grown up some, but she couldn't think of him as anything other than a tagalong that never shut up.

"I hear you've been drilling oil wells," Ewing said.

"Yes. Papa has a rig over on Twelfth, though it has yet to produce."

"How far down are they?"

"I'm not really sure."

"Who's working the rig?"

She pulled a section of Harley's hair up with her comb, trapping it between her fingers before snipping off its ends. "Jeremy Gillespie and a man by the name of Cal Redding."

"Redding? Who's that?"

"He's new to town. Only been here a month or so."

"Who worked the rig before that?"

"A drifter."

"Adam, that cowboy I was tellin' ya about," Harley piped in.

Essie froze, wondering what Harley had said about Adam. She caught herself with idle hands and immediately resumed her cutting.

The silence was heavy and uncomfortable. But no, she was just imagining it. Ewing had no reason to suspect anything out of the ordinary about Adam. The girl washing the windows headed back to the kitchen with her bucket and rag.

"Tell me about him, Essie," Ewing said, his voice soft.

She glanced at him briefly, then began to cut a section around Harley's ears. "There is nothing to tell, really. He was a drifter. Came to town, worked for a while, then left."

"Golly, Miss Essie, that ain't true. He petted Colonel. He helped us catch them mice. He bought me sarsaparillas. He could rope anything that moved. And you ran over him with your wheeled feet. Remember?"

She swallowed. "Put your chin down, Harley, and quit talking so I can even out the back."

She cut the back, the silence worse now. Much worse.

"Okay. You can raise your chin."

He lifted his head and she parted his hair, combing it to one side.

"There," she said. "All done." She untied the sheet from around his neck.

Harley jumped off the stool. "How do I look?"

"Handsome," she answered. "You look very handsome."

"Handsomer than Adam?"

Her lips parted. "Yes."

He puffed out his chest. "Thank ya, Miss Essie. Can I go now?"
"Yes."

He raced out the door, letting it bang closed behind him. She stared at it, the sheet hanging limp in her hand.

"Adam was handsome?" Ewing asked.

Essie lowered her gaze. "Yes," she whispered.

He stood. "I'll go get the broom so we can sweep up this mess."

chapter TWENTY-TWO

IT FELT FUNNY ENTERING the Slap Out from the front door instead of the back. Essie paused a moment just inside the threshold, inhaling the familiar scent of molasses, leather, and grain. She took in the store and the changes that had been made.

The corner shelf and table she had once arranged to hold sewing and millinery items now held a hodgepodge of goods—sewing notions, cookware, even farming supplies. The medicinals were no longer grouped according to ailments, nor even grouped alphabetically. She could not tell if there was any rhyme or reason whatsoever to their order on the shelf.

No items had been set out on the front porch to lure customers in, nor did the windows hold anything of particular interest.

The stove at the back was still there, though, with a hot pot of coffee and cups hanging in invitation. Huddled over a barrel, Mr. Vandervoort jumped his black disk across the checkerboard, spit into a spittoon, then gloated while Mr. Owen crowned him. Hamilton displayed an array of grommets for Mr. Bunert, the harness maker. Heads together, Katherine and Sadie Tyner studied the catalog.

Essie took a close look at Sadie and wondered, not for the first time, if she was the mysterious owner of the "mouse catcher." If she was, it hadn't done the girl much good.

"Essie," Hamilton exclaimed, looking up. "It's good to see you. Come on in. You know where the coffee is." He smiled. "And I guess you know where everything else is, too. Katherine or I will be with you in a moment."

"I'm fine, Hamilton, take your time." She glanced at Katherine.

The petite woman, wearing a stiff white apron Essie had donned many a time, was whispering to Sadie. The girl giggled and glanced over her shoulder, then turned back to Katherine, leaning close to give her response.

"Miss Essie," Mr. Vandervoort boomed. "This is the third time today I've beaten Lafoon. Come over here and give me some competition."

She draped her cloak on a hat rack, then wove around barrels, crates, and tables. "Is he cheating, Mr. Owen?"

"I believe he is, Miss Essie, I just cain't quite figure out how. He always straightens up when you come round, though. So maybe my luck will improve now."

She picked up the coffee kettle, but only the dregs remained. She moved to the coffee grinder, poured in some beans and cranked the handle, the potent aroma soothing and familiar.

Katherine hurried to her side. "That's my job. If you'll just wait until I'm through with Miss Tyner, I will take care of this."

Essie released the grinder and took a step back.

"Oh, let her do it, Katherine," Hamilton said from across the room. "Nobody can brew a pot of coffee the way Essie can."

"What do you want?" Katherine hissed.

"Some fabric."

She waved her hand in the general direction of the cloth. "Well, when you find what you are looking for, *I* will cut it off the bolt. Is that clear?"

"Certainly," Essie said, averting her gaze. "Please, excuse me." She moved to the alcove housing the cloth. The selection had diminished considerably. Replacement bolts should have long ago been ordered.

Katherine returned to help Sadie. The men resumed their game.

Hamilton filled out a credit slip for Mr. Bunert.

A few moments later, the bell on the door jingled and the harness maker left. She fingered a corner of some black India lawn.

"Find what you're looking for?" Hamilton asked softly, slipping up behind her.

"Didn't we used to have some brown worsted wool?" she asked.

"Why, yes." He scanned the stacked bolts. "Hmmm. I don't see any, but I'd have ordered it if we'd been low."

He rummaged through the cloth, lifting up a bolt here and there. Finally, he straightened and sighed. "I'm sorry. We must be out. I had no idea."

"It's all right."

"It's not all right. This never used to happen when you were here." He flashed a glance at Katherine, then stepped farther into the alcove and out of his wife's view. "Would you consider coming back, Essie? Things haven't been the same since you left."

"It's not even been a full three months, Hamilton," she said, lowering her voice. "Give her some time."

"It didn't take you more than a week to have this place running like clockwork."

"She's had a lot to adjust to. A new husband, a new baby, a new town. You must be patient."

"But look at this place. It's a mess."

"Hamilton, please. You're embarrassing me."

"Well," Katherine said, causing both of them to jump. "Isn't this cozy?"

The woman stood just outside the alcove, her body stiff, her lips pursed.

"Where's the brown worsted wool?" Hamilton snapped.

"Why don't you ask Miss Spreckelmeyer? She seems to know where everything is, now, doesn't she?"

Hamilton's cheeks flushed, and Essie felt the heat rising to her own, as well.

"I believe the men are in need of coffee," he said. "Why don't you go and make it, Katherine?"

She jerked loose the strings behind her waist and yanked off her apron. "Why don't you?" She shoved the apron against his chest. "I'm going upstairs to check on Mae and Mrs. Peterson."

She marched away, leaving the two of them alone in the alcove. Her bootheels cracked against the wooden floor, heralding her path from the store to the stairs, until finally a door slammed in the distance.

"Do not ever put me in such an awkward position again, Hamilton."

"I'm sorry." His glasses magnified his brown eyes and the distress within them.

"Comparing your new wife with another is the height of foolishness."

"I haven't said anything."

"You've done nothing but sing my praises since the moment I walked through the door. I'd thank you not to let it happen again." She stormed to the front, grabbed her cloak, and left without even saying good-bye to the men in the back.

Furious, Essie strode toward the Flour, Feed and Liquor Store. She could not decide who she was more irritated with—Hamilton for being so clumsy or Katherine for being unhappy with the man she had stolen right out from under Essie's nose.

Crossing the street, she dodged horse droppings, swatted at flies, squinted against the dust kicked up by traffic, barged into the Feed Store, and ran smack into a solid male body.

"Whoa!" the man said, encircling her with his arms to keep them both from falling. He quickly released her and stepped back. "Why, Essie. Are you all right?"

She took a deep breath. "I'm sorry, Ewing. I wasn't watching where I was going."

"Well, if I'd known it was you, I might not have let go so fast."

She frowned. She understood exactly what he was implying but couldn't reconcile the fact that it was Ewing talking to her this way.

The teasing glint in his eye was not at all patronizing, but instead glowed with obvious male interest. Her first thought was exasperation, followed by a bit of panic. There was simply something amiss about being admired by a man whose nappies she used to change when his mother was too busy.

"I think you must have jarred something loose in our collision," she said.

He chuckled. "I assure you, ma'am, I am in full use of my faculties."

She gave a short huff.

"What are you doing here?" he asked. "Is it anything I can assist you home with?"

"No, I was just going to pick up some wool. I wanted to make Harley a few pairs of pants and a shirt or two before winter set in."

"Did you, now? How very good of you."

She waved her hand in a dismissive gesture. "He's a sweet boy. Now, if you will excuse me?"

He tipped his hat. "Of course. Good afternoon." He opened the door, glanced back at her and winked.

She gave him a frown, but he smiled in return—completely unrepentant.

Essie stepped into the kitchen, cold from the walk home but anxious to start on Harley's trousers.

Mother came around the corner, pulling up short when she saw Essie. "Where have you been?"

"At the Flour, Feed and Liquor Store," she said, setting her cloth and cake on the table. "Then I stopped by Mr. Weidmann's bakery. What's the matter?"

"Your father wants to see you."

She paused in the unbuttoning of her cloak. "Why?"

Mother unfastened the final button for her, then slipped the cloak from Essie's shoulders. "Go on, dear. He said to send you in the moment you arrived home."

"Why?"

"You never used to question me when he wanted to see you."

235

"He hasn't asked to see me since Adam's desertion and since he banished me from the oil fields."

"Nevertheless, you'd best not tarry."

Essie turned around.

Papa stood in the archway separating the hall from the kitchen. "I need to speak with you," he said quietly. "Please."

Was he going to reinstate her in his oil business? He'd mellowed somewhat since he'd been reelected, but she hadn't expected him to give into her wishes quite so soon.

He stepped back from the archway, allowing her to sweep past and precede him into his office. When the door clicked shut behind him, he placed his hands on one of the upholstered chairs designated for guests and pulled it back slightly.

She sat, expecting him to circle around his desk. Instead, he sat in the matching chair beside hers.

For a long time he said nothing. She did not squirm. Nor did she make eye contact, choosing instead to look straight ahead in an effort to appear nonchalant.

"Ewing Wortham came by to see me."

She whipped her head around. Ewing? Papa called her in here to talk about Ewing?

"It's not public yet, but our church board has asked him to be its pastor as soon as Preacher Bogart retires at the beginning of the year. Now that Ewing has a means of support, he asked me for permission to court you."

She didn't know which alarmed her more—the idea of Ewing being her pastor or of Papa giving him permission to court her. "You told him no, I trust?"

"I did not."

She sucked in her breath. "Why not?"

"Because he's a good man."

"Which is precisely why you should have refused his request." Her eyes widened. "Please do not tell me you *accepted* on my behalf? Surely, if you did not refuse him outright, you told him you would think about it, knowing full well you would refuse him later?"

"I didn't need to think about it."

She shot up from her chair. "Papa, what are you saying? Are you saying you said yes?!"

"He came all the way back for you."

"He *what*?"

"He came back home from Tennessee because he wanted you. He said he'd been confident God would keep you available for him."

She shook, unable to believe this was happening. "If I have remained unmarried all these years because that snotty-nosed brat has been praying that I be here for him when he returned, then I will personally go and wring his sorry neck!"

"Come now, you can't be surprised. He's been infatuated with you since he was ten. He's written you every quarter since his departure and you've answered his letters."

"His letters were no more than two paragraphs long and I only answered him three times. And I only did that out of courtesy. Out of friendship. Never once did he intimate any romantic feelings for me. I thought he'd outgrown all that!"

A hint of humor touched Papa's face. "Apparently not."

"This is not the least bit funny. Have you forgotten that I am ruined? *Ruined*."

Papa surged to his feet. "You are nothing of the kind."

"How can you even say that? You know I am."

"You made a mistake, as has many an innocent girl."

"I'm not a girl. I'm a full-grown woman and I certainly am no longer innocent!"

"God is merciful. He gives second chances."

"Well, *God* is not asking to court me."

"Are you sure?" Papa set his jaw.

Heaven help her, he could not be serious. "Think, Papa. Ewing is going to be a preacher. A *preacher*. That would make me a preacher's wife. A preacher's wife does not go to her marriage bed soiled!"

He slammed his fist on the desk. "Do not speak of that again."

"But it *happened*. You cannot pretend it didn't simply because you want to."

"You have been forgiven. In God's eyes you are as pure as snow."

She pressed a hand to her forehead. "Perhaps that is so, Papa. But in Ewing's eyes, I'd be used goods."

"Enough!" he roared. "I gave him permission to court you. He will be here at five o'clock to take you for a ride."

"Well, I hope you and he enjoy your little outing, then, because I am not going."

He took a menacing step toward her. It took every bit of self-control she had to hold her ground.

"You are going, Esther Spreckelmeyer. Make no mistake. Your bread, your butter, and the clothes on your back are provided by me. And if I say you go, you go. Do you understand?"

An overwhelming fury consumed her.

"Do you?!" he shouted.

Mother burst into the room.

Essie whirled toward her. "Did you know about this?"

"Of course."

"And you *agreed*?"

"I did."

"How could you?"

"Because your father is correct. You have every right to be courted by a man."

"I do not! I gave up that right to Adam Currington. Are you suggesting I conceal that truth from Ewing? That I, in essence, lead him on some merry chase all the while knowing he thinks I'm untainted?"

"Well, no, of course not. But there's no need to be rash. No need to put the cart before the horse."

"And what happens if the cart and horse line up? What happens if the courtship progresses to the point that he makes an offer? What then?"

Mother wrung her hands. "Your father will handle that when the time comes."

"I won't do it." Essie rushed past her mother. "I'm not going," she cried, running up the stairs and slamming herself into her bedroom.

chapter **TWENTY-THREE**

ESSIE COULD NOT SIT still. She paced round and round the perimeter of her room, stunned at her parents' maneuverings. Papa should never have accepted Ewing's request. It was nothing short of dishonest.

In her heart of hearts, she still wanted to marry and have children, but she knew that was no longer a possibility. No matter what Mother and Papa thought, no decent man—especially not a preacher—would want a woman who'd lain with another.

She stopped at her window, looking out at the myriad of leaves covering the ground. What on earth was she going to do? If she outright refused to accompany him today as she threatened, he'd no doubt take it personally. She didn't want to hurt Ewing's feelings. Nor did she want to encourage him.

Papa had said Ewing came back for her. All the way from Nashville. She shook her head. He'd hung on to his feelings for her all this time? It was simply too preposterous to comprehend.

She began to circle her room again. Finally she decided she would go on that ride today. And she would tell Ewing the truth. About her and about Adam. She would not wait as her parents suggested.

And after that, perhaps Papa would think twice about granting anyone permission to court her. Not that anyone would be asking.

Sighing, she went to her wardrobe and tried to decide what a woman should wear on her first outing with a man who was about to be given the shock of his life.

———

At five o'clock, Essie opened her door, stepped to the top of the stairs, and made her way down. Papa stood at the entryway with Ewing. Both turned when they heard her descending.

Papa looked ready to collapse with relief.

Ewing looked like Harley when someone gave him a sarsaparilla. "Hello, Essie," he said.

"Ewing," she responded. His clay worsted frock coat was a perfectly respectable jacket but would have been better suited to someone with more height, what with its hem coming down to his knees and all.

"You look lovely," he said.

She tugged on the edge of her carriage cloak. The black satin was trimmed with black marten fur that descended down the front and about the hem like a round boa. Rather than a hat, she wore a simple beaded clip above her Empire twist.

He held out a bouquet of white chrysanthemums.

It was the first time in her life a man had brought her flowers. She faltered. "Oh. My goodness. Why, thank you. I . . . well, how very thoughtful. Thank you."

"You're welcome."

She touched her nose to the flowers, inhaling their light, refreshing scent.

"Here, my dear," Mother said, joining them. "Shall I put those in some water for you?"

"Yes, please."

Ewing made a small bow. "Good evening, Mrs. Spreckelmeyer."

"Hello, Ewing. It's good to see you again. Welcome home."

"Thank you, ma'am."

The four of them stood in the foyer, awkward and uncertain.

Ewing put his hat on. "Shall we go?"

He held out his arm. Essie placed hers atop it, feeling like an actress in a performance.

"I'll have her home before dark, sir," he said to Papa, then they stepped out of the house and headed to the fence where his rig was waiting.

She was surprised to see it was an actual top buggy as opposed to a road wagon and wondered if the church had given him an advance on his salary. He placed a hand beneath her elbow and helped her up before moving around to his side of the rig. The seat creaked and tilted when he pulled himself up.

He did not reach for the reins right away but instead sat looking at her, a smile on his face. "I can't believe I am here, with you, in this carriage. I cannot tell you how many times I have dreamed of this moment."

She flushed, knowing she'd had no such longings for him.

He searched her eyes. "You take my breath away. You always have. Did you know that?"

No.

"I know you'd probably rather go fishing than riding in a carriage, but now that we're courting, I don't think it would be wise. I'm afraid being alone together like that might damage your reputation."

She gave him a weak smile, wondering if there had been some gossip to prompt his statement. Gossip from Katherine Crook, perhaps?

"Well," he said, rubbing his thighs, "I suppose we ought to get going."

He unwound the reins, gave the horse a "giddy-up" and headed toward downtown. His gift of gab had been perfected and honed over the years he'd been gone. He elaborated on his letters, entertaining her with stories of his train rides to and from Tennessee, his adjustment to living so far from home, and the pranks he and his schoolmates had played upon one another. She'd never dreamed Bible college could be so rambunctious.

The familiarity the two of them had shared as children made a resurgence, but this time she found herself laughing and chattering and teasing. They'd circled all the way through town before she even took note of her surroundings. Once she did, however, she became conscious of the townsfolk.

They openly stared. What on earth was an old maid like her doing with a youth like Ewing? That's what they were wondering, she knew. Her cheeks burned under the scrutiny, and she couldn't bring herself to meet their gazes.

As the buggy swayed, the two of them inched unconsciously toward the center of the bench, until finally their shoulders touched. Shocked by the contact, Essie reached for the wing and pulled herself to her side of the seat.

He pinched a corner of her cloak and tugged it softly toward him. "Where ya going?"

"We were, I didn't realize—"

"I did. And it was nice."

"Ewing, I . . . well . . ." She sighed. How in the world did you tell a man you'd been ruined and he ought to turn his attentions elsewhere? She couldn't exactly blurt it out right here in the middle of town.

"Let go, Essie," he said, his voice quiet, persuasive, full of invitation.

She didn't answer, just intensified her grip on the arm rail.

"Don't be scared."

"I'm not scared."

"You look scared."

"Well, I'm not." She turned her attention to the street and saw Mrs. Lockhart standing on the walkway, handkerchief in hand. She waved it at Essie, a delighted smile on her face, a knowing look in her eyes.

Good heavens. "I'm ready to go home now, please."

"What's the matter?"

"Nothing."

"No, it's something. What is it?"

She tucked her chin.

The next opportunity he had, he guided the buggy in a northwesterly direction, pointing them toward home. The route took them right past the Merchants' Opera House.

The orchestra gathered at the grand entry, and Essie realized with a start that it must be ten-cent night. She remembered the way the "society belle" had flashed her ankle and bare foot in front of the braying crowd, and how she'd allowed Adam to embrace her in the balcony. Then kiss her, touch her. Were his intentions dishonorable even back then?

They reached the railroad tracks on the edge of town, but instead of turning north, Ewing prodded the horse to cross them.

"Where are we going?" she asked.

"Somewhere we can talk."

"I thought you said we needed to avoid being alone."

"We do, but there's something wrong and whatever it is, I don't want to sort it out on your front porch with all the windows open."

She made no protest, for she, too, abhorred the thought of telling him about her sordid past within earshot of her parents. That he could read her so well was unsettling and comforting all at the same time.

They traveled in silence, twilight beginning to fall. With its approach came the sounds of nature and her inhabitants—some preparing for bed, others just awakening. He turned into an unobtrusive break in the tangled growth that lined the road. It quickly led them to a copse of trees just wide and long enough to completely conceal their vehicle from casual passersby.

"Whoa," he said, stopping the horse.

In front of them was an opening that overlooked a pond she'd fished at many a time. Yet she had never noticed this spot. A spot perfect for lovers who did not want to be discovered.

"You've been here before," she said.

He turned. "Is that an accusation?"

"No! No, of course not. Just an observation, I suppose."

He wrapped the reins around the dash rail, then rested his elbows on his knees. Bullfrogs made their low, vibrant call of *jug-o-rum, jug-o-rum.* Crickets buzzed and trilled. A gathering of ducks squawked, loud and out of sync.

She moistened her lips, having no idea where to begin.

"Are you angry with me?" Ewing asked.

"No," she whispered. "Not at all."

"Then what's the matter?"

The pond picked up the pinks and purples touching the sky and duplicated them on its shimmery surface.

"Ewing, I . . ."

He studied his fingernails. "You don't like me."

"No, no. I do, I like you just fine, but . . ."

"But what?"

"But Papa has not been completely honest with you."

He sat up, frowning. "What?"

"He should never have granted you permission to court me. He should never grant permission for *anyone* to court me."

Confusion traveled across his features before alarm replaced it. "Essie, are you ill? Are you . . . dying?"

"No, no." She shook her head. "Nothing like that."

"Then, what?"

O Lord, help me. Her throat filled, requiring force to push the words out. "I am not marriageable, Ewing. Not to you, not to anyone."

He grasped both her hands and turned her toward him. "You are barren?"

She slid her eyes closed and shook her head.

He briefly tightened his hold. "If you aren't dying and you aren't barren, then what are you?"

"Ruined," she choked, a tear splashing onto their intertwined hands.

His grip relaxed, then withdrew.

She couldn't bring herself to look at him at first. But she decided that, whatever else she might be, she was no coward. She wiped the tear from her cheek and lifted her gaze—only to wish she hadn't.

His jaw was tight with shock, a tremor running under his skin.

His eyes sparkled dully, like they'd been forced to see too much and then had stopped seeing altogether.

He looked away, running a hand over his mouth. His Adam's apple bobbed. He stared at the pond as if mesmerized. "Who all knows?"

"My parents and the sheriff."

"No one else?"

"No one else."

He pinched the bridge of his nose. "Do I know him? Is he someone I will see at church, at the store, at the club?"

"No. You never knew him."

"Was it the drifter?"

She sucked in her breath but said nothing. Finally she touched his sleeve. "I'm sorry."

He jerked away from her touch. "I waited for you, Essie," he said, anguish coating his words. "Do you have any idea how many opportunities I've had to be with other women? Yet I never betrayed you. Not once. I held myself back. For you. For *us*."

"I didn't know," she said, the tears coming more rapidly now. "We had no understanding between us."

"You shouldn't need one. You should have waited on principle alone for whatever man God had for you."

"I know, I know. I'm sorry."

He jumped from the buggy, striding down the slope to the pond, kicking a log here, a rock there. At the bottom of the hill, he plopped down and propped his head in his hands. She watched his shoulders bounce.

I'm sorry, Ewing. I'm sorry, Lord. It wasn't worth it. The few moments of bliss I shared with Adam, they weren't worth all the torment I have caused my parents, my friend, myself, and you. Oh, if I could do it over, I would make a much different choice. Forgive me, Lord. Forgive me.

But even if He granted such a thing, she would never forgive herself.

It was dark before Ewing climbed back up the hill and joined her in the carriage. She could no longer see his face, but the stiffness in his body spoke for itself.

He drove her home with unbearable slowness, keeping the buggy at a sedate and calm pace. He didn't say a word to her or even glance her way. She kept religiously to her side of the seat. When they finally pulled up in front of her house, she prepared to jump down.

He touched her arm. "No."

He circled around and helped her to the ground, then took her elbow and walked her clear to the door.

"Good night, Essie," he said in a pleasant voice plenty loud enough to be heard through the windows.

"Good-bye," she whispered.

He tipped his hat and returned to the rig.

Papa was standing in front of his office door when she entered. "He said he would have you home before dark. Where have you been?"

Resentment surged through her, momentarily overshadowing her fragile bid toward repentance. "Where do you think I've been?"

"I have no idea."

She released the ties of her cloak, letting him think what he would.

"What is it?" Mother asked, stepping into the hall. "Has something happened?"

"I told him."

She hurried forward. "What do you mean, you told him?"

"I mean, I told him." Essie looked her father in the eye. "I told him I was ruined."

Mother gasped. "You didn't."

"I did."

"Why on earth would you do such a thing?"

Instead of answering, she slipped off her cloak, smoothed it over her arm, then returned her attention to Papa. "Do not accept another request for courtship on my behalf. I will never marry and I do not want to have to go through something like that ever again."

Katherine Crook knelt beside a bucket of oatmeal, carefully packing a half-dozen eggs inside. Lizzie was a careless girl, and Katherine didn't want the eggs to crack before they made it home to the child's mother. She glanced up when Hamilton entered the storage room and lifted the long, wooden bar from their barn-like door.

"Quickly," he said, "Mrs. Bogart has brought in a box of butter, but I need to receive a delivery."

Katherine placed the final egg in the bucket, then scrambled to her feet. The preacher's wife made the best butter for miles around. Not every woman scrubbed her churn out before each use or washed the buttermilk out of the butter. Mrs. Bogart not only did that but she also churned her butter twice a week while the cream was still fresh. Her trays would sell for double the normal price before the day was through.

Brushing oatmeal off her hands, Katherine picked up the bucket and entered the store. "Here are your eggs, Lizzie."

"Thank you, ma'am."

She nodded to the girl, then made her way to the preacher's wife, who had placed her butter chest on the counter.

"Good morning, Mrs. Bogart. How are you?"

The elderly woman's face and chin above her collar held as many wrinkles and sags as a mastiff. Her eyes were barely visible beneath the folds of her skin, but her smile was warm as ever. "I'm fine, dear. How is that beautiful baby?"

"Growing every day."

"I'll just bet she is."

Katherine opened the chest and began to remove trays of butter from inside. Each tray was dovetailed together and made with white wood, which kept its contents free from taint or smell. "I heard Preacher Bogart will be retiring soon?"

The woman rested her clasped, gloved hands against her waist. "Yes. I still can't quite believe it."

"How long has Preacher Bogart been at the pulpit?"

"Nearly fifty years now. And did you know that the young man the elders are bringing in as our new shepherd is barely out of school?"

"No. I hadn't heard a thing. Who is it?"

"Ewing Wortham. The son of the couple who run the orphanage?"

Katherine hesitated. "Yes, of course. I met him for the first time last week."

Mrs. Bogart tugged a handkerchief from her sleeve and dabbed at her eyes. "I just don't know how in the world I'll be able to sit in those pews and listen to someone my grandson's age give the message." She shook her head, sending the flaps along her chin to swinging. "I can't imagine what the elders were thinking to entrust our flock to such an untried fellow. Can you?"

Katherine covered the woman's hand and squeezed. "I cannot. And a couple of days ago I saw him driving Essie Spreckelmeyer through town. He's not thinking to court her, is he?"

A poignant smile stacked the wrinkles on each side of Mrs. Bogart's mouth. "If he is, that is his saving grace. Anyone smart enough to snatch up that sweet little thing clearly has more intelligence than most of the other men in this town."

Katherine stiffened. Was that a hidden inference to Hamilton? She was so tired of hearing people speak of Essie with such regard. Oh, many made remarks about her choice of hats and her fancy attire and her penchant for pursuits more suited to men. But there were many more—including her husband—who were quick to defend the brazen woman, and Katherine had had about all she could take.

She closed the chest and opened their accounting book. "Well, I wouldn't say this to just anyone, but I'd hate for young Mr. Wortham to assume such an important position in town, only to find out he'd been led astray by the woman he was considering for marriage."

Frowning, Mrs. Bogart cocked her head. "What do you mean?"

Katherine moistened her lips. "I want you to understand I'm not gossiping. I just thought you might want to, um, pray about this."

"Pray about what?"

Katherine scanned the store, then moved around the counter to

Mrs. Bogart's side. "Do you remember when that cowboy who worked for the judge left town in a hurry?"

"No. Not particularly."

"Well, he did." She lowered her voice. "And I have it from a good source that it was because he compromised Miss Spreckelmeyer."

The woman regarded Katherine at length before exasperation transformed her face. "Of all the ridiculous . . ." She tugged her gloves more tightly into place. "I wouldn't believe everything I heard if I were you, Mrs. Crook."

The censure of the preacher's wife stung. Katherine straightened. "Think what you will, Mrs. Bogart. Hamilton told me Essie was so desperate for a husband that she threw herself at him—right here in this very store when no one else was around. Why, she even wrote down the names of the men in town she'd decided to try her wiles on. Hamilton saw it with his own eyes. As a matter of fact, he was one of the men on her list."

A troubled frown puckered Mrs. Bogart's brows.

Katherine lifted her chin. "And the cowboy I was telling you about told Hamilton she did the same thing to him. Only he was not as discerning as my husband, and when the sheriff caught that man and Essie in an, um, unfortunate encounter, he and the judge ran the fellow right out of town—as if he were the one at fault."

Mrs. Bogart searched Katherine's eyes. And though Katherine couldn't be certain of the details, she knew she wasn't far from the mark. Jeremy and Harley were as close to Essie as anyone and not nearly so guarded with their tongues. It didn't take much to put two and two together.

She picked up a pencil and handed it to the preacher's wife. "Your signature, Mrs. Bogart?"

The woman scribbled down her name, and for all her earlier bravado, her disorientation was such that she left the store without her butter box. No matter. Katherine would see that it was delivered to her before the next batch of cream was ready for churning.

chapter TWENTY-FOUR

HARLEY PRESSED HIMSELF against the arm of Essie's chair and watched every stitch she took. The fire popped, filling the parlor with warmth.

"Cain't ya take bigger stitches? Then you'd finish quicker."

"Smaller ones are better," she answered. "You want these trousers to hold up through the winter, don't you?"

"Well, shore. But I ain't never had brand-new pants before. Not even at Christmas."

"Well, in another hour or so, you will."

Pushing away from the chair, he wandered throughout the room. But instead of admiring the scenic painting above the secretary or the bronze cherub on the mantel, he squatted down and smoothed the tangled strands at the edge of their Axminster rug.

"Go into the kitchen and ask my mother for a fork," she said. "Tell her you are going to rake the fringe in the parlor for her."

He raced out to do her bidding, returning shortly with fork in hand. She expected him to tire of the chore, but he gave it his full attention, lining the threads up like teeth on a comb.

"Ewing's gonna take me hunting," he said without deviating from his task.

"Is he?" She paused, picturing Ewing's carefully controlled expression when he'd escorted her to the door last week after her confession. "Hunting for what?"

"Dove."

"Dove? But you'd need a gun to bring down one of those."

"I know. He's gonna teach me how ta shoot. I already know how to load."

"But you're only seven."

"Ewing says his daddy gave him his first gun when he was six."

She tried to remember when Grandpa had taught her to shoot, but she couldn't recall. Surely she'd been older than six or seven.

A knock at the front door interrupted her musings.

"Want me ta get it?" Harley asked.

"Please."

The boy loved to answer the door. Such a simple, ordinary thing, unless you were an orphan and had no door to open.

"Howdy, Ewing," she heard Harley say. "Come on in."

Essie stiffened. She'd been to the orphanage several times this past week but had not seen any sign of him there or anywhere else in town.

He stepped into the parlor, hat in hand, his strawberry blond hair neatly combed. A moment passed before it dawned on her how he was dressed.

He wore a black cutaway, black vest, black necktie, light-colored trousers, and pale gloves. The consummate dress for a gentleman caller.

"Hello, Essie."

She felt heat rush to her cheeks. "Ewing." She put down her sewing and stood. "My goodness. I . . . well, can I offer you something to drink?"

"No." He swallowed. "Actually, I was wondering if I could interest you in a carriage ride?"

Perplexed, she studied him. His face had cleared of all expression. She couldn't imagine his motive for asking such a thing. "Why?"

"Because that's what courting couples do."

Her lips parted. Surely he didn't still want to court her? Yet his rust-colored eyes were intense and determined.

"What are you saying, Ewing?"

"I'm saying my feelings haven't changed." He looked to the side, floundered a moment, then returned his gaze to hers. "Well, that's not exactly true."

She stood mute and completely caught off guard. Never in all her imaginings had she expected him to show up on her doorstep.

She glanced at Harley. The boy had stopped combing the fringe and placed his full attention onto them, his brown eyes alert.

"Harley?" Ewing said. "Run along to the kitchen for a moment and let me speak to Miss Spreckelmeyer. Would you?"

"She cain't go with ya right now. She's makin' me some pants."

"Go on, Harley," she said. "Tell Mother I said you've worked so hard you deserve a cookie."

His eyes lit up. "A cookie? Right now? Before supper?"

"Yes."

He raced from the room, his rapid footfalls echoing in his wake.

Essie indicated her father's chair on the opposite side of the hearth from hers, and the two of them sat down.

Ewing crinkled the brim of his hat and stared at the fire. "I'm not going to pretend I'm not devastated. I am. But my feelings, the ones that count, haven't changed."

She had no idea what to say. Those stolen moments beneath the magnolia tree had not been forced upon her. She'd been a willing participant. Not for one second had she considered how her actions might later affect Ewing or any other man. Of course, she hadn't thought there would ever be any other man. Yet now an honorable one sat before her, his heart in his hand.

"I've been doing a lot of thinking," he said, "and a lot of praying. I came to the conclusion that I wouldn't be much of a preacher if I held against you something God has already forgiven."

Forgiven? How could God forgive her when she hadn't even forgiven herself, not to mention Adam? Disbelief warred with shame and regret. "I'm unworthy of it," she whispered.

His expression softened. "None of us are worthy of it. That's not the point. The point is, I'm not perfect and you're not perfect. But that doesn't mean I don't have strong feelings for you, because I do. And I'd still like to court you. If you'll have me, anyway."

She could not reconcile the boy she'd known with this man. This amazingly gracious, poised, well-spoken man. He deserved better.

"But I'm so old."

"Old?" A hesitant smile lifted one corner of his mouth. "Are you telling me you have some gray hairs tucked up in that bun of yours?"

"Certainly not."

"Well, then. Let's not worry over trivialities such as how old you are and how old I am."

"Seven years is not trivial."

"It is to me."

And, of course, it probably was to him. Anyone who could overlook her unchaste life would certainly be able to overlook her advancing age.

"What's the matter?" he asked.

I don't know, she thought. This was what she'd always wanted. Ewing might not send her pulse skittering, but he was a good man and a cherished friend. He'd be an excellent father and provider. If he was willing to accept her the way she was, how could she turn him down?

He shifted in his chair. "We would, of course, need to be very circumspect in how we proceed."

She frowned, unsure of his point.

"What I mean to say is, now that I am aware of your, um, weakness, I think it is essential that we do everything we can to guard you from yourself." Both his tone and posture stiffened.

"Guard me from myself?" she asked.

"Yes." He cleared his throat. "As you know, I have been offered the position of pastor at our church. And as such, my actions and those of the woman I court must be above reproach."

A spurt of defensiveness leapt to the forefront. What exactly did he think she was going to do? Drag him to the nearest tree and have her way with him?

254

With effort, she squelched her uncharitable thoughts. After all, she was the confessed sinner here, not him. And if he was willing to overlook her transgression, she could at least remember he was only trying to do what he thought best. Still, he needn't sound so self-righteous about it.

"First," he said, "any . . . um, extravagant feelings we have must be carefully repressed."

The image of him as a youngster jumping from a tree in an effort to fly flashed into her mind, along with the shockingly coarse words he'd exclaimed after his subsequent fall. She pushed the memory aside.

"If we wish to express affectionate fondness in our visits," he continued, "then we must keep it a sentiment, not debase it with animal passions."

Animal passions? She might have regretted her tryst with Adam. She might have felt profound remorse for squandering the most precious gift she had to offer. But never once had she considered her actions with him *animal passions.*

"Also, a woman's dress," he said, "is an expression of her inner soul and should serve to heighten her charm, not draw attention to her . . . to her garments."

What on earth? Ewing was suddenly so stiff and upright, spouting rules as if he'd memorized them along with his Bible verses. She sighed. Had his Bible college impressed these ideals upon him? Was he trying to act the way he thought a preacher should?

She became conscious of her plain wool gown and gloveless hands. Not exactly an outfit she would have chosen to receive callers in. But she didn't know she was going to have any callers.

"Do you have some objection to the way I dress, Ewing?"

"Your hats are very extravagant," he answered with a gentle tone. "I think it might be best to tone them down a bit. Quite a bit."

She slowly straightened her spine. Tone down her hats? But they were her pride and joy. "You think they are excessive somehow?"

"I don't mind them, Essie. I'm just not sure they are fitting for a preacher's wife to wear."

"Well, I don't happen to be a preacher's wife," she snapped.

"Yet," he said softly.

Her breath caught. Well. If she'd had any question about his intentions, they were certainly clear now. But for heaven's sake, what could possibly be wrong with wearing a pretty hat?

"And though we have known each other for our whole lives," he continued, "I think it best to start using a more formal form of address. From now on, I will call you Miss Spreckelmeyer and you must call me Mr. Wortham."

She stopped just short of snorting. Hadn't he been the one to insist upon first names when he'd returned home? Still, she knew he was right, but it seemed so absurd. When he was a toddler, she'd slapped him on his backside for sticking his tongue out at her. She'd kissed his knee when he fell and scraped it raw. She'd quizzed him on his multiplication tables. She'd helped him place his first worm on a hook.

And now she must call him Mr. Wortham?

"Anything else?" she asked, trying to keep the exasperation out of her voice.

"Just one more thing."

She folded her hands in her lap and waited.

"You must give up bicycle riding."

She sucked in her breath.

"I know this is difficult for you," he said. "But there are doctors, well-respected doctors, who claim that the bicycle will ruin the feminine organs of matrimonial necessity." Color rushed to his face. "And it is believed to greatly increase the labor pains of childbirth. And it will develop muscular legs, which would be an unsightly contrast to underdeveloped feminine arms. Forgive me for mentioning such delicate subjects, but I wanted you to understand how serious this is and why I am so opposed to women riding."

His color remained high, attesting to his embarrassment.

Her high color had nothing to do with embarrassment and everything to do with total and complete outrage. "You cannot possibly believe that bunch of poppycock. *Cosmopolitan* trumpeted the benefits of riding for women just last month."

"*Cosmopolitan* is a magazine, Essie. Hardly the same as a doctor."

"You are to call me 'Miss Spreckelmeyer,' if I am not mistaken." She sat stiff, her fingernails making indentations in her hands as she clasped them tightly.

He sighed. "You are angry. I knew this last one would be a touchy one."

"Touchy? It is outrageous. And you are living in the Dark Ages."

"Lower your voice," he whispered. "You know good and well that the leaders of God's church have a completely different set of expectations to adhere to."

"Are you now going to try and tell me the Bible says I cannot ride a bike?"

He searched her eyes. "You yourself have admitted to stumbling, Essie—Miss Spreckelmeyer. I am merely trying to keep us both on the straight and narrow."

Sputtering, she strove to collect her thoughts but could think of no polite way to express them.

He sighed. "The honest truth is that the elders were very reluctant to appoint someone my age to such an important position in the community. But it was either that or hire someone who was less qualified or who'd not been born and raised in Corsicana."

She held herself still, neither encouraging nor discouraging him.

"I can't afford to do anything the least bit controversial," he said, combing his fingers through his hair. "I have to show them my age is nothing to be concerned about. And while I am courting you, everything you do reflects back on me."

She pictured Preacher Bogart and the church elders. They were indeed an intimidating force and should not be taken lightly.

Her heart pounded as her mother's words came whistling back through her mind. *"Is that bicycle so important you'd rather have it than a man? Than babies of your own?"*

She wouldn't, of course. It wasn't really the bike, though, so much as what it represented. Freedom. Independence. Progress.

On the other hand, if she did sacrifice those things, she would reap a harvest of untold value. She'd have a husband, a home, a place in the community, children.

Wilting a little, she lowered her chin. "All right, Mr. Wortham. I will put away my wheels for now—but not necessarily forever."

"Thank you." He stood and offered her a gloved hand. "I'd like to take you for a carriage ride, Miss Spreckelmeyer. Will you do me the honor?"

After a charged moment, she allowed him to assist her to her feet. "If you would excuse me for a moment, I must go and change first."

She made her way to her room, telling herself this was exactly what she'd been wishing for. But instead of a weight being lifted, she felt heavy and burdened.

———

The sun provided Essie with warmth, while Ewing provided her with conversation. He kept the carriage close to the sidewalk, restraining the horses from using undue speed.

Making their way down Eleventh Street, the false fronts of town began to be replaced with quiet homes and picket fences. A scattering of crimson clover lined the road.

Ewing pointed to a flock of birds flying in V formation. The lead bird dropped off to the back of the line, allowing another to take its place.

"I wonder how they know when their turn at the front of the line is up," he said. "I wonder if some birds are lazier than others and don't fight the wind as long as they should. What would the other birds do, do you think?"

Essie followed their progress across the blanket of blue overhead. "I have no idea. I never thought about it before."

"Look," Ewing said, spotting some black huckleberries in a vacant lot and pulling over. "Want some?"

It took them ten minutes to pick a handful and less than a minute to eat them.

"I wish they weren't so tedious to harvest," he said. "I haven't had any of those since before I left."

"They don't have any huckleberries in Tennessee?"

"In the mountains they do."

"You've been on a mountain?"

Shaking out his handkerchief, he laid it across his hands and presented it to her. She placed her hand inside and allowed him to wipe her fingers clean of huckleberry juice.

"I didn't like being on it," he said. "Those misty mountains are beautiful from a distance, but when I got up on them, I felt surrounded and hemmed in." He began to wipe her other hand. "No, I prefer wide-open spaces."

He'd cleaned four of her fingers and reached for her thumb. She immediately moved it and tried to pin his down. Within seconds the handkerchief had floated to the ground and a thumb war began in earnest.

He pinned her thumbs in record time.

"Oh no!" she squealed. "I always used to win."

"I've grown up some since the last time we played."

"Don't get mouthy with me, youngster. I bet I can still beat you at the hand-slap game."

Grinning, he held out his hands. She lightly touched her palms to his and held fast his gaze. Quick as lightning, she struck and just barely caught the tips of his fingers.

They reversed positions. It took him four tries before he could catch her. But instead of slapping her hands, he grabbed them and did not let go. They stood in the middle of the lot, the breeze cold against their faces, the laughter of a moment before melting away.

"Your cheeks are all red," he said, studying her.

"My nose, too, I'd wager."

"Yes. But it's becoming. You have a lovely nose."

She gave a short huff.

He moved his gaze to her lips and she felt a moment of panic.

Gently tugging her hands free, she glanced at the carriage. "We should probably be getting back."

He walked her to the rig. And though he took her elbow, he did not immediately help her up. "Can I see you tomorrow?"

"The Ladies' Garden Club is cleaning the Methodist church sanctuary tomorrow."

"What about during the evening?"

"I'm substituting for Mrs. Quigley who can't make it to Mrs. Lockhart's whist game."

"Wednesday?"

"I'm helping Mother with the washing and ironing."

"Perhaps the following day, then?"

"Yes. Thursday should be fine."

"Good."

No words were spoken on the rest of the ride home. He pulled to a stop in front of her gate, then alighted. Placing her hands on his shoulders, she allowed him to assist her to the ground, his hands under her elbows.

"I'll see you Thursday." Touching his hat, he returned to the carriage seat.

She watched as he turned the rig and disappeared around the bend. It had been a lovely afternoon and an invigorating ride. She headed toward her front door, wondering what she would do if Ewing tried to kiss her.

She enjoyed his company, but she had no desire whatsoever to introduce anything physical into the relationship. It wasn't because she didn't enjoy those intimacies. She did. Very much.

She just couldn't muster up any enthusiasm for sharing them with Ewing. He was a pleasant-looking man. Amiable. Easy to get along with. She just wasn't attracted to him in that way.

Maybe that would come. Maybe the feelings she had for Adam weren't a one-time thing. Or maybe Ewing would be too fearful of arousing her "weakness" to risk kissing her.

Sighing, she entered the house. She needed to finish those trousers of Harley's.

chapter TWENTY-FIVE

EIGHT LADIES FROM the Garden Club had gathered early in the morning to clean the First Methodist Church. The noon hour found the sanctuary's leaded windows sparkling, the floor pristine, and the choir and amen corners shining. Only the pews were left.

Three more and they'd be done. Essie rubbed her polishing cloth against the varnished oak, praying the task would soon come to completion.

The church held the distinct honor of having housed the first democratic convention in Texas after the Civil War. At the time, a host of hogs had made their home beneath the building, and the convention had to be stopped several times due to the ruckus the hogs had made.

Essie fervently wished those hogs were still present today. Anything to stop the direction of today's conversation.

"I always knew the Lord had someone for you," Mrs. Owen sighed. "And didn't that Ewing turn out to be the most handsome thing you ever did see? Even if he's not very tall."

"The thing to remember, Essie," Shirley Bunting's mother interjected, "is a happy courtship promotes conjugal felicity more than anything else. So don't spoil it."

"She's right, dear," said Mrs. Shaw. President of the Garden Club, she never took a wrong step or had a hair out of place. Even now, after a morning of scrubbing, her apron was still stiff and her coif tidy. "So of course you want to look your best when he's courting you, but keep in mind that ornamentation that has no use is never, in any high sense, beautiful."

Essie frowned in confusion. Then why did Mrs. Shaw put so much effort into her ornamental flower garden, which, after all, had no purpose but beauty?

"What she means is," said the undertaker's wife, "buttons that fasten nothing should never be scattered over a garment. And bows, which are simply strings tied together, should only be placed where there is some possible use for, well, strings tied together."

Known as a woman of few words, the blacksmith's wife added, "In short, Esther, anything that looks useful, but is useless, is in bad taste."

Essie resumed her polishing, wondering if these women had bothered to look at *Godey's Lady's Book* sometime in the last few decades.

"More important than your attire, though, is your general treatment of each other." This from Mrs. Richie, who harangued her poor husband so much that he spent most of his waking hours at the Slap Out whittling and playing checkers. "You must tell Ewing that you should like to be treated thus, but not so, and that he must let you do this, but not that. It is much better to arrange these things now than for them to be left for future contention."

"Love will not bear neglect, however," said Mrs. Lockhart, settling herself on the first pew while the rest of the ladies finished up. "It should not be second in anything. You must spend a great deal of time together. Once love's fires have been lit, they must be perpetually resupplied with their natural fuel, or else they die down, go out or . . . go elsewhere." She looked over the rim of her glasses meaningfully.

The other matrons nodded in agreement. The only person who had yet to offer any advice was Mrs. Bogart. A worried frown puckered the woman's brows as she collected the dirty rags and dropped them into a bucket. The members of the Garden Club were set to clean her church at the beginning of the year. By then, though, Ewing would be their preacher.

Essie sighed, wondering what these ladies would do if she were to tell them how troubled and unsure she was over her blossoming relationship with Preacher Wortham.

———

Pumping the handle above the kitchen's washbasin, Essie filled a bowl with water, then splashed her face. She was glad to be finished with the cleaning and with hearing unwanted advice.

"Oh, thank goodness you're home," Mother said, entering the room and handing Essie a towel.

"What's the matter?" she asked, dabbing her face.

"Nothing. Your father is in his office with Melvin. They have something they'd like to, um, show you."

"I thought Uncle Melvin was out of town," she said, hanging the towel over a rod.

"He's back."

Essie frowned. "Is anything wrong?"

"No. Nothing at all."

Essie sighed. All morning she'd felt like a carcass that had been pecked and gouged. She wasn't sure she was up to facing Papa or even Uncle Melvin. Squaring her shoulders, she took a deep breath and headed toward the hallway.

"Perhaps you should freshen up a bit first," Mother said.

"No, I'm sure they won't mind either way."

Mother grabbed her hand. "Actually, I insist. Come on, I'll help you change."

Too tired to argue, Essie allowed her mother to pull her up the stairs and assist her in replacing work clothes with a simple white shirtwaist and wool skirt. Mother took the pins out of Essie's hair, brushing it with long, slow strokes.

Essie closed her eyes, relishing the unexpected treat of having someone else see to her needs. "The church cleaning this morning was awful."

"Awful? Why? What happened?"

"Every single one of those women had advice to offer me on my courtship with Ewing. Seems the entire town has us married already."

"Oh dear. I'm sorry I wasn't there."

"It's all right. I'm just glad the morning's over."

She opened her eyes. Mother had styled her hair in a loose bun at the back with soft tendrils framing her face.

"There." Her mother set the silver brush on the toilet table. "Ready?"

Essie met her gaze in the mirror. "Ready for what?"

"For your, um, meeting with your father and uncle."

Essie swiveled around on her stool. "What is going on, Mother?"

"Nothing. Now come along." But she was blushing and Essie found herself reluctant to follow.

Still, they made their way down the stairs and Mother opened the door to Papa's study. "She's home."

Essie stepped through the door. The neat and orderly office provided an unlikely backdrop for Uncle Melvin's slouching form. Covered with dust and dirt, he looked as tired as she'd ever seen him—eyes bloodshot, shoulders wilted, mouth sagging.

"What happened?" she asked, going straight to him. "Are you all right?"

"Just a little tuckered out."

"Where on earth have you been? You look like you rode clear to China and back."

He pushed a smile onto his face, but it didn't stay there long. She turned to ask Papa what this was all about and froze.

Behind her and leaning against the north wall, one hip cocked, was Adam Currington, hat in hand. He was just as filthy as Uncle Melvin, the starch long since gone from his handkerchief and blue shirt.

His eyes stayed on her face, never once venturing to places they ought not go. They were as clear and pretty as ever, but their sparkle had dulled.

"How's your nose?" she asked.

It was a ridiculous question, all things considered, but his nose was so crooked and bruised. Even after six weeks, hints of purple still hovered in the circles beneath his eyes.

He gave a slight smile. "It's fine. How's yours?"

She smiled back, but her good humor slowly dissolved as she remembered his perfidy. "Where have you been?"

His gaze dropped and he pulled away from the wall. "I owe you an apology, Essie."

An apology? He thought to waltz in here with an apology and all would be forgiven?

"Would you like to sit down?" he asked, pulling out one of Papa's chairs.

"No, thank you." She held herself still and straight.

"You're angry. And I can't say I blame ya." He swallowed. "I've come back to do right by ya. I've offered fer your hand, but your pa won't give it without your consent."

She sank into the previously offered chair, her eyes locking with Papa's. He'd erected a wall of indifference around him, refusing to let her see what he was thinking. She had no idea if he was angry, relieved, or anxious. But one thing was certain. He wasn't indifferent, no matter what he pretended.

She turned to Uncle Melvin. "You went after him, didn't you? That's where you've been."

He said nothing.

"Where did you find him?"

No one answered.

Adam pulled out the chair next to hers and sat down facing her, his spurs jingling. "None of that is important. What matters is that I'm back. And I'm back for good. Ready to do the honorable thing."

"Did Uncle Melvin have to threaten you?" she asked. "Cuff you and force you here by gunpoint?"

Hurt and irritation mingled, providing her heart some protection against the shock of seeing him again. She'd dreamed so often of his return that she could hardly credit the fact that he was actually here. Still, she'd never considered he would have to be tracked down and dragged back.

"No, Essie. Not at all. I'm here of my own free will."

He must think she was an idiot. And not surprisingly, considering the poor decisions she'd made concerning him. "Really? What took so long?"

He glanced at Melvin.

"Don't look over there for help," she said. "It's me who's asking and me whom you'll be answering to."

"Essie," he said, rotating his hat round and round in his big, bronzed hands, "I have no excuse to offer other than cowardice. The thought of being hogtied by matrimonial ropes made me as nervous as a long-tailed cat under a rockin' chair. So I left in such a hurry I forgot to take my right mind with me."

She waited, but no more was forthcoming. "That's it? That's your excuse?"

He frowned. "I'm back, ain't I?"

"Oh, for heaven's sake." She jumped out of her chair. "Surely you don't think I'm going to crumple at your feet for doing me the great service of returning, do you?"

"Well," he drawled, glancing at Melvin, then back at her. "Yes, ma'am. I guess I sorta did."

He was serious. Completely serious. An initial rush of anger was quickly replaced with disappointment.

"I'd like to speak to Adam alone," she said.

"Absolutely not," Papa answered.

Her heart softened toward her father for the first time in over a month. Walking to his desk, she held out her hand. He enveloped it in his.

"If he tries anything," she said, her voice gentle, "I will break his nose again myself."

She squeezed Papa's hand. He looked at Melvin, then the two of them left the study, closing the door behind them.

Essie sat in Papa's throne, hoping the position would imbue her with the strength she suddenly needed. "Where were you?"

"Dallas."

"Doing what?"

"It don't matter."

"It does to me."

"Well, it shouldn't. What should matter is that I'm back."

"Why? Why did you return?"

"To marry you."

She leaned against the warmth of Papa's chair. The fire crackled in the hearth. "What changed your mind?"

He paused. "The sheriff changed my mind, but not how you'd think. He didn't threaten me or try to whup me. He just talked to me, is all."

"About what?"

"You."

She studied him. So serious, so solemn. "I heard you were supposed to take Shirley Bunting to the Harvest Festival."

He slowly straightened. "Who told you that?"

"Is it true?"

His gaze darted about the room.

"Before you answer, please do not insult me with a falsehood. Furthermore, remember that this is a very small town and most everyone knows everyone else's business."

He wiped a hand across his mouth. "I might've led Shirley to believe I might possibly escort her to the festival, but I wouldn't have."

She didn't miss the ease with which he used the girl's first name. "Did her father know you were calling on her?"

"I wasn't callin' on her."

Shooting to her feet, Essie pressed her hands against the giant desk, a horrible thought robbing her of breath. "Did you compromise Shirley, too?"

"No, ma'am," he said, standing as soon as she did.

Relief swept through her, but only momentarily. "Were you thinking to?"

He didn't answer. His disheveled hair grazed his forehead. Several days' worth of whiskers shadowed his jaw. His broad shoulders stretched taut the blue shirt he wore. He was such a gorgeous man, even after riding for days on end. But he was not so handsome on the inside—and she didn't need to look in his mouth to determine as much. The thought of spending the rest of her life with him was rapidly losing its appeal.

"How many others, Adam? How many other women in this town were you carrying on with?"

Tunneling his fingers through his hair, he moved to the window. "Don't ya want to get married, Essie?"

"Yes. Oh yes. More than anything in the world. I'm just not sure anymore that it's *you* I want to marry. A man who has such a voracious appetite for the female gender. A man who prefers wandering to planting down roots. A man who would run out on a woman he'd said he would marry and who might have been carrying his babe. A man who may not even believe in Jesus Christ."

He looked down at his fingernails. "I'd be true to ya, Essie. Once we was wed, I'd be true."

"How many illegitimate children have you sired?"

He looked at her then, his eyes bleak with regret. "I don't rightly know," he whispered.

Sorrow crashed through her. "Oh, Adam."

"I think about it all the time. Wonderin'." He blinked several times. "Might be none, ya know." His voice was sandpaper rough. "And I'd have done all that worryin' fer nothing."

She went to him then. He folded her into his embrace and she felt moisture from his eyes slide against her cheek.

"I want you to stop carrying on with women who aren't your wife."

Pulling back, he untied his neckerchief and wiped his eyes and nose. "I done told you already, I wouldn't cheat on ya."

She gave him a sad smile.

He stilled. "You ain't gonna marry me, are ya?"

"I'm sorry."

He searched her eyes. "Why not?"

"Marriage is a sacred and blessed thing. I'm beginning to realize entering into it only because we had relations would be a very foolish thing indeed."

"Then why did the sheriff traipse all over the state just to track me down?"

"Because he loves me and I'm sure he thought you were what I wanted. So he must have decided to go and get you for me."

He nodded. "Yer lucky to have him. And your ma and pa, too."

"You have a father and grandfather who love you. Perhaps you should go and see them."

Lifting her hand to his lips, he placed a soft kiss against her knuckles. "Maybe I'll do that, Miss Spreckelmeyer. Maybe I'll do that very thing."

She gently withdrew her hand. "Good-bye, Adam."

He put on his hat and tugged its brim. "Miss Spreckelmeyer, I'll never forget ya and I wish you nothin' but the very, very best."

―――――

Essie scrubbed Papa's shirt against the washboard, her hands shriveled from being in the water so long. Washing was never pleasant, but washing when the weather turned wintry was downright onerous. The hot water burned her fingers, the cold breezes chafed her skin.

She glanced at the back door. Inside, Papa sat cloistered with Mr. Davidson, the oil scout, discussing the future of the still-dry well. The well she'd been forbidden to so much as inquire about.

Mother wrung out the clothes, then hung them on the line.

The back door slammed.

"Doreen?" Papa called from the porch.

Mother stopped.

"I need you to take a message to Melvin for me. Tell him I'm with Mr. Davidson right now, but that I'll collect everyone and meet him at the jailhouse in thirty minutes."

"What's happened?" Mother asked.

"Looks like Harley's gotten himself into some trouble."

Essie released the shirt she'd been cleaning, allowing it to slide into the water. "*My* Harley? Harley North?"

"I'm afraid so."

Drying her hands with her apron, she crossed the yard. "What kind of trouble? What did he do?"

"It's a long story. Melvin's got him locked up for now."

"Locked up! He can't put a seven-year-old in jail."

"He can if the boy committed a crime. He can if he wants to scare the living daylights out of him."

Essie quickly removed her apron and flung it over the back-porch rail. "I'll go."

"Would you like me to go with you?" Mother asked.

"No. I'll send word if I need you."

She raced to the barn, not bothering to change out of her work dress or to remove the handkerchief from around her head. "When will you be done?" she hollered back at Papa.

"Hopefully within half an hour."

———————

She had to hike her skirts clear up to her knees in order to keep them from tangling in Peg's chains. With one hand holding her skirts and the other on the handlebars, she couldn't go as rapidly as she wanted, but it was quicker than saddling Cocoa. Ewing would just have to understand this was an emergency. After this, though, she'd put the bike away.

She whizzed through the heart of town. Katherine Crook swept leaves from the Slap Out's porch, gasping when she saw the spectacle Essie made. Mr. Klocker's horse became spooked by the bike and pranced to the side, forcing an oncoming buggy to swerve out of the way.

Essie didn't slow so much as a mite. She had to reach Harley. She turned onto Jefferson Avenue, spotting the sheriff's office and jailhouse.

Ever since Uncle Melvin had returned with Adam in tow, things had smoothed out between her, her uncle, and her parents. Both Melvin and Papa were relieved she wasn't going to marry the cowboy and they had wasted no time in sending Adam on his way. She hoped this time he had gone home to his family.

The bike had not come to a complete stop when she jumped off and barreled up the steps leading to a small red-brick structure. An oversized, five-pointed star emblazoned with the word SHERIFF was attached to the brown wooden door she burst through.

Uncle Melvin looked up from a modest, scarred desk stacked with papers and books. A kerosene lamp cast a golden glow over his half-empty bottle of stomach bitters and a crusted mug of coffee. A pair of handcuffs and a set of keys doubled as paperweights.

"Papa said he'd have everyone you needed in thirty minutes. What has happened?"

Melvin tipped his chair back on two legs and hooked his thumbs into his vest pockets. The movement caused his impressive shoulders to expand, displaying his badge to advantage. It also disclosed the gun strapped across his waist—a waist that was perhaps even broader than his chest.

"Well, Mr. Harley North has broken the law," he boomed, combing the edge of his bushy moustache with his bottom teeth. "And folks who break the law go to jail."

Essie recognized this performance for what it was. And it wasn't for her benefit but for Harley's. She glanced over at the cell in the back corner of the room. Harley had wedged himself on the floor between the cot and the opposite wall. He sat huddled, his arms wrapped around his legs, his head resting against his knees.

"May I see him?" she asked.

Melvin stayed as he was for a moment, then dropped his chair with a thud and grabbed the keys. "I want you to be careful. He might be dangerous. If he gives you any trouble, I'll be right here within shoutin' distance."

Her heart squeezed with compassion. Whatever trouble Harley had gotten himself into, it was serious. Otherwise, Melvin would not have been so unsympathetic.

"I'll be careful."

Melvin opened the cell door, locked her in, then returned to his desk. The small cubicle had unpainted, barren plaster walls barely wide enough for a folding cot to fit between. Beneath it sat a gray enamel chamber pail with no lid. And in the corner was Harley.

What on earth had happened between yesterday, when the boy had swung by the house to pick up his new trousers, and now?

She butted the cot up against the far wall, then bent down next to him. "Harley? It's me, Miss Essie." She stroked the mop of hair on his head. "What happened, honey?"

He lifted his head, tears streaking down his face. "I ruined my new pants," he cried.

"You did? Let me see."

Straightening his legs, he pointed to a jagged tear in the fabric of his trousers. But it was the large stain of blood that captured her attention.

She gasped. "My stars and garters. Are you hurt?"

"No, ma'am. That ain't my blood. It's Mr. Vandervoort's."

"Mr. Vandervoort's?! How did his blood get onto your clothes?"

"I shot him, Miss Essie. I killed him dead."

chapter TWENTY-SIX

ESSIE TWISTED AROUND to look at Melvin. *Did he kill Mr. Vandervoort?* She didn't say the words out loud. She didn't have to. Melvin knew what she wanted to know.

He gave a very slight negative shake with his head.

Releasing the pent-up breath within her, she turned back around and settled herself on the floor, legs crossed. "Tell me everything that happened. Start at the beginning."

"Ewing was supposed to take me huntin' today. But somebody in Cryer Creek needed a preacher to say some words over a fella who died. So he went there instead. Said he didn't know when he'd be back. Maybe tomorrow, maybe not."

"Yes, he told me the same thing. Were you disappointed you couldn't go hunting?"

"I guess so. Then I thunk to myself, I could go without him. I mean, how hard could it be to shoot a gun? You jus' point and pull the trigger. Thing is, I didn't have no gun."

"Go on."

He stuck his finger in the hole of his trousers, tugging at it. "So I borrowed one."

"From who?"

"From the Slap Out."

"You stole a gun from Mr. Crook's store?" she exclaimed.

"I didn't steal it. I jus' told you. I *borrowed* it. I was gonna bring it back."

"And the shot?"

"I borrowed that, too."

"And just how were you planning on bringing that back?"

He leaned forward and lowered his voice. "It weren't shot. It were bullets. Colts don't use shot. I was gonna dig the bullet outta the bird, wash it off, and put it back in the box."

"A Colt? You took a *Colt?* You thought to use a revolver for shooting dove?"

"What's wrong with that?"

Good heavens. "So what happened?"

"Well, I would've gotten clean away, but that Mr. Vandervoort saw me and I didn't know it." His little eyebrows furrowed with indignation. "He followed me, only when I heard him, I thought he was a big bear or somethin'. So I shot him."

"Heavens to mercy. And you hit him?"

"'Courst I hit 'im. You just aim and pull."

"Oh, Harley. What happened then?"

"Well, he hollered, that's what. And there was blood everywhere. Lots and lots o' blood." He crooked his finger.

She leaned in close.

"And lots o' swearin'," he whispered. "Lots and lots o' swearing. Then his eyes rolled back and he died. Just like that."

"What did you do?"

"I ran, Miss Essie. I ran as fast and as far as I could. I emptied the gun and I snuck it back in the Slap Out and put it back in that glass shelf. The bullets, too. Only, I was too scared to get the one I used on Mr. Vandervoort. So the box full o' bullets is missin' one."

"Did you find a doctor for Mr. Vandervoort?"

"He didn't need a doctor, he needed the grave-man."

"Did you go to Mr. McCabe's funeral parlor, then?"

"I couldn't. Just as I was putting the bullets where they go, that mean ol' Mrs. Crook grabbed my arm and started screamin' she was being robbed. She must be dead between the ears or something 'cause she weren't bein' robbed, I was puttin' the stuff *back*."

"Oh dear."

"That's when I tore my pants. She was tryin' to take me to the sheriff. I wrestled her somethin' good."

"You wrestled with Mrs. Crook?"

"Yep. And she's a fair ta middlin' wrestler, Miss Essie. I had to work awful hard to escape her."

"You got away?"

"Shore did. But the sheriff caught up to me. And ain't nobody wrestles with the sheriff. I been in jail ever since."

Now that the telling was over, the magnitude of what he'd done seemed to hit him again. His eyes filled with tears, his lips quivered. "I didn't mean to hurt nobody. I 'specially didn't mean to kill Mr. Vandervoort."

"I know you didn't."

"They're gonna send me to the big jail or the cottonwood tree or the Poor House. Mr. Wortham, he don't put up with no funny business."

She didn't agree or disagree with him, for part of what he said was true. The State Orphan's Home was not for boys who misbehaved, but for children with no relatives. And the two did not mix.

The front door opened. Papa, Hamilton, Katherine, and Mrs. Vandervoort all crowded into the small building. Essie quickly rose to her feet, prompting Harley to do the same.

Melvin greeted everyone, then slipped a key into the keyhole, unbolting the lock with a loud thump. The door squeaked open. He stepped into the cell and reached for Harley's hands, cuffing them and squeezing the ratchets until they fit his tiny wrists.

"Is that really necessary?" Essie asked quietly.

This Melvin was not the amiable man who'd once bounced her on his knee. Nor was he the outraged uncle who had discovered her with her lover.

This Melvin was an unbending man who fought for law and order. A man who showed no weaknesses, no sympathy.

"He robbed the Slap Out, shot Mr. Vandervoort, left him for dead, and attacked Mrs. Crook. He's lucky I'm not putting him in leg irons."

Essie searched Melvin's eyes, but this was not a performance. The charges against Harley were hanging offenses, and though Essie knew it would not come to that, she was unsure of what it would come to.

"Come on, son," Melvin said, placing his large, calloused hand on the boy's head and guiding him to the center of his office.

Papa set a Colt revolver and a box of bullets on the sheriff's desk, then offered seats to Katherine and Mrs. Vandervoort. When they were settled in stark bentwood chairs, he looked at Essie.

She shook her head. She had no intention of sitting down to watch these proceedings like some spectator. She'd stand beside Harley throughout the entire thing. Her only regret was that she would do so in a worn brown work dress and headscarf. Not the best costume when needing to put her best face forward, but there was nothing she could do about it now.

A wall of accusers faced them. Her father was front and center, Melvin on his right, the Crooks on his left. Hamilton stood with his hand on Katherine's shoulder. For someone who'd been in a tussle, she looked very put together with not a hair out of place.

Mrs. Vandervoort, however, looked a mess. The barrel-shaped elderly woman had dressed in her best, but she'd obviously done so in a rush. Her clothing was wrinkled and smelled of camphor. She dabbed her eyes with a handkerchief.

"State your name," Papa said.

"Harley North." His little voice came out plenty loud, if a bit quivery.

"*Sir,*" Melvin scolded. "That's the judge you're talking to."

"Harley North, *sir,*" the boy corrected.

"Your full name," Papa said.

"I don't remember it and nobody else knows what it is, neither."

Papa waited.

"Oh! I mean, I don't remember, *sir.*"

"Your age?"

"I think I'm seven, but I don't know fer shore, sir. Mr. Wortham just kinda guessed when they brought me to the Home."

Essie's heart squeezed. It had never occurred to her that he didn't know his real age or, she imagined, even his birthday.

"Did you rob the Slap Out?" Papa asked.

"I borrowed somethin', then put it right back where I found it, sir."

"Mr. Crook?" Papa asked without breaking eye contact with Harley. "Are you in the business of loaning out goods, or of selling goods?"

"I sell goods, sir," Hamilton answered.

"Is anyone ever allowed to take stock from your store without paying or signing for it?"

"No, sir."

"Harley," Papa said, "what's it called when a person secretly takes something that doesn't belong to him?"

"But I gave it back."

"Did you or did you not take a Colt revolver and a box of bullets out of the Slap Out in secret and without paying for it?"

"I took the Colt, sir, but I didn't take the whole box o' bullets, only a handful."

"Did you do it in secret and without permission?"

Harley glanced at Hamilton. "Yes, sir," he mumbled.

"Speak up!"

"Yes, sir," he repeated, overly loud and thus magnifying the ensuing silence.

"Then you are guilty of stealing."

Harley looked up at Essie, his expression full of distress, but there was nothing she could do. What Papa said was right, and they both knew it.

"And did you shoot Mr. Vandervoort with that same gun?" Papa asked.

The boy looked at Mrs. Vandervoort. She was watching him, her handkerchief now pressed against her mouth. And though she was clearly upset, her eyes conveyed a touch of compassion.

"Not on purpose, ma'am. I liked Mr. Vandervoort. He was always real nice and gave me a 'howdy' whenever he saw me. I didn't know it was him comin' up behind me. I thought it was a bear."

The woman's eyes flickered with the faintest amount of understanding.

"And when you shot him," Papa continued, "did you run away and leave him for dead?"

"No, sir. He died first and then I run off."

A stunned silence filled the room.

"And did you run off in order to go and get help?" Papa asked, softening his voice for the first time.

"No, sir. I run off 'cause I was scared. I didn't want the sheriff to play cat's cradle with my neck, so I decided to run away fer good. Start fresh somewheres else. But I needed to give Mr. Crook his Colt and bullets back. And I needed to tell the grave-man about Mr. Vandervoort. But I never got to warn the grave-man 'cause that woman grabbed me and started in with her caterwaulin'."

He'd pointed his finger at Katherine, but because his hands were cuffed, both came up together.

She stiffened in her chair. "Well, I never."

Essie gently pushed Harley's hands back down. "It's not polite to point," she whispered.

"Mrs. Crook thought you were robbing her," Papa said.

"Well, she must not have anything under that hat but hair, then, 'cause I was puttin' everything back."

Katherine sucked in her breath. Hamilton scowled. And Papa exchanged glances with the sheriff.

"Watch your tongue," Melvin said.

"Meant no offense," Harley said to Hamilton.

"She said you attacked her," Papa accused.

Harley's shock was evident. "I didn't attack her, she attacked *me*. Look what she done with her fingernails!" He pointed to the tear in his trousers. "She ruined my brand-new pants. And she grabbed my arms, too, shakin' me so hard I thought my eyeballs were gonna fly right outta my head. When I broke free, she jumped on me. I tried to get away, but she wrestles better than all the boys at the Home. And she cheats, too."

Katherine gasped.

"When clawin' me didn't work, she bit me." He pulled up his sleeve with his teeth. Moon-shaped punctures decorated his arm. "See? Everybody knows yer not allowed to bite when yer wrestlin'."

Papa kept his expression firm, but Essie could tell the boy's outrage had struck a chord with him.

"A woman can do anything she wants if a man is attacking her," Papa said gently.

"But I weren't attackin' her, she was attackin' me!"

"*Sir*," Melvin interjected.

"Sir," Harley repeated.

Hamilton looked down at Katherine. "You bit him? Why did you bite him?"

Turning almost purple, she jumped to her feet. Harley reacted as if he'd been shot, stumbling back, then darting to Melvin and taking cover behind him.

"Don't let her git me, Sheriff. She chews up nails and spits out tacks."

"Harley," Essie hissed.

Katherine yanked her cloak together and strode out the door, slamming it behind her.

"She's overwrought," Hamilton said in a conciliatory tone.

Melvin put his hand on Harley's shoulder and nudged him back to where he had been.

Papa studied the boy for a long, quiet moment. Harley looked down, scuffing the floor with the toe of his boot.

"You see those pictures there?" Papa asked, pointing to the Wanted posters tacked up on the wall behind the sheriff's desk. "That fella on the left? He stole something that didn't belong to him. When he's caught, he'll be hanged."

Harley's eyes grew large.

"The one toward the middle? He shot a man. When he's caught, he'll be hanged."

Tears rushed to the boy's eyes.

"The one next to him? He attacked a woman. When he's caught, he'll be hanged."

"I didn't mean nothin' by it. I didn't." Tears spurted from his eyes, and he covered his face with his cuffed hands.

Essie felt her own eyes water.

"Lock him up, Sheriff. I'll have a decision before nightfall."

chapter TWENTY-SEVEN

"WHAT ARE YOU GOING to do?" Essie asked, following Papa out of the sheriff's office.

The activity on this end of the street was minimal, with an occasional carriage or pedestrian passing by. Papa's rig sat parked beside the building. The town stray, Cat, darted out from underneath it, startling Essie. Meowing, the tabby wove a figure eight between her ankles.

"I don't know what I'm going to do," Papa answered. "I haven't decided."

"He's only a child."

"If he's old enough to steal, he's old enough to suffer the consequences."

"Reasonable consequences."

"I'd like to think all my decisions are reasonable."

The door opened. Hamilton escorted Mrs. Vandervoort down the steps.

"How's Mr. Vandervoort?" Essie asked her.

"Worried about Harley," the woman said, the space between her thin gray eyebrows crinkling. "He feels worse about all this than the boy, I think. I told him he should have known better than to sneak up on a hunter like that."

"It wasn't Ludwig's fault," Papa said.

"Well, he could have gone about it differently, is all."

"He's mending all right, though?" Essie asked.

"Yes, dear. Don't you worry. The bullet merely winged him. The doc says he'll be fine in no time." She nodded to the two of them, then allowed Hamilton to walk her to the judge's chaise.

"Papa?" She touched his sleeve, stalling him.

"I won't discuss it with you, Essie. And I don't want you telling the boy that Vandervoort is alive."

"Why not?"

"Because he could have been killed. I want Harley to remember for a long, long time what it feels like to rob someone of his life."

Much as she hated to burden Harley with such heavy thoughts, she knew Papa would brook no argument from her. "All right, then. If you think it's best. But you'll be lenient with your verdict?"

He put on his hat. "I'll see you at supper." Then he headed to his shay and left her standing on the street with no clue as to how he would handle the matter.

———

Uncle Melvin locked the cell door behind Essie. Frigid temperatures from the rugless floor seeped through the soles of her boots as she approached the cot. There was no blanket, no pillow, no nothing. Only Harley, curled up tightly and facing the wall.

She didn't know what to say, yet she understood what it was like to feel all alone. Sitting on the edge of the makeshift bed, she stroked his hair, his arm, his back. Slowly, tension eased from his little body.

He rolled over, his eyes swollen and red. "I hope they hang me."

"Don't say that."

"I mean it. The only thing worse than a orphan is a cracksman. And now I'm both."

"Listen to me." She gathered his hands in hers. "You did something you weren't supposed to and you'll have to suffer some consequences. But once you've fulfilled your obligations, you'll get to start over, fresh and new."

"There ain't no such thing as startin' over. Folks got long memories. Everywheres I go, they'll be whisperin', 'That there's Harley North, the murderin', area-sneak.' See if they don't."

No matter how badly she wanted to argue with him, she knew there was some truth to what he said.

"What other people think doesn't matter."

He rolled his eyes. "'Course it matters."

She propped her hands on either side of his prone form, bracketing him. "You are very mistaken, Harley North. All that matters is what Jesus Christ thinks. Remember all those Bible stories you've heard in Sunday school, where Jesus met up with sinners? Do you recall what He told them?"

The boy said nothing, but he was listening.

"He told them that what had happened in the past was not of consequence. It was their new relationship with Him that mattered. You are just as valuable to Christ right this moment as you were before any of this happened."

As are you.

The thought was so strong, so powerful, that Essie stilled, listening to her own words echoing in the silence.

"Not of consequence . . . just as valuable . . . before any of this happened."

What Harley had done was nothing compared to what she had done, though. Or wasn't it? Didn't the Bible say one sin was no worse than another? Was she really as valuable to Christ now as she was before?

An overwhelming sense of peace and affirmation poured through her. And she knew. She knew she most certainly was.

"Jesus don't care nothin' about me. If He did, He would've gave me a mama and a papa."

"He did give you a mother and father. They just went up to heaven sooner than most parents do. But He cares about you, Harley. And if you tell Him you're sorry and you truly mean not to steal or sneak again, then He'll forgive you. Completely and totally."

"I *am* sorry," he whispered. "And I *won't* never do that again."

She pulled him up and into her embrace. "Then tell Him, Harley. In the quiet part of your heart, tell Him what you just told me."

And while she hugged him against her, she, too, confessed and repented. After a few moments, she opened her eyes, basking in the unfathomable knowledge that in the only way that really mattered, she was no longer "ruined." But was instead as pure and as white as the newly fallen snow.

And if that was how the God of the Universe saw her, then who was she to argue?

Melvin cut short her visit with Harley. He didn't give any reasons, but she guessed he wanted the boy to have a taste of life behind bars.

Papa shut himself in his office, asking that he not be disturbed. At suppertime, instead of joining Mother and her, he put on his coat and hat, then left without sharing his destination.

Essie quickly finished her meal, put on a simple woolen jacket and skirt, then went down to the State Orphan's Home to find something clean for Harley to wear. Ewing had not yet returned from Cryer Creek, and the Worthams displayed concern over what was to be done with "that North boy."

Back at the jail, Essie dipped a comb into a basin of water, slicking down Harley's black hair. He wore ill-fitting pants and a blue percale blouse she had brought for him. It showed little wear, and no wonder. No boy in his right mind would want to be dressed in it. The blouse had a ruffled sailor collar, a double-ruffled front, and ruffled cuffs.

"I look like a girl," he said, tugging at the collar and poking himself with the ruffles on his cuff. The tension in his face suggested he was worried about much more than his attire, however.

"It is a very becoming blouse," she said. "Any mother would be proud to have her son wear it."

"Then how come she gave it to the orphans?"

Ah. Smart boy. "You be sure to answer with respect when you address the adults. Understand?"

"Who all's comin'?"

"Same as before, I imagine."

She smoothed down his collar just as the sheriff's door opened. The Crooks, Mrs. Vandervoort, and Papa entered. The ladies wore the same costumes they'd had on earlier, though Mrs. Vandervoort had taken the time to iron hers.

Both women immediately sought Harley out with their gazes. Katherine looked him up and down but gave no indication of her thoughts.

When Mrs. Vandervoort saw his shirt, though, she pressed a hand to her heart and said, "Awwwww. Doesn't he look precious?"

Papa assisted the ladies into chairs while Melvin unlocked the cell and handcuffed the boy, ruffles and all.

"Essie," Papa said, "you will sit here with the other ladies."

She stiffened, not wishing to leave Harley to face everyone alone. "I'm fine, thank you."

"It was not a request."

Melvin placed a bentwood chair next to Mrs. Vandervoort. Essie gave Harley's shoulder a reassuring squeeze, then settled herself into the proffered chair.

"Harley North," Papa began, "I have found you guilty of stealing, guilty of shooting a man, and guilty of manhandling a woman. Any one of those offenses would be plenty serious on its own, but all three put together are very condemning, indeed."

Essie clasped her hands in her lap and held her breath. Harley swallowed.

"When considering my options for your sentence, I did take into account that you returned the goods you'd stolen, minus one bullet, and that you did not intend to harm Mr. Vandervoort and that you felt you were acting in self-defense with Mrs. Crook."

Katherine gasped and, with face flushing, frowned up at Papa. He didn't even notice.

"As it turns out," he continued, "Mr. Vandervoort did not die."

Harley's mouth fell open. "Are ya sure?" he asked, his voice cracking.

"Quite sure. He could have, but the Lord spared him."

The boy immediately turned to Mrs. Vandervoort. "He didn't take off his boots at the Pearly Gates?"

She shook her head.

"I'm right glad about that, ma'am."

"Me too, son," she answered quietly. "Me too."

"Does this mean you ain't gonna hang me?" he asked Papa.

"I am not going to have you hanged."

Harley sneaked a glance at Essie. She wanted to give him a wink, but she didn't dare.

"Thank ya, sir," he said, returning his attention to Papa.

"There will be consequences for your actions, though."

He puffed out his little ruffled chest. "I'm ready, sir. Just say it straight out."

"Very well." Papa slipped his hands into his trouser pockets. "With Mr. Vandervoort incapacitated, his missus will need help around their place. So from sunup to sundown, every Monday through Friday, you are to take care of anything and everything that Mrs. Vandervoort asks of you, for as long as it takes for Mr. Vandervoort to recover."

"Yes, sir."

"And on Saturdays, you will do cleaning and sorting and running for the Crooks at the Slap Out."

The boy was not nearly as quick to respond to this sentence. He looked at Katherine, then at Hamilton. Neither offered him any encouragement.

"Yes, sir," he repeated, a bit more subdued this time.

"On Sundays, you will go to church, then finish out the day doing chores at the Orphan's Home."

Harley frowned. "When do I get to go fishin'?"

"There will be no free time. In addition, until further notice, you will spend your nights in the jail."

His eyes widened and he glanced at the cell. "By myself?"

"By yourself."

He looked at Essie, his eyes full of fear. Her heart squeezed, and she gave him a reassuring nod.

"Yes, sir," he whispered.

"At the end of your sentence, it will be up to the Worthams to decide if you will be welcomed back at the Orphan's Home or if you will be reassigned to the Poor House. I imagine much of their decision will be based on how well you do your duties for the Vandervoorts and the Crooks."

Harley's lip quivered, but he did not cry.

"Do you have any questions?" Papa asked.

"How long am I punished fer?"

"Until Mr. Vandervoort is completely healed."

"Am I supposed to go to the Slap Out and play checkers fer him, too?"

Mrs. Vandervoort gave a hint of a smile.

"No," Papa said. "That will not be necessary."

"I don't have no more questions, then."

"Very well. You will spend the rest of this day and night in the jail, and come morning you will report to Mrs. Vandervoort's house. Do you know where it is?"

"Yes, sir."

"Then these proceedings are over."

———

Essie began again at the top of the page, trying once more to concentrate on the words of *Robinson Crusoe*. But her eyes kept straying to the parlor windows closed tight against the night air. The brocade drapes were parted, allowing the glass panes to reflect back a wavy image of the room.

She thought of Harley in that dark cell all by himself. She'd taken him a pillow and several quilts, but she still wasn't convinced he'd be warm enough without a stove or fire.

So far away was she in thought, that she had no notion of Ewing's presence until he was standing before her.

"Oh! My goodness. You're back." She put the book aside and

stood, looking to see who had shown him in, but the two of them were alone.

He took both her hands. "I returned as soon as I heard."

"Heard? You mean word has traveled all the way to Cryer Creek about Harley?"

"No. Father sent me a telegram."

She nodded. "How long have you been home?"

"About an hour. I went straight to the jailhouse."

"How is he?"

"Putting up a good front but scared to death underneath."

"Oh, Ewing."

He squeezed her hands. "Come sit on the porch with me?"

"Let me grab my cloak."

She had planned to sit in one of the rattan rockers, but Ewing steered her to the porch settee, then settled in next to her.

"Tell me what happened," he said.

She relayed the story, ending with Papa's all-work-and-no-play determination. They sat knee-to-knee, Ewing's arm stretched along the back of the two-seater. During the telling, he had captured a tendril of her hair at the nape, coiling it and uncoiling it with his finger.

"I think having Harley work at the Vandervoorts' will be just as good for them as it will be for the boy," he said.

"Yes, I had that same thought."

"He's not going to like working for the Crooks."

"That will be good for him, too, though. He needs to learn he can't charm everyone."

His finger strayed from her hair to her neck, grazing it lightly. "How are you holding up?"

Light from the parlor window behind them sliced his features in half, revealing only the right side of his face. The shadowing accentuated the angles and planes of his visage, calling attention to his masculinity.

The feathered caress of his finger began to coax a response from her that had heretofore been absent. Was it simply because her body now knew what it was missing and any man could rouse a reaction from her? Or was it Ewing himself that prompted this feeling?

"It's been a long day, that's for certain," she answered.

"You rode your bike through town."

She stiffened. "It was an emergency. I had to get to Harley as soon as I could and I didn't have time to saddle Cocoa."

"I heard that you weren't even wearing a split skirt. That you hiked up your hems, exposing your ankles and calves."

"Who told you that?"

"Is it true?"

"Well, yes," she sputtered. "And I'm sorry, but I only did it that once. When I went to the jailhouse later for the sentencing, I rode Cocoa."

"I want you to give me your bike."

She gasped. "What?"

"I want you to let me keep your bike in my barn so it won't tempt you anymore."

She glanced toward her own barn, where inside Peg was lovingly draped with a protective blanket. "I won't ride her again. I promise."

"Then you shouldn't mind giving it to me."

"*Her*. Her name is Pegasus."

For the longest time he said nothing. Just continued to finger her hair before finally urging her again. "Will you give her to me?"

"Do you really think that's necessary?" she asked, clasping her hands.

"It's for your own good."

She held her reaction in check. *It's just a machine*, she told herself. *It's not even a real animal, like a horse or a parrot or a snake*. And, truly, she probably would be tempted to ride again.

Sighing, she swallowed. "Yes, Mr. Wortham. I will hand her over to you for safekeeping."

He laid his palm on the side of her face, sliding his thumb from her cheek to the corner of her lips and back. "I missed you."

Pushing her thoughts of Peg aside, she considered him seriously for the very first time. The very first time since she'd dismissed Adam from her life and since she'd felt God's forgiveness for her sin. And she realized that she might never be *in* love with Ewing, but she could certainly love him. In fact, she was sure she already did.

"I'm glad you're back." And she meant that. Not just because Harley now had another staunch supporter close by, but because she really did enjoy his company.

He hesitated, then slid his hand to the back of her head and pulled her toward him. The kiss was tender, chaste, and very precious.

"Can I see you tomorrow?" he asked, the cold air making their breath visible as it blended together.

"Yes. I think I would like that."

He kissed her again, allowing a little intensity this time, but couching it with restraint.

chapter TWENTY-EIGHT

ESSIE ONLY SAW Harley on Sundays when he escorted Mrs. Vandervoort to church. This past Sunday, Mr. Vandervoort's health had improved enough for the three of them to attend together.

It was clear the older couple adored the boy, and he blossomed under their attention. On Thanksgiving, Mr. Vandervoort asked Papa if Harley could spend the nights at their home instead of in jail.

"He's so lonesome there," Mr. Vandervoort had said. "It's not right. A boy his age, all alone in a cell like that."

So Papa relented, and had the elderly man been able to dance a jig, she felt sure he would've. She wished she could have seen Harley's reaction. It must have been something to behold.

Meanwhile, Ewing had pressed his suit to the point that he came by the house every day, sometimes twice. So she had curtailed her visits to the State Orphan's Home. She didn't want to accelerate their courtship any further by going out to where he lived.

But it looked as if their connection was gaining momentum regardless of what she did or did not do. He had been very deliberate in his pursuit of her, going to great efforts to ensure the townsfolk saw them as a couple—carriage rides down Main Street, now decorated with a series of berried Christmas garlands spanning its width. Sitting beside her family at church and sharing a hymnal with her.

Showering her with flowers, candy, and books of poetry he'd purchased from the Slap Out.

And the town was all abuzz with the news. Just yesterday, Mrs. Lockhart had loaned Essie a novel by Mrs. Bertha Clay called *On Her Wedding Morn*. A little something she thought Essie might like to read.

However, one of Mrs. Clay's books was enough. Essie had no intention of ever reading another. But as she stared at its slate blue cover decorated with red medallions, its pages called to her, like a siren singing with bewitching sweetness. She picked it up off her nightstand and opened it to the middle.

> How was I to warn Miss Dalrymple? To tell her bluntly that her lover was a scamp, simply would not do. Did she still love him? Had she ever really loved him?
>
> I was inclined to answer no to both questions. I believed that as of yet she had really loved no one.

"Essie?" her mother called. "Ewing is here."

Slamming the book closed, Essie shoved it under the bed. Ewing was supposed to take her to Keber & Cobb's Confectionery for a sweet. Grabbing her cloak, she hurried to the stairs, only to pull up short, halfway down.

Ewing looked absolutely splendid. He wore a brown wool dress suit richly piped with satin. The pattern fit him with meticulous precision, showing off his young, muscular physique. He had a tan cassimere coat tucked in the crook of his elbow and a derby tucked under that same arm. His smile was warm, his gaze possessive.

He'd told her that in between his classes in Nashville he'd worked for a tailor. At first he'd wrapped up the orders, made deliveries, and swept the store. Then, little by little, his employer had taught him how to measure, how to cut, and how to construct their customers' garments.

He'd had free use of any of their damaged fabrics or spares. She was certain the fine clothes he wore now were of his own making. Otherwise, he'd never have been able to afford them.

He plucked off one of his gloves. "You are beautiful. What a lovely hat."

She smoothed the twist at the nape of her neck. The hat was decidedly dull, but her reservations were soothed by his obvious appreciation.

He took her hand in his and brought it to his lips. "Good evening." His breath was warm, his lips smooth. "Allow me to help you with your wrap."

After draping it over her shoulders, he shrugged on his jacket, set his derby at a jaunty angle upon his head, and escorted her to his buggy.

The drive to the confectionery was slow and easy as Ewing pointed to the Big Dipper and Orion's Belt. Then the two of them made up constellations of their own, connecting some of the brilliant dots God had strewn across the night sky. They discovered an umbrella, a boot, and a sled before arriving at the confectionery.

The bell on its door ting-a-linged as they entered. The aromas of chocolate, nuts, and melted sugar lay heavy in the air. Mr. Keber welcomed them and suggested they look around while he finished serving his current customer.

The glass display cases were lined with every kind of candy imaginable in an assortment of colors. All looked heavenly. She decided on a cherry walnut divinity. Ewing ordered a cream caramel.

"Would you put them in a box for us, please? We'll not have time to enjoy them here, I'm afraid."

Startled, Essie looked at Ewing but said nothing.

Mr. Keber's eyes held a twinkle as he winked and handed Ewing their order. "You two have a good evenin', now, ya hear?"

When they were back inside the buggy, she slipped her hands inside an ermine muff she had brought with her. "Where are we going?"

"It's a surprise," he said.

He placed his arm along the back of the buggy seat, content to move slowly through town while guiding the horse with one hand.

At Twelfth Street, they left the busy part of town behind and passed Papa's oil field and cable-tool rig, sitting silent and still in the quiet night. The magnolia tree's silhouette was barely discernable.

Images filled her. Adam, bandanna around his neck, sleeves rolled up as he hung suspended in the stirrup and kicked down the rig. Adam practicing tricks with his lasso. Adam admitting he had no idea how many children he might have fathered along the way.

"Where are we going?" she whispered.

"Just a little farther."

She rolled the muff back and forth against her skirt. "I thought we needed to avoid being alone."

He gave her shoulder a squeeze. "Just this once I think it'll be all right."

But instead of being reassured, she grew increasingly more alarmed as he turned the buggy off the road and headed toward Two Bit Creek. He pulled to a halt in front of the slope where she'd taught Adam to ride a bicycle.

Ewing jumped from the seat, then reached up for her. Grasping her elbows, he lifted her to the ground, his hands lingering before finally releasing her.

He swiped the box of confections from the floor of the buggy, took her hand and guided her down the slope. The evening rang with sounds of crickets, frogs, and woodcocks. The temperature had dropped with the approach of winter, but Essie loved the crispness of December's air. Always had.

Beside the giant tree stump where Adam had crashed her bike was a blanket. Open, waiting, and all spread out on the ground. Ewing lit two lanterns that held down the corners of the cloth. A handful of mums lay on top of it, scattered from the breeze.

He gathered them and handed them to her. "Would you join me?"

She hesitated. The last time a man had spread a blanket in advance of her arrival, things had turned out disastrously.

But this was Ewing, not Adam. And this was the new Essie, not the old one. Accepting the flowers, she settled onto the blanket. He lifted the lid to the confections and picked up her divinity.

"Open up," he said, his large, tanned hand dwarfing the tiny delectable.

Keeping her hands burrowed inside the muff, she took a bite, her teeth grazing his fingers. The brown sugar dissolved in her mouth, leaving behind candied cherries and walnuts. With his intense gaze on hers, he took the other half of the divinity into his mouth.

Her stomach quivered in response.

"Do you like cream caramels?" he asked.

She nodded. They shared it in the same manner, but once she took her half into her mouth, she bit down on something hard and inedible. He handed her a handkerchief.

Frowning, she used her tongue to clean the candy from the object within her mouth before transferring it to the handkerchief. Opening the crumpled cloth, she discovered a gold band.

"Will you do me the honor of becoming my wife?" he asked.

Her lips parted, confusion gripping her. She had no idea what to say.

Ewing took the ring, handkerchief and all, wiped it off, then tugged on her right hand, removing it from the muff.

It was acceptable for a man whose means were limited to offer a gold band as an engagement ring. It was worn on the third finger of his intended's right hand until the wedding, at which time it was transferred to her left.

"May I?" he asked, holding the ring in readiness.

Her throat swelled. "Don't you think you should speak with my father first?"

"I have."

"And he approves?"

"He does."

"He didn't say a word to me."

"I asked him not to."

She stood transfixed by the shiny sparkle of lantern light glancing off the gold ring. The gold ring she'd been longing for her whole entire life.

She curled her hand around his and brought it against her waist. "I'm scared."

"Don't be scared."

"Can I think about it?"

He slowly lowered the ring. "You have to think about it? Surely you knew I was going to ask you."

Licking her lips, she nodded. "Yes. Yes, I knew. I just, well, I wasn't expecting this panic, this uncertainty." She pressed his fist more solidly against her stomach. "Can you feel it? Can you feel the mayhem going on inside of me?"

He stretched his fingers, freeing himself from her grip, and flicked her cloak open. He pressed his hand flat against her shirtwaist, covering as much of her stomach as he could. The gesture was possessive and terribly intimate.

"All I feel is a woman I want very much. A woman I have wanted almost my whole life."

"Oh, Ewing." She clamped her lower lip between her teeth.

He placed a kiss on the palm of her hand, then held it against his cheek. "Please say yes, Essie. Please. I need you. I love you. Please."

"You must give me some time."

"How much time?"

"Two days? Three?"

"Not a minute more."

"All right."

Leaning forward, he kissed her. But she did not open her lips or lean into his chest. She knew now where that led and she'd committed to wait. And wait she would.

———————

The next day, Essie sat at the kitchen table, polishing silver fruit spoons, trying to sort out her feelings.

Papa stepped through the back door, a blast of cold air wafting through the kitchen and causing the fire to gutter. He hooked his coat on a peg, along with his hat, then poured himself a cup of coffee from the stove.

"Are you trying to shine those or obliterate their engravings?" he asked.

Essie looked up.

"You've been working on that same spoon ever since I came in."

"Have I? I wasn't paying attention."

Each spoon held on its bowl depictions of the fruit to be consumed. This one was for strawberries.

Papa pulled out a chair and settled himself into its rickety form. The sound of her rubbing was drowned out by the brisk winter wind whistling past their window and back door.

"Is something wrong?" he asked.

She shot him a quick glance. "Why do you ask?"

"Because you seem distracted. Quiet. You shut yourself in your room last night—"

"I was reading *Robinson Crusoe*."

"And Ewing hasn't come by all day."

"He had some things he needed to do." She dipped the spoon she was working on in a bowl of water, swishing it around before drying it off. "What do you think of Ewing, Papa? I mean what do you *really* think?"

"I think he is an excellent young man with a great deal of potential. Always has been." He paused. "What do you think of him?"

"The same, I guess."

He took a sip from his cup. "You guess? You don't know?"

"He's asked me to marry him."

Papa nodded. "Well. I had wondered. He'd requested my permission nearly a week ago."

Essie picked up the next spoon. This one had peaches on it.

"What did you say?" he asked.

"That I had to think about it."

"I imagine that wasn't the answer he was hoping for."

"No. I'm afraid it wasn't."

"Do you have some objection to him?"

Essie sighed. "That's just it, Papa. There is nothing wrong with him. He is perfect. He is a man of God. He has forgiven me for giving myself to Adam. He is nice-looking. He has a good heart. What, then, am I waiting for?"

"Perhaps someone you are in love with? Someone who isn't trying to mold you into being something you are not?" His words were quiet, gentle, yet very potent.

"But I've been waiting for this opportunity my whole life. Ever since I was a little girl, all I ever wanted was to grow up and be some-one's wife, the mother of someone's children. Now here is a perfectly fine man being handed to me on a silver platter, and I am hesitating."

Papa set down his cup. "Sounds like you are trying to convince yourself that if you could just marry Ewing—any man, really—you would be fulfilled. But you won't, Essie."

"But if Ewing had asked me this past summer, I'd have said yes without a moment's hesitation. It's what I want and what I've been praying for."

"You've been praying for something you *thought* would make you happy. But God may have something else in store for you. Remember, an 'eye has not seen, nor ear heard . . . the things which God has prepared for those who love Him.'"

Essie nodded and picked up another spoon. "But I could easily make my life with him. I could. We have been friends for years. I'm sure that over time my feelings for him would grow."

"You're still justifying. Is it because you're trying to convince me— and yourself—that a man and marriage will make you complete and happy?" He placed his large hand over her delicate one, halting her ministrations. "They won't, you know. Nothing can truly fill you other than Christ."

"Can't I have both? A man and Christ, I mean?"

"Not if you prefer marriage above all else. God must come first. He must be even more important to you than marriage."

"But God's not flesh and blood." She felt her eyes pool. "And I'm lonely."

Papa removed the cloth and spoon from her fingers, then clasped her hands. "Essie, my girl, there is no aloneness like being married and alone."

"How could that be?"

"It is that way for many, many couples, I'm afraid. There is no rapport between the partners. Or the man makes decisions the woman can't walk in. Or the woman henpecks the man to death. Or the man spends his time east of Beaton Street while the woman is left at home and alone with the children."

"None of that would happen to Ewing and me. And many folks say that friendship is the very best basis for marriage."

"Friendship is important, very important, I'll grant you that. But am I wrong in my estimation when I say that Ewing is trying to press you into some mold that you don't fit into very well?"

"What do you mean?"

"I mean, why have you quit bicycling? Quit practicing on your wheeled feet? Quit hunting and fishing? And why have you quit wearing those hats that suit you like no others?"

"Ewing is afraid the church will rescind their offer if I don't maintain the strictest of standards in ladylike behavior."

"So you are giving up the very things that make you *you*?"

"Only temporarily."

"Don't fool yourself, Essie. If that's what those elders require now, they will most assuredly hold you to those same restrictions and more after Ewing is their preacher."

"But Mother says a bicycle shouldn't be more important than getting married and having children. Besides, this is what I've been praying for, crying out for, hoping for."

Sorrow etched the lines in Papa's face. "You do not need a man to be a whole person."

"Then why would God send me Ewing if not for the purpose of marrying him?"

"Perhaps because the Lord wants to see if you will trust Him. If you will choose Him over being married."

"But marriage was His idea. He sanctified it."

"Marriage is a good thing, but it may not be the highest and best for you. Are you willing to give it up for Him, if that is what He wishes?"

Moisture once again rushed to her eyes. "But I don't want Him to wish that for me. Why would He?"

"I don't know. All I'm saying is, if you truly trust God, and if He is the most important thing in your entire life, then you will accept and believe that He knows what is best for you. And you will accept it joyfully. Willingly."

She pulled her hands away, propping an elbow on the table and resting her head against her palm. "Who will hug me in my old age? Who will eat at my table when you and Mother are gone?"

"Christ will meet your needs, Essie. If you let Him."

"But I can't touch Him with my hands or see Him with my eyes or hear Him with my ears."

Papa sighed. "So you would pretend to be something you aren't and marry a man you're not in love with?"

"I don't know," she whispered. "Maybe. Except . . . except I want something more."

"Of course you do. So, for now, why not embrace Christ fully and with abandon? Then see how you feel about marriage to Ewing?"

"How? How do I *embrace* Christ?"

"You obey Him. Dwell on His Word. Do every single thing for His glory. And I'm not talking about serving the church or caring for orphans. I'm talking about everyday things. When you ride your bike, do it for His enjoyment. Talk to Him, praise Him, delight in His creation. When you wear a hat, do it for His pleasure. When you polish the silver, sing to Him. Make Him the love of your life."

Those words were so easy for him to say. He had a wife. And a child. How could he possibly understand what he was suggesting?

He drained the last of his coffee. "Whatever you decide, honey, your mother and I will support you."

Standing, he squeezed her neck and left. Leaving her to decide if Christ as her lifelong groom would truly be enough.

chapter TWENTY-NINE

EWING TRIED NOT TO study Preacher Bogart's office too closely. He didn't want the old man to think he was coveting—though, in all likelihood, he was.

He took quick note of the open bookshelves along the north wall, the fireplace adjacent to the man's substantial desk, and the small prayer table holding an open Bible. Not much had changed—other than his age—since the last time he'd visited this office. The last time he'd stood here he was a youngster who, during church, had shaped his fingers into a gun, pointed them at an elder collecting the offering, and said, "Stick 'em up."

Ewing shook the memory free and cleared his throat.

"Come in, son," the preacher said, looking up and placing his pen in a holder. Nose and ears dominated a kind face framed by a head of pure white hair so thick he was the envy of many men half his age. Large blue eyes that missed nothing conveyed pleasure as he offered Ewing a seat.

Other memories of old flashed through Ewing's mind. Preacher Bogart shooting BBs at him the night he stole a watermelon from the man's garden. Arm wrestling him after rendering a hog to see who would keep the animal's bladder for a game of catch. Squaring off with him at age fifteen when—tired of being asked to do more than his share of chores around the church—he hollered, "My name is *not* 'Get Wood!'"

Removing his hat, Ewing settled into the wooden chair the preacher had indicated.

"You're looking well, Getwood."

Ewing smiled. "Thank you, sir. As are you."

"I haven't had a chance to tell you privately how pleased I am the elders chose you as my replacement."

"Thank you, sir. I'm still trying to decide which I'm feeling more—anticipation or terror. You've left some mighty big shoes to fill."

"No need to put on these old things when you have an excellent pair of your own." He leaned back in his chair. "Many of your professors at the Nashville Bible College are colleagues of mine. They had very complimentary and remarkable things to say about you."

"I learned a lot while I was there, sir. I'm anxious to do God's work here at home."

They spoke of the church's mission. They discussed the differences between Bible college now and when Bogart had attended. They debated about closed communion and whether or not nonmembers of faith should be allowed to receive communion.

As the conversation wound down, Bogart moved aside some papers on his desk. "The elders and I have noticed you courting our Miss Essie rather doggedly these last few weeks."

"Yes, sir. It is my hope she will agree to be my wife."

He nodded. "She's a strong woman from a good family, and the two of you have been friends a long time."

"My whole life, actually. Some of my earliest memories hearken back to her."

"I assume you have discussed your intentions with her father?"

"Of course."

Bogart rested his arms on top of his desk. "As you well know, the Lord has revealed to us through His Word that His expectations for His leaders are higher and more stringent than for those in His congregation."

"Yes, sir. First Timothy."

"Then you'll remember one of those qualifications is that their wives be above reproach and worthy of respect."

He nodded.

"Son," the preacher said, steepling his fingers, "it has come to the attention of myself and the elders that Miss Spreckelmeyer might not be as above reproach as one might think."

Ewing stiffened. "I don't understand."

"There is an unconfirmed rumor concerning an illicit affair she supposedly had with one of her father's employees."

His first reaction was outrage, followed swiftly by a need to vehemently deny the accusation. His third was panic. He forced himself to remain calm.

"Rumor?" he asked, putting as much disparagement on the word as he dared. "Well, I would venture to guess that, depending upon who you talk to, there are rumors about every person in this town."

"You're probably right. But not everyone in town is being considered for a position as our pastor."

"What are you saying?"

"I'm saying that before we can move any further in our dealings, we must first verify the rumor."

"How do you plan to do that?"

"We plan to ask Miss Spreckelmeyer to either deny or verify it."

He shot to his feet. "I won't have it. I will not subject her to such a thing simply because some busybody is spreading falsehoods about her."

"Calm down, Ewing. If they are falsehoods, all she need do is tell us and we will accept her word as absolute truth."

Ewing lowered himself back into his chair. "But don't you see how humiliating that will be for her?"

"Yes, yes I do. And it is unfortunate. But there is no other way. Too much is at stake."

"And if I refuse to subject her to an interrogation?"

"It won't be an interrogation, just a simple question put to her."

"The question will be anything but simple."

He acknowledged Ewing's statement with a nod. "Be that as it may, we must put it to her."

"We? Who is we?"

"The elders and myself."

"You cannot be serious. She would die of mortification. I will not permit it."

"Then our offer to you will be revoked."

Had the preacher walloped Ewing in the stomach, he'd have been less shocked. Revoked? The elders planned to revoke their offer if Essie didn't come in for questioning?

"What if I speak on her behalf?" he asked.

"I'm sorry. We must hear it from her."

He swallowed. "And what if it is true, this whatever it is? What if it did happen and she has confessed and repented and been forgiven?"

Bogart's eyes widened in alarm. "If it is true and you intend to marry her, then you'd best look for another profession. We cannot in good conscience allow you to pastor this church or any other if your wife is less than what she should be."

"You've known her longer than I," Ewing spat. "You know her family. She is a wonderful, good, wholesome woman."

Bogart's expression softened. "Then there should be no problem. But we must speak with her first."

"How prevalent is the rumor?"

"We have only heard the accusation from one source."

"Who?"

He shook his head. "That is not of importance."

"And if Essie is guiltless, what then? Will this person spreading malicious gossip be permitted to continue?"

"We will talk with her."

"Her?" He tightened his lips. "Figures."

Bogart's eyes became troubled.

Ewing reined in his anger and gentled his tone. "Miss Spreckel-meyer hasn't even consented to be my wife yet."

"Perhaps, then, you should have a talk with her before she does."

Curled up beneath the feather coverlet on her bed, Essie stared through the darkness. Beams of orange shot from the grate of her heating stove before dissipating into thin air. She wondered what time it was—other than well past bedtime and well before sunrise.

Still, she was wide awake. No longer able to hide from her thoughts. Could she really be so selfish as to marry Ewing just for the sake of achieving a state of matrimony? She moaned.

The outline of her Bible was barely discernible on her nightstand. Reaching over, she lifted the Book and plopped it beside her on top of the coverlet.

The cushioned leather was cool to the touch.

I've read this from front to back. I've memorized verses. Entire chapters, even. I've given my time to the widows and orphans and church. I've honored my parents—for the most part. I've not stolen or murdered or taken your name in vain. I have committed fornication, yes, but you pronounced me clean.

Grasping the volume tightly in her hand, she hurled it across the room. It crashed into the wall with a loud *thunk* before banging to the floor.

So where's my man? A man whom I not only like, but whom I love? And who loves me in return? And who doesn't ask me to be something that I'm not?

Anguished sobs burst from her. She smothered her face within the downy embrace of her pillow. *Why? Why?!*

You shall have no other gods before me.

It's not a god, she insisted, addressing in her heart the powerful, non-audible voice resonating inside her soul. *It's a dream. A desire. A hope.*

Your hope is not in me.

It is!

But she knew that wasn't entirely true. From the moment she had turned thirty, she'd decided she was through "waiting on the Lord" for a husband. She'd decided to take matters into her own hands.

And what a fine muck she'd made of things. She'd packed more heartache into six months than she'd experienced in a lifetime.

Rubbing the edge of the soft, unbleached bedsheet against her lips, remorse swept through her.

She slithered out from under the covers and onto the wool rug surrounding her bed, then hurried to the wall, picked up her Bible and cradled it within her arms. She placed it back on the nightstand where it belonged and stroked its cover, thanking God for providing it for her. Then she crouched over, face to the floor, tears of sorrow rushing to her eyes.

Forgive my pride, Lord. I'm willing to deny myself of the things I desire most—a man, a marriage, and children.

She sobbed, the ramifications of her prayer squeezing her with grief. For though she desperately wanted to please God, she'd been holding fast to this particular dream since childhood. The thought of living her entire earthly life without a man, without children, broke her heart.

Especially when she knew there was nothing wrong with wanting a man and marriage. The problem had occurred when she'd allowed it to consume her, rule her, orchestrate her every action.

Yet she was determined to have no other gods before Him. To be satisfied with whatever He had for her. No, not just satisfied or content. She wanted to rejoice in His plans for her.

She took a trembling breath. *I will embrace the life you have laid out for me, Lord, and I will live it joyfully so that I may be a witness to how great you are.*

Her tears slowed to a trickle, leaving her cheeks slick and salty. She wondered if she really could live the life of a spinster with joy.

Images of herself old and gray, of this house empty and quiet, rattled her resolve. How could she embrace such a thing?

Help me be joyful, Lord. I'm afraid. Afraid of being alone.

I will never leave you.

What if that wasn't enough? She scoured her memory for characters in the Bible who had been alone or isolated. Joseph immediately came to mind, for he had been abandoned by his loved ones and sold into slavery. David had been unaccompanied as he faced Goliath. Rahab had single-handedly risked death to shelter two spies. Daniel had been thrown into a lion's den.

Yet they'd not really been alone. God had been with them. And every one of them had experienced victory. Great victory. Her determination resurfaced.

I want to do your will, Lord, and I want to do it with joy. Use me for your glory. I am yours. Amen.

Slipping back into bed, she tarried in that place with Him. But this time she let Him do the talking. And what He had to say was the very last thing she expected.

But she acquiesced and promised to speak with Papa as soon as she had everything prepared.

You will need to soften his heart, though, Lord. And if this is not your will—close the doors. Amen.

chapter THIRTY

EWING GAVE ROSEBUD her head as he made his way to Essie's home. It had been three days since he'd proposed. Two days since Preacher Bogart's ultimatum.

He'd prayed. He'd fasted. He'd railed at God. But he was no closer to a palatable solution than he was before. He was going to have to choose between his calling and Essie.

He supposed he could marry her and then move somewhere else. But it would have to be outside the county, maybe even outside the state. But Essie had lived here all her life. He couldn't imagine her being willing to move away. And truthfully, he didn't want to live anywhere else, either.

He drug his hand down his face. If he were really honest with himself, he'd admit that Essie wasn't everything he'd remembered her to be. He'd left home a child and had carried with him an image of Essie that didn't quite translate into reality when he'd returned.

He realized now that all the things he'd loved about her were from a child's perspective. She'd fished with him. Swam with him. Climbed trees with him. Hunted with him. Played ball with him.

He'd absolutely adored her. Worshiped her, even. And had decided at a very early age that he wanted to spend the rest of his days with her.

Looking back, he realized now how unorthodox her behavior really had been. Shocking, even. She thought nothing of hiking up her skirts or soiling her clothing or barreling headlong into danger.

She thought only of adventure. What boy wouldn't fall in love with her?

But he was a man now. A man who desperately wanted to fulfill the Great Commission that Christ had given him. And when it came time for him to stand before God Almighty, what would he say?

That he had given up his calling so he could marry a woman whose everyday behavior bordered on the scandalous? Whose secrets were so shocking that the church would revoke their offer if and when they found out?

And what would he do for a living? He'd spent all his adult years preparing to be a pastor. How would he provide for Essie if he couldn't preach? Especially when that's all he wanted to do. He had a burning desire to serve God. The thought of not preaching was simply not to be borne.

Pulling Rosebud to a stop in front of the Spreckelmeyer house, Ewing stared at the two-story Georgian, shaded by giant pecan trees on a spacious lot and surrounded by a white picket fence. He'd banged in and out of that house more times than he could count. The Spreckelmeyers had been more than tolerant of him over the years and had acted as surrogate parents in many ways.

He sighed. A proposal of marriage was almost as binding as speaking the actual vows. What would the Spreckelmeyers think of him if he withdrew his offer? What if word got out? Would the elders decide that any man who broke his word was unworthy of pastoring a church?

If they did, he'd have to tell them the truth about Essie. And he did not want to do that. The risk of those men telling their wives and those wives telling others was too great.

Lord, help me, he prayed. Because as he swung off of his horse and tied her to a rail, he knew that the only thing he could do was to take back his offer of marriage. And it would very likely ruin lifelong friendships that he treasured.

"It's Ewing," Mother said, returning to the kitchen after answering the door. "He's in the parlor, waiting for you."

Essie slowly removed the apron from around her waist. It was all well and good for her to give up her wants and needs to the Lord. It was something totally different to refuse Ewing his.

She re-pinned a loose piece of hair. How on earth would she tell him she couldn't marry him? Especially after he'd extended her such grace?

He'd be so hurt. And she knew all too well what that particular kind of hurt and rejection felt like.

Yet she also knew that if she tried not to hurt him, she'd end up hurting him even more. So she'd have to tell him the truth.

Still, she couldn't admit he had been the means to an end for her. Though, he had.

She couldn't say the Lord had called her to give marriage up as a sacrifice to Him. Though, He had.

She couldn't say she wasn't in love with him. Though, she wasn't.

So what could she say? That he was asking her to pretend to be something she was not?

She shook her head. No. There was nothing. No easy, pat answer she could offer without injury.

Give me the words, Lord.

He stopped his pacing when she entered. He'd dressed more casually today in a pair of wool trousers and a navy hand-knit pullover sweater that suited him quite nicely.

"Hello," she said.

"Hello." He crushed the hat in his hands. "You look lovely."

She smiled. She'd been filling lamps in the kitchen and wore an ordinary black serge skirt and white shirtwaist. But she could see he meant his words and they warmed her.

"Thank you."

"We need to talk," he prompted.

"Yes. Yes, we do. Won't you sit down?"

He joined her on the settee and must have read the distress in her eyes.

"What is it?" he asked. "What has happened?"

"Ewing, I'm so sorry, but I'm afraid I won't be able to marry you."

His face registered shock. "You won't?"

"It's nothing you've done," she quickly assured him. "Nothing at all. You have been . . . wonderful to me." She swallowed. "I just do not have the kind of feelings for you that a bride should have for her groom."

"You don't?"

She slipped her hand between his clasped ones. "You are truly one of my dearest and most beloved friends and I treasure you beyond belief, but . . ."

"But. . . ?"

"But," she said, taking a deep breath, "I don't think I would make a very good preacher's wife. I'm too, too . . ."

"Impulsive?"

"Yes. And outdoorsy. And independent. I'm afraid my impetuous-ness would provide the gossip mill with so much material that it could hurt the church. And you. And your work. I really don't want to do that."

They sat in silence, the fire in the hearth crackling. The sounds of Mother's puttering in the kitchen now and again reached them.

He opened his palm, entwining their fingers together. "Do you love me, Essie?"

"Yes, of course. But I don't believe I'm *in* love with you. And there's . . . well, there's a difference."

"Yes," he whispered, "there is definitely a difference."

She squeezed his fingers.

He lifted their interlocked hands, resting his lips upon her knobby knuckles. "You are an amazing woman."

"Oh, Ewing."

"Can I make a confession?" he asked.

Blinking, she nodded.

"I think you are right."

She sucked in her breath. "You do?"

"Yes." He rubbed his cheek with their clasped hands, his closely shaven whiskers like the mildest of sandpaper against her fingers. "Yes, I do. And I would hate to see you have to suppress your vivaciousness. It wouldn't be right."

"You aren't angry with me, then?"

"Not at all." Kissing her knuckles one more time, he swallowed, then relinquished his hold.

She walked him to the door. "We can still be friends?"

"Of course," he said, tugging on his gloves. "I would consider it an honor."

But as she watched him stride down the sidewalk and swing up onto Rosebud, she knew that the relationship they'd shared since childhood would forever be altered.

———

Journal in hand, Essie knocked softly on Papa's door.

"Come in."

She slipped in, then closed the door behind her but did not advance.

Twilight streamed in from the big bay window, casting shadows about the room. An assortment of rugs covered the polished wooden floor, and a fur skin provided warmth for Papa's feet. Gilt-backed books lined rows upon rows of shelves without glass or coverings of any kind so Papa could remove his books without key and lock. The uppermost shelves had been designed for easy retrieval of his volumes with an outstretched arm.

The fire had recently been stoked, combating the end-of-the-day chill brought on by the setting sun and tingeing the air with smoke.

Papa's eyes displayed deep circles beneath them. Putting his pen back in its holder, he indicated a chair.

"Am I disturbing you?" she asked. "I can return later."

"No, it's almost time for supper anyway. What's on your mind?"

Smoothing her skirts beneath her, she sat and addressed the subject she'd not yet broached with him. "I, um, have a business proposition for you."

"You may not go back to the oil field, Essie. You can do all the paper work you want here in my office, but no field work. I won't change my mind on that."

"Oh." She looked toward the window. "That's not what I was going to ask, but I have wondered how it was going. You never talk about it at the supper table."

"It was a dry hole."

"No! You mean there was not any oil in that well at all?"

"Not a drop."

"Oh, Papa. All that work. How disappointing. I'm so terribly sorry."

He shrugged. "That's the way it is in any prospecting venture. I finally called the boys off the rig today and am moving them to another location Davidson suggested."

"Are you sure you trust his scouting instincts after this?"

"We'll give him another try before I call in somebody else. Now, what proposition did you have for me?"

She had dressed carefully for this meeting, wearing her green-and-gray tailored suit, blazer-style. Her hat was modest, decorated only by an ostrich demi-plume for some added height.

Straightening her backbone, she looked him directly in the eye. "I'd like to use my dowry to purchase the abandoned seed house, please."

He sat nonplussed for a moment. "Your dowry?"

"Yes. I'm through waiting for a husband. It's time to move forward."

"Now, Essie—"

"No, Papa. I'm officially setting my cap on the shelf. But if it's all right, I'd still like to invest my dowry. Just not in a husband."

"What if one comes along?"

"Then he'll have himself a very nice seed house."

"A seed house." It wasn't a question but a statement. A confirmation that he understood her correctly.

"Yes."

He rubbed his temples. "You want to go into the cotton business?"

"No. I'd like to found a bicycle club."

"A bicycle club?" he asked, clearly puzzled.

"That's right. I'd like to renovate the seed house and use it one night a week for members to ride in while a band plays. During the days, I'll give lessons."

"But you're the only person in town who owns a bicycle."

"I know. I'll have to rent or sell bikes to any members who don't have one of their own."

"So you want to buy not only the seed house but several bicycles?"

"For starters."

"Why? Why now?"

"Because I'm good at both teaching and bicycling and I can use the talents the Lord blessed me with to bless others."

He leaned back in his chair.

If you were serious about this, Lord, you will have to see it done.

"I believe," Papa said, "I had deferred these kinds of decisions to your mother."

"She's all for it."

He blinked. "You've discussed this with your mother?"

"At length."

He placed his arms on the desk. "What did she say?"

"That she'd like to sign up for lessons."

"Doreen wants to ride a bike?" Stiffening, he scowled. "I won't have it. She'll break her neck."

"No, she won't. I'm an excellent teacher."

"What would she wear? I will not have her riding about town in those short skirts."

Essie smiled. "You let me."

"That's different. Entirely different. I can't even fathom what Doreen was thinking."

Crossing her arms, Essie cocked her head. "She was thinking it looked like fun. And she's right. It is. I cannot believe you are being so stuffy about this."

"I'm not being stuffy."

She lifted an eyebrow.

"What would she wear?" he repeated.

"A costume with a series of drawstrings that will convert her skirt into bloomers while riding and can then be released to re-create the skirt."

He frowned. "Where would she get that?"

"She'll have to buy or make one. But that will be no problem. You see, I'm also going to sell patterns and bicycle-wear in my club."

"A seed house. Bicycles. Patterns. Ready-made clothing. Anything else you want to purchase while you're at it?"

"Quite a bit, actually."

He shook his head. "You are talking about a great deal of money. Your dowry is generous, but not that generous. I cannot see myself investing such a sum. Not for a business that is doomed to failure."

Picking her journal up off the floor, she set it on the edge of his desk. "Inside here I have a list of several hundred *profitable* bicycle clubs from all around our country. I have marked a section that lists what my club will entail, how it will work, and what it will cost to convert the seed house. I've gone into great detail about what I will charge for membership, bike rentals, and lessons. I have inserted an article from one of your old *New York Times* that cites, 'The bicycle is of more importance to mankind than all the victories and defeats of Napoleon, with the First and Second Punic Wars thrown in.'" She slid the bound book closer to him. "I have also listed my costs and how I will pay them back to you with interest."

He didn't even look at the journal. "Are you concerned with how you will live once I am gone? You needn't be. I have listed you as beneficiary in all my dealings, including Sullivan Oil. You will be well taken care of."

"Thank you, Papa. And I am most appreciative. But in the meanwhile, I'd like to have something that is mine." She leaned forward to emphasize her point. "The bicycle is the way of the future. Don't you see? It is better than a horse because it costs almost nothing and is never tired. It will take its rider three times as far as a horse in the same number of days or weeks. The *Times* says that the value of horseflesh will drop to almost nothing within the next twenty years."

"I'm sorry, Essie, but that is rather hard to imagine. Wheels may be a mode of transportation for some, but not the majority. Consider Mr. Fouty or Mrs. Vandervoort. Do you really believe they would give up their horses for a bike?"

"Yes, I do. Did you know in Brooklyn they have a Fat Man's Bicycle Club, where members must weigh over 250 pounds to join?"

He looked at her with skepticism. "But so many doctors and churches are against it. You won't be able to drum up enough business to support your venture."

"The folks in town are simply uninformed. I can show them article after article by doctors and clergymen who are not only proponents of bicycling for both men and women, but who actually make their rounds on bikes."

He harrumphed. "And will you tell me next that you'll pull a wagon with it?"

"Of course not, but the papers say you can make fifty miles a day as comfortably as twenty miles on foot while carrying all the clothing you need, besides a camera and other traps. And the exercise is more invigorating than walking."

He opened her journal and perused the first few pages. "What's this about social activities? I thought the main focus was bicycling."

"It is, but other clubs around the country offer banquets and bicycle debating societies and cycle races. In order to increase my yield, I thought I should do the same."

He continued to read, and after a while she quietly let herself out of the room, but not before she caught the slightest sparkle in Papa's eyes as he turned the pages of her journal.

chapter THIRTY-ONE

FIVE MONTHS LATER

ESSIE TOOK PEG FOR another turn around the Corsicana Velocipede Club. After an adjustment to the frame of her bike, the blacksmith had been able to eliminate the click that had resulted from Peg's fall. Now the wheels of her machine hummed with each rotation of the pedals.

Light poured in from long, narrow windows lining the ceiling of the one-hundred-fifty-foot structure, spotlighting her ride. The plank flooring offered an escape from the dirt roads outside, though the smell of cottonseed still tinted the club's air.

Today was to be her grand opening. She had, so far, seventy-eight paying members, and private lessons would start this morning. This would give her two months to teach her members the rudiments before the Fourth of July when she would host their inaugural "group ride"—band and all.

Shirley Bunting and Sadie Tyner entered from the back, their giggles and excited whispers echoing throughout the vast room. Essie steered her bike toward them.

She still marveled at Papa's cleverness in soliciting Mr. Bunting as an investor. He and Shirley had evidently been in Dallas and had seen for themselves the bicycle craze that had begun to grip the big city, and they were eager to participate.

With one of the town's most prominent bankers not only blessing her venture but backing it, the rest of the community responded in kind, many of them signing up for a membership.

Shirley lifted her arm and waved. "Helloooooooooooo."

. . . *helloooo . . . helloooo* . . . echoed in the vast space.

What a surprise the lovely young blonde had turned out to be. In many ways, she was as lonely as Essie had been. But her loneliness was due to an overabundance of suitors, who—attracted superficially to her beauty—offered her no real companionship.

Her closest chum, Sadie Tyner, was as sharp as they came but had been suppressed by a mother who had convinced the poor girl she was unattractive and too smart and would, therefore, never land a husband if she didn't do something about it.

Essie had hired the girls as a personal favor to Mr. Bunting. And what a gift from God they were. Both were quick, enthusiastic learners and had blossomed under her tutelage. For she had not only taught them the thrill and exhilaration of mastering a bicycle but also the sense of freedom and accomplishment a woman could achieve through it.

Of course, convincing Shirley to wear simple, lightweight clothing had so far been the most challenging task. She'd wanted to wear a fancy bicycle suit and hat, but Essie forbade it. The men and women in town were not yet comfortable with such fashions and she did not want to alienate them.

She drew up next to the girls. "Are you ready for a long day of work?"

"We can't wait," Shirley said. Sadie nodded her agreement.

She hoped that would still be the case at the end of the day. Once word had gotten out that the charming Miss Bunting would be assisting in lessons, the youth of Corsicana—male and female alike—had signed up in droves.

Gliding to a stop, Essie jumped from Peg.

"I'm wearing my bicycle corset," Sadie whispered, smoothing down the front of her shirtwaist, "just like you told me to. Can you tell?"

"Not a'tall. What about you, Shirley?" Essie asked.

"I feel downright scandalous. I cannot imagine how you are going to convince our mothers to do the same."

"We won't have to. They won't be able to breathe if they don't."

The door at the front of the building opened, and an elderly woman with a cane entered.

"Hello, Mrs. Lockhart," Essie said. "You are right on time. Welcome to the Corsicana Velocipede Club."

"A bunch of foolishness," she answered. "I'm going to break every bone in my body."

"Nonsense." Essie hugged the woman, the smell of lilacs teasing her nose. "Tumbling off your bicycle is inexcusable. All you need do is decide you won't fall and you won't."

"I had better not."

"Shall we begin right away?" she asked, taking the woman's shawl.

"If we must."

"Very well. First, let's watch Miss Bunting demonstrate."

Shirley mounted a Ladies Yukon with grace and ease, pedaling it away from them and toward the back wall of the building.

"By July Fourth you will know how to sit, pedal, balance, steer, turn, and dismount," Essie said. "Do you see that black thing attached to the front of the machine that looks a bit like bat wings?"

"Yes."

"That's called a Cherry Screen, and its purpose is to block the view of Miss Bunting's ankles and feet and to prevent her skirt from blowing about."

Shirley turned and headed back toward them, as pretty and engaging a sight as ever. There wasn't a woman under ninety who wouldn't want to look just like her.

"Notice how she isn't looking down," Essie continued, "but is looking up and off, on and out. Her forehead and feet all in line."

Shirley waved.

Mrs. Lockhart gasped. "Good heavens. Hold on, child."

. . . *child . . . child . . .* Her exclamation bounced off the walls throughout the building.

Swinging her legs to the side, Shirley jumped to the ground and jogged to a stop while still holding the handlebars.

Mrs. Lockhart turned around. "That is it. Never in all my days will I be able to do that. I'm leaving."

Essie took her elbow and brought her back. "'Except ye become as little children,'" she quoted.

"I'm too old to remember that far back."

"We will be beside you the entire time."

Shirley turned the wheel around and waited.

Sadie took Mrs. Lockhart's cane. Essie expected the woman to lean more heavily into her, but that did not occur. Why, the woman didn't need the cane at all. She obviously carried it for effect—or as a tool to whack misbehaving boys.

Essie suppressed her smile. "You remember Miss Tyner?"

"Of course. It's my body that's old. Not my mind."

Sadie placed a step stool next to the bike.

"For now, you will use a stool to help you mount. Are you ready?"

The woman tightened her grip on Essie. "I don't believe I can do it."

"It is all right," Essie said. "All three of us will be right beside you. You needn't ride today, just mount and dismount. That's all."

She placed her right foot on the stool.

"Other foot. You will need to straddle the seat."

Pressing a hand to her throat, Mrs. Lockhart stared at the machine as if it were the devil himself. "I've never done such a thing in my life. What will people think?"

"Princesses Louise and Beatrice both ride at Balmoral. You will be in fine company indeed."

The woman's eyebrows raised just a mite before she lifted her chin and placed her left foot on the stool. With Shirley on one side, Essie on the other, and Sadie holding the seat, they assisted her onto the saddle.

"Good heavens. Don't let go. Don't let go."

The grip she had on Essie's arm cut off her blood flow and crushed Shirley's leg o' mutton sleeve.

"We're not going anywhere, Mrs. Lockhart," Essie said, "but you must release us and take hold of the crossbar. Letting loose of the handles is the equivalent of dropping the bridle of a spirited steed. If you remember nothing else, you must forever keep your main hold, else your horse is not bitted and will shy to a dead certainty."

Mrs. Lockhart grasped the handlebars.

"Excellent work. Now, rest your feet on the stirrups, but do not exert any pressure on them."

She placed her black pointed boots on the pedals.

"This is downright wicked," she whispered.

Sadie giggled.

"It most certainly is not," Essie insisted. "Your position equally distributes your muscles so that when the exercise begins you will not overuse any one muscle. Now, would you like to move forward or sit awhile longer?"

"I'll just sit awhile, thank you."

"Of course."

She waited for Mrs. Lockhart to become accustomed to sitting astride the animal. Black draped the woman like a mantle—black shirtwaist and skirt, black gloves, black hat, black boots. Yet Essie knew behind all those morose clothes lived a heart that loved intrigue and risk.

The extra folds of skin below the woman's brows gave her eyes a beady look, but they were alight with anticipation.

"Better?" Essie asked.

Mrs. Lockhart gave a slight nod.

"All right, then. Shall we give her a try?"

Squeezing the handlebars, she nodded again.

"Excellent. Now, there are two things that must occupy your thinking powers at all times: the goal and the momentum required to reach it."

"What is my goal, again?" she asked, voice trembling.

"Today your goal is to ride, with our assistance, six feet. The momentum required will be one turn of the pedal. Are you ready?"

A fine sheen of perspiration gathered along her white hairline. "I am ready."

Essie signaled the girls and they walked several feet. Mrs. Lockhart exerted pressure on the pedals for one rotation, propelling her forward.

"Oh heavens," the woman said, surprise and delight transforming her wrinkled face. "Oh my. Goodness gracious. Don't let go."

"You did it," Essie exclaimed. "That's all there is to it. Congratulations. You have taken your first ride on a velocipede."

Sadie grabbed the stool, and the three of them helped Mrs. Lockhart dismount.

Pulling a handkerchief from her sleeve, she patted her hairline, cheeks, and lips. "That was the most exciting thing I have done in years. When can I do it again?"

"Miss Tyner keeps track of our lessons. If you will go with her to the front, she will tell you when your next appointment is."

They'd gone several yards before Essie stopped her. "Oh my. Don't forget your cane."

Mrs. Lockhart turned around and walked in perfect form back to Essie. "Thank you, my dear." She squeezed Essie's hand. "For everything."

———

July 4, 1895

Uncle Melvin pressed his tongue against his teeth and let loose a piercing whistle that bounced off the walls of the Corsicana Velocipede Club and silenced the excited mumblings of the crowd. All eyes turned to the source of the noise—a platform in the corner of the building. Members of the Merchants' Opera House orchestra shifted in their chairs.

Uncle Melvin offered Essie a hand up onto the platform. She wore a new pink-and-white-spotted taffeta dress with wide, leg o' mutton sleeves and elbow-length gloves, bracelets dangling over the top.

Her wide-brimmed hat of straw was one of the most spectacular she'd ever owned with pleated chiffon, ribbon loops, a steel buckle, and a bouquet of American beauties turned up slightly at the back.

"Ladies and gentlemen," she projected across the assembly. "Welcome to the Corsicana Velocipede Club's inaugural Group Ride."

The crowd applauded, whooped, whistled and stomped. Essie smiled, waiting for them to settle down. Her students had worked long and hard in preparation for this event. She felt like a mother watching her offspring perform in the annual school play.

Splashes of color from the ladies' garments were juxtaposed with the men's brown and black suits. Though a few of the younger, more fashionable men were wearing red-and-white striped jackets with white trousers.

Her pupils stood scattered around the track, bicycles in hand, while spectators lined the perimeters of her building.

"Ladies," she said, "prepare your skirts."

The crowd murmured as the men held both their bikes and the women's. A rustling of fabric ensued and her female students pulled up the drawstrings in their hems, transforming their skirts into bloomers. When all stilled, she turned her back to the audience and faced the band.

"Are you ready?" she whispered, raising her hands.

They lifted their instruments into place, poised and waiting.

She gave them four counts, then swept her hands down and up. The strains of "A Bicycle Built for Two" filled the cavernous room. She nodded to the director, Mr. Creiz, and he took her place. Spinning around, she watched the bicyclists mount and ride. The crowd cheered, then sang with gusto to the band's tune.

"Daisy, Daisy,
Give me your answer do.
I'm half crazy,
All for the love of you.
It won't be a stylish marriage,
I can't afford a carriage
But you'll look sweet upon the seat
Of a bicycle built for two."

Mr. Vandervoort whizzed by, with his newly adopted son, Harley, balanced on the handlebars and squealing in delight. He was followed by Mr. Baumgartner, Mr. Pickens of the Flour, Feed and Liquor Store, Miss Lillie Sue, the doctor's daughter, and Mrs. Peterson, the Crooks' nanny.

Shirley looked as if she were being escorted by an army of men as they flanked her on all sides with their machines. Mayor Whiteselle and his wife sang and wheeled in time to the music.

Mrs. Lockhart reigned over all, though. Her head high, her bearing regal. She commanded her wheel with ease, but it was her new bicycle costume complete with wide knickerbockers and colored stockings that garnered the most attention.

Essie moved from the platform and made her way toward the front of the building. Mr. Weidmann handed out free samples of his fruitcake, along with some new items on his menu of sweets. Mother poured punch for those with parched throats. Young Lawrence passed out flat fans to the ladies, the backs of which had been printed with *The Corsicana Velocipede Club*.

The song came to a close and the roar of the assembly momentarily deafened Essie's ears. Some of her pupils parked their bikes and went in search of family. Others continued to ride.

In the center, Sadie and Shirley began free instruction to the lucky two winners whose names had been drawn earlier. Jeremy Gillespie had been one of them. He'd made no delay in getting to Shirley's side.

She scowled at him and Essie stiffened. It hadn't occurred to her that Shirley would resent teaching the town drunk's grandson. Jeremy leaned over and said something to the girl. Her eyes widened.

He smiled, winked, and straddled the bike. Long hours kicking down the oil rig had broadened his shoulders, chest, and legs. It had also given him a confidence and cockiness he'd not had before. He wore a smart suit and straw boater. The transformation from boy to man boggled the mind.

". . . the conclusion that bicycles are just as good company as most husbands."

Essie recognized Mrs. Lockhart's voice at once and turned to see her waving her cane at a group of elderly widows.

"Why, you can dispose of it and get a new one without shocking the entire community," she concluded.

The band reached the chorus of "Say 'Au Revoir' But Not 'Good-Bye'," and the crowd's voices in song drowned out whatever response the women had to Mrs. Lockhart's sentiment. But their expressions of horror and disbelief were enough.

Essie choked back a snort.

"Looks like your big debut is a success," Papa said in her ear.

She looked over her shoulder and smiled. "I think so, too. I had no idea folks would turn out in such numbers."

He gave her waist a squeeze. "Perhaps I should have you pick the location of my next well."

"You hit oil this last time."

"I don't know if I'd call twenty-two barrels of oil a day hitting much of anything."

"Pishposh. You can't expect to find a gusher the first couple of tries. Where will you drill next?"

"I'm open to suggestions."

"Essie?" Ewing said, touching her elbow.

"Ewing! I didn't expect to see you." She grasped his hands and touched her cheek to his. He was dressed in black, as befitted his station, his hair neatly combed, his jacket crisp and neat.

"Almost the whole town is here," he said, "including a good portion of my flock." Leaning forward, he winked, a teasing note entering his voice. "I thought I'd best come to make sure some calamity didn't befall them."

Papa extended a hand. "Hello, Preacher. I must admit you do a mighty fine job in the pulpit. Mighty fine."

"Thank you, sir."

Someone called Papa's name and he turned.

Ewing squeezed Essie's elbow. "Congratulations. I'm exceedingly proud of you."

"Thank you."

He searched her face. "You look as fetching as ever. I particularly like your hat. Is it new?"

"It is."

"Will your box supper have ribbon to match it?"

"It will."

"Then I'll be sure to watch for it."

She shook her head. "I'm not entering it in the auction."

"Not entering it?" His crestfallen expression surprised her. "But why not? Surely—"

"Miss Spreckelmeyer?" Mrs. Fowler called. "Where can I sign up for membership?"

Essie glanced at the blacksmith's wife, then back at Ewing. "I'm sorry. Would you excuse me?"

He reluctantly released her and she hurried to Mrs. Fowler's side, guiding her to the front desk.

The rest of the two-hour event passed in a blur as she handed out membership cards, answered questions, accepted compliments on her club, and calmed naysayers.

After the final song, Uncle Melvin informed the crowd the box-supper auction would begin at the park in thirty minutes' time. The building emptied as fast as it had filled.

Essie thanked the band, picked up some fans that had been trampled upon, and locked up.

———

A large oak at the crest of a hill offered both shade and a view. Essie shook out her blanket, set her box supper on top of it and sat down.

Oh, it felt good to get off her feet. Mr. Roland's voice floated up the hill as he enticed the crowd with Miss Lizzie's basket. Bidding began in earnest.

Pulling the covering from her basket decorated with pink-and-white polka-dotted ribbon, she withdrew her journal, a pencil, and some cheese.

Jesus Christ

She formed the letters of His name with careful script.

Points of Merit:

- *Will never leave me*
- *Nothing can separate me from His love*
- *Took my sins upon himself*
- *Forgave me*
- *Turns my darkness into light*
- *Cares about everything I do, even knows how many hairs are on my head.*

Drawbacks:

She took a bite of cheese, then tapped the top of her pencil against her lips.

- *Can't see Him, touch Him, or hear Him with my physical body*

Yes, but blessed are those who have not seen and yet have believed.

- *Is always right about everything*

True. But if you depend on me and trust me, I will take care of you.

- *Expects absolute obedience*

I have warned man that it is better to live in a desert than with a quarrelsome and ill-tempered woman. It's in Proverbs, in case you've forgotten.

She took another bite of cheese and suppressed a smile.

- *Has a droll sense of humor*

A feeling of shared warmth and amusement washed over her. She giggled. Wrapping her arms around herself, she basked in the warmth of His love. It was more fulfilling than she had ever thought possible.

She knew, of course, that she would still go through difficult times. But she also knew she would not be alone. Smiling, she closed the journal and bowed her head before partaking of her meal. She thanked the Lord for her daily bread, for blessing the bicycle club and, most of all, for being her One and Only.

AUTHOR'S NOTE

Corsicana, Texas, is passionate about its history. They have preserved it, celebrated it and made it extremely accessible for us to enjoy. They have a historic section downtown, a Pioneer's Village—that, in my opinion, ranks up there with the best I've seen in our entire country—and a Petroleum Park commemorating the location where oil was first discovered in Texas—by accident while drilling a water well. If you find yourself on that patch of road between Dallas and Houston, set aside some time to spend in Corsicana exploring all it has to offer while dining on some fruitcake from the historic Collin Street Bakery.

That said, the folks of Corsicana will notice that I bent their timeline in places in order to fit things into my novel that didn't really take place in 1894. For example, Adam's story of the Cowhead Trail was true—but it happened in 1860 and the trail boss was a fella by the name of Tom Hester. Oil was struck in 1894, but not in August. It was struck on June 9th. I needed my novel to start on the Fourth of July, though, so I bent the dates a bit.

Also, over a year passed before the second oil well was drilled (two hundred feet south of the original water well). Again, my story only spanned eight or so months, so I had to speed up the drilling process.

The peg-legged rope walker was true, but I found conflicting dates for the actual occurrence. Some sources said it was 1884, some said 1898. Either way, it didn't happen in 1894, but again, some events in history call to be included even if we have to bend the timeline a little bit.

And before I get emails from all those snake lovers out there who know that snakes can go for quite some time without eating—please forgive my rush to release Colonel. I just couldn't bear to leave him at Katherine Crook's mercy, and it would have been too cumbersome to the story for Essie to take him home with her.

I look forward to spending another year with Essie in Corsicana as I write *Deep in the Heart of Trouble*, the sequel to *Courting Trouble*. It will take place four years later (1898) and in that time, Corsicana's population exploded—becoming the first oil boomtown in Texas, complete with derricks in almost everyone's backyard.

And Don't Miss
Essie's Next Escapade When
She Finds Herself…

Deep in the Heart of Trouble!

Coming Summer 2008!

But You Don't Have to Wait That Long….

Join Dee at *www.deeannegist.com* to:

- Discuss what should happen next with Essie
- Get early glimpses as the book takes shape
- Share your favorite moments with other fans
- Chat with Dee about books, writing, and more!

Looking for More Good Books to Read?

You can find out what is new and exciting with previews, descriptions, and reviews by signing up for Bethany House newsletters at

www.bethanynewsletters.com

We will send you updates for as many authors or categories as you desire so you get only the information you really want.

Sign up today!